1950, although more than thirty years ago, was nevertheless a wonderful year for science fiction very much in the modern manner. It produced stories still considered among the best ever written and it lists authors who are still today among the giants of the 1980's. Look down the list of the contributors to this Asimov selection and see for yourself:

RAY BRADBURY

DAMON KNIGHT

A.E. VAN VOGT

ISAAC ASIMOV

JOHN D. MACDONALD

FRITZ LEIBER

CHARLES L. HARNESS

ALFRED BESTER

RICHARD MATHESON

CORDWAINER SMITH

C.M. KORNBLUTH

ETC.

*Anthologies from DAW
include*

ASIMOV PRESENTS THE GREAT SF STORIES
The best stories of the last four decades.
Edited by Isaac Asimov and Martin H. Greenberg.

THE ANNUAL WORLD'S BEST SF
The best of the current year.
Edited by Donald A. Wollheim with Arthur W. Saha.

THE YEAR'S BEST HORROR STORIES
An annual of gooseflesh tales.
Edited by Karl Edward Wagner.

THE YEAR'S BEST FANTASY STORIES
An annual of high imagination.
Edited by Arthur W. Saha.

TERRA SF
The best SF from Western Europe.
Edited by Richard D. Nolane.

ISAAC ASIMOV

PRESENTS

THE GREAT SF STORIES

12

(1950)

EDITED BY ISAAC ASIMOV AND MARTIN H. GREENBERG

DAW BOOKS, INC.

DONALD A. WOLLHEIM, PUBLISHER

1633 Broadway, New York, NY 10019

DAW Book Collectors' Number 594

First Printing, September 1984.

1   2   3   4   5   6   7   8   9

PRINTED IN U. S. A.

ACKNOWLEDGMENTS

CONTENTS

1
Not With a Bang
Damon Knight
13

2
Spectator Sport
John D. MacDonald
19

3
There Will Come Soft Rains
Ray Bradbury
26

4
Dear Devil
Eric Frank Russell
34

5
Scanners Live in Vain
Cordwainer Smith
70

6
Born of Man and Woman
Richard Matheson
105

7
The Little Black Bag
C. M. Kornbluth
109

8
Enchanted Village
A. E. van Vogt
138

9

Oddy and Id
Alfred Bester
154

10

The Sack
William Morrison
170

11

The Silly Season
C. M. Kornbluth
190

12

Misbegotten Missionary
Isaac Asimov
205

13

To Serve Man
Damon Knight
221

14

Coming Attraction
Fritz Leiber
230

15

A Subway Named Mobius
A. J. Deutsch
244

16

Process
A. E. van Vogt
260

17

The Mindworm
C. M. Kornbluth
267

18

The New Reality
Charles L. Harness
281

1950 INTRODUCTION

In the world outside reality it was a very violent year. On June 25 North Korean troops crossed the 38th parallel and invaded South Korea. The United States, under the banner of the United Nations (the Soviets were out of the building protesting something else, and couldn't use their veto), went to the assistance of South Korea with air strikes and an expeditionary force. The North Koreans advanced steadily, forcing the U.S. and Republic of Korea troops back to a small area on the southern coast of the peninsula. Defeat was narrowly averted when General Douglas MacArthur engineered a remarkable landing far behind enemy lines at Inchon. Allied forces then pushed the North Koreans back across the border, pursuing them all the way to within a few miles of the border with the People's Republic of China at the Yalu River. However, on December 28 hundreds of thousands of Chinese troops crossed the Yalu and began to force the Allies back as the year ended.

Earlier, on January 25, Alger Hiss was convicted of perjury in testimony regarding his membership in the American Communist Party. Anti-communism reached fever pitch with the emergence of Senator Joseph McCarthy of Wisconsin, who charged in a speech that he had a list of "known communists" working for the State Department, and the passage on September 20 of the McCarran Act, which forced even suspected communists and former Party members out of government service. Especially vicious was the publication *Red Channels*, a book that accused

American citizens, particularly figures in the entertainment industry, of communist connections. Careers and lives were ruined on hearsay and through guilt by association.

Other highlights of the year included American recognition of Vietnam, the seizure of Tibet by Chinese Communist forces, and the formal decision by the Truman administration to develop the hydrogen bomb. The biggest heist in American history occurred when seven men took $2,700,000 in cash and money orders from the Brink's Express Company in Boston. French Foreign Minister Robert Schuman advocated a plan for the sharing of Europe's coal and iron ore deposits—this proposal would eventually lead to the formation of the European Economic Community or "Common Market."

On August 25 President Truman ordered Federal troops to seize the railroads in order to prevent a threatened strike. The President was the object of an assassination attempt on November 1, when Puerto Rican nationalists attempted to break into Blair House, where the Trumans were staying—one guard and one attacker were killed.

During 1950 the mambo became a dance craze in the United States. Uruguay defeated Brazil 5-4 to win soccer's World Cup. The Federal Bureau of Investigation issued its first "Most Wanted" list, while *What's My Line* and *Your Show of Shows*, the latter starring Sid Caeser, were hits on television. Minute Rice and Sugar Pops appeared on grocery shelves. Pablo Picasso sculpted "The Goat" as Charles M. Schulz's *Peanuts* debuted in the newspapers. Outstanding novels included *The Wall* by John Hersey, *A Town Like Alice* by Nevil Shute, *The Short Life* by Juan Carlos Onetti, and *Across The River and Through The Woods* by Ernest Hemingway. There were 8,000,000 television sets in the United States, serviced by over 100 TV stations. Orlon was introduced by DuPont.

Joe Louis attempted to regain his heavyweight boxing championship, but lost a decision to Ezzard Charles. Americans were the mostly proud owners of over 40,000,000 cars. Top films of the year included *The Asphalt Jungle, All About Eve, Sunset Boulevard* starring Gloria Swanson, Jean Cocteau's *Orpheus, Kind Hearts and Coronets,* and the wonderful *The Lavender Hill Mob*. The last two featured Alec Guinness. The Cleveland Browns won the National Football League Championship, while the New York Yankees defeated the surprising Philadelphia Phillies four games to none to take baseball's World Series. Cyclamates and

Sucaryl were introduced, and the Wallace and Wyeth laboratories developed tranquilizers. Two of the most influential books were *The Human Uses of Human Beings* by Norbert Wiener and *The Lonely Crowd* by David Riesman, Reuel Denney and Nathan Glazer.

The Haloid Company of Rochester, New York, produced the first Xerox copying machine. Middleground won the Kentucky Derby, while Al Rosen and Ralph Kiner led the American and National Leagues in home runs. Marc Chagall painted "King David." It was a wonderful year for the theater as *The Country Girl* by Clifford Odets, *Come Back Little Sheba* by William Inge, and *Member of the Wedding* by Carson McCullers all opened on Broadway. The Diners Club was founded as book publishers rejoiced. Popular musicals included Irving Berlin's *Call Me Madam*, and Frank Loesser's *Guys and Dolls*. America was singing "Cherry Pink and Apple Blossom White," "It's So Nice to Have a Man Around the House," and "If I Knew You Were Comin' I'd Have Baked a Cake."

Florence Chadwick broke the record for swimming the English Channel. Smokey the Bear became the symbol for fighting forest fires. There were about 2,520,000,000 people in the world. Death took George Bernard Shaw and painter Max Beckmann.

Mel Brooks may have still been Melvin Kaminsky.

In the real world it was a simply terrific year.

In the real world the eighth World Science Fiction Convention (the Norwescon) was held in far away Portland, Oregon. Also in the real world *Galaxy Science Fiction* was born and under the editorship of H. L. Gold quickly established itself as one of the premier magazines in the field. If this was not enough, *The Magazine of Fantasy*, launched the year before, changed its name to *The Magazine of Fantasy and Science Fiction*, and also rapidly achieved excellence, transforming *Astounding Science Fiction* from the "Big One," to one of the "Big Three." The tide continued to rise with the appearance of Damon Knight's excellent *Worlds Beyond*, Raymond Palmer's/Beatrice Mahaffey's *Imagination*, Malcolm Reiss' *Two Complete Science Adventure Books*, and a refurbished *Future Combined With Science Fiction Stories*. In England, Walter H. Gillings started *Science-Fantasy*, an uneven magazine but one that would enjoy a long life. These events overshadowed the folding of *A. Merritt's Fantasy Magazine* in October.

In the real world, more important people made their maiden

voyages into reality: in January—Cordwainer Smith with "Scanners Live in Vain", in February—Paul Fairman with "No Teeth for the Tiger"; in March—Gordon R. Dickson (co-authored with Poul Anderson) with "Trespass!"; in April—Mack Reynolds with "Isolationist"; in the summer—Richard Matheson with "Born of Man and Woman"; in November—Chad Oliver with "The Land of Lost Content"; and in December—J. T. McIntosh with "The Curfew Tolls."

More wondrous things happened in the real world as outstanding novels, stories and collections were published in magazines and in book form: James Blish began his "Oakie" series of novelettes, while L. Sprague de Camp and Fletcher Pratt published their first "Gavagan's Bar" story. *The Dreaming Jewels* by Theodore Sturgeon appeared in *Fantastic Adventures*, Judith Merril's first anthology, *Shot in the Dark*, appeared in paperback, and sf fans had the pleasure of reading *Pebble in the Sky* by Isaac Asimov and *The Martian Chronicles* by Ray Bradbury as part of Doubleday's new science fiction line. A. E. van Vogt brought together earlier stories in an attractive package and produced *The Voyage of the Space Beagle*. On a more serious note, veteran science fiction writer L. Ron Hubbard published an article entitled "Dianetics, the Evolution of a Science" in *Astounding*, which eventually led to controversy, to the distraction and temporary loss to sf of several important writers, and, incidentally to the establishment of something that considered itself a new religion.

The non-print media began to embrace science fiction with the release of *Destination Moon*, (based very loosely on Robert A. Heinlein's juvenile novel *Rocketship Galileo*), *The Flying Saucer*, *The Perfect Woman*, the unforgettable *Prehistoric Women*, and the moody *Rocketship* XM. *Tom Corbett: Space Cadet* debuted on television.

Let us travel back to that honored year of 1950 and enjoy the best stories that the real world bequeathed to us.

1

NOT WITH A BANG

Damon Knight (1922–   )

THE MAGAZINE OF FANTASY AND SCIENCE FICTION
Winter

The extinction of the human species has interested and frightened science fiction writers since at least Mary Shelley's The Last Man *of 1826. It is a subject that has produced moving, nostalgic, and powerful stories. Here, the urbane Damon Knight tackles the subject with somewhat different results.*

—M.H.G.

T. S. Eliot in 1925 published a poem called "The Hollow Men" of which the most famous lines are:

> This is the way the world ends
> Not with a bang but a whimper.

People who don't read science fiction think of T. S. Eliot when those lines are quoted. I think of Damon Knight because he composed "Not With a Bang," which expresses those lines perfectly.

Only one thing bothers me. How did Damon mean the phrase "Not With a Bang"? If we consider it as a vulgarism, the story illustrates that perfectly, too. Is that just a coincidence? Is it possible that Damon never thought of the other meaning?

And if Damon missed it, I cannot conceive that Tony Boucher, the editor of the magazine in which it appeared, missed it. I knew Tony too well in those old days to believe that for a minute.

—I. A.

Ten months after the last plane passed over, Rolf Smith knew beyond doubt that only one other human being had survived. Her name was Louise Oliver, and he was sitting opposite her in a department-store cafe in Salt Lake City. They were eating canned Vienna sausages and drinking coffee.

Sunlight struck through a broken pane, lying like a judgment on the cloudy air of the room. Inside and outside, there was no sound; only a stifling rumor of absence. The clatter of dishware in the kitchen, the heavy rumble of streetcars: never again. There was sunlight; and silence; and the watery, astonished eyes of Louise Oliver.

He leaned forward, trying to capture the attention of those fishlike eyes for a second. "Darling," he said, "I respect your views, naturally. But I've got to make you see that they're impractical."

She looked at him with faint surprise, then away again. Her head shook slightly: No. *No, Rolf. I will not live with you in sin.*

Smith thought of the women of France, of Russia, of Mexico, of the South Seas. He had spent three months in the ruined studios of a radio station in Rochester, listening to the voices until they stopped. There had been a large colony in Sweden, including an English cabinet minister. They reported that Europe was gone. Simply gone; there was not an acre that had not been swept clean by radioactive dust. They had two planes and enough fuel to take them anywhere on the Continent; but there was nowhere to go. Three of them had the plague; then eleven; then all.

There was a bomber pilot who had fallen near a government radio in Palestine. He did not last long, because he had broken some bones in the crash; but he had seen the vacant waters where the Pacific Islands should have been. It was his guess that the Arctic ice-fields had been bombed. He did not know whether that had been a mistake or not.

There were no reports from Washington, from New York, from London, Paris, Moscow, Chungking, Sydney. You could not tell who had been destroyed by disease, who by the dust, who by bombs.

Smith himself had been a laboratory assistant in a team that was trying to find an antibiotic for the plague. His superiors had found one that worked sometimes, but it was a little too late. When he left, Smith took along with him all there was of it—forty ampoules, enough to last him for years.

Louise had been a nurse in a genteel hospital near Denver. According to her, something rather odd had happened to the hospital as she was approaching it the morning of the attack. She was quite calm when she said this, but a vague look came into her eyes and her shattered expression seemed to slip a little more. Smith did not press her for an explanation.

Like himself, she had found a radio station which still functioned, and when Smith discovered that she had not contracted the plague, he agreed to meet her. She was, apparently, naturally immune. There must have been others, a few at least; but the bombs and the dust had not spared them.

It seemed very awkward to Louise that not one Protestant minister was left alive.

The trouble was, she really meant it. It had taken Smith a long time to believe it, but it was true. She would not sleep in the same hotel with him, either; she expected, and received, the utmost courtesy and decorum. Smith had learned his lesson. He walked on the outside of the rubble-heaped sidewalks; he opened doors for her, when there were still doors; he held her chair; he refrained from swearing. He courted her.

Louise was forty or thereabouts, at least five years older than Smith. He often wondered how old she thought she was. The shock of seeing whatever it was that had happened to the hospital, the patients she had cared for, had sent her mind scuttling back to her childhood. She tacitly admitted that everyone else in the world was dead, but she seemed to regard it as something one did not mention.

A hundred times in the last three weeks, Smith had felt an almost irresistible impulse to break her thin neck and go his own way. But there was no help for it; she was the only woman in the world, and he needed her. If she died, or left him, he died. *Old bitch!* he thought to himself furiously, and carefully kept the thought from showing on his face.

"Louise, honey," he told her gently, "I want to spare your feelings as much as I can. You know that."

"Yes, Rolf," she said, staring at him with the face of a hypnotized chicken.

Smith forced himself to go on. "We've got to face the facts, unpleasant as they may be. Honey, we're the only man and the only woman there are. We're like Adam and Eve in the Garden of Eden."

Louise's face took on a slightly disgusted expression. She was obviously thinking of fig-leaves.

"Think of the generations unborn," Smith told her, with a tremor in his voice. *Think about me for once. Maybe you're good for another ten years, maybe not.* Shuddering, he thought of the second stage of the disease—the helpless rigidity, striking without warning. He'd had one such attack already, and Louise had helped him out of it. Without her, he would have stayed like that till he died, the hypodermic that would save him within inches of his rigid hand. He thought desperately, *If I'm lucky, I'll get at least two kids out of you before you croak. Then I'll be safe.*

He went on, "God didn't mean for the human race to end like this. He spared us, you and me, to—" He paused; how could he say it without offending her? "Parents" wouldn't do—too suggestive. "—to carry on the torch of life," he ended. There. That was sticky enough.

Louise was staring vaguely over his shoulder. Her eyelids blinked regularly, and her mouth made little rabbit-like motions in the same rhythm.

Smith looked down at his wasted thighs under the tabletop. *I'm not strong enough to force her,* he thought. *Christ, if I were strong enough!*

He felt the futile rage again, and stifled it. He had to keep his head, because this might be his last chance. Louise had been talking lately, in the cloudy language she used about everything, of going up in the mountains to pray for guidance. She had not said, "alone," but it was easy enough to see that she pictured it that way. He had to argue her around before her resolve stiffened. He concentrated furiously, and tried once more.

The pattern of words went by like a distant rumbling. Louise heard a phrase here and there; each of them fathered chains of thought, binding her reverie tighter. "Our duty to humanity . . ." Mama had often said—that was in the old house on Waterbury Street of course, before Mama had taken sick—she had said, "Child, your duty is to be clean, polite, and God-fearing. Pretty doesn't matter. There's a plenty of plain women that have got themselves good, Christian husbands."

Husbands . . . To have and to hold . . . Orange blossoms, and the bridesmaids; the organ music. Through the haze, she saw Rolf's lean, wolfish face. Of course, he was the only one she'd ever get; *she* knew that well enough. Gracious, when a girl was past twenty-five, she had to take what she could get.

But I sometimes wonder if he's really a nice man, she thought.

". . . in the eyes of God . . ." She remembered the stained glass windows in the old First Episcopalian Church, and how she always thought God was looking down at her through that brilliant transparency. Perhaps He was still looking at her, though it seemed sometimes that He had forgotten. Well, of course she realized that marriage customs changed, and if you couldn't have a regular minister. . . . But it was really a shame, an outrage almost, that if she were actually going to marry this man, she couldn't have all those nice things . . . There wouldn't even be any wedding presents. Not even that. But of course Rolf would give her anything she wanted. She saw his face again, noticed the narrow black eyes staring at her with ferocious purpose, the thin mouth that jerked in a slow, regular tic, the hairy lobes of the ears below the tangle of black hair.

He oughtn't to let his hair grow so long, she thought, *it isn't quite decent.* Well, she could change all that. If she did marry him, she'd certainly make him change his ways. It was no more than her duty.

He was talking now about a farm he'd seen outside town—a good big house and a barn. There was no stock, he said, but they could get some later. And they'd plant things, and have their own food to eat, not go to restaurants all the time.

She felt a touch on her hand, lying pale before her on the table. Rolf's brown, stubby fingers, black-haired above and below the knuckles, were touching hers. He had stopped talking for a moment, but now he was speaking again, still more urgently. She drew her hand away.

He was saying, ". . . and you'll have the finest wedding dress you ever saw, with a bouquet. Everything you want, Louise, everything . . ."

A wedding dress! And flowers, even if there couldn't be any minister! Well, why hadn't the fool said so before?

Rolf stopped halfway through a sentence, aware that Louise had said quite clearly, "Yes, Rolf, I will marry you if you wish."

Stunned, he wanted her to repeat it, but dared not ask, "What did you say?" for fear of getting some fantastic answer, or none at all. He breathed deeply. He said, "Today, Louise?"

She said, "Well, *today* . . . I don't know quite . . . Of course, if you think you can make all the arrangements in time, but it does seem . . ."

Triumph surged through Smith's body. He had the advantage now, and he'd ride it. "Say you will, dear," he urged her; "say yes, and make me the happiest man . . ."

Even then, his tongue balked at the rest of it; but it didn't matter. She nodded submissively. "Whatever you think best, Rolf."

He rose, and she allowed him to kiss her pale, sapless cheek. "We'll leave right away," he said. "If you'll excuse me for just a minute, dear?"

He waited for her "Of course" and then left her, making footprints in the furred carpet of dust down toward the end of the room. Just a few more hours he'd have to speak to her like that, and then, in her eyes, she'd be committed to him forever. Afterwards, he could do with her as he liked—beat her when he pleased, submit her to any proof of his scorn and revulsion, use her. Then it would not be too bad, being the last man on Earth—not bad at all. She might even have a daughter . . .

He found the washroom door and entered. He took a step inside, and froze, balanced by a trick of motion, upright but helpless. Panic struck at his throat as he tried to turn his head and failed; tried to scream, and failed. Behind him, he was aware of a tiny click as the door, cushioned by the hydraulic check, shut forever. It was not locked; but its other side bore the warning: MEN.

2

SPECTATOR SPORT

John D. MacDonald (1916–   )

THRILLING WONDER STORIES
February

For those of you new to this series, this is the same John D. MacDonald responsible for the Travis Magee novels and several dozen other terrific suspense tales. Although he left the science fiction field (for the most part) in the early 1950s, he still has great affection for sf and the people who write and read it. His book-length science fiction is confined to the novels Wine of the Dreamers *(1951),* Ballroom of the Skies *(1952),* The Girl, The Gold Watch, and Everything *(1962) and the collection* Other Times, Other Worlds *(1978).*

"Spectator Sport" is a minor classic, a story with strong political overtones as well as some important observations on the nature of reality.

—M.H.G.

Science fiction, though usually dealing with the future, can't help but be rooted in its present.

In 1950, for instance, Americans began to realize that television was not just a fad, not just an oddity, but was going to alter society as deeply and permanently as the automobile had. Many intellectuals viewed it with a kind of horrified despair and began to foresee an unbearable future, as MacDonald does in "Spectator Sport."

Oddly enough, I think we fear television less now than we did a third of a century ago. (Heavens, is television that old?)

Custom hardens us. Nevertheless, we are still capable of being devastated by novelty. Ask people over forty what they think of video games.

—*I.A.*

Dr. Rufus Maddon was not generally considered to be an impatient man—or addicted to physical violence.

But when the tenth man he tried to stop on the street brushed by him with a mutter of annoyance Rufus Maddon grabbed the eleventh man, swung him around and held him with his shoulders against a crumbling wall.

He said, "You will listen to me, sir! I am the first man to travel into the future and I will not stand—"

The man pushed him away, turned around and said, "You got this dust on my suit. Now brush it off."

Rufus Maddon brushed mechanically. He said, with a faint uncontrollable tremble in his voice, "But nobody seems to care."

The man peered back over his shoulder. "Good enough, chum. Better go get yourself lobed. The first time I saw the one on time travel it didn't get to me at all. Too hammy for me. Give me those murder jobs. Every time I have one of those I twitch for twenty hours."

Rufus made another try. "Sir, I am physical living proof that the future is predetermined. I can explain the energy equations, redesign the warp projector, send myself from your day further into the future—"

The man walked away. "Go get a lobe job," he said.

"But don't I look different to you?" Rufus called after him, a plaintive note in his voice.

The man, twenty feet away, turned and grinned at him. "How?"

When the man had gone Rufus Maddon looked down at his neat grey suit, stared at the men and women in the street. It was not fair of the future to be so—so dismally normal.

Four hundred years of progress? The others had resented the experience that was to be his. In those last few weeks there had been many discussions of how the people four hundred years in the future would look on Rufus Maddon as a barbarian.

Once again he continued his aimless walk down the streets of the familiar city. There was a general air of disrepair. Shops were boarded up. The pavement was broken and potholed. A few automobiles traveled on the broken streets. They, at least, appeared to be of a slightly advanced design but they were dented, dirty and noisy.

The man who had spoken to him had made no sense. "Lobe job?" And what was "the one on time travel"?

He stopped in consternation as he reached the familiar park. His consternation arose from the fact that the park was all too familiar. Though it was a tangle of weeds the equestrian statue of General Murdy was still there in deathless bronze, liberally decorated by pigeons.

Clothes had not changed nor had common speech. He wondered if the transfer had gone awry, if this world were something he was dreaming.

He pushed through the knee-high tangle of grass to a wrought-iron bench. Four hundred years before he had sat on that same bench. He sat down again. The metal powdered and collapsed under his weight, one end of the bench dropping with a painful thump.

Dr. Rufus Maddon was not generally considered to be a man subject to fits of rage. He stood up, rubbing his bruised elbow, and heartily kicked the offending bench. The part he kicked was all too solid.

He limped out of the park, muttering, wondering why the park wasn't used, why everyone seemed to be in a hurry.

It appeared that in four hundred years nothing at all had been accomplished. Many familiar buildings had collapsed. Others still stood. He looked in vain for a newspaper or a magazine.

One new element of this world of the future bothered him considerably. That was the number of low-slung white-panel delivery trucks. They seemed to be in better condition than the other vehicles. Each bore in fairly large gilt letters the legend WORLD SENSEWAYS. But he noticed that the smaller print underneath the large inscription varied. Some read, *Feeder Division*—others, *Hookup Division*.

The one that stopped at the curb beside him read, *Lobotomy Division*. Two husky men got out and smiled at him and one said, "You've been taking too much of that stuff, Doc."

"How did you know my title?" Rufus asked, thoroughly puzzled.

The other man smiled wolfishly, patted the side of the truck.

"Nice truck, pretty truck. Climb in, bud. We'll take you down and make you feel wonderful, hey?"

Dr. Rufus Maddon suddenly had a horrid suspicion that he knew what a lobe job might be. He started to back away. They grabbed him quickly and expertly and dumped him into the truck.

The sign on the front of the building said WORLD SENSEWAYS. The most luxurious office inside was lettered, *Regional Director— Roger K. Handriss*.

Roger K. Handriss sat behind his handsome desk. He was a florid grey-haired man with keen grey eyes. He was examining his bank book thinking that in another year he'd have enough money to retire and buy a permanent hookup. Permanent was so much better than the Temp stuff you could get on the home sets. The nerve ends was what did it, of course.

The girl came in and placed several objects on the desk in front of him. She said, "Mr. Handriss, these just came up from LD. They took them out of the pockets of a man reported as wandering in the street in need of a lobe job."

She had left the office door open. Cramer, deputy chief of LD, sauntered in and said, "The guy was really off. He was yammering about being from the past and not to destroy his mind."

Roger Handriss poked the objects with a manicured finger. He said, "Small pocket change from the twentieth century, Cramer. Membership cards in professional organizations of that era. Ah, here's a letter."

As Cramer and the girl waited, Roger Handriss read the letter through twice. He gave Cramer an uncomfortable smile and said, "This appears to be a letter from a technical publishing house telling Mr.—ah—Maddon that they intend to reprint his book, Suggestions on Time Focus in February of nineteen hundred and fifty. Miss Hart, get on the phone and see if you can raise anyone at the library who can look this up for us. I want to know if such a book was published."

Miss Hart hastened out of the office.

As they waited, Handriss motioned to a chair. Cramer sat down. Handriss said, "Imagine what it must have been like in those days, Al. They had the secrets but they didn't begin to use them until—let me see—four years later. Aldous Huxley had already given them their clue with his literary invention of the Feelies. But they ignored them.

"All their energies went into wars and rumors of wars and random scientific advancement and sociological disruptions. Of course, with Video on the march at that time, they were beginning to get a little preview. Millions of people were beginning to sit in front of the Video screens, content even with that crude excuse for entertainment."

Cramer suppressed a yawn. Handriss was known to go on like that for hours.

"Now," Handriss continued, "all the efforts of a world society are channeled into World Senseways. There is no waste of effort changing a perfectly acceptable status quo. Every man can have Temp and if you save your money you can have Permanent, which they say is as close to heaven as man can get. Uh—what was that, Miss Hart?"

"There is such a book, Mr. Handriss, and it was published at that time. A Dr. Rufus Maddon wrote it."

Handriss sighed and clucked. "Well," he said, "have Maddon brought up here."

Maddon was brought into the office by an attendant. He wore a wide foolish smile and a tiny bandage on his temple. He walked with the clumsiness of an overgrown child.

"Blast it, Al," Handriss said, "why couldn't your people have been more careful! He looks as if he might have been intelligent."

Al shrugged. "Do they come here from the past every couple of minutes? He didn't look any different than any other lobey to me."

"I suppose it couldn't be helped," Handriss said. "We've done this man a great wrong. We can wait and reeducate, I suppose. But that seems to be treating him rather shabbily."

"We can't send him back," Al Cramer said.

Handriss stood up, his eyes glowing. "But it is within my authority to grant him one of the Perm setups given me. World Senseways knows that Regional Directors make mistakes. This will rectify any mistake to an individual."

"Is it fair he should get it for free?" Cramer asked. "And besides, maybe the people who helped send him up here into the future would like to know what goes on."

Handriss smiled shrewdly. "And if they knew, what would stop them from flooding in on us? Have Hookup install him immediately."

The subterranean corridor had once been used for underground trains. But with the reduction in population it had ceased to pay its way and had been taken over by World Senseways to house the sixty-five thousand Perms.

Dr. Rufus Maddon was taken, in his new shambling walk, to the shining cubicle. His name and the date of installation were written on a card and inserted in the door slot. Handriss stood enviously aside and watched the process.

The bored technicians worked rapidly. They stripped the un-protesting Rufus Maddon, took him inside his cubicle, forced him down onto the foam couch. They rolled him over onto his side, made the usual incision at the back of his neck, carefully slit the main motor nerves, leaving the senses, the heart and lungs intact. They checked the air conditioning and plugged him into the feeding schedule for that bank of Perms.

Next they swung the handrods and the footplates into position, gave him injections of local anesthetic, expertly flayed the palms of his hands and the soles of his feet, painted the raw flesh with the sticky nerve graft and held his hands closed around the rods, his feet against the plates until they adhered in the proper position.

Handriss glanced at his watch.

"Guess that's all we can watch, Al. Come along."

The two men walked back down the long corridor. Handriss said, "The lucky so and so. We have to work for it. I get my Perm in another year—right down here beside him. In the mean-time we'll have to content ourselves with the hand sets, holding onto those blasted knobs that don't let enough through to hardly raise the hair on the back of your neck."

Al sighed enviously. "Nothing to do for as long as he lives except twenty-four hours a day of being the hero of the most adventurous and glamorous and exciting stories that the race has been able to devise. No memories. I told them to dial him in on the Cowboy series. There's seven years of that now. It'll be more familiar to him. I'm electing Crime and Detection. Eleven years of that now, you know."

Roger Handriss chuckled and jabbed Al with his elbow. "Be smart, Al. Pick the Harem series."

Back in the cubicle the technicians were making the final adjustments. They inserted the sound buttons in Rufus Maddon's ears, deftly removed his eyelids, moved his head into just the right position and then pulled down the deeply concave shining screen so that Rufus Maddon's staring eyes looked directly into it.

The elder technician pulled the wall switch. He bent and peered into the screen. "Color okay, three dimensions okay. Come on, Joe, we got another to do before quitting."

They left, closed the metal door, locked it.

Inside the cubicle, Dr. Rufus Maddon was riding slowly down the steep trail from the mesa to the cattle town on the plains. He was trail-weary and sun-blackened. There was an old score to settle. Feeney was about to foreclose on Mary Ann's spread and Buck Hoskie, Mary Ann's crooked foreman, had threatened to shoot on sight.

Rufus Maddon wiped the sweat from his forehead on the back of a lean hard brown hero's hand.

3

THERE WILL COME SOFT RAINS

Ray Bradbury (1920–   )

COLLIER'S
May

1950 was a banner year for the thirty-year-old Bradbury. It saw the publication of The Martian Chronicles, *the work for which he is still famous. The stories that comprise it were partly written in the second half of the 40s while others appeared in the volume for the first time. In spite of its impossible astronomy, it remains a landmark work in the history of modern science fiction. Obviously influenced by American history and the movement of the frontier westward as well as Bradbury's own midwestern childhood, the book established his reputation as a major American literary figure.*

"There Will Come Soft Rains" contains some of the most haunting scenes in sf, images that I have retained for more than thirty years. It was published in Collier's, *a Saturday Evening Post-like family magazine of beloved memory—Bradbury, along with Robert A. Heinlein, brought science fiction to its slick pages.*

—M.H.G.

One of the turning points of modern science fiction came in late 1949. Doubleday and Co., the largest of the trade publishers, actually decided to put out a line of hard-cover science fiction books.

This was unheard-of. For twenty-three years, American science fiction existed almost entirely in the magazines. There were some hard-cover books put out by fans, but they were curios more

26

than anything else. There were also a couple of paperbacks put out, and one or two anthologies, but these were all exceptional.

Doubleday planned to put out science fiction books on a regular basis and use their expertise and facilities to publicize and sell them. Wow!

The first book they published was The Big Eye *by Max Ehrlich (who died recently). The second book—the first by a recognized science fiction writer—was* Pebble in the Sky *by Isaac Asimov (my first book). But what really established Doubleday's line and made a permanent thing of it (it still exists a third of a century later) was the third book, which was* The Martian Chronicles *by Ray Bradbury. It was an instant classic.*

But was I jealous?

Of course.

—I.A.

In the living room the voice-clock sang, *Tick-tock, seven o'clock, time to get up, time to get up, seven o'clock!* as if it were afraid that nobody would. The morning house lay empty. The clock ticked on, repeating and repeating its sounds into the emptiness. *Seven-nine, breakfast time, seven-nine!*

In the kitchen the breakfast stove gave a hissing sigh and ejected from its warm interior eight pieces of perfectly browned toast, eight eggs sunnyside up, sixteen slices of bacon, two coffees, and two cool glasses of milk.

"Today is August 4, 2026," said a second voice from the kitchen ceiling, "in the city of Allendale, California." It repeated the date three times for memory's sake. "Today is Mr. Featherstone's birthday. Today is the anniversary of Tilita's marriage. Insurance is payable, as are the water, gas, and light bills."

Somewhere in the walls, relays clicked, memory tapes glided under electric eyes.

Eight-one, tick-tock, eight-one o'clock, off to school, off to work, run, run, eight-one! But no doors slammed, no carpets took the soft tread of rubber heels. It was raining outside. The weather box on the front door sang quietly: "Rain, rain, go away; rubbers, raincoats for today . . ." And the rain tapped on the empty house, echoing.

Outside, the garage chimed and lifted its door to reveal the waiting car. After a long wait the door swung down again.

At eight-thirty the eggs were shriveled and the toast was like stone. An aluminum wedge scraped them into the sink, where hot water whirled them down a metal throat which digested and flushed them away to the distant sea. The dirty dishes were dropped into a hot washer and emerged twinkling dry.

Nine-fifteen, sang the clock, *time to clean.*

Out of warrens in the wall, tiny robot mice darted. The rooms were acrawl with the small cleaning animals, all rubber and metal. They thudded against chairs, whirling their mustached runners, kneading the rug nap, sucking gently at hidden dust. Then, like mysterious invaders, they popped into their burrows. Their pink electric eyes faded. The house was clean.

Ten o'clock. The sun came out from behind the rain. The house stood alone in a city of rubble and ashes. This was the one house left standing. At night the ruined city gave off a radioactive glow which could be seen for miles.

Ten-fifteen. the garden sprinklers whirled up in golden founts, filling the soft morning air with scatterings of brightness. The water pelted windowpanes, running down the charred west side where the house had been burned evenly free of its white paint. The entire west face of the house was black, save for five places. Here the silhouette in paint of a man mowing a lawn. Here, as in a photograph, a woman bent to pick flowers. Still farther over, their images burned on wood in one titanic instant, a small boy, hands flung into the air; higher up, the image of a thrown ball, and opposite him a girl, hands raised to catch a ball which never came down.

The five spots of paint—the man, the woman, the children, the ball—remained. The rest was a thin charcoaled layer.

The gentle sprinkler rain filled the garden with falling light.

Until this day, how well the house had kept its peace. How carefully it had inquired, "Who goes there? What's the password?" and, getting no answer from lonely foxes and whining cats, it had shut up its windows and drawn shades in an old-maidenly preoccupation with self-protection which bordered on a mechanical paranoia.

It quivered at each sound, the house did. If a sparrow brushed a window, the shade snapped up. The bird, startled, flew off! No, not even a bird must touch the house!

The house was an altar with ten thousand attendants, big,

small, servicing, attending, in choirs. But the gods had gone away, and the ritual of the religion continued senselessly, uselessly.

Twelve noon.

A dog whined, shivering, on the front porch.

The front door recognized the dog voice and opened. The dog, once huge and fleshy, but now gone to bone and covered with sores, moved in and through the house, tracking mud. Behind it whirred angry mice, angry at having to pick up mud, angry at inconvenience.

For not a leaf fragment blew under the door but what the wall panels flipped open and the copper scrap rats flashed swiftly out. The offending dust, hair, or paper, seized in miniature steel jaws, was raced back to the burrows. There, down tubes which fed into the cellar, it was dropped into the sighing vent of an incinerator which sat like a evil Baal in a dark corner.

The dog ran upstairs, hysterically yelping to each door, at last realizing, as the house realized, that only silence was here.

It sniffed the air and scratched the kitchen door. Behind the door, the stove was making pancakes which filled the house with a rich baked odor and the scent of maple syrup.

The dog frothed at the mouth, lying at the door, sniffing, its eyes turned to fire. It ran wildly in circles, biting at its tail, spun in a frenzy, and died. It lay in the parlor for an hour.

Two o'clock, sang a voice.

Delicately sensing decay at last, the regiments of mice hummed out as softly as blown gray leaves in an electrical wind.

Two-fifteen.

The dog was gone.

In the cellar, the incinerator glowed suddenly and a whirl of sparks leaped up the chimney.

Two thirty-five.

Bridge tables sprouted from patio walls. Playing cards fluttered onto pads in a shower of pips. Martinis manifested on an oaken bench with egg-salad sandwiches. Music played.

But the tables were silent and the cards untouched.

At four o'clock the tables folded like great butterflies back through the paneled walls.

Four-thirty.

The nursery walls glowed.

Animals took shape: yellow giraffes, blue lions, pink antelopes, lilac panthers cavorting in crystal substance. The walls were glass. They looked out upon color and fantasy. Hidden films clocked through well-oiled sprockets, and the walls lived. The nursery floor was woven to resemble a crisp, cereal meadow. Over this ran aluminum roaches and iron crickets, and in the hot still air butterflies of delicate red tissue wavered among the sharp aroma of animal spoors! There was the sound like a great matted yellow hive of bees within a dark bellows, the lazy bumble of a purring lion. And there was the patter of okapi feet and the murmur of a fresh jungle rain, like other hoofs, falling upon the summer-starched grass. Now the walls dissolved into distances of parched weed, mile on mile, and warm endless sky. The animals drew away into thorn brakes and water holes.

It was the children's hour.

Five o'clock. The bath filled with clear hot water.

Six, seven, eight o'clock. The dinner dishes manipulated like magic tricks, and in the study a *click.* In the metal stand opposite the hearth where a fire now blazed up warmly, a cigar popped out, half an inch of soft gray ash on it, smoking, waiting.

Nine o'clock. The beds warmed their hidden circuits, for nights were cool here.

Nine-five. A voice spoke from the study ceiling:

"Mrs. McClellan, which poem would you like this evening?"

The house was silent.

The voice said at last, "Since you express no preference, I shall select a poem at random." Quiet music rose to back the voice. "Sara Teasdale. As I recall, your favorite. . . .

"There will come soft rains and the smell of the ground,
And swallows circling with their shimmering sound;

And frogs in the pools singing at night,
And wild plum trees in tremulous white;

Robins will wear their feathery fire,
Whistling their whims on a low fence-wire;

And not one will know of the war, not one
Will care at last when it is done.

Not one would mind, neither bird nor tree,
If mankind perished utterly;

And Spring herself, when she woke at dawn
Would scarcely know that we were gone."

The fire burned on the stone hearth and the cigar fell away
into a mound of quiet ash on its tray. The empty chairs
faced each other between the silent walls, and the music
played.

At ten o'clock the house began to die.
The wind blew. A falling tree bough crashed through the
kitchen window. Cleaning solvent, bottled, shattered over the
stove. The room was ablaze in an instant!
"Fire!" screamed a voice. The house lights flashed, water
pumps shot water from the ceilings. But the solvent spread on
the linoleum, licking, eating, under the kitchen door, while the
voices took it up in chorus: "Fire, fire, fire!"
The house tried to save itself. Doors sprang tightly shut, but
the windows were broken by the heat and the wind blew and
sucked upon the fire.
The house gave ground as the fire in ten billion angry sparks
moved with flaming ease from room to room and then up the
stairs. While scurrying water rats squeaked from the walls,
pistoled their water, and ran for more. And the wall sprays let
down showers of mechanical rain.
But too late. Somewhere, sighing, a pump shrugged to a stop.
The quenching rain ceased. The reserve water supply which had
filled baths and washed dishes for many quiet days was gone.
The fire crackled up the stairs. It fed upon Picassos and
Matisses in the upper halls, like delicacies, baking off the oily
flesh, tenderly crisping the canvases into black shavings.
Now the fire lay in beds, stood in windows, changed the
colors of drapes!
And then, reinforcements.
From attic trapdoors, blind robot faces peered down with
faucet mouths gushing green chemical.
The fire backed off, as even an elephant must at the sight of
a dead snake. Now there were twenty snakes whipping over
the floor, killing the fire with a clear cold venom of green
froth.
But the fire was clever. It had sent flame outside the house, up
through the attic to the pumps there. An explosion! The attic

brain which directed the pumps was shattered into bronze shrap-
nel on the beams.

The fire rushed back into every closet and felt of the clothes
hung there.

The house shuddered, oak bone on bone, its bared skeleton
cringing from the heat, its wire, its nerves revealed as if a
surgeon had torn the skin off to let the red veins and capillaries
quiver in the scalded air. Help, help! Fire! Run, run! Heat
snapped mirrors like the first brittle winter ice. And the voices
wailed Fire, fire, run, run, like a tragic nursery rhyme, a dozen
voices, high, low, like children dying in a forest, alone, alone.
And the voices fading as the wires popped their sheathings like
hot chestnuts. One, two, three, four, five voices died.

In the nursery the jungle burned. Blue lions roared, purple
giraffes bounded off. The panthers ran in circles, changing color,
and ten million animals, running before the fire, vanished off
toward a distant steaming river. . . .

Ten more voices died. In the last instant under the fire avalanche,
other chorusus, oblivious, could be heard announcing the time,
playing music, cutting the lawn by remote-control mower, or
setting an umbrella frantically out and in the slamming and
opening front door, a thousand things happening, like a clock
shop when each clock strikes the hour insanely before or after
the other, a scene of maniac confusion, yet unity; singing,
screaming, a few last cleaning mice darting bravely out to carry
the horrid ashes away! And one voice, with sublime disregard
for the situation, read poetry aloud in the fiery study, until all the
film spools burned, until all the wires withered and the circuits
cracked.

The fire burst the house and let it slam flat down, puffing out
skirts of spark and smoke.

In the kitchen, an instant before the rain of fire and timber, the
stove could be seen making breakfasts at a psychopathic rate, ten
dozen eggs, six loaves of toast, twenty dozen bacon strips,
which, eaten by fire, started the stove working again, hysterically hissing!

The crash. The attic smashing into kitchen and parlor. The
parlor into cellar, cellar into sub-cellar. Deep freeze, armchair,
film tapes, circuits, beds, and all like skeletons thrown in a
cluttered mound deep under.

Smoke and silence. A great quantity of smoke.

Dawn showed faintly in the east. Among the ruins, one wall stood alone. Within the wall, a last voice said, over and over again and again, even as the sun rose to shine upon the heaped rubble and steam:

"Today is August 5, 2026, today is August 5, 2026, today is ..."

4

DEAR DEVIL

Eric Frank Russell (1905–1978)

OTHER WORLDS
May

The wonderful and underrated Eric Frank Russell returns to this
series with one of his best stories (and that is very high praise).
It concerns one of his favorite themes, Earthman against alien.
Russell could write almost any kind of science fiction—he ex-
celled at adventure and action—but he seemed to really enjoy the
automatic dramatic tension of encounters between two different
intelligent species. "Dear Devil" contains the warmth and compassion that he often brought to his work, attributes not com-
monly found in the science fiction of his day. The title character
in this story should remain in your mind for a long time—if he
doesn't, you may need some professional help.

—M.H.G.

In the earliest tales of interplanetary travel, natives of other
worlds were usually presented as reasonably friendly. Earthmen
visited them as inquisitive travelers; they visited us likewise. The
first case of a hostile encounter was The War of the Worlds, by
H. G. Wells, published in 1898.
   That did it. The tale of interplanetary warfare was so dramatic
that it set the fashion for what followed. Interplanetary warfare
and nothing but interplanetary warfare. And Mars was always
particularly demonic; partly because of Wells's tale, partly because of the association with the god of war.
   It took some courage, then, for Russell to reverse this, but the
result was a terrific story, and a moving one. And a recipe for

34

success, as well, as Steven Spielberg recently demonstrated with the motion picture E.T.

And there's a moral, too. I hate pointing out morals, but this one is so important I don't want anyone to miss it. If the great difference between Martian and Earthman could be bridged, did it make sense to destroy a planet over much smaller differences?

—I.A.

The first Martian vessel descended upon Earth with the slow, stately fall of a grounded balloon. It did resemble a large balloon in that it was spherical and had a strange buoyance out of keeping with its metallic construction. Beyond this superficial appearance all similarity to anything Terrestrial ceased.

There were no rockets, no crimson venturis, no external projections other than several solaradiant distorting grids which boosted the ship in any desired direction through the cosmic field. There were no observation ports. All viewing was done through a transparent band running right around the fat belly of the sphere. The bluish, nightmarish crew was assembled behind that band, surveying the world with great multifaceted eyes.

They gazed through the band in utter silence as they examined this world which was Terra. Even if they had been capable of speech they would have said nothing. But none among them had a talkative facility in any sonic sense. At this quiet moment none needed it.

The scene outside was one of the untrammeled desolation. Scraggy blue-green grass clung to tired ground right away to the horizon scarred by ragged mountains. Dismal bushes struggled for life here and there, some with the pathetic air of striving to become trees as once their ancestors had been. To the right, a long, straight scar through the grass betrayed the sterile lumpiness of rocks at odd places. Too rugged and too narrow ever to have been a road, it suggested no more than the desiccating remnants of a long-gone wall. And over all this loomed a ghastly sky.

Captain Skhiva eyed his crew, spoke to them with his sign-talking tentacle. The alternative was contact-telepathy which required physical touch.

"It is obvious that we are out of luck. We could have done r

worse had we landed on the empty satellite. However, it is safe
to go out. Anyone who wishes to explore a little while may do
so.''

One of them gesticulated back at him. "Captain, don't you
wish to be the first to step upon this world?''

"It is of no consequence. If anyone deems it an honor, he is
welcome to it.'' He pulled the lever opening both air-lock doors.
Thicker, heavier air crowded in and pressure went up a little.
"Beware of overexertion,'' he warned as they went out.

Poet Fander touched him, tentacles tip to tip as he sent his
thoughts racing through their nerve ends. "This confirms all that
we saw as we approached. A stricken planet far gone in its death
throes. What do you suppose caused it?''

"I have not the remotest idea. I would like to know. If it has
been smitten by natural forces, what might they do to Mars?''
His troubled mind sent its throb of worry up Fander's contacting
tentacle. "A pity that this planet had not been farther out instead
of closer in; we might then have observed the preceding phenomena from the surface of Mars. It is so difficult properly to view
this one against the Sun.''

"That applies still more to the next world, the misty one,''
observed Poet Fander.

"I know it. I am beginning to fear what we may find there. If
it proves to be equally dead, then we are stalled until we can
make the big jump outward.''

"Which won't be in our lifetimes.''

"I doubt it,'' agreed Captain Skhiva. "We might move fast
with the help of friends. We shall be slow—alone.'' He turned to
watch his crew writhing in various directions across the grim
landscape. "They find it good to be on firm ground. But what is
a world without life and beauty? In a short time they will grow
tired of it.''

Fander said thoughtfully, "Nevertheless, I would like to see
more of it. May I take out the lifeboat?''

"You are a songbird, not a pilot,'' reproved Captain Skhiva.
"Your function is to maintain morale by entertaining us, not to
roam around in a lifeboat.''

"But I know how to handle it. Every one of us was trained to
handle it. Let me take it that I may see more.''

"Haven't we seen enough, even before we landed? What else
is there to see? Cracked and distorted roads about to dissolve into
nothingness. Ages-old cities, torn and broken, crumbling into

dust. Shattered mountains and charred forests and craters little smaller than those upon the Moon. No sign of any superior lifeform still surviving. Only the grass, the shrubs, and various animals, two- or four-legged, that flee at our approach. Why do you wish to see more?''

"There is poetry even in death," said Fander.

"Even so, it remains repulsive." Skhiva gave a little shiver. "All right. Take the lifeboat. Who am I to question the weird workings of the nontechnical mind?''

"Thank you, Captain.''

"It is nothing. See that you are back by dusk.'' Breaking contact, he went to the lock, curled snakishly on its outer rim and brooded, still without bothering to touch the new world. So much attempted, so much done—for so poor reward.

He was still pondering it when the lifeboat soared out of its lock. Expressionlessly, his multifaceted eyes watched the ener- gized grids change angle as the boat swung into a curve and floated away like a little bubble. Skhiva was sensitive to futility.

The crew came back well before darkness. A few hours were enough. Just grass and shrubs and child-trees straining to grow up. One had discovered a grassless oblong that once might have been the site of a dwelling. He brought back a small piece of its foundation, a lump of perished concrete which Skhiva put by for later analysis.

Another had found a small, brown, six-legged insect, but his nerve ends had heard it crying when he picked it up, so hastily he had put it down and let it go free. Small, clumsily moving animals had been seen hopping in the distance, but all had dived down holes in the ground before any Martian could get near. All the crew were agreed upon one thing: the silence and solemnity of a people's passing was unendurable.

Fander beat the sinking of the sun by half a time-unit. His bubble drifted under a great, black cloud, sank to ship level, came in. The rain started a moment later, roaring down in frenzied torrents while they stood behind the transparent band and mar- veled at so much water.

After a while, Captain Skhiva told them, "We must accept what we find. We have drawn a blank. The cause of this world's condition is a mystery to be solved by others with more time and better equipment. It is for us to abandon this graveyard and try the misty planet. We will take off early in the morning.''

None commented, but Fander followed him to his room, made contact with a tentacle-touch.

"One could live here, Captain."

"I am not so sure of that." Skhiva coiled on his couch, suspending his tentacles on the various limb-rests. The blue sheen of him was reflected by the back wall. "In some places are rocks emitting alpha sparks. They are dangerous."

"Of course, Captain. But I can sense them and avoid them."

"*You?*" Skhiva stared up at him.

"Yes, Captain. I wish to be left here."

"What? In this place of appalling repulsiveness?"

"It has an all-pervading air of ugliness and despair," admitted Poet Fander. "All destruction is ugly. But by accident I have found a little beauty. It heartens me. I would like to seek its source."

"To what beauty do you refer?" Skhiva demanded.

Fander tried to explain the alien in nonalien terms.

"Draw it for me," ordered Skhiva.

Fander drew it, gave him the picture, said, "There!"

Gazing at it for a long time, Skhiva handed it back, mused awhile, then spoke along the other's nerves. "We are individuals with all the rights of individuals. As an individual, I don't think that picture sufficiently beautiful to be worth the tail-tip of a domestic *arlan*. I will admit that it is not ugly, even that it is pleasing."

"But, Captain—"

"As an individual," Skhiva went on, "you have an equal right to your opinions, strange though they may be. If you really wish to stay I cannot refuse you. I am entitled only to think you a little crazy." He eyed Fander again. "When do you hope to be picked up?"

"This year, next year, sometime, never."

"It may well be never," Skhiva reminded him. "Are you prepared to face that prospect?"

"One must always be prepared to face the consequences of his own actions," Fander pointed out.

"True." Skhiva was reluctant to surrender. "But have you given the matter serious thought?"

"I am a nontechnical component. I am not guided by thought."

"Then by what?"

"By my desires, emotions, instincts. By my inward feelings."

Skhiva said fervently, "The twin moons preserve us!"

"Captain, sing me a song of home and play me the tinkling harp."

"Don't be silly. I have not the ability."

"Captain, if it required no more than careful thought you would be able to do it?"

"Doubtlessly," agreed Skhiva, seeing the trap but unable to avoid it.

"There you are!" said Fander pointedly.

"I give up. I cannot argue with someone who casts aside the accepted rules of logic and invents his own. You are governed by notions that defeat me."

"It is not a matter of logic or illogic," Fander told him. "It is merely a matter of viewpoint. You see certain angles; I see others."

"For example?"

"You won't pin me down that way. I can find examples. For instance, do you remember the formula for determining the phase of a series tuned circuit?"

"Most certainly."

"I felt sure you would. You are a technician. You have registered it for all time as a matter of technical utility." He paused, staring at Skhiva. "I know that formula, too. It was mentioned to me, casually, many years ago. It is of no use to me—yet I have never forgotten it."

"Why?"

"Because it holds the beauty of rhythm. It is a poem," Fander explained.

Skhiva sighed and said, "I don't get it."

"One upon R into omega L minus one upon omega C," recited Fander. "A perfect hexameter." He showed his amusement as the other rocked back.

After a while Skhiva remarked, "It could be sung. One could dance to it."

"Same with this." Fander exhibited his rough sketch. "This holds beauty. Where there is beauty there once was talent—may still be talent for all we know. Where talent abides is also greatness. In the realms of greatness we may find powerful friends. We *need* such friends."

"You win." Skhiva made a gesture of defeat. "We leave you to your self-chosen fate in the morning."

"Thank you, Captain."

* * *

That same streak of stubbornness which made Skhiva a worthy commander induced him to take one final crack at Fander shortly before departure. Summoning him to his room, he eyed the poet calculatingly.

"You are still of the same mind?"

"Yes, Captain."

"Then does it not occur to you as strange that I should be so content to abandon this planet if indeed it does hold the remnants of greatness?"

"No."

"Why not?" Skhiva stiffened slightly.

"Captain, I think you are a little afraid because you suspect what I suspect—that there was no natural disaster. They did it themselves, to themselves."

"We have no proof of it," said Skhiva uneasily.

"No, Captain." Fander paused there without desire to add more.

"*If* this is their own sad handiwork," Skhiva commented at length, "what are our chances of finding friends among people so much to be feared?"

"Poor," admitted Fander. "But that—being the product of cold thought—means little to me. I am animated by warm hopes."

"There you go again, blatantly discarding reason in favor of an idle dream. Hoping, hoping, hoping—to achieve the impossible."

Fander said, "The difficult can be done at once; the impossible takes a little longer."

"Your thoughts make my orderly mind feel lopsided. Every remark is a flat denial of something that makes sense." Skhiva transmitted the sensation of a lugubrious chuckle. "Oh, well, we live and learn." He came forward, moving closer to the other. "All your supplies are assembled outside. Nothing remains but to bid you goodby."

They embraced in the Martian manner. Leaving the lock, Poet Fander watched the big sphere shudder and glide up. It soared without sound, shrinking steadily until it was a mere dot entering a cloud. A moment later it had gone.

He remained there, looking at the cloud, for a long, long time. Then he turned his attention to the load-sled holding his supplies. Climbing onto its tiny, exposed front seat, he shifted the control which energized the flotation-grids, let it rise a few feet. The higher the rise the greater the expenditure of power.

He wished to conserve power; there was no knowing how long he might need it. So at low alttude and gentle pace he let the sled glide in the general direction of the thing of beauty.

Later, he found a dry cave in the hill on which his objective stood. It took him two days of careful, cautious raying to square its walls, ceiling and floor, plus half a day with a powered fan driving out silicate dust. After that, he stowed his supplies at the back, parked the sled near the front, set up a curtaining force-screen across the entrance. The hole in the hill was now home.

Slumber did not come easily that first night. He lay within the cave, a ropy, knotted thing of glowing blue with enormous, beelike eyes, and found himself listening for harps that played sixty million miles away. His tentacle-ends twitched in involuntary search of the telepathic-contact songs that would go with the harps, and twitched in vain. Darkness grew deep, and all the world a monstrous stillness held. His hearing organs craved for the eventide flip-flop of sand-frogs, but there were no frogs. He wanted the homely drone of night beetles, but none droned. Except for once when something faraway howled its heart at the Moon, there was nothing, nothing.

In the morning he washed, ate, took out the sled and explored the site of a small town. He found little to satisfy his curiosity, no more than mounds of shapeless rubble on ragged, faintly oblong foundations. It was a graveyard of long-dead domiciles, rotting, weedy, near to complete oblivion. A view from five hundred feet up gave him only one piece of information: the orderliness of outlines showed that these people had been tidy, methodical.

But tidiness is not beauty in itself. He came back to the top of his hill and sought solace with the thing that was beauty.

His explorations continued, not systematically as Skhiva would have performed them, but in accordance with his own mercurial whims. At times he saw many animals, singly or in groups, none resembling anything Martian. Some scattered at full gallop when his sled swooped over them. Some dived into groundholes, showing a brief flash of white, absurd tails, Others, four-footed, long-faced, sharp-toothed, hunted in gangs and bayed at him in concert with harsh, defiant voices.

On the seventieth day, in a deep, shadowed glade to the north, he spotted a small group of new shapes slinking along in single file. He recognized them at a glance, knew them so well that his searching eyes sent an immediate thrill of triumph into his mind.

They were ragged, dirty, and no more than half grown, but the thing of beauty had told him what they were.

Hugging the ground low, he swept around in a wide curve that brought him to the farther end of the glade. His sled sloped slightly into the drop as it entered the glade. He could see them better now, even the soiled pinkishness of their thin legs. They were moving away from him, with fearful caution, but the silence of his swoop gave them no warning.

The rearmost one of the stealthy file fooled him at the last moment. He was hanging over the side of the sled, tentacles outstretched in readiness to snatch the end one with the wild mop of yellow hair when, responding to some sixth sense, his intended victim threw itself flat. His grasp shot past a couple of feet short, and he got a glimpse of frightened gray eyes two seconds before a dexterous side-tilt of the sled enabled him to make good his loss by grabbing the less wary next in line.

This one was dark-haired, a bit bigger, and sturdier. It fought madly at his holding limbs while he gained altitude. Then suddenly, realizing the queer nature of its bonds, it writhed around and looked straight at him. The result was unexpected; it closed its eyes and went completely limp.

It was still limp when he bore it into the cave, but its heart continued to beat and its lungs to draw. Laying it carefully on the softness of his bed, he moved to the cave's entrance and waited for it to recover. Eventually it stirred, sat up, gazed confusedly at the facing wall. Its black eyes moved slowly around, taking in the surroundings. Then they saw Fander. They widened tremendously, and their owner began to make high-pitched, unpleasant noises as it tried to back away through the solid wall. It screamed so much, in one rising throb after another, that Fander slithered out of the cave, right out of sight, and sat in the cold winds until the noises had died down.

A couple of hours later he made cautious reappearance to offer it food, but its reaction was so swift, hysterical, and heartrending that he dropped his load and hid himself as though the fear were his own. The food remained untouched for two full days. On the third, a little of it was eaten. Fander ventured within.

Although the Martian did not go near, the boy cowered away, murmuring, "Devil! Devil!" His eyes were red, with dark discoloration beneath them.

"Devil!" thought Fander, totally unable to repeat the alien word, but wondering what it meant. He used his sign-talking tentacle in valiant effort to convey something reassuring. The attempt was wasted. The other watched its writhings half in fear, half with distaste, and showed complete lack of comprehension. He let the tentacle gently slither forward across the floor, hoping to make thought-contact. The other recoiled from it as from a striking snake.

"Patience," he reminded himself. "The impossible takes a little longer."

Periodically he showed himself with food and drink, and nighttimes he slept fitfully on the coarse, damp grass beneath lowering skies—while the prisoner who was his guest enjoyed the softness of the bed, the warmth of the cave, the security of the force-screen.

Time came when Fander betrayed an unpoetic shrewdness by using the other's belly to estimate the ripeness of the moment. When, on the eighth day, he noted that his food-offerings were now being taken regularly, he took a meal of his own at the edge of the cave, within plain sight, and observed that the other's appetite was not spoiled. That night he slept just within the cave, close to the force-screen, and as far from the boy as possible. The boy stayed awake late, watching him, always watching him, but gave way to slumber in the small hours.

A fresh attempt at sign-talking brought no better results than before, and the boy still refused to touch his offered tentacle. All the same, he was gaining ground slowly. His overtures still were rejected, but with less revulsion. Gradually, ever so gradually, the Martian shape was becoming familiar, almost acceptable.

The sweet savor of success was Fander's in the middle of the next day. The boy had displayed several spells of emotional sickness during which he lay on his front with shaking body and emitted low noises while his eyes watered profusely. At such times the Martian felt strangely helpless and inadequate. On this occasion, during another attack, he took advantage of the sufferer's lack of attention and slid near enough to snatch away the box by the bed.

From the box he drew his tiny electroharp, plugged its connectors, switched it on, touched its strings with delicate affection. Slowly he began to play, singing an accompaniment deep inside himself. For he had no voice with which to sing out loud, but the harp sang it for him. The boy ceased his quiverings, sat up, all his attention upon the dexterous play of the tentacles and the music they conjured forth. And when he judged that at last the listener's mind was captured, Fander ceased with easy, quieting strokes, gently offered him the harp. The boy registered interest and reluctance. Careful not to move nearer, not an inch nearer, Fander offered it at full tentacle length. The boy had to take four steps to get it. He took them.

That was the start. They played together, day after day and sometimes a little into the night, while almost imperceptibly the distance between them was reduced. Finally they sat together, side by side, and the boy had not yet learned to laugh but no longer did he show unease. He could now extract a simple tune from the instrument and was pleased with his own aptitude in a solemn sort of way.

One evening as darkness grew, and the things that sometimes howled at the moon were howling again, Fander offered his tentacle-tip for the hundredth time. Always the gesture had been unmistakable even if its motive was not clear, yet always it had been rebuffed. But now, now, five fingers curled around it in shy desire to please.

With a fervent prayer that human nerves would function just like Martian ones, Fander poured his thoughts through, swiftly, lest the warm grip be loosened too soon.

"Do not fear me. I cannot help my shape any more than you can help yours. I am your friend, your father, your mother. I need you as much as you need me."

The boy let go of him, began quiet, half-stifled whimpering noises. Fander put a tentacle on his shoulder, made little patting motions that he imagined were wholly Martian. For some inexplicable reason, this made matters worse. At his wits' end what to do for the best, what action to take that might be understandable in Terrestrial terms, he gave the problem up, surrendered to his instinct, put a long, ropy limb around the boy and held him close until the noises ceased and slumber came. It was then he realized the child he had taken was much younger than he had estimated. He nursed him through the night.

Much practice was necessary to make conversation. The boy had to learn to put mental drive behind his thoughts, for it was beyond Fander's power to suck them out of him.

"What is your name?"

Fander got a picture of thin legs running rapidly.

He returned it in question form. "Speedy?"

An affirmative.

"What name do you call me?"

An unflattering montage of monsters.

"Devil?"

The picture whirled around, became confused. There was a trace of embarrassment.

"Devil will do," assured Fander. He went on. "Where are your parents?"

More confusion.

"You must have had parents. Everyone has a father and mother, haven't they? Don't you remember yours?"

Muddled ghost-pictures. Grown-ups leaving children. Grown-ups avoiding children, as if they feared them.

"What is the first thing you remember?"

"Big man walking with me. Carried me a bit. Walked again."

"What happened to him?"

"Went away. Said he was sick. Might make me sick too."

"Long ago?"

Confusion.

Fander changed his aim. "What of those other children—have they no parents either?"

"All got nobody."

"But you've got somebody now, haven't you, Speedy?"

Doubtfully. "Yes."

Fander pushed it further. "Would you rather have me, or those other children?" He let it rest a moment before he added, "Or both?"

"Both," said Speedy with no hesitation. His fingers toyed with the harp.

"Would you like to help me look for them tomorrow and bring them here? And if they are scared of me will you help them not to be afraid?"

"Sure!" said Speedy, licking his lips and sticking his chest out.

"Then," said Fander, "perhaps you would like to go for a walk today? You've been too long in this cave. Will you come for a walk with me?"

"Y'betcha!"

Side by side they went for a short walk, one trotting rapidly along, the other slithering. The child's spirits perked up with this trip in the open; it was as if the sight of the sky and the feel of the grass made him realize at last that he was not exactly a prisoner. His formerly solemn features became animated, he made exclamations that Fander could not understand, and once he laughed at nothing for the sheer joy of it. On two occasions he grabbed a tentacle-tip in order to tell Fander something, performing the action as if it were in every way as natural as his own speech.

They got out the load-sled in the morning. Fander took the front seat and the controls; Speedy squatted behind him with hands gripping his harness-belt. With a shallow soar, they headed for the glade. Many small, white-tailed animals bolted down holes as they passed over.

"Good for dinner," remarked Speedy, touching him and speaking through the touch.

Fander felt sickened. Meat-eaters! It was not until a queer feeling of shame and apology came back at him that he knew the other had felt his revulsion. He wished he'd been swift to blanket that reaction before the boy could sense it, but he could not be blamed for the effect of so bald a statement taking him so completely unaware. However, it had produced another step forward in their mutual relationship—Speedy desired his good opinion.

Within fifteen minutes they struck it lucky. At a point half a mile south of the glade Speedy let out a shrill yell and pointed downward. A small, golden-haired figure was standing there on a slight rise, staring fascinatedly upward at the phenomenon in the sky. A second tiny shape, with red but equally long hair, was at the bottom of the slope gazing in similar wonderment. Both came to their senses and turned to flee as the sled tilted toward them.

Ignoring the yelps of excitement close behind him and the pulls upon his belt, Fander swooped, got first one, then the other. This left him with only one limb to right the sled and gain height. If the victims had fought he would have had his work cut out to make it. They did not fight. They shrieked as he snatched them and then relaxed with closed eyes.

The sled climbed, glided a mile at five hundred feet. Fander's attention was divided between his limp prizes, the controls and the horizon when suddenly a thunderous rattling sounded on the metal base on the sled, the entire framework shuddered, a strip of metal flew from its leading edge and things made whining sounds toward the clouds.

"Old Graypate," bawled Speedy, jigging around but keeping away from the rim. "He's shooting at us."

The spoken words meant nothing to the Martian, and he could not spare a limb for the contact the other had forgotten to make. Grimly righting the sled, he gave it full power. Whatever damage it had suffered had not affected its efficiency; it shot forward at a pace that set the red and golden hair of the captives streaming in the wind. Perforce his landing by the cave was clumsy. The sled bumped down and lurched across forty yards of grass.

First things first. Taking the quiet pair into the cave, he made them comfortable on the bed, came out and examined the sled. There were half a dozen deep dents in its flat underside, two bright furrows angling across one rim. He made contact with Speedy.

"What were you trying to tell me?"

"Old Graypate shot at us."

The mind-picture burst upon him vividly and with electrifying effect: a vision of a tall, white-haired, stern-faced old man with a tubular weapon propped upon his shoulder while it spat fire upward. A white-haired old man! An adult!

His grip was tight on the other's arm. "What is this oldster to you?"

"Nothing much. He lives near us in the shelters."

Picture of a long, dusty concrete burrow, badly damaged, its ceiling marked with the scars of a lighting system which had rotted away to nothing. The old man living hermitlike at one end; the children at the other. The old man was sour, taciturn, kept the children at a distance, spoke to them seldom but was quick to respond when they were menaced. He had guns. Once, he had killed many wild dogs that had eaten two children.

"People left us near shelters because Old Graypate was there, and had guns," informed Speedy.

"But why does he keep away from children? Doesn't he like children?"

"Don't know." He mused a moment. "Once told us that old people could get very sick and make young ones sick—and then we'd all die. Maybe he's afraid of making us die." Speedy wasn't very sure about it.

So there was some much-feared disease around, something

contagious, to which adults were peculiarly susceptible. Without hesitation they abandoned their young at the first onslaught, hoping that at least the children would live. Sacrifice after sacrifice that the remnants of the race might survive. Heartbreak after heartbreak as elders chose death alone rather than death together.

Yet Graypate himself was depicted as very old. Was this an exaggeration of the child-mind?

"I must meet Graypate."

"He will shoot," declared Speedy positively. "He knows by now that you took me. He saw you take the others. He will wait for you and shoot."

"We will find some way to avoid that."

"How?"

"When these two have become my friends, just as you have become my friend, I will take all three of you back to the shelters. You can find Graypate for me and tell him that I am not as ugly as I look."

"I don't think you're ugly," denied Speedy.

The picture Fander got along with that gave him the weirdest sensation of pleasure. It was of a vague, shadowy but distorted body with a clear human face.

The new prisoners were female. Fander knew it without being told because they were daintier than Speedy and had the warm, sweet smell of females. That meant complications. Maybe they were mere children, and maybe they lived together in the shelter, but he was permitting none of that while they were in his charge. Fander might be outlandish by other standards but he had a certain primness. Forthwith he cut another and smaller cave for Speedy and himself.

Neither of the girls saw him for two days. Keeping well out of their sight, he let Speedy take them food, talk to them, prepare them for the shape of the thing to come. On the third day he presented himself for inspection at a distance. Despite forewarnings they went sheet-white, clung together, but uttered no distressing sounds. He played his harp a little while, withdrew, came back in the evening and played for them again.

Encouraged by Speedy's constant and self-assured flow of propaganda, one of them grasped a tentacle-tip next day. What came along the nerves was not a picture so much as an ache, a desire, a childish yearning. Fander backed out of the cave, found wood, spent the whole night using the sleepy Speedy as a model, and fashioned the wood into a tiny, jointed semblance of a human being. He was no sculptor, but he possessed a natural delicacy of touch, and the poet in him ran through his limbs and expressed itself in the model. Making a thorough job of it, he clothed it in Terrestrial fashion, colored its face, fixed upon its features the pleasure-grimace which humans call a smile.

He gave her the doll the moment she awakened in the morning. She took it eagerly, hungrily, with wide, glad eyes. Hugging it to her unformed bosom, she crooned over it—and he knew that the strange emptiness within her was gone.

Though Speedy was openly contemptuous of this manifest waste of effort, Fander set to and made a second mannikin. It did not take quite as long. Practice on the first had made him swifter, more dexterous. He was able to present it to the other child by midafternoon. Her acceptance was made with shy grace, she held the doll close as if it meant more than the whole of her sorry world. In her thrilled concentration upon the gift, she did not notice his nearness, his closeness, and when he offered a tentacle, she took it.

He said, simply, "I love you."

Her mind was too untrained to drive a response, but her great eyes warmed.

Fander sat on the grounded sled at a point a mile east of the glade and watched the three children walk hand in hand toward the hidden shelters. Speedy was the obvious leader, hurrying them onward, bossing them with the noisy assurance of one who has been around and considers himself sophisticated. In spite of this, the girls paused at intervals to turn and wave to the ropy, bee-eyed thing they'd left behind. And Fander dutifully waved back, always using his signal-tentacle because it had not occurred to him that any tentacle would serve.

They sank from sight behind a rise of ground. He remained on the sled, his multifaceted gaze going over his surroundings or studying the angry sky now threatening rain. The ground was a dull, dead gray-green all the way to the horizon. There was no relief from that drab color, not one shining patch of white, gold, or crimson such as dotted the meadows of Mars. There was only the eternal gray-green and his own brilliant blueness.

Before long a sharp-faced, four-footed thing revealed itself in the grass, raised its head and howled at him. The sound was an eerily urgent wail that ran across the grasses and moaned into the distance. It brought others of its kind, two, ten, twenty. Their defiance increased with their numbers until there was a large band of them edging toward him with lips drawn back, teeth exposed. Then there came a sudden and undetectable flock-command which caused them to cease their slinking and spring forward like one, slavering as they came. They did it with the hungry, red-eyed frenzy of animals motivated by something akin to madness.

Repulsive though it was, the sight of creatures craving meat— even strange blue meat—did not bother Fander. He slipped a control a notch, the flotation grids radiated, the sled soared twenty feet. So calm and easy an escape so casually performed infuriated the wild dog pack beyond all measure. Arriving beneath the sled, they made futile springs upward, fell back upon one another, bit and slashed each other, leaped again and again. The pandemonium they set up was a compound of snarls, yelps, barks, and growls, the ferocious expressions of extreme hate. They exuded a pungent odor of dry hair and animal sweat.

Reclining on the sled in a maddening pose of disdain, Fander let the insane ones rave below. They raced around in tight circles, shrieking insults at him and biting each other. This went on for some time and ended with a spurt of ultra-rapid cracks from the direction of the glade. Eight dogs fell dead. Two flopped and struggled to crawl away. Ten yelped in agony, made off on three legs. The unharmed ones flashed away to some place where they could make a meal of the escaping limpers. Fander lowered the sled.

Speedy stood on the rise with Graypate. The latter restored his weapon to the crook of his arm, rubbed his chin thoughtfully, ambled forward.

Stopping five yards from the Martian, the old Earthman again massaged his chin whiskers, then said, "It sure is the darnedest thing, just the darnedest thing!"

"No use talking *at* him," advised Speedy. "You've got to touch him, like I told you."

"I know, I know." Graypate betrayed a slight impatience. "All in good time. I'll touch him when I'm ready." He stood there, gazing at Fander with eyes that were very pale and very sharp. "Oh, well, here goes." He offered a hand.

Fander placed a tentacle end in it.

"Jeepers, he's cold," commented Graypate, closing his grip. "Colder than a snake."

"He isn't a snake," Speedy contradicted fiercely.

"Ease up, ease up—I didn't say he is." Graypate seemed fond of repetitive phrases.

"He doesn't feel like one, either," persisted Speedy, who had never felt a snake and did not wish to.

Fander boosted a thought through. "I come from the fourth planet. Do you know what that means?"

"I ain't ignorant," snapped Graypate aloud.

"No need to reply vocally. I receive your thoughts exactly as you receive mine. Your responses are much stronger than the boy's, and I can understand you easily."

"Humph!" said Graypate to the world at large.

"I have been anxious to find an adult because the children can tell me little. I would like to ask questions. Do you feel inclined to answer questions?"

"It depends," answered Graypate, becoming leery.

"Never mind. Answer them if you wish. My only desire is to help you."

"Why?" asked Graypate, searching around for a percentage.

"We need intelligent friends."

"Why?"

"Our numbers are small, our resources poor. In visiting this world and the misty one we've come near to the limit of our ability. But with assistance we could go farther. I think that if we could help you a time might come when you could help us."

Graypate pondered it cautiously, forgetting that the inward workings of his mind were wide open to the other. Chronic suspicion was the keynote of his thoughts, suspicion based on life experiences and recent history. But inward thoughts ran both ways, and his own mind detected the clear sincerity in Fander's.

So he said. "Fair enough. Say more."

"What caused all this?" inquired Fander, waving a limb at the world.

"War," said Graypate. "The last war we'll ever have. The entire place went nuts."

"How did that come about?"

"You've got me there." Graypate gave the problem grave consideration. "I reckon it wasn't just any one thing; it was a multitude of things sort of piling themselves up."

"Such as?"

"Differences in people. Some were colored differently in their bodies, others in their ideas, and they couldn't get along. Some bred faster than others, wanted more room, more food. There wasn't any more room or more food. The world was full, and nobody could shove in except by pushing another out. My old man told me plenty before he died, and he always maintained that if folk had had the hoss-sense to keep their numbers down, there might not—"

"Your old man?" interjected Fander. "Your father? Didn't all this occur in your own lifetime?"

"It did not. I saw none of it. I am the son of the son of a survivor."

"Let's go back to the cave," put in Speedy, bored with the silent contact-talk. "I want to show him our harp."

They took no notice, and Fander went on, "Do you think there might be a lot of others still living?"

"Who knows?" Graypate was moody about it. "There isn't any way of telling how many are wandering around the other side of the globe, maybe still killing each other, or starving to death, or dying of the sickness."

"What sickness is this?"

"I couldn't tell what it is called." Graypate scratched his head confusedly. "My old man told me a few times, but I've long forgotten. Knowing the name wouldn't do me any good, see? He said his father told him that it was part of the war, it got invented and was spread deliberately—and it's still with us."

"What are its symptoms?"

"You go hot and dizzy. You get black swellings in the armpits. In forty-eight hours you're dead. Old ones get it first. The kids then catch it unless you make away from them mighty fast."

"It is nothing familiar to me," said Fander, unable to recognize cultured bubonic. "In any case, I'm not a medical expert." He eyed Graypate. "But you seem to have avoided it."

"Sheer luck," opined Graypate. "Or maybe I can't get it. There was a story going around during the war that some folk might develop immunity to it, durned if I know why. Could be that I'm immune, but I don't count on it."

"So you keep your distance from these children?"

"Sure." He glanced at Speedy. "I shouldn't really have come along with this kid. He's got a lousy chance as it is without me increasing the odds."

"That is thoughtful of you," Fander put over softly. "Especially seeing that you must be lonely."

Graypate bristled and his thought-flow became aggressive. "I ain't grieving for company. I can look after myself, like I have done since my old man went away to curl up by himself. I'm on my own feet. So's every other guy."

"I believe that," said Fander. "You must pardon me—I'm a stranger here myself. I judged you by my own feelings. Now and again I get pretty lonely."

"How come?" demanded Graypate, staring at him. "You ain't telling me they dumped you and left you, on your own?"

"They did."

"Man!" exclaimed Graypate fervently.

Man! It was a picture resembling Speedy's conception, a vision elusive in form but firm and human in face. The oldster was reacting to what he considered a predicament rather than a choice, and the reaction came on a wave of sympathy.

Fander struck promptly and hard. "You see how I'm fixed. The companionship of wild animals is nothing to me. I need someone intelligent enough to like my music and forget my looks, someone intelligent enough to—"

"I ain't so sure we're that smart," Graypate chipped in. He let his gaze swing morbidly around the landscape. "Not when I see this graveyard and think of how it looked in granpop's days."

"Every flower blooms from the dust of a hundred dead ones," answered Fander.

"What are flowers?"

It shocked the Martian. He had projected a mind-picture of a trumpet lily, crimson and shining, and Graypate's brain had juggled it around, uncertain whether it was fish, flesh, or fowl.

"Vegetable growths, like these." Fander plucked half a dozen blades of blue-green grass. "But more colorful, and sweet-scented." He transmitted the brilliant vision of a mile-square field of trumpet lilies, red and glowing.

"Glory be!" said Graypate. "We've nothing like those."

"Not here," agreed Fander. "Not here." He gestured toward the horizon. "Elsewhere may be plenty. If we got together we could be company for each other, we could learn things from each other. We could pool our ideas, our efforts, and search for flowers far away—also for more people."

"Folk just won't get together in large bunches. They stick to each other in family groups until the plague breaks them up. Then they abandon the kids. The bigger the crowd, the bigger the risk of someone contaminating the lot.'' He leaned on his gun, staring at the other, his thought-forms shaping themselves in dull solemnity. ''When a guy gets hit, he goes away and takes it on his own. The end is a personal contract between him and his God, with no witnesses. Death's a pretty private affair these days.''

''What, after all these years? Don't you think that by this time the disease may have run its course and exhausted itself?''

''Nobody knows—and nobody's gambling on it.''

''I would gamble,'' said Fander.

''You ain't like us. You mightn't be able to catch it.''

''Or I might get it worse, and die more painfully.''

''Mebbe,'' admitted Graypate, doubtfully. ''Anyway, you're looking at it from a different angle. You've been dumped on your own some. What've you got to lose?''

''My life,'' said Fander.

Graypate rocked back on his heels, then said, ''Yes, sir, that is a gamble. A guy can't bet any heavier than that.'' He rubbed his chin whiskers as before. ''All right, all right, I'll take you up on that. You come right here and live with us.'' His grip tightened on his gun, his knuckles showing white. ''On this understanding: The moment you feel sick you get out fast, and for keeps. If you don't, I'll bump you and drag you away myself, even if that makes me get it too. The kids come first, see?''

The shelters were far roomier than the cave. There were eighteen children living in them, all skinny with their prolonged diet of roots, edible herbs, and an occasional rabbit. The youngest and most sensitive of them ceased to be terrified of Fander after ten days. Within four months his slithering shape of blue ropiness had become a normal adjunct to their small, limited world.

Six of the youngsters were males older than Speedy, one of them much older but not yet adult. He beguiled them with his harp, teaching them to play, and now and again giving them ten-minute rides on the load-sled as a special treat. He made dolls for the girls and queer, cone-shaped little houses for the dolls, and fan-backed chairs of woven grass for the houses. None of these toys was truly Martian in design, and none was Terrestrial.

They represented a pathetic compromise within his imagination; the Martian notion of what Terrestrial models might have looked like had there been any in existence.

But surreptitiously, without seeming to give any less attention to the younger ones, he directed his main efforts upon the six older boys and Speedy. To his mind, these were the hope of the world—and of Mars. At no time did he bother to ponder that the nontechnical brain is not without its virtues, or that there are times and circumstances when it is worth dropping the short view of what is practicable for the sake of the long view of what is remotely possible. So as best he could he concentrated upon the elder seven, educating them through the dragging months, stimulating their minds, encouraging their curiosity, and continually impressing upon them the idea that fear of disease can become a folk-separating dogma unless they conquered it within their souls.

He taught them that death is death, a natural process to be accepted philosophically and met with dignity—and there were times when he suspected that he was teaching them nothing, he was merely reminding them, for deep within their growing minds was the ancestral strain of Terrestrialism which had mulled its way to the same conclusions ten or twenty thousands of years before. Still, he was helping to remove this disease-block from the path of the stream, and was driving child-logic more rapidly toward adult outlook. In that respect he was satisfied. He could do little more.

In time, they organized group concerts, humming or making singing noises to the accompaniment of the harp, now and again improvising lines to suit Fander's tunes, arguing out the respective merits of chosen words until by process of elimination they had a complete song. As songs grew to a repertoire and singing grew more adept, more polished, Old Graypate displayed interest, came to one performance, then another, until by custom he had established his own place as a one-man audience.

One day the eldest boy, who was named Redhead, came to Fander and grasped a tentacle-tip. "Devil, may I operate your food-machine?"

"You mean you would like me to show you how to work it?"

"No, Devil, I know how to work it." The boy gazed self-assuredly into the other's great bee-eyes.

"Then how is it operated?"

"You fill its container with the tenderest blades of grass,

being careful not to include roots. You are equally careful not to turn a switch before the container is full and its door completely closed. You then turn the red switch for a count of two hundred eighty, reverse the container, turn the green switch for a count of forty-seven. You then close both switches, empty the container's warm pulp into the end molds and apply the press until the biscuits are firm and dry.''

"How have you discovered all this?"

"I have watched you make biscuits for us many times. This morning, while you were busy, I tried it myself." He extended a hand. It held a biscuit. Taking it from him, Fander examined it. Firm, crisp, well-shaped. He tasted it. Perfect.

Redhead became the first mechanic to operate and service a Martian lifeboat's emergency premasticator. Seven years later, long after the machine had ceased to function, he managed to repower it, weakly but effectively, with dust that gave forth alpha sparks. In another five years he had improved it, speeded it up. In twenty years he had duplicated it and had all the know-how needed to turn out premasticators on a large scale. Fander could not have equalled this performance for, as a nontechnician, he'd no better notion than the average Terrestrial of the principles upon which the machine worked, neither did he know what was meant by radiant digestion or protein enrichment. He could do little more than urge Redhead along and leave the rest to whatever inherent genius the boy possessed—which was plenty.

In similar manner, Speedy and two youths named Blacky and Bigears took the load-sled out of his charge. On rare occasions, as a great privilege, Fander had permitted them to take up the sled for one-hour trips, alone. This time they were gone from dawn to dusk. Graypate mooched around, gun under arm, another smaller one stuck in his belt, going frequently to the top of a rise and scanning the skies in all directions. The delinquents swooped in at sunset, bringing with them a strange boy.

Fander summoned them to him. They held hands so that his touch would give him simultaneous contact with all three.

"I am a little worried. The sled has only so much power. When it is all gone there will be no more."

They eyed each other aghast.

"Unfortunately, I have neither the knowledge nor the ability to energize the sled once its power is exhausted. I lack the wisdom of the friends who left me here—and that is my shame.''

He paused, watching them dolefully, then went on, "All I do know is that its power does not leak away. If not used much, the reserves will remain for many years." Another pause before he added, "And in a few years you will be men."

Blacky said, "But, Devil, when we are men we'll be much heavier, and the sled will use so much more power."

"How do you know that?" Fander put it sharply.

"More weight, more power to sustain it," opined Blacky with the air of one whose logic is incontrovertible. "It doesn't need thinking out. *It's obvious.*"

Very slowly and softly, Fander told him, "You'll do. May the twin moons shine upon you someday, for I know you'll do."

"Do what, Devil?"

"Build a thousand sleds like this one, or better—and explore the whole world."

From that time onward they confined their trips strictly to one hour, making them less frequently than of yore, spending more time poking and prying around the sled's innards.

Graypate changed character with the slow reluctance of the aged. Leastways, as two years then three rolled past, he came gradually out of his shell, was less taciturn, more willing to mix with those swiftly growing up to his own height. Without fully realizing what he was doing he joined forces with Fander, gave the children the remnants of Earthly wisdom passed down from his father's father. He taught the boys how to use the guns of which he had as many as eleven, some maintained mostly as a source of spares for others. He took them shell-hunting; digging deep beneath rotting foundations into stale, half-filled cellars in search of ammunition not too far corroded for use.

"Guns ain't no use without shells, and shells don't last forever."

Neither do buried shells. They found not one.

Of his own wisdom Graypate stubbornly withheld but a single item until the day when Speedy and Redhead and Blacky chivvied it out of him. Then, like a father facing the hangman, he gave them the truth about babies. He made no comparative mention of bees because there were no bees, nor of flowers because there were no flowers. One cannot analogize the nonexistent. Nevertheless he managed to explain the matter more or less to their satisfaction, after which he mopped his forehead and went to Fander.

"These youngsters are getting too nosy for my comfort. They've been asking me how kids come along."

"Did you tell them?"

"I sure did." He sat down, staring at the Martian, his pale gray eyes bothered. "I don't mind giving in to the boys when I can't beat 'em off any longer, but I'm durned if I'm going to tell the girls."

Fander said, "I have been asked about this many a time before. I could not tell much because I was by no means certain whether you breed precisely as we breed. But I told them how *we* breed."

"The girls too?"

"Of course."

"Jeepers!" Graypate mopped his forehead again. "How did they take it?"

"Just as if I'd told them why the sky is blue or why water is wet."

"Must've been something in the way you put it to them," opined Graypate.

"I told them it was poetry between persons."

Throughout the course of history, Martian, Venusian, or Terrestrial, some years are more noteworthy than others. The twelfth one after Fander's marooning was outstanding for its series of events, each of which was pitifully insignificant by cosmic standards but loomed enormously in this small community life.

To start with, on the basis of Redhead's improvements to the premasticator, the older seven—now bearded men—contrived to repower the exhausted sled and again took to the air for the first time in forty months. Experiments showed that the Martian load-carrier was now slower, could bear less weight, but had far longer range. They used it to visit the ruins of distant cities in search of metallic junk suitable for the building of more sleds, and by early summer they had constructed another, larger than the original, clumsy to the verge of dangerousness, but still a sled.

On several occasions they failed to find metal but did find people, odd families surviving in under-surface shelters, clinging grimly to life and passed-down scraps of knowledge. Since all these new contacts were strictly human to human, with no weirdly tentacled shape to scare off the parties of the second part, and since many were finding fear of plague more to be endured than their terrible loneliness, many families returned with the explorers, settled in the shelters, accepted Fander, added their surviving skills to the community's riches.

Thus local population grew to seventy adults and four hundred children. They compounded with their plague-fear by spreading through the shelters, digging through half-wrecked and formerly unused expanses, and moving apart to form twenty or thirty lesser communities each one of which could be isolated should death reappear.

Growing morale born of added strength and confidence in numbers soon resulted in four more sleds, still clumsy but slightly less dangerous to manage. There also appeared the first rock house above ground, standing four-square and solidly under the gray skies, a defiant witness that mankind still considered itself a cut above the rats and rabbits. The community presented the house to Blacky and Sweetvoice, who had announced their desire to associate. An adult who claimed to know the conventional routine spoke solemn words over the happy couple before many witnesses, while Fander attended the groom as best Martian.

Toward summer's end Speedy returned from a solo sled trip of many days, brought with him one old man, one boy and four girls, all of strange, outlandish countenance. They were yellow in complexion, had black hair, black, almond-shaped eyes, and spoke a language that none could understand. Until these newcomers had picked up the local speech, Fander had to act as interpreter, for his mind-pictures and theirs were independent of vocal sounds. The four girls were quiet, modest, and very beautiful. Within a month Speedy had married one of them whose name was a gentle clucking sound which meant Precious Jewel Ling.

After this wedding, Fander sought Graypate, placed a tentacle-tip in his right hand. "There were differences between the man and the girl, distinctive features wider apart than any we know upon Mars. Are these some of the differences which caused your war?"

"I dunno. I've never seen one of these yellow folk before. They must live mighty far off." He rubbed his chin to help his thoughts along. "I only know what my old man told me and his old man told him. There were too many folk of too many different sorts."

"They can't be all that different if they can fall in love."

"Mebbe not," agreed Graypate.

"Supposing most of the people still in this world could assemble here, breed together, and have less different children; the children breed others still less different. Wouldn't they eventually become all much the same—just Earth-people?''

"Mebbe so."

"All speaking the same language, sharing the same culture? If they spread out slowly from a central source, always in contact by sled, continually sharing the same knowledge, same progress, would there be any room for new differences to arise?"

"I dunno," said Graypate evasively. "I'm not so young as I used to be, and I can't dream as far ahead as I used to do."

"It doesn't matter so long as the young ones can dream it." Fander mused a moment. "If you're beginning to think yourself a back number, you're in good company. Things are getting somewhat out of hand as far as I'm concerned. The onlooker sees the most of the game, and perhaps that's why I'm more sensitive than you to a certain peculiar feeling."

"To what feeling?" inquired Graypate, eyeing him.

"That Terra is on the move once more. There are now many people where there were few. A house is up and more are to follow. They talk of six more. After the six they will talk of sixty, then six hundred, then six thousand. Some are planning to haul up sunken conduits and use them to pipe water from the northward lake. Sleds are being built. Premasticators will soon be built, and force-screens likewise. Children are being taught. Less and less is being heard of your plague, and so far no more have died of it. I feel a dynamic surge of energy and ambition and genius which may grow with appalling rapidity until it becomes a mighty flood. I feel that I, too, am a back number."

"Bunk!" said Graypate. He spat on the ground. "If you dream often enough, you're bound to have a bad one once in a while."

"Perhaps it is because so many of my tasks have been taken over and done better than I was doing them. I have failed to seek new tasks. Were I a technician I'd have discovered a dozen by now. Reckon this is as good a time as any to turn to a job with which you can help me."

"What is that?"

"A long, long time ago I made a poem. It was for the beautiful thing that first impelled me to stay here. I do not know exactly what its maker had in mind, nor whether my eyes see it as he wished it to be seen, but I have made a poem to express what I feel when I look upon his work."

"Humph!" said Graypate, not very interested.

"There is an outcrop of solid rock beneath its base which I can shave smooth and use as a plinth on which to inscribe my words. I would like to put them down twice—in the script of Mars and the script of Earth." Fander hesitated a moment, then went on. "Perhaps this is presumptuous of me, but it is many years since I wrote for all to read—and my chance may never come again."

Graypate said, "I get the idea. You want me to put down your notions in our writing so you can copy it."

"Yes."

"Give me your stylus and pad." Taking them, Graypate squatted on a rock, lowering himself stiffly, for he was feeling the weight of his years. Resting the pad on his knees, he held the writing instrument in his right hand while his left continued to grasp a tentacle-tip. "Go ahead."

He started drawing thick, laborious marks as Fander's mind-pictures came through, enlarging the letters and keeping them well separated. When he had finished he handed the pad over.

"Asymmetrical," decided Fander, staring at the queer letters and wishing for the first time that he had taken up the study of Earth-writing. "Cannot you make this part balance with that, and this with this?"

"It's what you said."

"It is your own translation of what I said. I would like it better balanced. Do you mind if we try again?"

They tried again. They made fourteen attempts before Fander was satisfied with the perfunctory appearance of letters and words he could not understand.

Taking the paper, he found his ray-gun, went to the base-rock of the beautiful thing and sheared the whole front to a flat, even surface. Adjusting his beam to cut a V-shaped channel one inch deep, he inscribed his poem on the rock in long, unpunctuated lines of neat Martian curlicues. With less confidence and much greater care, he repeated the verse in Earth's awkward, angular hieroglyphics. The task took him quite a time, and there were fifty people watching him when he finished. They said nothing. In utter silence they looked at the poem and at the beautiful thing, and were still standing there brooding solemnly when he went away.

One by one the rest of the community visited the site next day, going and coming with the air of pilgrims attending an ancient shrine. All stood there a long time, returned without comment.

Nobody praised Fander's work, nobody damned it, nobody re-
proached him for alienizing something wholly Earth's. The only
effect—too subtle to be noteworthy—was a greater and still
growing grimness and determination that boosted the already
swelling Earth-dynamic.

In that respect, Fander wrought better than he knew.

A plague-scare came in the fourteenth year. Two sleds had
brought back families from afar, and within a week of their
arrival the children sickened, became spotted.

Metal gongs sounded the alarm, all work ceased, the affected
section was cut off and guarded, the majority prepared to flee. It
was a threatening reversal of all the things for which many had
toiled so long; a destructive scattering of the tender roots of new
civilization.

Fander found Graypate, Speedy, and Blacky, armed to the
teeth, facing a drawn-faced and restless crowd.

"There's most of a hundred folk in that isolated part," Graypate
was telling them. "They ain't all got it. Maybe they won't get it.
If they don't it ain't so likely you'll go down either. We ought to
wait and see. Stick around a bit."

"Listen who's talking," invited a voice in the crowd. "If you
weren't immune you'd have been planted thirty-forty years ago."

"Same goes for near everybody," snapped Graypate. He
glared around, his gun under one arm, his pale blue eyes bellicose.
"I ain't much use at speechifying, so I'm just saying flatly that
nobody goes before we know whether this really is the plague."
He hefted his weapon in one hand, held it forward. "Anyone
fancy himself at beating a bullet?"

The heckler in the audience muscled his way to the front. He
was a swarthy man of muscular build, and his dark eyes looked
belligerently into Graypate's. "While there's life there's hope. If
we beat it, we live to come back, when it's safe to come back, if
ever—and you know it. So I'm calling your bluff, see?" Squar-
ing his shoulders, he began to walk off.

Graypate's gun already was halfway up when he felt the touch
of Fander's tentacle on his arm. He lowered the weapon, called
after the escapee.

"I'm going into that cut-off section and the Devil is going
with me. We're running into things, not away from them. I
never did like running away." Several of the audience fidgeted,
murmuring approval. He went on, "We'll see for ourselves just

what's wrong. We mightn't be able to put it right, but we'll find out what's the matter."

The walker paused, turned, eyed him, eyed Fander, and said, "You can't do that."

"Why not?"

"You'll get it yourself—and a heck of a lot of use you'll be dead and stinking."

"What, and me immune?" cracked Graypate grinning.

"The Devil will get it," hedged the other.

Graypate was about to retort, "What do *you* care?" but altered it slightly in response to Fander's contacting thoughts. He said, more softly, "Do you *care?*"

It caught the other off-balance. He fumbled embarrassedly within his own mind, avoided looking at the Martian, said lamely, "I don't see reason for any guy to take risks."

"He's taking them, because *he* cares," Graypate gave back. "And I'm taking them because I'm too old and useless to give a darn."

With that, he stepped down, marched stubbornly toward the isolated section, Fander slithered by his side, tentacle in hand. The one who wished to flee stayed put, staring after them. The crowd shuffled uneasily, seemed in two minds whether to accept the situation and stick around, or to rush Graypate and Fander and drag them away. Speedy and Blacky made to follow the pair but were ordered off.

No adult sickened; nobody died. Children in the affected sector went one after another through the same routine of liverishness, high temperature, and spots, until the epidemic of measles had died out. Not until a month after the last case had been cured by something within its own constitution did Graypate and Fander emerge.

The innocuous course and eventual disappearance of this suspected plague gave the pendulum of confidence a push, swinging it farther. Morale boosted itself almost to the verge of arrogance. More sleds appeared, more mechanics serviced them, more pilots rode them. More people flowed in; more oddments of past knowledge came with them.

Humanity was off to a flying start with the salvaged seeds of past wisdom and the urge to do. The tormented ones of Earth were not primitive savages, but surviving organisms of a greatness nine-tenths destroyed but still remembered, each contributing his mite of know-how to restore at least some of those things which had been boiled away in atomic fires.

When, in the twentieth year, Redhead duplicated the premasticator, there were eight thousand stone houses standing around the hill. A community hall seventy times the size of a house, with a great green dome of copper, reared itself upon the eastward fringe. A dam held the lake to the north. A hospital was going up in the west. The nuances and energies and talents of fifty races had built this town and were still building it. Among them were ten Polynesians and four Icelanders and one lean, dusky child who was the last of the Seminoles.

Farms spread wide. One thousand heads of Indian corn rescued from a sheltered valley in the Andes had grown to ten thousand acres. Water buffaloes and goats had been brought from afar to serve in lieu of the horses and sheep that would never be seen again—and no man knew why one species survived while another did not. The horses had died; the water buffaloes lived. The canines hunted in ferocious packs; the felines had departed from existence. The small herbs, some tubers, and a few seedy things could be rescued and cultivated for hungry bellies; but there were no flowers for the hungry mind. Humanity carried on, making do with what was available. No more than that could be done.

Fander was a back-number. He had nothing left for which to live but his songs and the affection of the others. In everthing but his harp and his songs the Terrans were way ahead of him. He could do no more than give of his own affection in return for theirs and wait with the patience of one whose work is done.

At the end of that year they buried Graypate. He died in his sleep, passing with the undramatic casualness of one who ain't much use at speechifying. They put him to rest on a knoll behind the community hall, and Fander played his mourning song, and Precious Jewel, who was Speedy's wife, planted the grave with sweet herbs.

In the spring of the following year Fander summoned Speedy and Blacky and Redhead. He was coiled on a couch, blue and shivering. They held hands so that his touch would speak to them simultaneously.

"I am about to undergo my *amafa*."

He had great difficulty in putting it over in understandable thought forms, for this was something beyond their Earthly experience.

"It is an unavoidable change of age during which my kind must sleep undisturbed." They reacted as if the casual reference to his kind was a strange and startling revelation, a new aspect previously unthought-of. He continued, "I must be left alone until this hibernation has run its natural course."

"For how long, Devil?" asked Speedy, with anxiety.

"It may stretch from four of your months to a full year, or—"

"Or what?" Speedy did not wait for a reassuring reply. His agile mind was swift to sense the spice of danger lying far back in the Martian's thoughts. "Or it may never end?"

"It may never," admitted Fander, reluctantly. He shivered again, drew his tentacles around himself. The brilliance of his blueness was fading visibly. "The possibility is small, but it is there."

Speedy's eyes widened and his breath was taken in a short gasp. His mind was striving to readjust itself and accept the appalling idea that Fander might not be a fixture, permanent, established for all time. Blacky and Redhead were equally aghast.

"We Martians do not last forever," Fander pointed out, gently. "All are mortal, here and there. He who survives his *amafa* has many happy years to follow, but some do not survive. It is a trial that must be faced as everything from beginning to end must be faced."

"But—"

"Our numbers are not large," Fander went on. "We breed slowly and some of us die halfway through the normal span. By cosmic standards we are a weak and foolish people much in need of the support of the clever and the strong. You are clever and strong. Whenever my people visit you again, or any other still stranger people come, always remember that you are clever and strong."

"We are strong," echoed Speedy, dreamily. His gaze swung around to take in the thousands of roofs, the copper dome, the thing of beauty on the hill. "We are strong."

A prolonged shudder went through the ropy, bee-eyed creature on the couch.

"I do not wish to be left here, an idle sleeper in the midst of life, posing like a bad example to the young. I would rather rest within the little cave where first we made friends and grew to know and understand each other. Wall it up and fix a door for me. Forbid anyone to touch me or let the light of day fall upon me until such time as I emerge of my own accord." Fander stirred sluggishly, his limbs uncoiling with noticeable lack of sinuousness. "I regret I must ask you to carry me there. Please forgive me; I have left it a little late and cannot . . . cannot . . . make it by myself."

Their faces were pictures of alarm, their minds bells of sorrow. Running for poles, they made a stretcher, edged him onto it, bore him to the cave. A long procession was following by the time they reached it. As they settled him comfortably and began to wall up the entrance, the crowd watched in the same solemn silence with which they had looked upon his verse.

He was already a tightly rolled ball of dull blueness, with filmed eyes, when they fitted the door and closed it, leaving him to darkness and slumber. Next day a tiny, brown-skinned man with eight children, all hugging dolls, came to the door. While the youngsters stared huge-eyed at the door, he fixed upon it a two-word name in metal letters, taking great pains over his self-imposed task and making a neat job of it.

The Martian vessel came from the stratosphere with the slow, stately fall of a grounding balloon. Behind the transparent band its bluish, nightmarish crew were assembled and looking with great, multifaceted eyes at the upper surface of the clouds. The scene resembled a pink-tinged snowfield beneath which the planet still remained concealed.

Captain Rdina could feel this as a tense, exciting moment even though his vessel had not the honor to be the first with such an approach. One Captain Skhiva, now long retired, had done it many years before. Nevertheless, this second venture retained its own exploratory thrill.

Someone stationed a third of the way around the vessel's belly came writhing at top pace toward him as their drop brought them near to the pinkish clouds. The oncomer's signaling tentacle was jiggling at a seldom-used rate.

"Captain, we have just seen an object swoop across the horizon."

"What sort of an object?"

"It looked like a gigantic load-sled."

"It couldn't have been."

"No, Captain, of course not—but that is exactly what it appeared to be."

"Where is it now?" demanded Rdina, gazing toward the side from which the other had come.

"It dived into the mists below."

"You must have been mistaken. Long-standing anticipation can encourage the strangest delusions." He stopped a moment as the observation band became shrouded in the vapor of a cloud. Musingly, he watched the gray wall of fog slide upward as his vessel continued its descent. "That old report says definitely that there is nothing but desolation and wild animals. There is no intelligent life except some fool of a minor poet whom Skhiva left behind, and twelve to one he's dead by now. The animals may have eaten him."

"Eaten him? Eaten *meat?*" exclaimed the other, thoroughly revolted.

"Anything is possible," assured Rdina, pleased with the extreme to which his imagination could be stretched. "Except a load-sled. That was plain silly."

At which point he had no choice but to let the subject drop for the simple and compelling reason that the ship came out of the base of the cloud, and the sled in question was floating alongside. It could be seen in complete detail, and even their own instruments were responding to the powerful output of its numerous flotation-grids.

The twenty Martians aboard the sphere sat staring bee-eyed at this enormous thing which was half the size of their own vessel, and the forty humans on the sled stared back with equal intentness. Ship and sled continued to descend side by side, while both crews studied each other with dumb fascination which persisted until simultaneously they touched ground.

It was not until he felt the slight jolt of landing that Captain Rdina recovered sufficiently to look elsewhere. He saw the houses, the green-domed building, the thing of beauty poised upon its hill, the many hundreds of Earth-people streaming out of their town and toward his vessel.

None of these queer, two-legged life forms, he noted, betrayed the slightest sign of revulsion or fear. They galloped to the tryst with a bumptious self-confidence which would still be evident any place the other side of the cosmos.

It shook him a little, and he kept saying to himself, again and again, "They're not scared—why should you be? They're not scared—why should you be?"

He went out personally to meet the first of them, suppressing his own apprehensions and ignoring the fact that many of them bore weapons. The leading Earthman, a big-built, spade-bearded two-legger, grasped his tentacle as to the manner born.

There came a picture of swiftly moving limbs. "My name is Speedy."

The ship emptied itself within ten minutes. No Martian would stay inside who was free to smell new air. Their first visit, in a slithering bunch, was to the thing of beauty. Rdina stood quietly looking at it, his crew clustered in a half-circle around him, the Earth-folk a silent audience behind.

It was a great rock statue of a female of Earth. She was broad-shouldered, full-bosomed, wide-hipped, and wore voluminous skirts that came right down to her heavy-soled shoes. Her back was a little bent, her head a little bowed, and her face was hidden in her hands, deep in her toilworn hands. Rdina tried in vain to gain some glimpse of the tired features behind those hiding hands. He looked at her a long while before his eyes lowered to read the script beneath, ignoring the Earth-lettering, running easily over the flowing Martian curlicues:

> *Weep, my country, for your sons asleep,*
> *The ashes of your homes, your tottering towers.*
> *Weep, my country, O, my country, weep!*
> *For birds that cannot sing, for vanished flowers,*
> > *The end of everything,*
> > *The silenced hours.*
> > *Weep! my country.*

There was no signature. Rdina mulled it through many minutes while the others remained passive. Then he turned to Speedy, pointed to the Martian script.

"Who wrote this?"

"One of your people. He is dead."

"Ah!" said Rdina. "That songbird of Skhiva's. I have forgotten his name. I doubt whether many remember it. He was only a very small poet. How did he die?"

"He ordered us to enclose him for some long and urgent sleep he must have, and—"

"The *amafa*," put in Rdina, comprehendingly. "And then?"

"We did as he asked. He warned us that he might never come out." Speedy gazed at the sky, unconscious that Rdina was picking up his sorrowful thoughts. "He has been there nearly two years and has not emerged." The eyes came down to Rdina.

"I don't know whether you can understand me, but he was one of us."

"I think I understand." Rdina was thoughtful. He asked, "How long is this period you call nearly two years?"

They managed to work it out between them, translating it from Terran to Martian time-terms.

"It is long," pronounced Rdina. "Much longer than the usual *amafa*, but not unique. Occasionally, for no known reason, someone takes even longer. Besides, Earth is Earth and Mars is Mars." He became swift, energetic as he called to one of his crew. "Physician Traith, we have a prolonged-*amafa* case. Get your oils and essences and come with me." When the other had returned, he said to Speedy, "Take us to where he sleeps."

Reaching the door to the walled-up cave, Rdina paused to look at the names fixed upon it in neat but incomprehensible letters. They read: DEAR DEVIL.

"What do those mean?" asked Physician Traith, pointing.

"Do not disturb," guessed Rdina carelessly. Pushing open the door, he let the other enter first, closed it behind him to keep all others outside.

They reappeared an hour later. The total population of the city had congregated outside the cave to see the Martians. Rdina wondered why they had not permitted his crew to satisfy their natural curiosity, since it was unlikely that they would be more interested in other things—such as the fate of one small poet. Ten thousand eyes were upon them as they came into the sunlight and fastened the cave's door. Rdina made contact with Speedy, gave him the news.

Stretching himself in the light as if reaching toward the sun, Speedy shouted in a voice of tremendous gladness which all could hear.

"He will be out again within twenty days."

At that, a mild form of madness seemed to overcome the two-leggers. They made pleasure-grimaces, piercing mouth-noises, and some went so far as to beat each other.

Twenty Martians felt like joining Fander that same night. The Martian constitution is peculiarly susceptible to emotion.

5

SCANNERS LIVE IN VAIN

Cordwainer Smith
(Paul M. A. Linebarger, 1913–1966)

FANTASY BOOK
June

"Cordwainer Smith" makes his debut in this series with one of the most famous first stories in the history of science fiction. "Smith's" true identity was a closely guarded secret for many years; the author was Professor of Asiatic Politics at the Johns Hopkins University School of Advanced International Studies and one of the leading experts in the world on political propaganda, a man who moved somewhat mysteriously through the Middle East and Southeast Asia during and after World War II. As a science fiction writer his work was poetic, imaginative, and mind-bending. Most of it is set in his own universe, a civilization called the "Instrumentality of Mankind," a wonderful creation that has attracted the notice of critics and readers since his too-early death in 1966. Its incomplete story can be found in about ten books, all collections or fix-ups of previously published material. The Best of Cordwainer Smith is a treasure that should be on the shelf of every sf reader.

"Scanners Live in VAin." contains a stunning first line that opened the sf career of a remarkable man and a remarkable writer. Fantasy Book appeared irregularly over a five year period, with a total of only eight issues.

—M.H.G.

Let me tell you a little story. In 1940, Frederik Pohl wrote a story called "Little Man on the Subway." He couldn't sell it anywhere (he was only 20 years old at the time). So he asked me

70

to try to revise it. In January 1941 (I had just turned 21), I rewrote the story. It still couldn't sell anywhere.

Years later, we managed to sell it to Fantasy Book, *a semi-professional science fiction magazine. There it appeared as the lead novelette because by that time my name and Fred's meant something.*

Would you like to know the third story in that same issue of that same magazine? I'll tell you. It was "Scanners Live in Vain" which is now universally recognized as a classic and which obviously must have been as unable to find a home as my stinkeroo had.

I tell you this just in case you think that editors always know what they're doing.

—I.A.

Martel was angry. He did not even adjust his blood away from anger. He stamped across the room by judgment, not by sight. When he saw the table hit the floor, and could tell by the expression on Luci's face that the table must have made a loud crash, he looked down to see if his leg was broken. It was not. Scanner to the core, he had to scan himself. The action was reflex and automatic. The inventory included his legs, abdomen, chestbox of instruments, hands, arms, face and back with the mirror. Only then did Martel go back to being angry. He talked with his voice, even though he knew that his wife hated its blare and preferred to have him write.

"I tell you, I must cranch. I have to cranch. It's my worry, isn't it?"

When Luci answered, he saw only a part of her words as he read her lips: "Darling . . . you're my husband . . . right to love you . . . dangerous . . . do it . . . dangerous . . . wait . . ."

He faced her, but put sound in his voice, letting the blare hurt her again: "I tell you, I'm going to cranch."

Catching her expression, he became rueful and a little tender: "Can't you understand what it means to me? To get out of this horrible prison in my own head? To be a man again—hearing your voice, smelling smoke? To *feel* again—to feel my feet on the ground, to feel the air move against my face? Don't you know what it means?"

Her wide-eyed worrisome concern thrust him back into pure annoyance. He read only a few words as her lips moved: ". . . love you . . . your own good . . . don't you think I want you to be human? . . . your own good . . . too much . . . he said . . . they said . . ."

When he roared at her, he realized that his voice must be particularly bad. He knew that the sound hurt her no less than did the words: "Do you think I wanted you to marry a scanner? Didn't I tell you we're almost as low as the habermans? We're dead, I tell you. We've got to be dead to do our work. How can anybody go to the up-and-out? Can you dream what raw space is? I warned you. But you married me. All right, you married a man. Please, darling, let me be a man. Let me hear your voice, let me feel the warmth of being alive, of being human. Let me!"

He saw by her look of stricken assent that he had won the argument. He did not use his voice again. Instead, he pulled his tablet up from where it hung against his chest. He wrote on it, using the pointed fingernail of his right forefinger—the talking nail of a scanner—in quick cleancut script: *Pls, drlng, whrs crnching wire?*

She pulled the long gold-sheathed wire out of the pocket of her apron. She let its field sphere fall to the carpeted floor. Swiftly, dutifully, with the deft obedience of a scanner's wife, she wound the cranching wire around his head, spirally around his neck and chest. She avoided the instruments set in his chest. She even avoided the radiating scars around the instruments, the stigmata of men who had gone up and into the out. Mechanically he lifted a foot as she slipped the wire between his feet. She drew the wire taut. She snapped the small plug into the high-burden control next to his heart-reader. She helped him to sit down, arranging his hands for him, pushing his head back into the cup at the top of the chair. She turned then, full-face toward him, so that he could read her lips easily. Her expression was composed.

She knelt, scooped up the sphere at the other end of the wire, stood erect calmly, her back to him. He scanned her, and saw nothing in her posture but grief which would have escaped the eye of anyone but a scanner. She spoke: he could see her chest-muscles moving. She realized that she was not facing him, and turned so that he could see her lips.

"Ready at last?"

He smiled a *yes*.

She turned her back to him again. (Luci could never bear to

watch him go under the wire.) She tossed the wire-sphere into the air. It caught in the force-field, and hung there. Suddenly it glowed. That was all. All—except for the sudden red stinking roar of coming back to his senses. Coming back, across the wild threshold of pain.

When he awakened, under the wire, he did not feel as though he had just cranched. Even though it was the second cranching within the week, he felt fit. He lay in the chair. His ears drank in the sound of air touching things in the room. He heard Luci breathing in the next room, where she was hanging up the wire to cool. He smelt the thousand and one smells that are in anybody's room: the crisp freshness of the germ-burner, the sour-sweet tang of the humidifier, the odor of the dinner they had just eaten, the smells of clothes, furniture, of people themselves. All these were pure delight. He sang a phrase or two of his favorite song:

> *"Here's to the haberman, up-and-out!*
> *"Up—oh!—and out—oh!—up-and-out! . . ."*

He heard Luci chuckle in the next room. He gloated over the sounds of her dress as she swished to the doorway.

She gave him her crooked little smile. "You sound all right. Are you all right, really?"

Even with this luxury of senses, he scanned. He took the flash-quick inventory which constituted his professional skill. His eyes swept in the news of the instruments. Nothing showed off scale, beyond the nerve compression hanging in the edge of *Danger*. But he could not worry about the nerve-box. That always came through cranching. You couldn't get under the wire without having it show on the nerve-box. Some day the box would go to *Overload* and drop back down to *Dead*. That was the way a haberman ended. But you couldn't have everything. People who went to the up-and-out had to pay the price for space.

Anyhow, he should worry! He was a scanner. A good one, and he knew it. If he couldn't scan himself, who could? This cranching wasn't too dangerous. Dangerous, but not too dangerous.

Luci put out her hand and ruffled his hair as if she had been reading his thoughts, instead of just following them: "But you know you shouldn't have! You shouldn't!"

"But I did!" He grinned at her.

Her gaiety still forced, she said: "Come on, darling, let's have a good time. I have almost everything there is in the icebox—all your favorite tastes. And I have two new records just full of smells. I tried them out myself, and even I liked them. And you know me—"

"Which?"

"Which what, you old darling?"

He slipped his hand over her shoulders as he limped out of the room. (He could never go back to feeling the floor beneath his feet, feeling the air against his face, without being bewildered and clumsy. As if cranching was real, and being a haberman was a bad dream. But he *was* a haberman, and a scanner.) "You know what I meant, Luci . . . the smells, which you have. Which one did you like, on the record?"

"Well-l-l," said she, judiciously, "there were some lamb chops that were the strangest things—"

He interrupted: "What are lambtchots?"

"Wait till you smell them. Then guess. I'll tell you this much. It's a smell hundreds and hundreds of years old. They found out about it in the old books."

"Is a bambtchot a Beast?"

"I won't tell you. You've got to wait," she laughed, as she helped him sit down and spread his tasting dishes before him. He wanted to go back over the dinner first, sampling all the pretty things he had eaten, and savoring them this time with his now-living lips and tongue.

When Luci had found the music wire and had thrown its sphere up into the force-field, he reminded her of the new smells. She took out the long glass records and set the first one into a transmitter.

"Now sniff!"

A queer, frightening, exciting smell came over the room. It seemed like nothing in this world, nor like anything from the up-and-out. Yet it was familiar. His mouth watered. His pulse beat a little faster; he scanned his heartbox. (Faster, sure enough.) But that smell, what was it? In mock perplexity, he grabbed her hands, looked into her eyes, and growled:

"Tell me, darling! Tell me, or I'll eat you up!"

"That's just right!"

"What?"

"You're right. It should make you want to eat me. It's meat."

"Meat. Who?"

"Not a person," said she, knowledgeably, "a Beast. A Beast

which people used to eat. A lamb was a small sheep—you've seen sheep out in the Wild, haven't you?—and a chop is part of its middle—here!'' She pointed at her chest.

Martel did not hear her. All his boxes had swung over toward *Alarm,* some to *Danger.* He fought against the roar of his own mind, forcing his body into excess excitement. How easy it was to be a scanner when you really stood outside your own body, haberman-fashion, and looked back into it with your eyes alone. Then you could manage the body, rule it coldly even in the enduring agony of space. But to realize that you *were* a body, that this thing was ruling you, that the mind could kick the flesh and send it roaring off into panic! That was bad.

He tried to remember the days before he had gone into the haberman device, before he had been cut apart for the up-and-out. Had he always been subject to the rush of his emotions from his mind to his body, from his body back to his mind, confounding him so that he couldn't scan? But he hadn't been a scanner then.

He knew what had hit him. Amid the roar of his own pulse, he knew. In the nightmare of the up-and-out, that smell had forced its way through to him, while their ship burned off Venus and the habermans fought the collapsing metal with their bare hands. He had scanned then: all were in *Danger.* Chestboxes went up to *Overload* and dropped to *Dead* all around him as he had moved from man to man, shoving the drifting corpses out of his way as he fought to scan each man in turn, to clamp vises on unnoticed broken legs, to snap the sleeping valve on men whose instruments showed they were hopelessly near *Overload.* With men trying to work and cursing him for a scanner while he, professional zeal aroused, fought to do his job and keep them alive in the great pain of space, he had smelled that smell. It had fought its way along his rebuilt nerves, past the haberman cuts, past all the safeguards of physical and mental discipline. In the wildest hour of tragedy, he had smelled aloud. He remembered it was like a bad cranching, connected with the fury and nightmare all around him. He had even stopped his work to scan himself, fearful that the first effect might come, breaking past all haberman cuts and ruining him with the pain of space. But he had come through. His own instruments stayed and stayed at *Danger,* without nearing *Overload.* He had done his job, and won a commendation for it. He had even forgotten the burning ship.

All except the smell.

And here the smell was all over again—the smell of meat-with-fire . . .

Luci looked at him with wifely concern. She obviously thought he had cranched too much, and was about to haberman back. She tried to be cheerful: "You'd better rest, honey."

He whispered to her: "Cut—off—that—smell."

She did not question his word. She cut the transmitter. She even crossed the room and stepped up the room controls until a small breeze flitted across the floor and drove the smells up to the ceiling.

He rose, tired and stiff. (His instruments were normal, except that heart was fast and nerves still hanging on the edge of *Danger*.) He spoke sadly:

"Forgive me, Luci. I suppose I shouldn't have cranched. Not so soon again. But darling, I have to get out from being a haberman. How can I ever be near you? How can I be a man—not hearing my own voice, not even feeling my own life as it goes through my veins? I love you, darling. Can't I ever be near you?"

Her pride was disciplined and automatic: "But you're a scanner!"

"I know I'm a scanner. But so what?"

She went over the words, like a tale told a thousand times to reassure herself: "You are the bravest of the brave, the most skillful of the skilled. All mankind owes most honor to the scanner, who unites the Earths of mankind. Scanners are the protectors of the habermans. They are the judges in the up-and-out. They make men live in the place where men need desperately to die. They are the most honored of mankind, and even the chiefs of the Instrumentality are delighted to pay them homage!"

With obstinate sorrow he demurred: "Luci, we've heard that all before. But does it pay us back—"

" 'Scanners work for more than pay. They are the strong guards of mankind.' Don't you remember that?"

"But our lives, Luci. What can you get out of being the wife of a scanner? Why did you marry me? I'm human only when I cranch. The rest of the time—you know what I am. A machine. A man turned into a machine. A man who has been killed and kept alive for duty. Don't you realize what I miss?"

"Of course, darling, of course—"

He went on: "Don't you think I remember my childhood?

Don't you think I remember what it is to be a man and not a haberman? To walk and feel my feet on the ground? To feel a decent clean pain instead of watching my body every minute to see if I'm alive? How will I know if I'm dead? Did you ever think of that, Luci? How will I know if I'm dead?''

She ignored the unreasonableness of his outburst. Pacifyingly, she said: ''Sit down, darling. Let me make you some kind of a drink. You're overwrought.''

Automatically, he scanned. ''No I'm not! Listen to me. How do you think it feels to be in the up-and-out with the crew tied-for-space all around you? How do you think it feels to watch them sleep? How do you think I like scanning, scanning, scanning month after month, when I can feel the pain of space beating against every part of my body, trying to get past my haberman blocks? How do you think I like to wake the men when I have to, and have them hate me for it? Have you ever seen habermans fight—strong men fighting, and neither knowing pain, fighting until one touches *Overload*? Do you think about that, Luci?'' Triumphantly he added: ''Can you blame me if I cranch, and come back to being a man, just two days a month?''

''I'm not blaming you, darling. Let's enjoy your cranch. Sit down now, and have a drink.''

He was sitting down, resting his face in his hands, while she fixed the drink, using natural fruits out of bottles in addition to the secure alkaloids. He watched her restlessly and pitied her for marrying a scanner; and then, though it was unjust, resented having to pity her.

Just as she turned to hand him the drink, they both jumped a little as the phone rang. It should not have rung. They had turned it off. It rang again, obviously on the emergency circuit. Stepping ahead of Luci, Martel strode over to the phone and looked into it. Vomact was looking at him.

The custom of scanners entitled him to be brusque, even with a senior scanner, on certain given occasions. This was one.

Before Vomact could speak, Martel spoke two words into the plate, not caring whether the old man could read lips or not:

''Cranching. Busy.''

He cut the switch and went back to Luci.

The phone rang again.

Luci said, gently, ''I can find out what it is, darling. Here, take your drink and sit down.''

''Leave it alone'' said her husband. ''No one has a right to call when I'm cranching. He knows that. He ought to know that."

The phone rang again. In a fury, Martel rose and went to the plate. He cut it back on. Vomact was on the screen. Before Martel could speak, Vomact held up his talking nail in line with his heartbox. Martel reverted to discipline:

"Scanner Martel present and waiting, sir."

The lips moved solemnly: "Top emergency."

"Sir, I am under the wire."

"Top emergency."

"Sir, don't you understand?" Martel mouthed his words, so he could be sure that Vomact followed. "I . . . am . . . under . . . the . . . wire. Unfit . . . for . . . Space!"

Vomact repeated: "Top emergency. Report to Central Tie-in."

"But, sir, no emergency like this—"

"Right, Martel. No emergency like this, ever before. Report to Tie-in." With a faint glint of kindliness, Vomact added: "No need to decranch. Report as you are."

This time it was Martel whose phone was cut out. The screen went gray.

He turned to Luci. The temper had gone out of his voice. She came to him. She kissed him, and rumpled his hair. All she could say was,

"I'm sorry."

She kissed him again, knowing his disappointment. "Take good care of yourself, darling. I'll wait."

He scanned, and slipped into his transparent aircoat. At the window he paused, and waved. She called, "Good luck!" As the air flowed past him he said to himself,

"This is the first time I've felt flight in—eleven years. Lord, but it's easy to fly if you can feel yourself live!"

Central Tie-in glowed white and austere far ahead. Martel peered. He saw no glare of incoming ships from the up-and-out, no shuddering flare of space-fire out of control. Everything was quiet, as it should be on an off-duty night.

And yet Vomact had called. He had called an emergency higher than space. There was no such thing. But Vomact had called it.

When Martel got there, he found about half the scanners present, two dozen or so of them. He lifted the talking finger. Most of the scanners were standing face to face, talking in pairs as they read lips. A few of the old, impatient ones were scribbling on their tablets and then thrusting the tablets into other people's faces. All the faces wore the dull dead relaxed look of a haberman. When Martel entered the room, he knew that most of the others laughed in the deep isolated privacy of their own minds, each thinking things it would be useless to express in formal words. It had been a long time since a scanner showed up at a meeting cranched.

Vomact was not there; probably, thought Martel, he was still on the phone calling others. The light of the phone flashed on and off; the bell rang. Martel felt odd when he realized that of all those present, he was the only one to hear that loud bell. It made him realize why ordinary people did not like to be around groups of habermans or scanners. Martel looked around for company.

His friend Chang was there, busy explaining to some old and testy scanner that he did not know why Vomact had called. Martel looked farther and saw Parizianski. He walked over, threading his way past the others with a dexterity that showed he could feel his feet from the inside, and did not have to watch them. Several of the others stared at him with their dead faces, and tried to smile. But they lacked full muscular control and their faces twisted into horrid masks. (Scanners usually knew better than to show expression on faces which they could no longer govern. Martel added to himself, *I swear I'll never smile again unless I'm cranched.*)

Parizianski gave him the sign of the talking finger. Looking face to face, he spoke:

"You come here cranched?"

Parizianski could not hear his own voice, so the words roared like the words on a broken and screeching phone; Martel was startled, but knew that the inquiry was well meant. No one could be better-natured than the burly Pole.

"Vomact called. Top emergency."

"You told him you were cranched?"

"Yes."

"He still made you come?"

"Yes."

"Then all this—it is not for Space? You could not go up-and-out? You are like ordinary men?"

"That's right."

"Then why did he call us?" Some pre-haberman habit made Parizianski wave his arms in inquiry. The hand struck the back of the old man behind them. The slap could be heard throughout the room, but only Martel heard it. Instinctively, he scanned Parizianski and the old scanner, and they scanned him back. Only then did the old man ask why Martel had scanned him. When Martel explained that he was under the wire, the old man moved swiftly away to pass on the news that there was a cranched scanner present at the tie-in.

Even this minor sensation could not keep the attention of most of the scanners from the worry about the top emergency. One young man, who had scanned his first transit just the year before, dramatically interposed himself between Parizianski and Martel. He dramatically flashed his tablet at them:

Is Vmct mad?

The older men shook their heads. Martel, remembering that it had not been too long that the young man had been haberman, mitigated the dead solemnity of the denial with a friendly smile. He spoke in a normal voice, saying:

"Vomact is the senior of scanners. I am sure that he could not go mad. Would he not see it on his boxes first?"

Martel had to repeat the question, speaking slowly and mouthing his words before the young scanner could understand the comment. The young man tried to make his face smile, and twisted it into a comic mask. But he took up his tablet and scribbled:

Yr rght.

Chang broke away from his friend and came over, his half-Chinese face gleaming in the warm evening. (It's strange, thought Martel, that more Chinese don't become scanners. Or not so strange perhaps, if you think that they never fill their quota of habermans. Chinese love good living too much. The ones who do scan are all good ones.) Chang saw that Martel was cranched, and spoke with voice:

"You break precedents. Luci must be angry to lose you?"

"She took it well. Chang, that's strange."

"What?"

"I'm cranched, and I can hear. Your voice sounds all right. How did you learn to talk like—like an ordinary person?"

"I practiced with soundtracks. Funny you noticed it. I think I am the only scanner in or between the Earths who can pass for an ordinary man. Mirrors and soundtracks. I found out how to act."

"But you don't . . .?"

"No, I don't feel, or taste, or hear, or smell things, any more

than you do. Talking doesn't do me much good. But I notice that
it cheers up the people around me.''

"It would make a difference in the life of Luci.''

Chang nodded sagely. "My father insisted on it. He said,
'You may be proud of being a scanner. I am sorry you are not a
man. Conceal your defects.' So I tried. I wanted to tell the old
boy about the up-and-out, and what we did there, but it did not
matter. He said, 'Airplanes were good enough for Confucius,
and they are for me too.' The old humbug! He tries so hard to be
a Chinese when he can't even read Old Chinese. But he's got
wonderful good sense, and for somebody going on two hundred
he certainly gets around.''

Martel smiled at the thought: "In his airplane?''

Chang smiled back. This discipline of his facial muscles was
amazing; a bystander would not think that Chang was a haberman,
controlling his eyes, cheeks, and lips by cold intellectual means.
The expression had the spontaneity of life. Martel felt a flash of
envy for Chang when he looked at the dead cold faces of
Parizianski and the others. He knew that he himself looked fine:
but why shouldn't he? He was cranched. Turning to Parizianski
he said,

"Did you see what Chang said about his father? The old boy
uses an airplane.''

Parizianski made motions with his mouth, but the sounds
meant nothing. He took up his tablet and showed it to Martel and
Chang.

Bzz bzz. Ha ha. Gd ol' boy.

At that moment, Martel heard steps out in the corridor. He
could not help looking toward the door. Other eyes followed the
direction of his glance.

Vomact came in.

The group shuffled to attention in four parallel lines. They
scanned one another. Numerous hands reached across to adjust
the electrochemical controls on chestboxes which had begun to
load up. One scanner held out a broken finger which his counter-
scanner had discovered, and submitted it for treatment and
splinting.

Vomact had taken out his staff of office. The cube at the top
flashed red light through the room, the lines reformed, and all
scanners gave the sign meaning, *Present and ready!*

Vomact countered with the stance signifying, *I am the senior
and take command.*

Talking fingers rose in the counter-gesture, *We concur and commit ourselves.*

Vomact raised his right arm, dropped the wrist as though it were broken, in a queer searching gesture, meaning: *Any men around? Any habermans not tied? All clear for the scanners?*

Alone of all those present, the cranched Martel heard the queer rustle of feet as they all turned completely around without leaving position, looking sharply at one another and flashing their beltlights into the dark corners of the great room. When again they faced Vomact, he made a further sign:

All clear. Follow my words.

Martel noticed that he alone relaxed. The others could not know the meaning of relaxation with the minds blocked off up there in their skulls, connected only with the eyes, and the rest of the body connected with the mind only by controlling non-sensory nerves and the instrument boxes on their chests. Martel realized that, cranched as he was, he had expected to hear Vomact's voice: the senior had been talking for some time. No sound escaped his lips. (Vomact never bothered with sound.)

". . . and when the first men to go up-and-out went to the moon, what did they find?"

"Nothing," responded the silent chorus of lips.

"Therefore they went farther, to Mars and to Venus. The ships went out year by year, but they did not come back until the Year One of Space. Then did a ship come back with the first effect. Scanners, I ask you, what is the first effect?"

"No one knows. No one knows."

"No one will ever know. Too many are the variables. By what do we know the first effect?"

"By the great pain of space," came the chorus.

"And by what further sign?"

"By the need, oh the need for death."

Vomact again: "And who stopped the need for death?"

"Henry Haberman conquered the first effect, in the Year Eighty-three of Space."

"And, Scanners, I ask you, what did he do?"

"He made the habermans."

"How, O Scanners, are habermans made?"

"They are made with the cuts. The brain is cut from the heart, the lungs. The brain is cut from the ears, the nose. The brain is cut from the mouth, the belly. The brain is cut from desire, and pain. The brain is cut from the world. Save for the eyes. Save for the control of the living flesh."

"And how, O Scanners, is flesh controlled?"

"By the boxes set in the flesh, the controls set in the chest, the signs made to rule the living body, the signs by which the body lives."

"How does a haberman live and live?"

"The haberman lives by control of the boxes."

"Whence come the habermans?"

Martel felt in the coming response a great roar of broken voices echoing through the room as the scanners, habermans themselves, put sound behind their mouthings:

"Habermans are the scum of mankind. Habermans are the weak, the cruel, the credulous, and the unfit. Habermans are the sentenced-to-more-than-death. Habermans live in the mind alone. They are killed for space but they live for space. They master the ships that connect the Earths. They live in the great pain while ordinary men sleep in the cold, cold sleep of the transit."

"Brothers and Scanners, I ask you now: are we habermans or are we not?"

"We are habermans in the flesh. We are cut apart, brain and flesh. We are ready to go to the up-and-out. All of us have gone through the haberman device."

"We are habermans then?" Vomact's eyes flashed and glittered as he asked the ritual question.

Again the chorused answer was accompanied by a roar of voices heard only by Martel: "Habermans we are, and more, and more. We are the chosen who are habermans by our own free will. We are the agents of the Instrumentality of Mankind."

"What must the others say to us?"

"They must say to us, 'You are the bravest of the brave, the most skillful of the skilled. All mankind owes most honor to the scanner, who unites the Earths of mankind. Scanners are the protectors of the habermans. They are the judges in the up-and-out. They make men live in the place where men need desperately to die. They are the most honored of mankind, and even the chiefs of the Instrumentality are delighted to pay them homage!"

Vomact stood more erect: "What is the secret duty of the scanner?"

"To keep secret our law, and to destroy the acquirers thereof."

"How to destroy?"

"Twice to the *Overload*, back and *Dead*."

"If habermans die, what the duty then?"

The scanners all compressed their lips for answer. (Silence was the code.) Martel, who—long familiar with the code—was a little bored with the proceedings, noticed that Chang was breathing too heavily; he reached over and adjusted Chang's lung-control and received the thanks of Chang's eyes. Vomact observed the interruption and glared at them both. Martel relaxed, trying to imitate the dead cold stillness of the others. It was so hard to do, when you were cranched.

"If others die, what the duty then?" asked Vomact.

"Scanners together inform the Instrumentality. Scanners together accept the punishment. Scanners together settle the case."

"And if the punishment be severe?"

"Then no ships go."

"And if scanners be not honored?"

"Then no ships go."

"And if a scanner goes unpaid?"

"Then no ships go."

"And if the Others and the Instrumentality are not in all ways at all times mindful of their proper obligation to the scanners?"

"Then no ships go."

"And what, O Scanners, if no ships go?"

"The Earths fall apart. The Wild comes back in. The Old Machines and the Beasts return."

"What is the first known duty of a scanner?"

"Not to sleep in the up-and-out."

"What is the second duty of a scanner?"

"To keep forgotten the name of fear."

"What is the third duty of a scanner?"

"To use the wire of Eustace Cranch only with care, only with moderation." Several pairs of eyes looked quickly at Martel before the mouthed chorus went on. "To cranch only at home, only among friends, only for the purpose of remembering, of relaxing, or of begetting."

"What is the word of the scanner?"

"Faithful though surrounded by death."

"What is the motto of the scanner?"

"Awake though surrounded by silence."

"What is the work of the scanner?"

"Labor even in the heights of the up-and-out, loyalty even in the depths of the Earths."

"How do you know a scanner?"

"We know ourselves. We are dead though we live. And we talk with the tablet and the nail."

"What is this code?"

"This code is the friendly ancient wisdom of scanners; briefly put, that we may be mindful and be cheered by our loyalty to one another."

At this point the formula should have run: "We complete the code. Is there work or word for the scanners?" But Vomact said, and he repeated:

"Top emergency. Top emergency."

They gave him the sign, *Present and ready!*

He said, with every eye straining to follow his lips:

"Some of you know the work of Adam Stone?"

Martel saw lips move, saying: "The Red Asteroid. The Other who lives at the edge of Space."

"Adam Stone has gone to the Instrumentality, claiming success for his work. He says that he has found how to screen out the pain of space. He says that the up-and-out can be made safe for ordinary men to work in, to stay awake in. He says that there need be no more scanners."

Beltlights flashed on all over the room as scanners sought the right to speak. Vomact nodded to one of the older men. "Scanner Smith will speak."

Smith stepped slowly up into the light, watching his own feet. He turned so that they could see his face. He spoke: "I say that this is a lie. I say that Stone is a liar. I say that the Instrumentality must not be deceived."

He paused. Then, in answer to some question from the audience which most of the others did not see, he said:

"I invoke the secret duty of the scanners."

Smith raised his right hand for emergency attention:

"I say that Stone must die."

Martel, still cranched, shuddered as he heard the boos, groans, shouts, squeaks, grunts and moans which came from the scanners who forgot noise in their excitement and strove to make their dead bodies talk to one another's deaf ears. Beltlights flashed wildly all over the room. There was a rush for the rostrum and scanners milled around at the top, vying for attention until Parizianski—by sheer bulk—shoved the others aside and down, and turned to mouth at the group.

"Brother Scanners, I want your eyes."

The people on the floor kept moving, with their numb bodies jostling one another. Finally Vomact stepped up in front of Parizianski, faced the others, and said:

"Scanners, be scanners! Give him your eyes."

Parizianski was not good at public speaking. His lips moved too fast. He waved his hands, which took the eyes of the others away from his lips. Nevertheless, Martel was able to follow most of the message:

". . . can't do this. Stone may have succeeded. If he has succeeded, it means the end of the scanners. It means the end of the habermans, too. None of us will have to fight in the up-and-out. We won't have anybody else going under the wire for a few hours or days of being human. Everybody will be Other. Nobody will have to cranch, never again. Men can be men. The habermans can be killed decently and properly, the way men were killed in the old days, without anybody keeping them alive. They won't have to work in the up-and-out! There will be no more great pain—think of it! No . . . more . . . great . . . pain! How do we know that Stone is a liar—" Lights began flashing directly into his eyes. (The rudest insult of scanner to scanner was this.)

Vomact again exercised authority. He stepped in front of Parizianski and said something which the others could not see. Parizianski stepped down from the rostrum. Vomact again spoke:

"I think that some of the scanners disagree with our brother Parizianski. I say that the use of the rostrum be suspended till we have had a chance for private discussion. In fifteen minutes I will call the meeting back to order."

Martel looked around for Vomact when the senior had rejoined the group on the floor. Finding the senior, Martel wrote swift script on his tablet, waiting for a chance to thrust the tablet before the senior's eyes. He had written:

Am crnchd. Rspctfly requst prmissn lv now, stnd by fr orders.

Being cranched did strange things to Martel. Most meetings that he attended seemed formal, hearteningly ceremonial, lighting up the dark inward eternities of habermanhood. When he was not cranched, he noticed his body no more than a marble bust notices its marble pedestal. He had stood with them before. He had stood with them effortless hours, while the long-winded ritual broke through the terrible loneliness behind his eyes, and made him feel that the scanners, though a confraternity of the damned, were none the less forever honored by the professional requirements of their mutilation.

This time, it was different. Coming cranched, and in full possession of smell-sound-taste-feeling, he reacted more or less as a normal man would. He saw his friends and colleagues as a lot of cruelly driven ghosts, posturing out the meaningless ritual of their indefeasible damnation. What difference did anything make, once you were a haberman? Why all this talk about habermans and scanners? Habermans were criminals or heretics, and scanners were gentlemen-volunteers, but they were all in the same fix—except that scanners were deemed worthy of the short-time return of the cranching wire, while habermans were simply disconnected while the ships lay in port and were left suspended until they should be awakened, in some hour of emergency or trouble, to work out another spell of their damnation. It was a rare haberman that you saw on the street—someone of special merit or bravery, allowed to look at mankind from the terrible prison of his own mechanified body. And yet, what scanner ever pitied a haberman? What scanner ever honored a haberman except perfunctorily in the line of duty? What had the scanners as a guild and a class ever done for the habermans, except to murder them with a twist of the wrist whenever a haberman, too long beside a scanner, picked up the tricks of the scanning trade and learned how to live at his own will, not the will the scanners imposed? What could the Others, the ordinary men, know of what went on inside the ships? The Others slept in their cylinders, mercifully unconscious until they woke up on whatever other Earth they had consigned themselves to. What could the Others know of the men who had to stay alive within the ship?

What could any Other know of the up-and-out? What Other could look at the biting acid beauty of the stars in open space? What could they tell of the great pain, which started quietly in the marrow, like an ache, and proceeded by the fatigue and nausea of each separate nerve cell, brain cell, touchpoint in the body, until life itself became a terrible aching hunger for silence and for death?

He was a scanner. All right, he *was* a scanner. He had been a scanner from the moment when, wholly normal, he had stood in the sunlight before a subchief of the Instrumentality, and had sworn:

"I pledge my honor and my life to mankind. I sacrifice myself willingly for the welfare of mankind. In accepting the perilous austere honor, I yield all my rights without exception to the honorable chiefs of the Instrumentality and to the honored Confraternity of Scanners.''

He had pledged.

He had gone into the haberman device.

He had remembered his hell. He had not had such a bad one, even though it had seemed to last a hundred-million years, all of them without sleep. He had learned to feel with his eyes. He had learned to see despite the heavy eyeplates set back of his eyeballs to insulate his eyes from the rest of him. He had learned to watch his skin. He still remembered the time he had noticed dampness on his shirt, and had pulled out his scanning mirror only to discover that he had worn a hole in his side by leaning against a vibrating machine. (A thing like that could not happen to him now; he was too adept at reading his own instruments.) He remembered the way that he had gone up-and-out, and the way that the great pain beat into him, despite the fact that his touch, smell, feeling, and hearing were gone for all ordinary purposes. He remembered killing habermans, and keeping others alive, and standing for months beside the honorable scanner-pilot while neither of them slept. He remembered going ashore on Earth Four, and remembered that he had not enjoyed it, and had realized on that day that there was no reward.

Martel stood among the other scanners. He hated their awkwardness when they moved, their immobility when they stood still. He hated the queer assortment of smells which their bodies yielded unnoticed. He hated the grunts and groans and squawks which they emitted from their deafness. He hated them, and himself.

How could Luci stand him? He had kept his chestbox reading *Danger* for weeks while he courted her, carrying the cranch wire about with him most illegally, and going direct from one cranch to the other without worrying about the fact his indicators all crept up to the edge of *Overload*. He had wooed her without thinking of what would happen if she did say, ''Yes.'' She had.

''And they lived happily ever after.'' In old books they did, but how could they, in life? He had had eighteen days under the wire in the whole of the past year! Yet she had loved him. She still loved him. He knew it. She fretted about him through the long months that he was in the up-and-out. She tried to make home mean something to him even when he was haberman, make food pretty when it could not be tasted, make herself lovable when she could not be kissed—or might as well not, since a haberman body meant no more than furniture. Luci was patient.

And now, Adam Stone! (He let his tablet fade: how could he leave, now?)

God bless Adam Stone?

Martel could not help feeling a little sorry for himself. No longer would the high keen call of duty carry him through two hundred or so years of the Others' time, two million private eternities of his own. He could slouch and relax. He could forget high space, and let the up-and-out be tended by Others. He could cranch as much as he dared. He could be almost normal—almost—for one year or five years or no years. But at least he could stay with Luci. He could go with her into the Wild, where there were Beasts and Old Machines still roving the dark places. Perhaps he would die in the excitement of the hunt, throwing spears at an ancient manshonyagger as it leapt from its lair, or tossing hot spheres at the tribesmen of the Unforgiven who still roamed the Wild. There was still life to live, still a good normal death to die, not the moving of a needle out in the silence and agony of space!

He had been walking about restlessly. His ears were attuned to the sounds of normal speech, so that he did not feel like watching the mouthings of his brethren. Now they seemed to have come to a decision. Vomact was moving to the rostrum. Martel looked about for Chang, and went to stand beside him. Chang whispered.

"You're as restless as water in mid-air! What's the matter? Decranching?"

They both scanned Martel, but the instruments held steady and showed no sign of the cranch giving out.

The great light flared in its call to attention. Again they formed ranks. Vomact thrust his lean old face into the glare, and spoke:

"Scanners and Brothers, I call for a vote." He held himself in the stance which meant: *I am the senior and take command.*

A beltlight flashed in protest.

It was old Henderson. He moved to the rostrum, spoke to Vomact, and—with Vomact's nod of approval—turned full-face to repeat his question:

"Who speaks for the scanners out in space?"

No beltlight or hand answered.

Henderson and Vomact, face to face, conferred for a few moments. Then Henderson faced them again:

"I yield to the senior in command. But I do not yield to a meeting of the Confraternity. There are sixty-eight scanners, and only forty-seven present of whom one is cranched and U. D. I have therefore proposed that the senior in command assume authority only over an emergency committee of the Confraternity, not over a meeting. Is that agreed and understood by the honorable scanners?"

Hands rose in assent.

Chang murmured in Martel's ear, "Lot of difference that makes! Who can tell the difference between a meeting and a committee?" Martel agreed with the words, but was even more impressed with the way that Chang, while haberman, could control his own voice.

Vomact resumed chairmanship: "We now vote on the question of Adam Stone.

"First, we can assume that he has not succeeded, and that his claims are lies. We know that from our practical experience as scanners. The pain of space is only part of scanning," (*But the essential part, the basis of it all,* thought Martel.) "and we can rest assured that Stone cannot solve the problem of space discipline."

"That tripe again," whispered Chang, unheard save by Martel.

"The space discipline of our confraternity has kept high space clean of war and dispute. Sixty-eight disciplined men control all high space. We are removed by our oath and our haberman status from all Earthly passions.

"Therefore, if Adam Stone has conquered the pain of space, so that Others can wreck our confraternity and bring to space the trouble and ruin which afflicts Earths, I say that Adam Stone is wrong. If Adam Stone succeeds, scanners live in vain!

"Secondly, if Adam Stone has not conquered the pain of space, he will cause great trouble in all the Earths. The Instrumentality and the subchiefs may not give us as many habermans as we need to operate the ships of mankind. There will be wild stories, and fewer recruits, and, worst of all, the discipline of the Confraternity may relax if this kind of nonsensical heresy is spread around.

"Therefore, if Adam Stone has succeeded, he threatens the ruin of the Confraternity and should die.

"I move the death of Adam Stone."

And Vomact made the sign, *The honorable scanners are pleased to vote.*

Martel grabbed wildly for his beltlight. Chang, guessing ahead, had his light out and ready; its bright beam, voting *No*, shone straight up at the ceiling. Martel got his light out and threw its beam upward in dissent. Then he looked around. Out of the forty-seven present, he could see only five or six glittering.

Two more lights went on. Vomact stood as erect as a frozen corpse. Vomact's eyes flashed as he stared back and forth over the group, looking for lights. Several more went on. Finally Vomact took the closing stance:

May it please the scanners to count the vote.

Three of the older men went up on the rostrum with Vomact. They looked over the room. (Martel thought; *These damned ghosts are voting on the life of a real man, a live man! They have no right to do it. I'll tell the Instrumentality!* But he knew that he would not. He thought of Luci and what she might gain by the triumph of Adam Stone: the heart-breaking folly of the vote was then almost too much for Martel to bear.)

All three of the tellers held up their hands in unanimous agreement on the sign of the number: *Fifteen against.*

Vomact dismissed them with a bow of courtesy. He turned and again took the stance: *I am the senior and take command.*

Marveling at his own daring, Martel flashed his beltlight on. He knew that any one of the bystanders might reach over and twist his heartbox to *Overload* for such an act. He felt Chang's hand reaching to catch him by the aircoat. But he eluded Chang's grasp and ran, faster than a scanner should, to the platform. As he ran, he wondered what appeal to make. It was no use talking common sense. Not now. It had to be law.

He jumped up on the rostrum beside Vomact, and took the stance: *Scanners, a Illegality!*

He violated good custom while speaking, still in the stance: "A committee has no right to vote death by a majority vote. It takes two-thirds of a full meeting."

He felt Vomact's body lunge behind him, felt himself falling from the rostrum, hitting the floor, hurting his knees and his touch-aware hands. He was helped to his feet. He was scanned. Some scanner he scarcely knew took his instruments and toned him down.

Immediately Martel felt more calm, more detached, and hated himself for feeling so.

He looked up at the rostrum. Vomact maintained the stance signifying: *Order!*

The scanners adjusted their ranks. The two scanners next to Martel took his arms. He shouted at them, but they looked away, and cut themselves off from communication altogether.

Vomact spoke again when he saw the room was quiet: "A scanner came here cranched. Honorable Scanners, I apologize for this. It is not the fault of our great and worthy scanner and friend, Martel. He came here under orders. I told him not to de-cranch. I hoped to spare him an unnecessary haberman. We all know how happily Martel is married, and we wish his brave experiment well. I like Martel. I respect his judgment. I wanted him here. I knew you wanted him here. But he is cranched. He is in no mood to share in the lofty business of the scanners. I therefore propose a solution which will meet all the requirements of fairness. I propose that we rule Scanner Martel out of order for his violation of rules. This violation would be inexcusable if Martel were not cranched.

"But at the same time, in all fairness to Martel, I further propose that we deal with the points raised so improperly by our worthy but disqualified brother."

Vomact gave the sign, *The honorable scanners are pleased to vote*. Martel tried to reach his own beltlight; the dead strong hands held him tightly and he struggled in vain. One lone light shone high: Chang's, no doubt.

Vomact thrust his face into the light again: "Having the approval of our worthy scanners and present company for the general proposal, I now move that this committee declare itself to have the full authority of a meeting, and that this committee further make me responsible for all misdeeds which this committee may enact, to be held answerable before the next full meeting, but not before any other authority beyond the closed and secret ranks of scanners."

Flamboyantly this time, his triumph evident, Vomact assumed the *vote* stance.

Only a few lights shone: far less, patently, than a minority of one-fourth.

Vomact spoke again. The light shone on his high calm forehead, on his dead relaxed cheekbones. His lean cheeks and chin were half-shadowed, save where the lower light picked up and spot-lighted his mouth, cruel even in repose. (Vomact was said to be a descendant of some ancient lady who had traversed, in an illegitimate and inexplicable fashion, some hundreds of years of time in a single night. Her name, the Lady Vomact, had passed into legend; but her blood and her archaic lust for mastery lived on in the mute masterful body of her descendant. Martel could believe the old tales as he stared at the rostrum, wondering what untraceable mutation had left the Vomact kin as predators among mankind.) Calling loudly with the movement of his lips, but still without sound, Vomact appealed:

"The honorable committee is now pleased to reaffirm the sentence of death issued against the heretic and enemy, Adam Stone." Again the *vote* stance.

Again Chang's light shone lonely in its isolated protest.

Vomact then made his final move:

"I call for the designation of the senior scanner present as the manager of the sentence. I call for authorization to him to appoint executioners, one or many, who shall make evident the will and majesty of scanners. I ask that I be accountable for the deed, and not for the means. The deed is a noble deed, for the protection of mankind and for the honor of the scanners; but of the means it must be said that they are to be the best at hand, and no more. Who knows the true way to kill an Other, here on a crowded and watchful Earth? This is no mere matter of discharging a cylindered sleeper, no mere question of upgrading the needle of a haberman. When people die down here, it is not like the up-and-out. They die reluctantly. Killing within the Earth is not our usual business, O Brothers and Scanners, as you know well. You must choose me to choose my agent as I see fit. Otherwise the common knowledge will become the common betrayal whereas if I alone know the responsibility, I alone could betray us, and you will not have far to look in case the Instrumentality comes searching." (*What about the killer you choose?* thought Martel. *He too will know unless—unless you silence him forever.*)

Vomact went into the stance: *The honorable scanners are pleased to vote.*

One light of protest shone; Chang's, again.

Martel imagined that he could see a cruel joyful smile on Vomact's dead face—the smile of a man who knew himself righteous and who found his righteousness upheld and affirmed by militant authority.

Martel tried one last time to come free.

The dead hands held. They were locked like vises until their owners' eyes unlocked them; how else could they hold the piloting month by month?

Martel then shouted: "Honorable Scanners, this is judicial murder."

No ear heard him. He was cranched, and alone.

Nonetheless, he shouted again: "You endanger the Confraternity."

Nothing happened.

The echo of his voice sounded from one end of the room to the other. No head turned. No eyes met his.

Martel realized that as they paired for talk, the eyes of the scanners avoided him. He saw that no one desired to watch his speech. He knew that behind the cold faces of his friends there lay compassion or amusement. He knew that they knew him to be cranched—absurd, normal, manlike, temporarily no scanner. But he knew that in this matter the wisdom of scanners was nothing. He knew that only a cranched scanner could feel with his very blood the outrage and anger which deliberate murder would provoke among the Others. He knew that the Confraternity endangered itself, and knew that the most ancient prerogative of law was the monopoly of death. Even the ancient nations, in the times of the Wars, before the Beasts, before men went into the up-and-out—even the ancients had known this. How did they say it? *Only the state shall kill.* The states were gone but the Instrumentality remained, and the Instrumentality could not pardon things which occurred within the Earths but beyond its authority. Death in space was the business, the right of the scanners: how could the Instrumentality enforce its laws in a place where all men who wakened, wakened only to die in the great pain? Wisely did the Instrumentality leave space to the scanners, wisely had the Confraternity not meddled inside the Earths. And now the Confraternity itself was going to step forth as a outlaw band, as a gang of rogues as stupid and reckless as the tribes of the Unforgiven!

Martel knew this because he was cranched. Had he been haberman, he would have thought only with his mind, not with his heart and guts and blood. How could the other scanners know?

Vomact returned for the last time to the rostrum: *The committee has met and its will shall be done.* Verbally he added: "Senior among you, I ask your loyalty and your silence."

At that point, the two scanners let his arms go. Martel rubbed his numb hands, shaking his fingers to get the circulation back into the cold fingertips. With real freedom, he began to think of what he might still do. He scanned himself; the cranching held. He might have a day. Well, he could go on even if haberman, but it would be inconvenient, having to talk with finger and tablet. He looked about for Chang. He saw his friend standing patient and immobile in a quiet corner. Martel moved slowly, so as not to attract any more attention to himself than could be helped. He faced Chang, moved until his face was in the light, and then articulated:

"What are we going to do? You're not going to let them kill Adam Stone, are you? Don't you realize what Stone's work will mean to us, if it succeeds? No more scanners. No more habermans. No more pain in the up-and-out. I tell you, if the others were all cranched, as I am, they would see it in a human way, not with the narrow crazy logic which they used in the meeting. We've got to stop them. How can we do it? What are we going to do? What does Parizianski think? Who has been chosen?"

"Which question do you want me to answer?"

Martel laughed. (It felt good to laugh, even then; it felt like being a man.) "Will you help me?"

Chang's eyes flashed across Martel's face as Chang answered: "No. No. No."

"You won't help?"

"No."

"Why not, Chang? Why not?"

"I am a scanner. The vote has been taken. You would do the same if you were not in this unusual condition."

"I'm not in an unusual condition. I'm cranched. That merely means that I see things the way that the Others would. I see the stupidity. The recklessness. The selfishness. It is murder."

"What is murder? Have you not killed? You are not one of the Others. You are a scanner. You will be sorry for what you are about to do, if you do not watch out."

"But why did you vote against Vomact then? Didn't you too see what Adam Stone means to all of us? Scanners will live in vain. Thank God for that! Can't you see it?"

"No."

"But you talk to me, Chang. You are my friend?"

"I talk to you. I am your friend. Why not?"

"But what are you going to do?"

"Nothing, Martel. Nothing."

"Will you help me?"

"No."

"Not even to save Stone?"

"No."

"Then I will go to Parizianski for help."

"It will do you no good."

"Why not? He's more human than you, right now."

"He will not help you, because he has the job. Vomact designated him to kill Adam Stone."

Martel stopped speaking in mid-movement. He suddenly took the stance: *I thank you, Brother, and I depart.*

At the window he turned and faced the room. He saw that Vomact's eyes were upon him. He gave the stance, *I thank you, Brother, and I depart,* and added the flourish of respect which is shown when seniors are present. Vomact caught the sign, and Martel could see the cruel lips move. He thought he saw the words ". . . take good care of yourself . . ." but did not wait to inquire. He stepped backward and dropped out the window.

Once below the window and out of sight, he adjusted his aircoat to a maximum speed. He swam lazily in the air, scanning himself thoroughly, and adjusting his adrenal intake down. He then made the movement of release, and felt the cold air rush past his face like running water.

Adam Stone had to be at Chief Downport.

Adam Stone had to be there.

Wouldn't Adam Stone be surprised in the night? Surprised to meet the strangest of beings, the first renegade among scanners. (Martel suddenly appreciated that it was of himself he was thinking. Martel the Traitor to Scanners! That sounded strange and bad. But what of Martel, the Loyal to Mankind? Was that not compensation? And if he won, he won Luci. If he lost, he lost nothing—an unconsidered and expendable haberman. It happened to be himself. But in contrast to the immense reward, to mankind, to the Confraternity, to Luci, what did that matter?)

Martel thought to himself: "Adam Stone will have two visitors tonight. Two scanners, who are the friends of one another." He hoped that Parizianski was still his friend.

"And the world," he added, "depends on which of us gets there first."

Multifaceted in their brightness, the lights of Chief Downport began to shine through the mist ahead. Martel could see the outer towers of the city and glimpsed the phosphorescent periphery which kept back the Wild, whether Beasts, Machines, or the Unforgiven.

Once more Martel invoked the lords of his chance: "Help me to pass for an Other!"

Within the Downport, Martel had less trouble than he thought. He draped his aircoat over his shoulder so that it concealed the instruments. He took up his scanning mirror, and made up his face from the inside, by adding tone and animation to his blood and nerves until the muscles of his face glowed and the skin gave out a healthy sweat. That way he looked like an ordinary man who had just completed a long night flight.

After straightening out his clothing, and hiding his tablet within his jacket, he faced the problem of what to do about the talking finger. If he kept the nail, it would show him to be a scanner. He would be respected, but he would be identified. He might be stopped by the guards whom the Instrumentality had undoubtedly set around the person of Adam Stone. If he broke the nail— But he couldn't! No scanner in the history of the Confraternity had ever willingly broken his nail. That would be resignation, and there was no such thing. The only way *out*, was in the up-and-out! Martel put his finger to his mouth and bit off the nail. He looked at the now-queer finger, and sighed to himself.

He stepped toward the city gate, slipping his hand into his jacket and running up his muscular strength to four times normal. He started to scan, and then realized that his instruments were masked. *Might as well take all the chances at once,* he thought.

The watcher stopped him with a searching wire. The sphere thumped suddenly against Martel's chest.

"Are you a man?" said the unseen voice. (Martel knew that as a scanner in haberman condition, his own field-charge would have illuminated the sphere.)

"I am a man." Martel knew that the timbre of his voice had been good; he hoped that it would not be taken for that of a manshonyagger or a Beast or an Unforgiven one, who with mimicry sought to enter the cities and ports of mankind.

"Name, number, rank, purpose, function, time departed."

"Martel." He had to remember his old number, not Scanner 34. "Sunward 4234, 782nd Year of Space. Rank, rising subchief." That was no lie, but his substantive rank. "Purpose, personal and lawful within the limits of this city. No function of the Instrumentality. Departed Chief Outport 2019 hours." Everything now depended on whether he was believed, or would be checked against Chief Outport.

The voice was flat and routine: "Time desired within the city."

Martel used the standard phrase: "Your honorable sufference is requested."

He stood in the cool night air, waiting. Far above him, through a gap in the mist, he could see the poisonous glittering in the sky of scanners. *The stars are my enemies,* he thought: *I have mastered the stars but they hate me. Ho, that sounds ancient! Like a book. Too much cranching.*

The voice returned: "Sunward 4234 dash 782 rising subchief Martel, enter the lawful gates of the city. Welcome. Do you desire food, raiment, money, or companionship?" The voice had no hospitality in it, just business. This was certainly different from entering a city in a scanner's role! Then the petty officers came out, and threw their beltlights on their fretful faces, and mouthed their words with preposterous deference, shouting against the stone deafness of scanner's ears. So that was the way that a subchief was treated: matter of fact, but not bad. Not bad.

Martel replied: "I have that which I need, but beg of the city a favor. My friend Adam Stone is here. I desire to see him, on urgent and personal lawful affairs."

The voice replied: "Did you have an appointment with Adam Stone?"

"No."

"The city will find him. What is his number?"

"I have forgotten it."

"You have forgotten it? Is not Adam Stone a magnate of the Instrumentality? Are you truly his friend?"

"Truly." Martel let a little annoyance creep into his voice. "Watcher, doubt me and call your subchief."

"No doubt implied. Why do you not know the number? This must go into the record," added the voice.

"We were friends in childhood. He has crossed the—" Martel started to say "the up-and-out" and remembered that the phrase was current only among scanners. "He has leapt from Earth to Earth, and has just now returned. I knew him well and I seek him out. I have word of his kith. May the Instrumentality protect us!"

"Heard and believed. Adam Stone will be searched."

At a risk, though a slight one, of having the sphere sound an alarm for *nonhuman,* Martel cut in on his scanner speaker within his jacket. He saw the trembling needle of light await his words and he started to write on it with his blunt finger. *That won't work,* he thought, and had a moment's panic until he found his comb, which had a sharp enough tooth to write. He wrote: "Emergency none. Martel Scanner calling Parizianski Scanner."

The needle quivered and the reply glowed and faded out: "Parizianski Scanner on duty and D.C. Calls taken by Scanner Relay."

Martel cut off his speaker.

Parizianski was somewhere around. Could he have crossed the direct way, right over the city wall, setting off the alert, and invoking official business when the petty officers overtook him in mid-air? Scarcely. That meant that a number of other scanners must have come in with Parizianski, all of them pretending to be in search of a few of the tenuous pleasures which could be enjoyed by a haberman, such as the sight of the newspictures or the viewing of beautiful women in the Pleasure Gallery. Parizianski was around, but he could not have moved privately, because Scanner Central registered him on duty and recorded his movements city by city.

The voice returned. Puzzlement was expressed in it. "Adam Stone is found and awakened. He has asked pardon of the Honorable, and says he knows no Martel. Will you see Adam Stone in the morning? The city will bid you welcome."

Martel ran out of resources. It was hard enough mimicking a man without having to tell lies in the guise of one. Martel could only repeat: "Tell him I am Martel. The husband of Luci."

"It will be done."

Again the silence, and the hostile stars, and the sense that Parizianski was somewhere near and getting nearer; Martel felt his heart beating faster. He stole a glimpse at his chestbox and set his heart down a point. He felt calmer, even though he had not been able to scan with care.

The voice this time was cheerful, as though an annoyance had been settled: "Adam Stone consents to see you. Enter Chief Downport, and welcome."

The little sphere dropped noiselessly to the ground and the wire whispered away into the darkness. A bright arc of narrow light rose from the ground in front of Martel and swept through the city to one of the higher towers—apparently a hostel, which Martel had never entered. Martel plucked his aircoat to his chest for ballast, stepped heel-and-toe on the beam, and felt himself whistle through the air to an entrance window which sprang up before him as suddenly as a devouring mouth.

A tower guard stood in the doorway. "You are awaited, sir. Do you bear weapons, sir?"

"None," said Martel, grateful that he was relying on his own strength.

The guard led him past the check-screen. Martel noticed the quick flight of a warning across the screen as his instruments registered and identified him as a scanner. But the guard had not noticed it.

The guard stopped at a door. "Adam Stone is armed. He is lawfully armed by authority of the Instrumentality and by the liberty of this city. All those who enter are given warning."

Martel nodded in understanding at the man and went in.

Adam Stone was a short man, stout and benign. His gray hair rose stiffly from a low forehead. His whole face was red and merry-looking. He looked like a jolly guide from the Pleasure Gallery, not like a man who had been at the edge of the up-and-out, fighting the great pain without haberman protection.

He stared at Martel. His look was puzzled, perhaps a little annoyed, but not hostile.

Martel came to the point. "You do not know me. I lied. My name is Martel, and I mean you no harm. But I lied. I beg the honorable gift of your hospitality. Remain armed. Direct your weapon against me—"

Stone smiled: "I am doing so," and Martel noticed the small wirepoint in Stone's capable, plump hand.

"Good. Keep on guard against me. It will give you confidence in what I shall say. But do, I beg of you, give us a screen of privacy. I want no casual lookers. This is a matter of life and death."

"First: whose life and death?" Stone's face remained calm, his voice even.

"Yours, and mine, and the worlds'."

"You are cryptic but I agree." Stone called through the doorway: "Privacy please." There was a sudden hum, and all the little noises of the night quickly vanished from the air of the room.

Said Adam Stone: "Sir, who are you? What brings you here?"

"I am Scanner 34."

"You a scanner? I don't believe it."

For an answer, Martel pulled his jacket open, showing his chestbox. Stone looked up at him, amazed. Martel explained:

"I am cranched. Have you never seen it before?"

"*Not with men*. On animals. Amazing! But—what do you want?"

"The truth. Do you fear me?"

"Not with this," said Stone, grasping the wirepoint. "But I shall tell you the truth."

"Is it true that you have conquered the great pain?"

Stone hesitated, seeking words for an answer.

"Quick, can you tell me how you have done it, so that I may believe you?"

"I have loaded the ships with life."

"Life?"

"Life. I don't know what the great pain is, but I did find that in the experiments, when I sent out masses of animals or plants, the life in the center of the mass lived longest. I built ships—small ones, of course—and sent them out with rabbits, with monkeys—"

"Those are Beasts?"

"Yes. With small Beasts. And the Beasts came back unhurt. They came back because the walls of the ships were filled with life. I tried many kinds, and finally found a sort of life which lives in the waters. Oysters. Oyster-beds. The outermost oysters died in the great pain. The inner ones lived. The passengers were unhurt."

"But they were Beasts?"

"Not only Beasts. Myself."

"You!"

"I came through space alone. Through what you call the up-and-out, alone. Awake and sleeping. I am unhurt. If you do not believe me, ask your brother scanners. Come and see my ship in the morning. I will be glad to see you then, along with your brother scanners. I am going to demonstrate before the chiefs of the Instrumentality."

Martel repeated his question: "You came here alone?"

Adam Stone grew testy: "Yes, alone. Go back and check your scanner's register if you do not believe me. You never put me in a bottle to cross Space."

Martel's face was radiant. "I believe you now. It is true. No more scanners. No more habermans. No more cranching."

Stone looked significantly toward the door.

Martel did not take the hint. "I must tell you that—"

"Sir, tell me in the morning. Go enjoy your cranch. Isn't it supposed to be pleasure? Medically I know it well. But not in practice."

"It is pleasure. It's normality—for a while. But listen. The scanners have sworn to destroy you, and your work."

"What!"

"They have met and have voted and sworn. You will make scanners unnecessary, they say. You will bring the ancient wars back to the world, if scanning is lost and the scanners live in vain!"

Adam Stone was nervous but kept his wits about him: "You're a scanner. Are you going to kill me—or try?"

"No, you fool. I have betrayed the Confraternity. Call guards the moment I escape. Keep guards around you. I will try to intercept the killer."

Martel saw a blur in the window. Before Stone could turn, the wirepoint was whipped out of his hand. The blur solidified and took form as Parizianski.

Martel recognized what Parizianski was doing: *High speed.*

Without thinking of his cranch, he thrust his hand to his chest, set himself up to *High speed* too. Waves of fire, like the great pain, but hotter, flooded over him. He fought to keep his face readable as he stepped in front of Parizianski and gave the sign, *Top emergency.*

Parizianski spoke, while the normally moving body of Stone stepped away from them as slowly as a drifting cloud: "Get out of my way. I am on a mission."

"I know it. I stop you here and now. Stop. Stop. Stop. Stone is right."

Parizianski's lips were barely readable in the haze of pain which flooded Martel. (He thought: *God, God, God of the ancients! Let me hold on! Let me live under* Overload *just long enough!*) Parizianski was saying: "Get out of my way. By order of the Confraternity, get out of my way!" And Parizianski gave the sign, *Help I demand in the name of my duty!*

Martel choked for breath in the syruplike air. He tried one last time: "Parizianski, friend, friend, my friend. Stop. Stop." (No scanner had ever murdered scanner before.)

Parizianski made the sign: *You are unfit for duty, and I will take over.*

Martel thought, *For the first time in the world!* as he reached over and twisted Parizianski's brainbox up to *Overload*. Parizianski's eyes glittered in terror and understanding. His body began to drift down toward the floor.

Martel had just strength to reach his own chestbox. As he faded into haberman or death, he knew not which, he felt his fingers turning on the control of speed, turning down. He tried to speak, to say, "Get a scanner, I need help, get a scanner . . ."

But the darkness rose about him, and the numb silence clasped him.

Martel awakened to see the face of Luci near his own.

He opened his eyes wider, and found that he was hearing—hearing the sound of her happy weeping, the sound of her chest as she caught the air back into her throat.

He spoke weakly: "Still cranched? Alive?"

Another face swam into the blur beside Luci's. It was Adam Stone. His deep voice rang across immensities of space before coming to Martel's hearing. Martel tried to read Stone's lips, but could not make them out. He went back to listening to the voice:

". . . not cranched. Do you understand me? Not cranched!"

Martel tried to say: "But I can hear! I can feel!" The others got his sense if not his words.

Adam Stone spoke again:

"You have gone back through the haberman. I put you back first. I didn't know how it would work in practice, but I had the theory all worked out. You don't think the Instrumentality would waste the scanners, do you? You go back to normality. We are letting the habermans die as fast as the ships come in. They don't need to live anymore. But we are restoring the scanners. You are the first. Do you understand? You are the first. Take it easy, now."

Adam Stone smiled. Dimly behind Stone, Martel thought that he saw the face of one of the chiefs of the Instrumentality. That face, too, smiled at him, and then both faces disappeared upward and away.

Martel tried to lift his head, to scan himself. He could not. Luci stared at him, calming herself, but with an expression of loving perplexity. She said,

"My darling husband! You're back again, to stay!"

Still, Martel tried to see his box. Finally he swept his hand across his chest with a clumsy motion. There was nothing there.

The instruments were gone. He was back to normality but still alive.

In the deep weak peacefulness of his mind, another troubling thought took shape. He tried to write with his finger, the way that Luci wanted him to, but he had neither pointed fingernail nor scanner's tablet. He had to use his voice. He summoned up his strength and whispered:

"Scanners?"

"Yes, darling? What is it?"

"Scanners?"

"Scanners. Oh, yes, darling, they're all right. They had to arrest some of them for going into *High speed* and running away. But the Instrumentality caught them all—all those on the ground— and they're happy now. Do you know, darling," she laughed, "some of them didn't want to be restored to normality. But Stone and the chiefs persuaded them."

"Vomact?"

"He's fine, too. He's staying cranched until he can be restored. Do you know, he has arranged for scanners to take new jobs. You're all to be deputy chiefs for Space. Isn't that nice? But he got himself made chief for Space. You're all going to be pilots, so that your fraternity and guild can go on. And Chang's getting changed right now. You'll see him soon."

Her face turned sad. She looked at him earnestly and said: "I might as well tell you now. You'll worry otherwise. There has been one accident. Only one. When you and your friend called on Adam Stone, your friend was so happy that he forgot to scan, and he let himself die of *Overload.*"

"Called on Stone?"

"Yes. Don't you remember? Your friend."

He still looked surprised, so she said:

"Parizianski."

6

BORN OF MAN AND WOMAN

Richard Matheson (1926–   )

THE MAGAZINE OF FANTASY AND SCIENCE FICTION
Summer

"Born of Man and Woman" was Richard Matheson's first sf story, and opened a rich career that includes such novels as I Am Legend *(1954) and* The Shrinking Man *(1956), both of which were filmed (the former twice, as* The Last Man on Earth *and* The Omega Man, *neither doing justice to the book). Matheson's connections with filmed sf and fantasy are considerable—he did many of the screenplays for Roger Corman's Poe movies, as well as for such television productions as the memorable* Duel *(later released theatrically),* The Night Stalker *series, and* The Enemy Within, *one of the best* Star Trek *scripts. His peers in the industry have recognized his talent with two Writers Guild of America Awards. He also has won a Hugo (for best screenplay) and the World Fantasy Award. Although he is often compared with Ray Bradbury and Charles Beaumont, his is a singular voice, and his early work was influential in the development of both science fiction and the contemporary horror story. His best short stories are scattered through six collections, and a definitive* Best of *book awaits publication.*

—M.H.G.

I'm ambivalent about first stories that are instantly recognized as classics. On the one hand, I turn slightly green, because my first published story was not a classic. (My fourteenth story was my first classic.) On the other hand, who wants to spend the rest of his life trying to repeat that first smash, though, as it turned out, Matheson didn't have much trouble with that.

Let me say this about "Born of Man and Woman": There are many stories I read thirty years ago and more, that I've liked and admired and felt I remembered. Usually, though, in preparing thses anthologies, I don't feel safe about it and must re-read it to make sure what I remember is actually so and that the story does hold up over the years. Not so in the case of "Born of Man and Woman"; I remembered every word and was never in any doubt it belonged here. Read it and you'll see.

—I.A.

X—— This day when it had light mother called me a retch. You retch she said. I saw in her eyes the anger. I wonder what is a retch.

This day it had water falling from upstairs. It fell all around. I saw that. The ground of the back I watched from the little window. The ground it sucked up the water like thirsty lips. It drank too much and it got sick and runny brown. I didn't like it.

Mother is a pretty I know. In my bed place with cold walls around I have a paper things that was behind the furnace. It says on it SCREENSTARS. I see in the pictures faces like of mother and father. Father says they are pretty. Once he said it.

And also mother he said. Mother so pretty and me decent enough. Look at you he said and didn't have the nice face. I touched his arm and said it is all right father. He shook and pulled away where I couldn't reach.

Today mother let me off the chain a little so I could look out the little window. That's how I saw the water falling from upstairs.

XX—— This day it had goldness in the upstairs. As I know, when I looked at it my eyes hurt. After I look at it the cellar is red.

I think this was church. They leave the upstairs. The big machine swallows them and rolls out past and is gone. In the back part is the *little* mother. She is much small than me. I am big. It is a secret but I have pulled the chain out of the wall. I can see out the little window all I like.

In this day when it got dark I had eat my food and some bugs.

I hear laughs upstairs. I like to know why there are laughs for. I took the chain from the wall and wrapped it around me. I walk squish to the stairs. They creak when I walk on them. My legs slip on them because I don't walk on stairs. My feet stick to the wood.

I went up and opened a door. It was a white place. White as white jewels that come from upstairs sometime. I went in and stood quiet. I hear the laughing some more. I walk to the sound and look through to the people. More people than I thought was. I thought I should laugh with them.

Mother came out and pushed the door in. It hit me and hurt. I fell back on the smooth floor and the chain made noise. I cried. She made a hissing noise into her and put her hand on her mouth. Her eyes got big.

She looked at me. I heard father call. What fell he called. She said an iron board. Come help pick it up she said. He came and said now is *that* so heavy you need. He saw me and grew big. The anger came in his eyes. He hit me. I spilled some of the drip on the floor from one arm. It was not nice. It made ugly green on the floor.

Father told me to go to the cellar. I had to go. The light it hurt some now in my eyes. It is not so like that in the cellar.

Father tied my legs and arms up. He put me on my bed. Upstairs I heard laughing while I was quiet there looking on a black spider that was swinging down to me. I thought what father said. Ohgod he said. And only eight.

XXX—— This day father hit in the chain again before it had light. I have to try pull it out again. He said I was bad to come upstairs. He said never do that again or he would beat me hard. That hurts.

I hurt. I slept the day and rested my head against the cold wall. I thought of the white place upstairs.

XXXX—— I got the chain from the wall out. Mother was upstairs. I heard little laughs very high. I looked out the window. I saw all little people like the little mother and little fathers too. They are pretty.

They were making nice noise and jumping around the ground. Their legs was moving hard. They are like mother and father. Mother says all right people look like they do.

One of the little fathers saw me. He pointed at the window. I let go and slid down the wall in the dark. I curled up as they would not see. I heard their talks by the window and foots running. Upstairs there was a door hitting. I heard the little mother call upstairs. I heard heavy steps and I rushed to my bed place. I hit the chain in the wall and lay down on my front.

I heard mother come down. Have you been at the window she said. I heard the anger. *Stay* away from the window. You have pulled the chain out again.

She took the stick and hit me with it. I didn't cry. I can't do that. But the drip ran all over the bed. She saw it and twisted away and made a noise. Oh mygod mygod she said why have you *done* this to me? I heard the stick go bounce on the stone floor. She ran upstairs. I slept the day.

XXX—— This day it had water again. When mother was upstairs I heard the little one come slow down the steps. I hidded myself in the coal bin for mother would have anger if the little mother saw me.

She had a little live thing with her. It walked on the arms and had pointy ears. She said things to it.

It was all right except the live thing smelled me. It ran up the coal and looked down at me. The hairs stood up. In the throat it made an angry noise. I hissed but it jumped on me.

I didn't want to hurt it. I got fear because it bit me harder than the rat does. I hurt and the little mother screamed. I grabbed the live thing tight. It made sounds I never heard. I pushed it all together. It was all lumpy and red on the black coal.

I hid there when mother called. I was afraid of the stick. She left. I crept over the coal with the thing. I hid it under my pillow and rested on it. I put the chain in the wall again.

X—— This is another times. Father chained me tight. I hurt because he beat me. This time I hit the stick out of his hands and made noise. He went away and his face was white. He ran out of my bed place and locked the door.

I am not so glad. All day it is cold in here. The chain comes slow out of the wall. And I have a bad anger with mother and father. I will show them. I will do what I did that once.

I will screech and laugh loud. I will run on the walls. Last I will hang head down by all my legs and laugh and drip green all over until they are sorry they didn't be nice to me.

If they try to beat me again I'll hurt them. I will.

THE LITTLE BLACK BAG

C. M. Kornbluth (1923–1958)

ASTOUNDING SCIENCE FICTION
July

Until his tragic death in 1958 at the age of 35, Cyril M. Kornbluth was one of the finest craftmen working in the science fiction field. He was also one of the most sardonic, both in real life and in his fiction, a man who had little faith in the ability of average people to understand the forces affecting their lives. He liked the masses in his stories, but his cynical views didn't permit him to respect them. Kornbluth is most famous for his very successful collaborative novels with Frederik Pohl, especially The Space Merchants *(1953),* Gladiator-at-Law *(1955), and* Wolfbane *(1959).*

Although he had published in the sf magazines in the 1940–42 period, World War II and other concerns kept him silent until 1949. However, once he resumed writing he returned in a major way, and we will meet him many times as this series works its way through the 1950s. 1950 was a particularly notable year for him, and "The Little Black Bag" is the first of three of his stories in this book.

—M.H.G.

The C. stands for Cyril and I met him in 1938, when the Futurians came into being. He was the youngest of us, being only 15 (three years younger than I was at the time) and the most brilliant and erratic of us all. I always seemed quite staid and normal by comparison when I was in his presence.

We didn't get along. I didn't know this at the time because I

*liked him. (I liked everybody. Still do.) The trouble is that I don't
think he liked me. I never really found out why, but I think it may
have been that I am always very noisy and happy at gatherings,
and he may well have thought I hurt his ears.*

*Anyway, about the time it began to dawn on me that he
disapproved of me, he died—precocious in that as in everything
else—and it was too late to get to the bottom of the matter and to
make up. I've always regretted that. Especially when I read
stories like "The Little Black Bag."*

—I.A.

Old Dr. Full felt the winter in his bones as he limped down the
alley. It was the alley and the back door he had chosen rather
than the sidewalk and the front door because of the brown paper
bag under his arm. He knew perfectly well that the flat-faced,
stringy-haired women of his street and their gap-toothed, sour-
smelling husbands did not notice if he brought a bottle of cheap
wine to his room. They all but lived on the stuff themselves,
varied with whiskey when pay checks were boosted by overtime.
But Dr. Full, unlike them, was ashamed. One of the neighborhood
dogs—a mean little black one he knew and hated, with its
teeth always bared and always snarling with menace—hurled at
his legs through a hole in the board fence that lined his path.
Dr. Full flinched, then swung his leg in what was to have
been a satisfying kick to the animal's gaunt ribs. But the winter
in his bones weighed down the leg. His foot failed to clear a
half-buried brick, and he sat down abruptly, cursing. When he
smelled unbottled wine and realized his brown paper package
had slipped from under his arm and smashed, his curses died on
his lips. The snarling black dog was circling him at a yard's
distance, tensely stalking, but he ignored it in the greater disaster.

With stiff fingers as he sat on the filth of the alley, Dr. Full
unfolded the brown paper bag's top, which had been crimped
over, grocer-wise. The early autumnal dusk had come; he could
not see plainly what was left. He lifted out the jug-handled top of
his half gallon, and some fragments, and then the bottom of the
bottle. Dr. Full was far too occupied to exult as he noted that
there was a good pint left. He had a problem, and emotions
could be deferred until the fitting time.

The dog closed in, its snarl rising in pitch. He set down the bottom of the bottle and pelted the dog with the curved triangular glass fragments of its top. One of them connected, and the dog ducked back through the fence, howling. Dr. Full then placed a razor-like edge of the half-gallon bottle's foundation to his lips and drank from it as though it were a giant's cup. Twice he had to put it down to rest his arms, but in one minute he had swallowed the pint of wine.

He thought of rising to his feet and walking through the alley to his room, but a flood of well-being drowned the notion. It was, after all, inexpressibly pleasant to sit there and feel the frost-hardened mud of the alley turn soft, or seem to, and to feel the winter evaporating from his bones under a warmth which spread from his stomach through his limbs.

A three-year-old girl in a cut-down winter coat squeezed through the same hole in the board fence from which the black dog had sprung its ambush. Gravely she toddled up to Dr. Full and inspected him with her dirty forefinger in her mouth. Dr. Full's happiness had been providentially made complete; he had been supplied with an audience.

"Ah, my dear," he said hoarsely. And then: "Preposserous accusation. 'If that's what you call evidence,' I should have told them, 'you better stick to your doctoring.' I should have told them: 'I was here before your County Medical Society. And the License Commissioner never proved a thing on me. So, gennulmen, doesn't it stand to reason? I appeal to you as fellow memmers of a great profession—' "

The little girl, bored, moved away, picking up one of the triangular pieces of glass to play with as she left. Dr. Full forgot her immediately, and continued to himself earnestly: "But so help me, they *couldn't* prove a thing. Hasn't a man got any *rights?*" He brooded over the question, of whose answer he was so sure, but on which the Committee on Ethics of the County Medical Society had been equally certain. The winter was creeping into his bones again, and he had no money and no more wine.

Dr. Full pretended to himself that there was a bottle of whiskey somewhere in the fearful litter of his room. It was an old and cruel trick he played on himself when he simply had to be galvanized into getting up and going home. He might freeze there in the alley. In his room he would be bitten by bugs and would cough at the moldy reek from his sink, but he would not freeze and be cheated of the hundreds of bottles of wine that he still might drink, the thousands of hours of glowing content he still might feel. He thought about that bottle of whiskey—was it back of a mounded heap of medical journals? No; he had looked there last time. Was it under the sink, shoved well to the rear, behind the rusty drain? The cruel trick began to play itself out again. Yes, he told himself with mounting excitement, yes, it might be! Your memory isn't so good nowadays, he told himself with rueful good fellowship. You know perfectly well you might have bought a bottle of whiskey and shoved it behind the sink drain for a moment just like this.

The amber bottle, the crisp snap of the sealing as he cut it, the pleasurable exertion of starting the screw cap on its threads, and then the refreshing tangs in his throat, the warmth in his stomach, the dark, dull happy oblivion of drunkenness—they became real to him. You *could* have, you know! You *could* have! he told himself. With the blessed conviction growing in his mind—It *could* have happened, you know! It *could* have!—he struggled to his right knee. As he did, he heard a yelp behind him, and curiously craned his neck around while resting. It was the little girl, who had cut her hand quite badly on her toy, the piece of glass. Dr. Full could see the rilling bright blood down her coat, pooling at her feet.

He almost felt inclined to defer the image of the amber bottle for her, but not seriously. He knew that it was there, shoved well to the rear under the sink, behind the rusty drain where he had hidden it. He would have a drink and then magnanimously return to help the child. Dr. Full got to his other knee and then his feet, and proceeded at a rapid totter down the littered alley toward his room, where he would hunt with calm optimism at first for the bottle that was not there, then with anxiety, and then with frantic violence. He would hurl books and dishes about before he was done looking for the amber bottle of whiskey, and finally would beat his swollen knuckles against the brick wall until old scars on them opened and his thick old blood oozed over his hands. Last of all, he would sit down somewhere on the floor, whimpering, and would plunge into the abyss of purgative nightmare that was his sleep.

After twenty generations of shilly-shallying and "we'll cross that bridge when we come to it," genus homo had bred himself into an impasse. Dogged biometricians had pointed out with irrefutable logic that mental subnormals were outbreeding mental normals and supernormals, and that the process was occurring on an exponential curve. Every fact that could be mustered in the argument proved the biometricians' case, and led inevitably to the conclusion that genus homo was going to wind up in a preposterous jam quite soon. If you think that had any effect on breeding practices, you do not know genus homo.

There was, of course, a sort of masking effect produced by that other exponential function, the accumulation of technological devices. A moron trained to punch an adding machine seems to be a more skillful computer than a medieval mathematician trained to count on his fingers. A moron trained to operate the twenty-first century equivalent of a linotype seems to be a better typographer than a Renaissance printer limited to a few fonts of movable type. This is also true of medical practice.

It was a complicated affair of many factors. The supernormals "improved the product" at greater speed than the subnormals degraded it, but in smaller quantity because elaborate training of their children was practiced on a custom-made basis. The fetish of higher education had some weird avatars by the twentieth generation: "colleges" where not a member of the student body could read words of three syllables; "universities" where such degrees as "Bachelor of Typewriting," "Master of Shorthand" and "Doctor of Philosophy (Card Filing)" were conferred with the traditional pomp. The handful of supernormals used such devices in order that the vast majority might keep some semblance of a social order going.

Some day the supernormals would mercilessly cross the bridge; at the twentieth generation they were standing irresolutely at its approaches wondering what had hit them. And the ghosts of twenty generations of biometricians chuckled malignantly.

It is a certain Doctor of Medicine of this twentieth generation that we are concerned with. His name was Hemingway—John Hemingway, B.Sc., M.D. He was a general practitioner, and did not hold with running to specialists with every trifling ailment. He often said as much, in approximately these words: "Now, uh, what I mean is you got a good old G.P. See what I mean? Well, uh, now a good old G.P. don't claim he knows all about lungs and glands and them things, get me? But you got a G.P., you got, uh, you got a, well, you got a . . . *all-around man!* That's what you got when you got a G.P.—you got a all-around man."

But from this, do not imagine that Dr. Hemingway was a poor

doctor. He could remove tonsils or appendixes, assist at practically any confinement and deliver a living, uninjured infant, correctly diagnose hundreds of ailments, and prescribe and administer the correct medication or treatment for each. There was, in fact, only one thing he could not do in the medical line, and that was violate the ancient canons of medical ethics. And Dr. Hemingway knew better than to try.

Dr. Hemingway and a few friends were chatting one evening when the event occurred that precipitates him into our story. He had been through a hard day at the clinic, and he wished his physicist friend Walter Gillis, B.Sc., M.Sc., Ph.D., would shut up so he could tell everybody about it. But Gillis kept rambling on, in his stilted fashion: "You got to hand it to old Mike; he don't have what we call the scientific method, but you got to hand it to him. There this poor little dope is, puttering around with some glassware and I come up and I ask him, kidding of course, 'How's about a time-travel machine, Mike?' "

Dr. Gillis was not aware of it, but "Mike" had an I.Q. six times his own, and was—to be blunt—his keeper. "Mike" rode herd on the pseudo-physicists in the pseudo-laboratory, in the guise of a bottle washer. It was a social waste—but as has been mentioned before, the supernormals were still standing at the approaches to a bridge. Their irresolution led to many such preposterous situations. And it happens that "Mike," having grown frantically bored with his task, was malevolent enough to—but let Dr. Gillis tell it:

"So he gives me these here tube numbers and says, 'Series circuit. Now stop bothering me. Build your time machine, sit down at it and turn on the switch. That's all I ask, Dr. Gillis—that's all I ask.' "

"Say," marveled a brittle and lovely blond guest, "you remember real good, don't you, doc.?" She gave him a melting smile.

"Heck," said Gillis modestly, "I always remember good. It's what you call an inherent facility. And besides I told it quick to my secretary, so she wrote it down. I don't read so good, but I sure remember good, all right. Now, where was I?"

Everybody thought hard, and there were various suggestions:

"Something about bottles, doc?"

"You was starting a fight. You said 'time somebody was traveling.' "

"Yeah—you called somebody a swish. Who did you call a swish?"

"Not swish—*switch*."

Dr. Gillis's noble brow grooved with thought, and he declared: "Switch is right. It was about time travel. What we call travel through time. So I took the tube numbers he gave me and I put them into the circuit builder; I set it for 'series' and there it is—my time-traveling machine. It travels things through time real good." He displayed a box.

"What's in the box?" asked the lovely blonde.

Dr. Hemingway told her: "Time travel. It travels things through time."

"Look," said Gillis, the physicist. He took Dr. Hemingway's little black bag and put in on the box. He turned on the switch and the little black bag vanished.

"Say," said Dr. Hemingway, "that was, uh, swell. Now bring it back."

"Huh?"

"Bring back my little black bag."

"Well," said Dr. Gillis, "they don't come back. I tried it backwards and they don't come back. I guess maybe that dummy Mike give me a bum steer."

There was wholesale condemnation of "Mike" but Dr. Hemingway took no part in it. He was nagged by a vague feeling that there was something he would have to do. He reasoned: "I am a doctor, and a doctor has got to have a little black bag. I ain't got a little black bag—so ain't I a doctor no more?" He decided that this was absurd. He *knew* he was a doctor. So it must be the bag's fault for not being there. It was no good, and he would get another one tomorrow from that dummy Al, at the clinic. Al could find things good, but he was a dummy—never liked to talk sociable to you.

So the next day Dr. Hemingway remembered to get another little black bag from his keeper—another little black bag with which he could perform tonsillectomies, appendectomies, and the most difficult confinements, and with which he could diagnose and cure his kind until the day when the supernormals could bring themselves to cross that bridge. Al was kinda nasty about the missing little black bag, but Dr. Hemmingway didn't exactly remember what had happened, so no tracer was sent out, so—

*   *   *

Old Dr. Full awoke from the horrors of the night to the horrors of the day. His gummy eyelashes pulled apart convulsively. He was propped against a corner of his room, and something was making a little drumming noise. He felt very cold and cramped. As his eyes focused on his lower body, he croaked out a laugh. The drumming noise was being made by his left heel, agitated by fine tremors against the bare floor. It was going to be the D.T.'s again, he decided dispassionately. He wiped his mouth with his bloody knuckles, and the fine tremor coarsened; the snare-drum beat became louder and slower. He was getting a break this fine morning, he decided sardonically. You didn't get the horrors until you had been tightened like a violin string, just to the breaking point. He had a reprieve, if a reprieve into his old body with the blazing, endless headache just back of the eyes and the screaming stiffness in the joints was anything to be thankful for.

There was something or other about a kid, he thought vaguely. He was going to doctor some kid. His eyes rested on a little black bag in the center of the room, and he forgot about the kid. "I could have sworn," said Dr. Full, "I hocked that two years ago!" He hitched over and reached the bag, and then realized it was some stranger's kit, arriving here he did not know how. He tentatively touched the lock and it snapped open and lay flat, rows and rows of instruments and medications tucked into loops in its four walls. It seemed vastly larger open than closed. He didn't see how it could possibly fold up into that compact size again, but decided it was some stunt of the instrument makers. Since his time—that made it worth more at the hock shop, he thought with satisfaction.

Just for old times' sake, he let his eyes and fingers rove over the instruments before he snapped the bag shut and headed for Uncle's. More than a few were a little hard to recognize—exactly that is. You could see the things with blades for cutting, the forceps for holding and pulling, the retractors for holding fast, the needles and gut for suturing, the hypos—a fleeting thought crossed his mind that he could peddle the hypos separately to drug addicts.

Let's go, he decided, and tried to fold up the case. It didn't fold until he happened to touch the lock, and then it folded all at once into a little black bag. Sure have forged ahead, he thought, almost able to forget that what he was primarily interested in was its pawn value.

With a definite objective, it was not too hard for him to get to his feet. He decided to go down the front steps, out the front door, and down the sidewalk. But first—

He snapped the bag open again on his kitchen table, and pored through the medication tubes. "Anything to sock the autonomic nervous system good and hard," he mumbled. The tubes were numbered, and there was a plastic card which seemed to list them. The left margin of the card was a run-down of the systems— vascular, muscular, nervous. He followed the last entry across to the right. There were columns for "stimulant," "depressant," and so on. Under "nervous system" and "depressant" he found the number 17, and shakily located the little glass tube which bore it. It was full of pretty blue pills and he took one.

It was like being struck by a thunderbolt.

Dr. Full had so long lacked any sense of well-being except the brief glow of alcohol that he had forgotten its very nature. He was panic-stricken for a long moment at the sensation that spread through him slowly, finally tingling in his fingertips. He straightened up, his pains gone and his leg tremor stilled.

That was great, he thought. He'd be able to *run* to the hock shop, pawn the little black bag, and get some booze. He started down the stairs. Not even the street, bright with mid-morning sun, into which he emerged, made him quail. The little black bag in his left hand had a satisfying, authoritative weight. He was walking erect, he noted, and not in the somewhat furtive crouch that had grown on him in recent years. A little self-respect, he told himself, that's what I need. Just because a man's down doesn't mean—

"Docta, please-a come wit'!" somebody yelled at him, tugging his arm. "Da litt-la girl, she's-a burn' up!" It was one of the slum's innumerable flat-faced, stringy-haired women, in a slovenly wrapper.

"Ah, I happen to be retired from practice—" he began hoarsely, but she would not be put off.

"In by here, Docta!" she urged, tugging him to a doorway. "You come look-a da litt-la girl. I got two dolla, you come look!" That put a different complexion on the matter. He allowed himself to be towed through the doorway into a mussy, cabbage-smelling flat. He knew the woman now, or rather knew who she must be—a new arrival who had moved in the other night. These people moved at night, in motorcades of battered cars supplied by friends and relations, with furniture lashed to the tops, swearing and drinking until the small hours. It explained why she had stopped him: she did not yet know he was old Dr. Full, a drunken reprobate whom nobody would trust. The little black bag had been his guarantee, outweighing his whiskery face and stained black suit.

He was looking down on a three-year-old girl who had, he rather suspected, just been placed in the mathematical center of a freshly changed double bed. God knew what sour and dirty mattress she usually slept on. He seemed to recognize her as he noted a crusted bandage on her right hand. Two dollars, he thought— An ugly flush had spread up her pipe-stem arm. He poked a finger into the socket of her elbow, and felt little spheres like marbles under the skin and ligaments roll apart. The child began to squall thinly; beside him, the woman gasped and began to weep herself.

"Out," he gestured briskly at her, and she thudded away, still sobbing.

Two dollars, he thought— Give her some mumbo jumbo, take the money and tell her to go to a clinic. Strep, I guess, from that stinking alley. It's a wonder any of them grow up. He put down the little black bag and forgetfully fumbled for his key, then remembered and touched the lock. It flew open, and he selected a bandage shears, with a blunt wafer for the lower jaw. He fitted the lower jaw under the bandage, trying not to hurt the kid by its pressure on the infection, and began to cut. It was amazing how easily and swiftly the shining shears snipped through the crusty rag around the wound. He hardly seemed to be driving the shears with fingers at all. It almost seemed as though the shears were driving his fingers instead as they scissored a clean, light line through the bandage.

Certainly have forged ahead since my time, he thought—sharper than a microtome knife. He replaced the shears in their loop on the extraordinarily big board that the little black bag turned into when it unfolded, and leaned over the wound. He whistled at the ugly gash, and the violent infection which had taken immediate root in the sickly child's thin body. Now what can you do with a thing like that? He pawed over the contents of the little black bag, nervously. If he lanced it and let some of the pus out, the old woman would think he'd done something for her and he'd get the two dollars. But at the clinic they'd want to know who did it and if they got sore enough they might send a cop around. Maybe there was something in the kit—

He ran down the left edge of the card to "lymphatic" and read across to the column under "infection." It didn't sound right at all to him; he checked again, but it still said that. In the square to which the line and column led were the symbols: "IV-g-3cc." He couldn't find any bottles marked with Roman numerals, and then noticed that that was how the hypodermic needles were designated. He lifted number IV from its loop, noting that it was fitted with a needle already and even seemed to be charged. What a way to carry those things around! So—three cc. of whatever was in hypo number IV ought to do something or other about infections settled in the lymphatic system—which, God knows, this one was. What did the lower-case "g" mean, though? He studied the glass hypo and saw letters engraved on what looked like a rotating disk at the top of the barrel. They ran from "a" to "i," and there was an index line engraved on the barrel on the opposite side from the calibrations.

Shrugging, old Dr. Full turned the disk until "g" coincided with the index line, and lifted the hypo to eye level. As he pressed in the plunger he did not see the tiny thread of fluid squirt from the tip of the needle. There was a sort of dark mist for a moment about the tip. A closer inspection showed that the needle was not even pierced at the tip. It had the usual slanting cut across the bias of the shaft, but the cut did not expose an oval hole. Baffled, he tried pressing the plunger again. Again *something* appeared around the tip and vanished. "We'll settle this," said the doctor. He slipped the needle into the skin of his forearm. He thought at first that he had missed—that the point had glided over the top of his skin instead of catching and slipping under it. But he saw a tiny blood-spot and realized that somehow he just hadn't felt the puncture. Whatever was in the barrel, he decided, couldn't do him any harm if it lived up to its billing—and if it could come out through a needle that had no hole. He gave himself three cc. and twitched the needle out. There was the swelling—painless, but otherwise typical.

Dr. Full decided it was his eyes or something, and gave three cc. of "g" from hypodermic IV to the feverish child. There was no interruption to her wailing as the needle went in and the swelling rose. But a long instant later, she gave a final gasp and was silent.

Well, he told himself, cold with horror, you did it that time. You killed her with that stuff.

Then the child sat up and said: "Where's my mommy?"

Incredulously, the doctor seized her arm and palpated the

elbow. The gland infection was zero, and the temperature seemed normal. The blood-congested tissues surrounding the wound were subsiding as he watched. The child's pulse was stronger and no faster than a child's should be. In the sudden silence of the room he could hear the little girl's mother sobbing in her kitchen, outside. And he also heard a girl's insinuating voice:

"She gonna be O.K., doc?"

He turned and saw a gaunt-faced, dirty-blond sloven of perhaps eighteen leaning in the doorway and eyeing him with amused contempt. She continued: "I heard about you, *Doc-tor* Full. So don't go try and put the bite on the old lady. You couldn't doctor up a sick cat."

"Indeed?" he rumbled. This young person was going to get a lesson she richly deserved. "Perhaps you would care to look at my patient?"

"Where's my mommy?" insisted the little girl, and the blonde's jaw fell. She went to the bed and cautiously asked: "You O.K. now, Teresa? You all fixed up?"

"Where's my mommy?" demanded Teresa. Then, accusingly, she gestured with her wounded hand at the doctor. "You *poke* me!" she complained, and giggled pointlessly.

"Well—" said the blond girl, "I guess I got to hand it to you, doc. These loud-mouth women around here said you didn't know your . . . I mean, didn't know how to cure people. They said you ain't a real doctor."

"I *have* retired from practice," he said. "But I happened to be taking this case to a colleague as a favor, your good mother noticed me, and—" a deprecating smile. He touched the lock of the case and it folded up into the little black bag again.

"You stole it," the girl said flatly.

He sputtered.

"Nobody'd trust you with a thing like that. It must be worth plenty. You stole that case. I was going to stop you when I come in and saw you working over Teresa, but it looked like you wasn't doing her any harm. But when you give me that line about taking that case to a colleague I know you stole it. You gimme a cut or I go to the cops. A thing like that must be worth twenty—thirty dollars."

The mother came timidly in, her eyes red. But she let out a whoop of joy when she saw the little girl sitting up and babbling to herself, embraced her madly, fell on her knees for a quick prayer, hopped up to kiss the doctor's hand, and then dragged him into the kitchen, all the while rattling in her native language while the blond girl let her eyes go cold with disgust. Dr. Full allowed himself to be towed into the kitchen, but flatly declined a cup of coffee and a plate of anise cakes and St. John's Bread.

"Try him on some wine, ma," said the girl sardonically.

"Hyass! Hyass!" breathed the woman delightedly. "You like-a wine, docta?" She had a carafe of purplish liquid before him in an instant, and the blond girl snickered as the doctor's hand twitched out at it. He drew his hand back, while there grew in his head the old image of how it would smell and then taste and then warm his stomach and limbs. He made the kind of calculation at which he was practiced; the delighted woman would not notice as he downed two tumblers, and he could overawe her through two tumblers more with his tale of Teresa's narrow brush with the Destroying Angel, and then—why, then it would not matter. He would be drunk.

But for the first time in years, there was a sort of counter-image: a blend of the rage he felt at the blond girl to whom he was so transparent, and of pride at the cure he had just effected. Much to his own surprise, he drew back his hand from the carafe and said, luxuriating in the words: "No, thank you. I don't believe I'd care for any so early in the day." He covertly watched the blond girl's face, and was gratified at her surprise. Then the mother was shyly handing him two bills and saying: "Is no much-a money, docta—but you come again, see Teresa?"

"I shall be glad to follow the case through," he said. "But now excuse me—I really must be running along." He grasped the little black bag firmly and got up; he wanted very much to get away from the wine and the older girl.

"Wait up, doc," said she, "I'm going your way." She followed him out and down the street. He ignored her until he felt her hand on the black bag. Then old Dr. Full stopped and tried to reason with her:

"Look, my dear. Perhaps you're right. I might have stolen it. To be perfectly frank, I don't remember how I got it. But you're young and you can earn your own money—"

"Fifty-fifty," she said, "or I go to the cops. And if I get another word outta you, it's sixty-forty. And you know who gets the short end, don't you, doc?"

Defeated, he marched to the pawnshop, her impudent hand still on the handle with his, and her heels beating out a tattoo against his stately tread.

In the pawnshop, they both got a shock.

"It ain't standard," said Uncle, unimpressed by the ingenious lock. "I ain't nevva seen one like it. Some cheap Jap stuff, maybe? Try down the street. This I nevva could sell."

Down the street they got an offer of one dollar. The same complaint was made: "I ain't a collecta, mista—I buy stuff that got resale value. Who could I sell this to, a Chinaman who don't know medical instruments? Every one of them looks funny. You sure you didn't make these yourself?" They didn't take the one-dollar offer.

The girl was baffled and angry; the doctor was baffled too, but triumphant. He had two dollars, and the girl had a half-interest in something nobody wanted. But, he suddenly marveled, the thing had been all right to cure the kid, hadn't it?

"Well," he asked her, "do you give up? As you see, the kit is practically valueless."

She was thinking hard. "Don't fly off the handle, doc. I don't get this, but something's going on all right . . . would those guys know good stuff if they saw it?"

"They would. They make a living from it. Wherever this kit came from—"

She seized on that, with a devilish faculty she seemed to have of eliciting answers without asking questions. "I thought so. You don't know either, huh? Well, maybe I can find out for you. C'mon in here. I ain't letting go of that thing. There's money in it—some way, I don't know how, there's money in it." He followed her into a cafeteria and to an almost-empty corner. She was oblivious to stares and snickers from the other customers as she opened the little black bag—it almost covered a cafeteria table—and ferreted through it. She picked out a retractor from a loop, scrutinized it, contemptuously threw it down, picked out a speculum, threw it down, picked out the lower half of an O.B. forceps, turned it over, close to her sharp young eyes—and saw what the doctor's dim old ones could not have seen.

All old Dr. Full knew was that she was peering at the neck of the forceps and then turned white. Very carefully, she placed the half of the forceps back in its loop of cloth and then replaced the retractor and the speculum. "Well?" he asked. "What did you see?"

" 'Made in U.S.A.,' " she quoted hoarsely. " 'Patent Applied for July 2450.' "

He wanted to tell her she must have misread the inscription, that it must be a practical joke, that—

But he knew she had read correctly. Those bandage shears: they *had* driven his fingers, rather than his fingers driving them. The hypo needle that had no hole. The pretty blue pill that had struck him like a thunderbolt.

"You know what I'm going to do?" asked the girl, with sudden animation. "I'm going to go to charm school. You'll like that, won't ya, doc? Because we're sure going to be seeing a lot of each other."

Old Dr. Full didn't answer. His hands had been playing idly with that plastic card from the kit on which had been printed the rows and columns that had guided him twice before. The card had a slight convexity; you could snap the convexity back and forth from one side to the other. He noted, in a daze, that with each snap a different text appeared on the cards. *Snap.* "The knife with the blue dot in the handle is for tumors only. Diagnose tumors with your Instrument Seven, the Swelling Tester. Place the Swelling Tester—" *Snap.* "An overdose of the pink pills in Bottle 3 can be fixed with one white pill from Bottle—" *Snap.* "Hold the suture needle by the end without the hole in it. Touch it to one end of the wound you want to close and let go. After it has made the knot, touch it—" *Snap.* "Place the top half of the O.B. Forceps near the opening. Let go. After it has entered and conformed to the shape of—" *Snap.*

The slot man saw "FLANNERY 1—MEDICAL" in the upper left corner of the hunk of copy. He automatically scribbled "trim to .75" on it and skimmed it across the horseshoe-shaped copy desk to Piper, who had been handling Edna Flannery's quack-exposé series. She was a nice youngster, he thought, but like all youngsters she overwrote. Hence, the "trim."

Piper dealt back a city hall story to the slot, pinned down Flannery's feature with one hand and began to tap his pencil across it, one tap to a word, at the same steady beat as a teletype carriage traveling across the roller. He wasn't exactly reading it this first time. He was just looking at the letters and words to find out whether, as letters and words, they conformed to *Herald* style. The steady tap of his pencil ceased at intervals as it drew a black line ending with a stylized letter "d" through the word "breast" and scribbled in "chest" instead, or knocked down the capital "E" in "East" to lower case with a diagonal, or closed up a split word—in whose middle Flannery had bumped the space bar of her typewriter—with two curved lines like parentheses rotated through ninety degrees. The thick black pencil zipped a ring around the "30," which, like all youngsters, she put at the end of her stories. He turned back to the first page for the second reading. This time the pencil drew lines with the stylized "d's" at the end of them through adjectives and whole phrases, printed big "L's" to mark paragraphs, hooked some of Flannery's own paragraphs together with swooping recurved lines.

At the bottom of "FLANNERY ADD 2—MEDICAL" the pencil slowed down and stopped. The slot man, sensitive to the rhythm of his beloved copy desk, looked up almost at once. He saw Piper squinting at the story, at a loss. Without wasting words, the copy reader skimmed it back across the Masonite horseshoe to the chief, caught a police story in return and buckled down, his pencil tapping. The slot man read as far as the fourth add, barked at Howard, on the rim: "Sit in for me," and stumped through the clattering city room toward the alcove where the managing editor presided over his own bedlam.

The copy chief waited his turn while the make-up editor, the pressroom foreman, and the chief photographer had words with the M.E. When his turn came, he dropped Flannery's copy on his desk and said: "She says this one isn't a quack."

The M.E. read:

"FLANNERY 1—MEDICAL, by Edna Flannery, *Herald* Staff Writer.

"The sordid tale of medical quackery which the *Herald* has exposed in this series of articles undergoes a change of pace today which the reporter found a welcome surprise. Her quest for the facts in the case of today's subject started just the same way that her exposure of one dozen shyster M.D.'s and faith-healing phonies did. But she can report for a change that Dr. Bayard Full is, despite unorthodox practices which have drawn the suspicion of the rightly hypersensitive medical associations, a true healer living up to the highest ideals of his profession.

"Dr. Full's name was given to the *Herald's* reporter by the ethical committee of a county medical association, which reported that he had been expelled from the association on July 18, 1941, for allegedly 'milking' several patients suffering from trivial complaints. According to sworn statements in the committee's files, Dr. Full had told them they suffered from cancer, and that he had a treatment which would prolong their lives. After his expulsion from the association, Dr. Full dropped out of their sight—until he opened a midtown 'sanitarium' in a brownstone front which had for years served as a rooming house.

"The *Herald's* reporter went to that sanitarium, on East 89th Street, with the full expectation of having numerous imaginary ailments diagnosed and of being promised a sure cure for a flat sum of money. She expected to find unkempt quarters, dirty instruments, and the mumbo-jumbo paraphernalia of the shyster M.D. which she had seen a dozen times before.

"She was wrong.

"Dr. Full's sanitarium is spotlessly clean, from its tastefully furnished entrance hall to its shining, white treatment rooms. The attractive, blond receptionist who greeted the reporter was soft-spoken and correct, asking only the reporter's name, address, and the general nature of her complaint. This was given, as usual, as 'nagging backache.' The receptionist asked the *Herald's* reporter to be seated, and a short while later conducted her to a second-floor treatment room and introduced her to Dr. Full.

"Dr. Full's alleged past, as described by the medical society spokesman, is hard to reconcile with his present appearance. He is a clear-eyed, white-haired man in his sixties, to judge by his appearance—a little above middle height and apparently in good physical condition. His voice was firm and friendly, untainted by the ingratiating whine of the shyster M.D. which the reporter has come to know too well.

"The receptionist did not leave the room as he began his examination after a few questions as to the nature and location of the pain. As the reporter lay face down on a treatment table the doctor pressed some instrument to the small of her back. In about one minute he made this astounding statement: 'Young woman, there is no reason for you to have any pain where you say you do. I understand they're saying nowadays that emotional upsets cause pains like that. You'd better go to a psychologist or psychiatrist if the pain keeps up. There is no physical cause for it, so I can do nothing for you.'

"His frankness took the reporter's breath away. Had he guessed she was, so to speak, a spy in his camp? She tried again: 'Well, doctor, perhaps you'd give me a physical checkup, I feel run down all the time, besides the pains. Maybe I need a tonic.' This is never-failing bait to shyster M.D.'s—an invitation for them to find all sorts of mysterious conditions wrong with a patient, each of which 'requires' an expensive treatment. As explained in the first article of this series, of course, the reporter underwent a thorough physical checkup before she embarked on her quack hunt, and was found to be in one hundred percent perfect condition, with the exception of a 'scarred' area at the bottom tip of her left lung resulting from a childhood attack of tuberculosis and a tendency toward 'hyperthyroidism'—overactivity of the thyroid gland which makes it difficult to put on weight and sometimes causes a slight shortness of breath.

"Dr. Full consented to perform the examination, and took a number of shining, spotlessly clean instruments from loops in a large board literally covered with instruments—most of them unfamiliar to the reporter. The instrument with which he approached first was a tube with a curved dial in its surface and two wires that ended on flat disks growing from its ends. He placed one of the disks on the back of the reporter's right hand and the other on the back of her left. 'Reading the meter,' he called out some number which the attentive receptionist took down on a ruled form. The same procedure was repeated several times, thoroughly covering the reporter's anatomy and thoroughly convincing her that the doctor was a complete quack. The reporter had never seen any such diagnostic procedure practiced during the weeks she put in preparing for this series.

"The doctor then took the ruled sheet from the receptionist, conferred with her in low tones, and said: 'You have a slightly overactive thyroid, young woman. And there's something wrong with your left lung—not seriously, but I'd like to take a closer look.'

"He selected an instrument from the board which, the reporter knew, is called a 'speculum'—a scissorlike device which spreads apart body openings such as the orifice of the ear, the nostril, and so on, so that a doctor can look in during an examination. The instrument was, however, too large to be an aural or nasal speculum but too small to be anything else. As the *Herald's* reporter was about to ask further questions, the attending receptionist told her: 'It's customary for us to blindfold our patients during lung examinations—do you mind?' The reporter, bewildered, allowed her to tie a spotlessly clean bandage over her eyes, and waited nervously for what would come next.

"She still cannot say exactly what happened while she was blindfolded—but X rays confirm her suspicions. She felt a cold sensation at her ribs on the left side—a cold that seemed to enter inside her body. Then there was a snapping feeling, and the cold sensation was gone. She heard Dr. Full say in a matter-of-fact voice: 'You have an old tubercular scar down there. It isn't doing any particular harm, but an active person like you needs all the oxygen she can get. Lie still and I'll fix it for you.'

"Then there was a repetition of the cold sensation, lasting for a longer time. 'Another batch of alveoli and some more vascular glue,' the *Herald's* reporter heard Dr. Full say, and the receptionist's crisp response to the order. Then the strange sensation departed and the eye bandage was removed. The reporter saw no scar on her ribs, and yet the doctor assured her: 'That did it. We took out the fibrosis—and a good fibrosis it was, too; it walled off the infection so you're still alive to tell the tale. Then we planted a few clumps of alveoli—they're the little gadgets that get the oxygen from the air you breathe into your blood. I won't monkey with your thyroxin supply. You've got used to being the kind of person you are, and if you suddenly found yourself easygoing and all the rest of it, chances are you'd only be upset. About the backache: just check with the county medical society for the name of a good psychologist or psychiatrist. And look out for quacks; the woods are full of them.'

"The doctor's self-assurance took the reporter's breath away. She asked what the charge would be, and was told to pay the receptionist fifty dollars. As usual, the reporter delayed paying until she got a receipt signed by the doctor himself, detailing the services for which it paid. Unlike most, the doctor cheerfully wrote: 'For removal of fibrosis from left lung and restoration of alveoli,' and signed it.

"The reporter's first move when she left the sanitarium was to head for the chest specialist who had examined her in preparation for this series. A comparison of X rays taken on the day of the 'operation' and those taken previously would, the *Herald's* reporter then thought, expose Dr. Full as a prince of shyster M.D.'s and quacks.

"The chest specialist made time on his crowded schedule for the reporter, in whose series he has shown a lively interest from the planning stage on. He laughed uproariously in his staid Park Avenue examining room as she described the weird procedure to which she had been subjected. But he did not laugh when he took a chest X ray of the reporter, developed it, dried it, and compared it with the ones he had taken earlier. The chest specialist took six more X rays that afternoon, but finally admitted that they all told the same story. The *Herald's* reporter has it on his authority that the scar she had eighteen days ago from her tuberculosis is now gone and has been replaced by healthy lung tissue. He declared that this is a happening unparalleled in medical history. He does not go along with the reporter in her firm conviction that Dr. Full is responsible for the change.

"The *Herald's* reporter, however, sees no two ways about it. She concludes that Dr. Bayard Full—whatever his alleged past may have been—is now an unorthodox but highly successful practitioner of medicine, to whose hands the reporter would trust herself in any emergency.

"Not so is the case of 'Rev.' Annie Dimsworth—a female harpy who, under the guise of 'faith' preys on the ignorant and suffering who come to her sordid 'healing parlor' for help and remain to feed 'Rev.' Annie's bank account, which now totals up to $53,238.64. Tomorrow's article will show, with photostats of bank statements and sworn testimony that—"

The managing editor turned down "FLANNERY LAST ADD—MEDICAL" and tapped his front teeth with a pencil, trying to think straight. He finally told the copy chief: "Kill the story. Run the teaser as a box." He tore off the last paragraph—the "teaser" about "Rev." Annie—and handed it to the desk man, who stumped back to his Masonite horseshoe.

The make-up editor was back, dancing with impatience as he tried to catch the M.E.'s eye. The interphone buzzed with the red light which indicated that the editor and publisher wanted to talk to him. The M.E. thought briefly of a special series on this Dr. Full, decided nobody would believe it and that he probably was a phony anyway. He spiked the story on the "dead" hook and answered his interphone.

Dr. Full had become almost fond of Angie. As his practice had grown to engross the neighborhood illnesses, and then to a corner suite in an uptown taxpayer building, and finally to the sanitarium, she seemed to have grown with it. Oh, he thought, we have our little disputes—

The girl, for instance, was too much interested in money. She had wanted to specialize in cosmetic surgery—removing wrinkles from wealthy old women and whatnot. She didn't realize, at first, that a thing like this was in their trust, that they were the stewards and not the owners of the little black bag and its fabulous contents.

THE LITTLE BLACK BAG 129

He had tried, ever so cautiously, to analyze them, but without success. All the instruments were slightly radioactive, for instance, but not quite so. They would make a Geiger-Mueller counter indicate, but they would not collapse the leaves of an electroscope. He didn't pretend to be up on the latest developments, but as he understood it, that was just plain *wrong*. Under the highest magnification there were lines on the instruments' superfinished surfaces: incredibly fine lines, engraved in random hatchments which made no particular sense. Their magnetic properties were preposterous. Sometimes the instruments were strongly attracted to magnets, sometimes less so, and sometimes not at all.

Dr. Full had taken X rays in fear and trembling lest he disrupt whatever delicate machinery worked in them. He was *sure* they were not solid, that the handles and perhaps the blades must be mere shells filled with busy little watchworks—but the X rays showed nothing of the sort. Oh, yes—and they were always sterile, and they wouldn't rust. Dust *fell* off them if you shook them: now, that was something he understood. They ionized the dust, or were ionized themselves, or something of the sort. At any rate, he had read of something similar that had to do with phonograph records.

She wouldn't know about that, he proudly thought. She kept the books well enough, and perhaps she gave him a useful prod now and then when he was inclined to settle down. The move from the neighborhood slum to the uptown quarters had been her idea, and so had the sanitarium. Good, good, it enlarged his sphere of usefulness. Let the child have her mink coats and her convertible, as they seemed to be calling roadsters nowadays. He himself was too busy and too old. He had so much to make up for.

Dr. Full thought happily of his Master Plan. She would not like it much, but she would have to see the logic of it. This marvelous thing that had happened to them must be handed on. She was herself no doctor; even though the instruments practically ran themselves, there was more to doctoring than skill. There were the ancient canons of the healing art. And so, having seen the logic of it, Angie would yield; she would assent to his turning over the little black bag to all humanity.

He would probably present it to the College of Surgeons, with as little fuss as possible—well, perhaps a *small* ceremony, and he would like a souvenir of the occasion, a cup or a framed testimonial. It would be a relief to have the thing out of his hands, in a way; let the giants of the healing art decide who was to have its benefits. No, Angie would understand. She was a goodhearted girl.

It was nice that she had been showing so much interest in the surgical side lately—asking about the instruments, reading the instruction card for hours, even practicing on guinea pigs. If something of his love for humanity had been communicated to her, old Dr. Full sentimentally thought, his life would not have been in vain. Surely she would realize that a greater good would be served by surrendering the instruments to wiser hands than theirs, and by throwing aside the cloak of secrecy necessary to work on their small scale.

Dr. Full was in the treatment room that had been the brownstone's front parlor; through the window he saw Angie's yellow convertible roll to a stop before the stoop. He liked the way she looked as she climbed the stairs; neat, not flashy, he thought. A sensible girl like her, she'd understand. There was somebody with her—a fat woman, puffing up the steps, overdressed and petulant. Now, what could she want?

Angie let herself in and went into the treatment room, followed by the fat woman. "Doctor," said the blond girl gravely, "may I present Mrs. Coleman?" Charm school had not taught her everything, but Mrs. Coleman, evidently *nouveau riche,* thought the doctor, did not notice the blunder.

"Miss Aquella told me *so* much about you, doctor, and your remarkable system!" she gushed.

Before he could answer, Angie smoothly interposed: "Would you excuse us for just a moment, Mrs. Coleman?"

She took the doctor's arm and led him into the reception hall. "Listen," she said swiftly, "I know this goes against your grain, but I couldn't pass it up. I met this old thing in the exercise class at Elizabeth Barton's. Nobody else'll talk to her there. She's a widow. I guess her husband was a black marketeer or something, and she has a pile of dough. I gave her a line about how you had a system of massaging wrinkles out. My idea is, you blindfold her, cut her neck open with the Cutaneous Series knife, shoot some Firmol into the muscles, spoon out some of that blubber with an Adipose Series curette and spray it all with Skintite. When you take the blindfold off she's got rid of a wrinkle and doesn't know what happened. She'll pay five hundred dollars. Now, don't say 'no,' doc. Just this once, let's do it my way, can't you? I've been working on this deal all along too, haven't I?''

"Oh," said the doctor, "very well." He was going to have to tell her about the Master Plan before long anyway. He would let her have it her way this time.

Back in the treatment room, Mrs. Coleman had been thinking things over. She told the doctor sternly as he entered: "Of course, your system is permanent, isn't it?''

"It is, madam," he said shortly. "Would you please lie down there? Miss Aquella, get a sterile three-inch bandage for Mrs. Coleman's eyes.'' He turned his back on the fat woman to avoid conversation, and pretended to be adjusting the lights. Angie blindfolded the woman, and the doctor selected the instruments he would need. He handed the blond girl a pair of retractors, and told her: "Just slip the corners of the blades in as I cut—'' She gave him an alarmed look, and gestured at the reclining woman. He lowered his voice: "Very well. Slip in the corners and rock them along the incision. I'll tell you when to pull them out.''

Dr. Full held the Cutaneous Series knife to his eyes as he adjusted the little slide for three centimeters depth. He sighed a little as he recalled that its last use had been in the extirpation of an "inoperable" tumor of the throat.

"Very well," he said, bending over the woman. He tried a tentative pass through her tissues. The blade dipped in and flowed through them, like a finger through quicksilver, with no wound left in the wake. Only the retractors could hold the edges of the incision apart.

Mrs. Coleman stirred and jabbered: "Doctor, that felt so peculiar! Are you sure you're rubbing the right way?''

"Quite sure, madam," said the doctor wearily. "Would you please try not to talk during the massage?''

He nodded at Angie, who stood ready with the retractors. The blade sank in to its three centimeters, miraculously cutting only the dead horny tissues of the epidermis and the live tissue of the dermis, pushing aside mysteriously all major and minor blood vessels and muscular tissue, declining to affect any system or organ except the one it was—tuned to, could you say? The doctor didn't know the answer, but he felt tired and bitter at this prostitution. Angie slipped in the retractor blades and rocked them as he withdrew the knife, then pulled to separate the lips of the incision. It bloodlessly exposed an unhealthy string of muscle, sagging in a dead-looking loop from blue-gray ligaments. The doctor took a hypo. Number IX, pre-set to "g," and raised it to his eye level. The mist came and went; there probably was no possibility of an embolus with one of these gadgets, but why take chances? He shot one cc. of "g"—identified as "Firmol" by the card—into the muscle. He and Angie watched as it tightened up against the pharynx.

He took the Adipose Series curette, a small one, and spooned out yellowish tissue, dropping it into the incinerator box, and then nodded to Angie. She eased out the retractors and the gaping incision slipped together into unbroken skin, sagging now. The doctor had the atomizer—dialed to "Skintite"—ready. He sprayed, and the skin shrank up into the new firm throat line.

As he replaced the instruments, Angie removed Mrs. Coleman's bandage and gaily announced: "We're finished! And there's a mirror in the reception hall—"

Mrs. Coleman didn't need to be invited twice. With incredulous fingers she felt her chin, and then dashed for the hall. The doctor grimaced as he heard her yelp of delight, and Angie turned to him with a tight smile. "I'll get the money and get her out," she said. "You won't have to be bothered with her any more."

He was grateful for that much.

She followed Mrs. Coleman into the reception hall, and the doctor dreamed over the case of instruments. A ceremony, certainly—he was *entitled* to one. Not everybody, he thought, would turn such a sure source of money over to the good of humanity. But you reached an age when money mattered less, and when you thought of these things you had done that *might* be open to misunderstanding if, just if, there chanced to be any of that, well, that judgment business. The doctor wasn't a religious man, but you certainly found yourself thinking hard about some things when your time drew near—

Angie was back, with a bit of paper in her hands. "Five hundred dollars," she said matter-of-factly. "And you realize, don't you, that we could go over her an inch at a time—at five hundred dollars an inch?"

"I've been meaning to talk to you about that," he said.

There was bright fear in her eyes, he thought—but why?

"Angie, you've been a good girl and an understanding girl, but we can't keep this up forever, you know."

"Let's talk about it some other time," she said flatly. "I'm tired now."

"No—I really feel we've gone far enough on our own. The instruments—"

"Don't say it, doc!" she hissed. "Don't say it, or you'll be sorry!" In her face there was a look that reminded him of the hollow-eyed, gaunt-faced, dirty-blond creature she had been. From under the charm-school finish there burned the guttersnipe whose infancy had been spent on a sour and filthy mattress, whose childhood had been play in the littered alley, and whose adolescence had been the sweat-shops and the aimless gatherings at night under the glaring street lamps.

He shook his head to dispel the puzzling notion. "It's this way," he patiently began. "I told you about the family that invented the O.B. forceps and kept them a secret for so many generations, how they could have given them to the world but didn't?"

"They knew what they were doing," said the guttersnipe flatly.

"Well, that's neither here nor there," said the doctor, irritated. "My mind is made up about it. I'm going to turn the instruments over to the College of Surgeons. We have enough money to be comfortable. You can even have the house. I've been thinking of going to a warmer climate, myself." He felt peeved with her for making the unpleasant scene. He was unprepared for what happened next.

Angie snatched the little black bag and dashed for the door, with panic in her eyes. He scrambled after her, catching her arm, twisting it in a sudden rage. She clawed at his face with her free hand, babbling curses. Somehow, somebody's finger touched the little black bag, and it opened grotesquely into the enormous board, covered with shining instruments, large and small. Half a dozen of them joggled loose and fell to the floor.

"*Now* see what you've done!" roared the doctor, unreasonably. Her hand was still viselike on the handle, but she was standing still, trembling with choked-up rage. The doctor bent stiffly to pick up the fallen instruments. Unreasonable girl! he thought bitterly. Making a scene—

Pain drove in between his shoulderblades and he fell face down. The light ebbed. "Unreasonable girl!" he tried to croak. And then: "They'll know I tried, anyway—"

Angie looked down on his prone body, with the handle of the

Number Six Cautery Series knife protruding from it. "—will cut through all tissues. Use for amputations before you spread on the Re-Gro. Extreme caution should be used in the vicinity of vital organs and major blood vessels or nerve trunks—"

"I didn't mean to do that," said Angie, dully, cold with horror. Now the detective would come, the implacable detective who would reconstruct the crime from the dust in the room. She would run and turn and twist, but the detective would find her out and she would be tried in a courtroom before a judge and jury; the lawyer would make speeches, but the jury would convict her anyway, and the headlines would scream: "BLOND KILLER GUILTY!" and she'd maybe get the chair, walking down a plain corridor where a beam of sunlight struck through the dusty air, with an iron door at the end of it. Her mink, her convertible, her dresses, the handsome man she was going to meet and marry—

The mist of cinematic clichés cleared, and she knew what she would do next. Quite steadily, she picked the incinerator box from its loop in the board—a metal cube with a different-textured spot on one side. "—to dispose of fibroses or other unwanted matter, simply touch the disk—" You dropped something in and touched the disk. There was a sort of soundless whistle, very powerful and unpleasant if you were too close, and a sort of lightless flash. When you opened the box again, the contents were gone. Angie took another of the Cautery Series knives and went grimly to work. Good thing there wasn't any blood to speak of— She finished the awful task in three hours.

She slept heavily that night, totally exhausted by the wringing emotional demands of the slaying and the subsequent horror. But in the morning, it was as though the doctor had never been there. She ate breakfast, then dressed with care. Nothing out of the ordinary, she told herself. Don't do one thing different from the way you would have done it before. After a day or two, you can phone the cops. Say he walked out spoiling for a drunk, and you're worried. But don't rush it, baby—*don't rush it*.

Mrs. Coleman was due at 10:00 a.m. Angie had counted on being able to talk the doctor into at least one more five-hundred-dollar session. She'd have to do it herself now—but she'd have to start sooner or later.

The woman arrived early. Angie explained smoothly: "The doctor asked me to take care of the massage today. Now that he has the tissue-firming process beginning, it only requires somebody trained in his methods—'' As she spoke, her eyes swiveled to the instrument case—open! She cursed herself for the single flaw as the woman followed her gaze and recoiled.

"What are those things!" she demanded. "Are you going to cut me with them? I *thought* there was something fishy—"

"Please, Mrs. Coleman," said Angie, "please, *dear* Mrs. Coleman—you don't understand about the . . . the massage instruments!"

"Massage instruments, my foot!" squabbled the woman shrilly. "That doctor *operated* on me. Why, he might have killed me!"

Angie wordlessly took one of the smaller Cutaneous Series knives and passed it through her forearm. The blade flowed like a finger through quicksilver, leaving no wound in its wake. *That* should convince the old cow!

It didn't convince her, but it did startle her. "What did you do with it? The blade folds up into the handle—that's it!"

"Now look closely, Mrs. Coleman," said Angie, thinking desperately of the five hundred dollars. "Look very closely and you'll see that the, uh, the sub-skin massager simply slips beneath the tissues without doing any harm, tightening and firming the muscles themselves instead of having to work through layers of skin and adipose tissue. It's the secret of the doctor's method. Now, how can outside massage have the effect that we got last night?"

Mrs. Coleman was beginning to calm down. "It *did* work, all right," she admitted, stroking the new line of her neck. But your arm's one thing and my neck's another! Let me see you do that with your neck!"

Angie smiled—

Al returned to the clinic after an excellent lunch that had almost reconciled him to three more months he would have to spend on duty. And then, he thought, and then a blessed year at the blessedly super-normal South Pole working on his specialty— which happened to be telekinesis exercises for ages three to six. Meanwhile, of course, the world had to go on and of course he had to shoulder his share in the running of it.

Before settling down to desk work he gave a routine glance at the bag board. What he saw made him stiffen with shocked surprise. A red light was on next to one of the numbers—the first since he couldn't think when. He read off the number and murmured "O.K., 674,101. That fixes *you*." He put the number on a card sorter and in a moment the record was in his hand. Oh, yes—Hemingway's bag. The big dummy didn't remember how or where he had lost it; none of them ever did. There were hundreds of them floating around.

Al's policy in such cases was to leave the bag turned on. The things practically ran themselves, it was practically impossible to do harm with them, so whoever found a lost one might as well be allowed to use it. You turn it off, you have a social loss—you leave it on, it may do some good. As he understood it, and not very well at that, the stuff wasn't "used up." A temporalist had tried to explain it to him with little success that the prototypes in the transmitter *had been transducted* through a series of point-events of transfinite cardinality. Al had innocently asked whether that meant prototypes had been stretched, so to speak, through all time, and the temporalist had thought he was joking and left in a huff.

"Like to see him do this," thought Al darkly, as he telekinized himself to the combox, after a cautious look to see that there were no medics around. To the box he said: "Police chief," and then to the police chief: "There's been a homicide committed with Medical Instrument Kit 674,101. It was lost some months ago by one of my people, Dr. John Hemingway. He didn't have a clear account of the circumstances."

The police chief groaned and said: "I'll call him in and question him." He was to be astonished by the answers, and was to learn that the homicide was well out of his jurisdiction.

Al stood for a moment at the bag board by the glowing red light that had been sparked into life by a departing vital force giving, as its last act, the warning that Kit 674,101 was in homicidal hands. With a sigh, Al pulled the plug and the light went out.

"Yah," jeered the woman. "You'd fool around with my neck, but you wouldn't risk your own with that thing!"

Angie smiled with serene confidence a smile that was to shock hardened morgue attendants. She set the Cutaneous Series knife to three centimeters before drawing it across her neck. Smiling, knowing the blade would cut only the dead horny tissue of the epidermis and the live tissue of the dermis, mysteriously push aside all major and minor blood vessels and muscular tissue—

Smiling, the knife plunging in and its microtomesharp metal

shearing through major and minor blood vessels and muscular tissue and pharynx, Angie cut her throat.

In the few minutes it took the police, summoned by the shrieking Mrs. Coleman, to arrive, the instruments had become crusted with rust, and the flasks which had held vascular glue and clumps of pink, rubbery alveoli and spare gray cells and coils of receptor nerves held only black slime, and from them when opened gushed the foul gases of decomposition.

8

ENCHANTED VILLAGE

A. E. van Vogt (1913–   )

OTHER WORLDS
July

The May 1950 issue of Astounding Science Fiction *contained an article by veteran sf writer L. Ron Hubbard called "Dianetics, The Evolution of a Science," which was destined to spawn one of the most controversial "movements" in American history. Initially championed by John W. Campbell, Jr., its pseudo-scientific claims of self-therapy found a willing audience, including several members of the science fiction community. Hubbard's 1950 book,* Dianetics: The Modern Science of Mental Health, *eventually sold in the millions. The movement was to cost A. E. van Vogt, one of the major figures of "Golden Age" sf, many potentially productive years away from his writing, and although he later returned, he never achieved the same level of fame and excellence.*

In 1950, however, van Vogt was still going strong, as "Enchanted Village" indicates—it was also the year that his The Voyage of the Space Beagle *(consisting of earlier stories with linking material) was published to excellent reviews.*

—M.H.G.

The advance of science does kill some romance. In 1950, it was still possible to think of a barely habitable Mars. There was still the possibility of canals, of liquid water, of a high civilization either alive or recently dead—at least there was no definite scientific evidence to the contrary.

Therefore we had the Mars of Edgar Rice Burroughs and of

Ray Bradbury, and to it, "Enchanted Village" is a worthy addition. Notice that the Earthman on Mars has no trouble breathing and he is not suffering unduly from cold. Notice that there is plant life on Mars and the remnants of an advanced technology.

It was only in 1969 that the Mars-probe, Mariner 4, gave the first hint that this was all wrong. Now we know that the Martian atmosphere is far too thin to breathe and lacks oxygen anyway, that the surface temperature is reminiscent of Antarctica, and that there is no sign of life.

Too bad, but in this book it's still 1950 so cling to the romance.

—I.A.

"Explorers of a new frontier" they had been called before they left for Mars.

For a while after the ship crashed into a Martian desert, killing all on board except—miraculously—this one man, Bill Jenner spat the words occasionally into the constant, sand-laden wind. He despised himself for the pride he had felt when he first heard them.

His fury faded with each mile that he walked, and his black grief for his friends became a gray ache. Slowly he realized that he had made a ruinous misjudgment.

He had underestimated the speed at which the rocketship had been traveling. He'd guessed that he would have to walk three hundred miles to reach the shallow, polar sea he and the others had observed as they glided in from outer space. Actually, the ship must have flashed an immensely greater distance before it hurtled down out of control.

The days stretched behind him, seemingly as numberless as the hot, red, alien sand that scorched through his tattered clothes. This huge scarecrow of a man kept moving across the endless, arid waste—he would not give up.

By the time he came to the mountain, his food had long been gone. Of his four water bags, only one remained, and that was so close to being empty that he merely wet his cracked lips and swollen tongue whenever his thirst became unbearable.

Jenner climbed high before he realized that it was not just

another dune that had barred his way. He paused, and as he gazed up at the mountain that towered above him, he cringed a little. For an instant he felt the hopelessness of this mad race he was making to nowhere—but he reached the top. He saw that below him was a depression surrounded by hills as high as or higher than the one on which he stood. Nestled in the valley they made was a village.

He could see trees and the marble floor of a courtyard. A score of buildings were clustered around what seemed to be a central square. They were mostly low-constructed, but there were four towers pointing gracefully into the sky. They shone in the sunlight with a marble luster.

Faintly, there came to Jenner's ears a thin, high-pitched whistling sound. It rose, fell, faded completely, then came up again clearly and unpleasantly. Even as Jenner ran toward it, the noise grated on his ears, eerie and unnatural.

He kept slipping on smooth rock, and bruised himself when he fell. He rolled halfway down into the valley. The buildings remained new and bright when seen from nearby. Their walls flashed with reflections. On every side was vegetation—reddish-green shrubbery, yellow-green trees laden with purple and red fruit.

With ravenous intent, Jenner headed for the nearest fruit tree. Close up, the tree looked dry and brittle. The large red fruit he tore from the lowest branch, however, was plump and juicy.

As he lifted it to his mouth, he remembered that he had been warned during his training period to taste nothing on Mars until it had been chemically examined. But that was meaningless advice to a man whose only chemical equipment was in his own body.

Nevertheless, the possibility of danger made him cautious. He took his first bite gingerly. It was bitter to his tongue, and he spat it out hastily. Some of the juice which remained in his mouth seared his gums. He felt the fire of it, and he reeled from nausea. His muscles began to jerk, and he lay down on the marble to keep himself from falling. After what seemed like hours to Jenner, the awful trembling finally went out of his body and he could see again. He looked up despisingly at the tree.

The pain finally left him, and slowly he relaxed. A soft breeze rustled the dry leaves. Nearby trees took up that gentle clamor, and it struck Jenner that the wind here in the valley was only a whisper of what it had been on the flat desert beyond the mountain.

There was no other sound now. Jenner abruptly remembered the high-pitched, ever-changing whistle he had heard. He lay very still, listening intently, but there was only the rustling of the leaves. The noisy shrilling had stopped. He wondered if it had been an alarm, to warn the villagers of his approach.

Anxiously he climbed to his feet and fumbled for his gun. A sense of disaster shocked through him. It wasn't there. His mind was a blank, and then he vaguely recalled that he had first missed the weapon more than a week before. He looked around him uneasily, but there was not a sign of creature life. He braced himself. He couldn't leave, as there was nowhere to go. If necessary, he would fight to the death to remain in the village.

Carefully Jenner took a sip from his water bag, moistening his cracked lips and his swollen tongue. Then he replaced the cap and started through a double line of trees toward the nearest building. He made a wide circle to observe it from several vantage points. On one side a low, broad archway opened into the interior. Through it, he could dimly make out the polished gleam of a marble floor.

Jenner explored the buildings from the outside, always keeping a respectful distance between him and any of the entrances. He saw no sign of animal life. He reached the far side of the marble platform on which the village was built, and turned back decisively. It was time to explore interiors.

He chose one of the four tower buildings. As he came within a dozen feet of it, he saw that he would have to stoop low to get inside.

Momentarily, the implications of that stopped him. These buildings had been constructed for a life form that must be very different from human beings.

He went forward again, bent down, and entered reluctantly, every muscle tensed.

He found himself in a room without furniture. However, there were several low marble fences projecting from one marble wall. They formed what looked like a group of four wide, low stalls. Each stall had an open trough carved out of the floor.

The second chamber was fitted with four inclined planes of marble, each of which slanted up to a dais. Altogether there were four rooms on the lower floor. From one of them a circular ramp mounted up, apparently to a tower room.

Jenner didn't investigate the upstairs. The earlier fear that he would find alien life was yielding to the deadly conviction that he wouldn't. No life meant no food or chance of getting any. In frantic haste he hurried from building to building, peering into the silent rooms, pausing now and then to shout hoarsely.

Finally there was no doubt. He was alone in a deserted village on a lifeless planet, without food, without water—except for the pitiful supply in his bag—and without hope.

He was in the fourth and smallest room of one of the tower buildings when he realized that he had come to the end of his search. The room had a single stall jutting out from one wall. Jenner lay down wearily in it. He must have fallen asleep instantly.

When he awoke he became aware of two things, one right after the other. The first realization occurred before he opened his eyes—the whistling sound was back; high and shrill, it wavered at the threshold of audibility.

The other was that a fine spray of liquid was being directed down at him from the ceiling. It had an odor, of which technician Jenner took a single whiff. Quickly he scrambled out of the room, coughing, tears in his eyes, his face already burning from chemical reaction.

He snatched his handkerchief and hastily wiped the exposed parts of his body and face.

He reached the outside and there paused, striving to understand what had happened.

The village seemed unchanged.

Leaves trembled in a gentle breeze. The sun was poised on a mountain peak. Jenner guessed from its position that it was morning again and that he had slept at least a dozen hours. The glazing white light suffused the valley. Half hidden by trees and shrubbery, the buildings flashed and shimmered.

He seemed to be in an oasis in a vast desert. It was an oasis, all right, Jenner reflected grimly, but not for a human being. For him, with its poisonous fruit, it was more like a tantalizing mirage.

He went back inside the building and cautiously peered into the room where he had slept. The spray of gas had stopped, not a bit of odor lingered, and the air was fresh and clean.

He edged over the threshold, half-inclined to make a test. He had a picture in his mind of a long-dead Martian creature lazing on the floor in the stall while a soothing chemical sprayed down on its body. The fact that the chemical was deadly to human beings merely emphasized how alien to man was the life that had spawned on Mars. But there seemed little doubt of the reason for the gas. The creature was accustomed to taking a morning shower.

Inside the "bathroom," Jenner eased himself feet first into the stall. As his hips came level with the stall entrance, the solid ceiling sprayed a jet of yellowish gas straight down upon his legs. Hastily Jenner pulled himself clear of the stall. The gas stopped as suddenly as it had started.

He tried it again, to make sure it was merely an automatic process. It turned on, then shut off.

Jenner's thirst-puffed lips parted with excitement. He thought, "If there can be one automatic process, there may be others."

Breathing heavily, he raced into the outer room. Carefully he shoved his legs into one of the two stalls. The moment his hips were in, a steaming gruel filled the trough beside the wall.

He stared at the greasy-looking stuff with a horrified fascination—food—and drink. He remembered the poison fruit and felt repelled, but he forced himself to bend down and put his finger into the hot, wet substance. He brought it up, dripping, to his mouth.

It tasted flat and pulpy, like boiled wood fiber. It trickled viscously into his throat. His eyes began to water and his lips drew back convulsively. He realized he was going to be sick, and ran for the outer door—but didn't quite make it.

When he finally got outside, he felt limp and unutterably listless. In that depressed state of mind, he grew aware again of the shrill sound.

He felt amazed that he could have ignored its rasping even for a few minutes. Sharply he glanced about, trying to determine its source, but it seemed to have none. Whenever he approached a point where it appeared to be loudest, then it would fade or shift, perhaps to the far side of the village.

He tried to imagine what an alien culture would want with a mind-shattering noise—although, of course, it would not necessarily have been unpleasant to them.

He stopped and snapped his fingers as a wild but nevertheless plausible notion entered his mind. Could this be music?

He toyed with the idea, trying to visualize the village as it had been long ago. Here a music-loving people had possibly gone about their daily tasks to the accompaniment of what was to them beautiful strains of melody.

The hideous whistling went on and on, waxing and waning. Jenner tried to put buildings between himself and the sound. He sought refuge in various rooms, hoping that at least one would be soundproof. None were. The whistle followed him wherever he went.

He retreated into the desert, and had to climb halfway up one of the slopes before the noise was low enough not to disturb him. Finally, breathless, but immeasurably relieved, he sank down on the sand and thought blankly:

What now?

The scene that spread before him had in it qualities of both heaven and hell. It was all too familiar now—the red sands, the stony dunes, the small, alien village promising so much and fulfilling so little.

Jenner looked down at it with his feverish eyes and ran his parched tongue over his cracked, dry lips. He knew that he was a dead man unless he could alter the automatic food-making machines that must be hidden somewhere in the walls and under the floors of the buildings.

In ancient days, a remnant of Martian civilization had survived here in this village. The inhabitants had died off, but the village lived on, keeping itself clean of sand, able to provide refuge for any Martian who might come along. But there were no Martians. There was only Bill Jenner, pilot of the first rocketship ever to land on Mars.

He had to make the village turn out food and drink that he could take. Without tools, except his hands, with scarcely any knowledge of chemistry, he must force it to change its habits.

Tensely he hefted his water bag. He took another sip and fought the same grim fight to prevent himself from guzzling it down to the last drop. And, when he had won the battle once more, he stood up and started down the slope.

He could last, he estimated, not more than three days. In that time he must conquer the village.

He was already among the trees when it suddenly struck him that the "music" had stopped. Relieved, he bent over a small shrub, took a good firm hold of it—and pulled.

It came up easily, and there was a slab of marble attached to it. Jenner stared at it, noting with surprise that he had been mistaken in thinking the stalk came up through a hole in the marble. It was merely stuck to the surface. Then he noticed something else—the shrub had no roots. Almost instinctively, Jenner looked down at the spot from which he had torn the slab of marble along with the plant. There was sand there.

He dropped the shrub, slipped to his knees, and plunged his fingers into the sand. Loose sand trickled through them. He reached deep, using all his strength to force his arm and hand down; sand—nothing but sand.

He stood up and frantically tore up another shrub. It also came easily, bringing with it a slab of marble. It had no roots, and where it had been was sand.

With a kind of mindless disbelief, Jenner rushed over to a fruit tree and shoved at it. There was a momentary resistance, and then the marble on which it stood split and lifted slowly into the air. The tree fell over with a swish and a crackle as its dry branches and leaves broke and crumbled into a thousand pieces. Underneath where it had been was sand.

Sand everywhere. A city built on sand. Mars, planet of sand. That was not completely true, of course. Seasonal vegetation had been observed near the polar icecaps. All but the hardiest of it died with the coming of summer. It had been intended that the rocketship land near one of those shallow, tideless seas.

By coming down out of control, the ship had wrecked more than itself. It had wrecked the chances for life of the only survivor of the voyage.

Jenner came slowly out of his daze. He had a thought then. He picked up one of the shrubs he had already torn loose, braced his foot against the marble to which it was attached, and tugged, gently at first, then with increasing strength.

It came loose finally, but there was no doubt that the two were part of a whole. The shrub was growing out of the marble.

Marble? Jenner knelt beside one of the holes from which he had torn a slab, and bent over an adjoining section. It was quite porous—calciferous rock, most likely, but not true marble at all. As he reached toward it, intending to break off a piece, it changed color. Astounded, Jenner drew back. Around the break, the stone was turning a bright orange-yellow. He studied it uncertainly, then tentatively he touched it.

It was as if he had dipped his fingers into searing acid. There was a sharp, biting, burning pain. With a gasp, Jenner jerked his hand clear.

The continuing anguish made him feel faint. He swayed and moaned, clutching the bruised members of his body. When the agony finally faded and he could look at the injury, he saw that the skin had peeled and that blood blisters had formed already. Grimly Jenner looked down at the break in the stone. The edges remained bright orange-yellow.

The village was alert, ready to defend itself from further attacks.

Suddenly weary, he crawled into the shade of a tree. There was only one possible conclusion to draw from what had happened, and it almost defied common sense. This lonely village was alive.

As he lay there, Jenner tried to imagine a great mass of living substance growing into the shape of buildings, adjusting itself to suit another life form, accepting the role of servant in the widest meaning of the term.

If it would serve one race, why not another? If it could adjust to Martians, why not to human beings?

There would be difficulties, of course. He guessed wearily that essential elements would not be available. The oxygen for water could come from the air . . . thousands of compounds could be made from sand. . . . Though it meant death if he failed to find a solution, he fell asleep even as he started to think about what they might be.

When he awoke it was quite dark.

Jenner climbed heavily to his feet. There was a drag to his muscles that alarmed him. He wet his mouth from his water bag and staggered toward the entrance of the nearest building. Except for the scraping of his shoes on the "marble," the silence was intense.

He stopped short, listened, and looked. The wind had died away. He couldn't see the mountains that rimmed the valley, but the buildings were still dimly visible, black shadows in a shadow world.

For the first time, it seemed to him that, in spite of his new hope, it might be better if he died. Even if he survived, what had he to look forward to? Only too well he recalled how hard it had been to rouse interest in the trip and to raise the large amount of money required. He remembered the colossal problems that had had to be solved in building the ship, and some of the men who had solved them were buried somewhere in the Martian desert.

It might be twenty years before another ship from Earth would try to reach the only other planet in the Solar System that had shown signs of being able to support life.

During those uncountable days and nights, those years, he would be here alone. That was the most he could hope for—if he lived. As he fumbled his way to a dais in one of the rooms, Jenner considered another problem: How did one let a living village know that it must alter its processes? In a way, it must already have grasped that it had a new tenant. How could he make it realize he needed food in a different chemical combination than that which it had served in the past; that he liked music, but on a different scale system; and that he could use a shower each morning—of water, not of poison gas?

He dozed fitfully, like a man who is sick rather than sleepy. Twice he wakened, his lips on fire, his eyes burning, his body bathed in perspiration. Several times he was startled into consciousness by the sound of his own harsh voice crying out in anger and fear at the night.

He guessed, then, that he was dying.

He spent the long hours of darkness tossing, turning, twisting, befuddled by waves of heat. As the light of morning came, he was vaguely surprised to realize that he was still alive. Restlessly he climbed off the dais and went to the door.

A bitingly cold wind blew, but it felt good to his hot face. He wondered if there were enough pneumococci in his blood for him to catch pneumonia. He decided not.

In a few moments he was shivering. He retreated back into the house, and for the first time noticed that, despite the doorless doorway, the wind did not come into the building at all. The rooms were cold but not draughty.

That started an association: Where had his terrible body heat come from? He teetered over to the dais where he had spent the night. Within seconds he was sweltering in a temperature of about one hundred and thirty.

He climbed off the dais, shaken by his own stupidity. He estimated that he had sweated at least two quarts of moisture out of his dried-up body on that furnace of a bed.

This village was not for human beings. Here even the beds were heated for creatures who needed temperatures far beyond the heat comfortable for men.

Jenner spent most of the day in the shade of a large tree. He felt exhausted, and only occasionally did he even remember that he had a problem. When the whistling started, it bothered him at first, but he was too tired to move away from it. There were long periods when he hardly heard it, so dulled were his senses.

Late in the afternoon he remembered the shrubs and the tree he had torn up the day before and wondered what had happened to them. He wet his swollen tongue with the last few drops of water in his bag, climbed lackadaisically to his feet, and went to look for the dried-up remains.

There weren't any. He couldn't even find the holes where he had torn them out. The living village had absorbed the dead tissue into itself and had repaired the breaks in its "body."

That galvanized Jenner. He began to think again . . . about mutations, genetic readjustment, life forms adapting to new environments. There'd been lectures on that before the ship left Earth, rather generalized talks designed to acquaint the explorers with the problems men might face on an alien planet. The important principle was quite simple: adjust or die.

The village had to adjust to him. He doubted if he could seriously damage it, but he could try. His own need to survive must be placed on as sharp and hostile a basis as that.

Frantically Jenner began to search his pockets. Before leaving the rocket he had loaded himself with odds and ends of small equipment. A jackknife, a folding metal cup, a printed radio, a tiny super-battery that could be charged by spinning an attached wheel—and for which he had brought along, among other things, a powerful electric fire lighter.

Jenner plugged the lighter into the battery and deliberately scraped the red-hot end along the surface of the "marble." The reaction was swift. The substance turned an angry purple this time. When an entire section of the floor had changed color, Jenner headed for the nearest stall trough, entering far enough to activate it.

There was a noticeable delay. When the food finally flowed into the trough, it was clear that the living village had realized the reason for what he had done. The food was a pale, creamy color, where earlier it had been a murky gray.

Jenner put his finger into it but withdrew it with a yell and wiped his finger. It continued to sting for several moments. The vital question was: Had it deliberately offered him food that would damage him, or was it trying to appease him without knowing what he could eat?

He decided to give it another chance, and entered the adjoining stall. The gritty stuff that flooded up this time was yellower. It didn't burn his finger, but Jenner took one taste and spat it out. He had the feeling that he had been offered a soup made of a greasy mixture of clay and gasoline.

He was thirsty now with a need heightened by the unpleasant taste in his mouth. Desperately he rushed outside and tore open the water bag, seeking the wetness inside. In his fumbling eagerness, he spilled a few precious drops onto the courtyard. Down he went on his face and licked them up.

Half a minute later, he was still licking, and there was still water.

The fact penetrated suddenly. He raised himself and gazed wonderingly at the droplets of water that sparkled on the smooth stone. As he watched, another one squeezed up from the apparently solid surface and shimmered in the light of the sinking sun.

He bent, and with the tip of his tongue sponged up each visible drop. For a long time he lay with his mouth pressed to the "marble," sucking up the tiny bits of water that the village doled out to him.

The glowing white sun disappeared behind a hill. Night fell, like the dropping of a black screen. The air turned cold, then icy. He shivered as the wind keened through his ragged clothes. But what finally stopped him was the collapse of the surface from which he had been drinking.

Jenner lifted himself in surprise, and in the darkness gingerly felt over the stone. It had genuinely crumbled. Evidently the substance had yielded up its available water and had disintegrated in the process. Jenner estimated that he had drunk altogether an ounce of water.

It was a convincing demonstration of the willingness of the village to please him, but there was another, less satisfying, implication. If the village had to destroy a part of itself every time it gave him a drink, then clearly the supply was not unlimited.

Jenner hurried inside the nearest building, climbed onto a dais—and climbed off again hastily, as the heat blazed up at him. He waited, to give the Intelligence a chance to realize he wanted a change, then lay down once more. The heat was as great as ever.

He gave that up because he was too tired to persist and too sleepy to think of a method that might let the village know he needed a different bedroom temperature. He slept on the floor with an uneasy conviction that it could *not* sustain him for long. He woke up many times during the night and thought, "Not enough water. No matter how hard it tries—" Then he would sleep again, only to wake once more, tense and unhappy.

Nevertheless, morning found him briefly alert; and all his steely determination was back—that iron will power that had brought him at least five hundred miles across an unknown desert.

He headed for the nearest trough. This time, after he had activated it, there was a pause of more than a minute; and then about a thimbleful of water made a wet splotch at the bottom.

Jenner licked it dry, then waited hopefully for more. When none came he reflected gloomily that somewhere in the village an entire group of cells had broken down and released their water for him.

Then and there he decided that it was up to the human being, who could move around, to find a new source of water for the village, which could not move.

In the interim, of course, the village would have to keep him alive, until he had investigated the possibilities. That meant, above everything else, he must have some food to sustain him while he looked around.

He began to search his pockets. Toward the end of his food supply, he had carried scraps and pieces wrapped in small bits of cloth. Crumbs had broken off into the pocket, and he had searched for them often during those long days in the desert. Now, by actually ripping the seams, he discovered tiny particles of meat and bread, little bits of grease and other unidentifiable substances.

Carefully he leaned over the adjoining stall and placed the scrappings in the trough there. The village would not be able to offer him more than a reasonable facsimile. If the spilling of a few drops on the courtyard could make it aware of his need for water, then a similar offering might give it the clue it needed as to the chemical nature of the food he could eat.

Jenner waited, then entered the second stall and activated it. About a pint of thick, creamy substance trickled into the bottom of the trough. The smallness of the quantity seemed evidence that perhaps it contained water.

He tasted it. It had a sharp, musty flavor and a stale odor. It was almost as dry as flour—but his stomach did not reject it.

Jenner ate slowly, acutely aware that at such moments as this the village had him at its mercy. He could never be sure that one of the food ingredients was not a slow-acting poison.

When he had finished the meal he went to a food trough in another building. He refused to eat the food that came up, but activated still another trough. This time he received a few drops of water.

He had come purposefully to one of the tower buildings. Now he started up the ramp that led to the upper floor. He paused only briefly in the room he came to, as he had already discovered that they seemed to be additional bedrooms. The familiar dais was there in a group of three.

What interested him was that the circular ramp continued to wind on upward. First to another, smaller room that seemed to have no particular reason for being. Then it wound on up to the top of the tower, some seventy feet above the ground. It was high enough for him to see beyond the rim of all the surrounding hilltops. He had thought it might be, but he had been too weak to make the climb before. Now he looked out to every horizon. Almost immediately the hope that had brought him up faded.

The view was immeasurably desolate. As far as he could see was an arid waste, and every horizon was hidden in a midst of wind-blown sand.

Jenner gazed with a sense of despair. If there was a Martian sea out there somewhere, it was beyond his reach.

Abruptly he clenched his hands in anger against his fate, which seemed inevitable now. At the very worst, he had hoped he would find himself in a mountainous region. Seas and mountains were generally the two main sources of water. He should have known, of course, that there were very few mountains on Mars. It would have been a wild coincidence if he had actually run into a mountain range.

His fury faded because he lacked the strength to sustain any emotion. Numbly he went down the ramp.

His vague plan to help the village ended as swiftly and finally as that.

The days drifted by, but as to how many he had no idea. Each time he went to eat, a smaller amount of water was doled out to him. Jenner kept telling himself that each meal would have to be his last. It was unreasonable for him to expect the village to destroy itself when his fate was certain now.

What was worse, it became increasingly clear that the food was not good for him. He had misled the village as to his needs by giving it stale, perhaps even tainted, samples, and prolonged the agony for himself. At times after he had eaten, Jenner felt dizzy for hours. All too frequently his head ached and his body shivered with fever.

The village was doing what it could. The rest was up to him, and he couldn't even adjust to an approximation of Earth food.

For two days he was too sick to drag himself to one of the troughs. Hour after hour he lay on the floor. Some time during the second night the pain in his body grew so terrible that he finally made up his mind.

"If I can get to a dais," he told himself, "the heat alone will kill me; and in absorbing my body, the village will get back some of its lost water."

He spent at least an hour crawling laboriously up the ramp of the nearest dais, and when he finally made it, he lay as one already dead. His last waking thought was: "Beloved friends, I'm coming."

The hallucination was so complete that momentarily he seemed to be back in the control room of the rocketship, and all around him were his former companions.

With a sigh of relief Jenner sank into a dreamless sleep.

He woke to the sound of a violin. It was a sad-sweet music that told of the rise and fall of a race long dead.

Jenner listened for a while and then with abrupt excitement realized the truth. This was a substitute for the whistling—the village had adjusted its music to him!

Other sensory phenomena stole in upon him. The dais felt comfortably warm, not hot at all. He had a feeling of wonderful physical well-being.

Eagerly he scrambled down the ramp to the nearest food stall. As he crawled forward, his nose close to the floor, the trough filled with a steamy mixture. The odor was so rich and pleasant that he plunged his face into it and slopped it up greedily. It had the flavor of thick, meaty soup and was warm and soothing to his lips and mouth. When he had eaten it all, for the first time he did not need a drink of water.

"I've won!" thought Jenner. "The village has found a way!"

After a while he remembered something and crawled to the bathroom. Cautiously, watching the ceiling, he eased himself backward into the shower stall. The yellowish spray came down, cool and delightful.

Ecstatically Jenner wriggled his four-foot tail and lifted his long snout to let the thin streams of liquid wash away the food impurities that clung to his sharp teeth.

Then he waddled out to bask in the sun and listen to the timeless music.

9

ODDY AND ID

Alfred Bester (1913–)

ASTOUNDING SCIENCE FICTION
August

Like C. M. Kornbluth, Alfred Bester had published science fiction in the early 1940s but then stopped for some eight years to pursue other interests. When he returned to sf in 1950 he quickly established himself as a unique and ambitious writer, but one who published far too little. Almost all of his post-1950 short stories are memorable, and most can be found in Starlight *(1976). His two great novels of the 1950s,* The Demolished Man *(1953) and* Tiger! Tiger! *(1956, better known as* The Stars My Destination, *the title of the 1957 American edition), are rightly considered to be seminal works in the field. He again left science fiction when he went to work for* Holiday *magazine, but returned in the mid-1970s with several interesting stories and two novels,* The Computer Connection *(1975) and* Golem 100 *(1980), neither of which could live up to the legendary reputation of his first two.*

—*M.H.G.*

The last time I saw Alfie was at a small convention in New York over the Independence Day weekend of 1983. When a panel fell apart because a couple of the participants had unaccountably failed to show up, Alfie and I, who were in the audience, dutifully agreed to substitute.

A question from the audience was addressed to Alfie. The questioner wanted to know how Alfred Bester reacted to rejections.

A queer look came over Alfie's face. He looked helplessly

*from side to side and then said in a nervous voice. "I don't
know. I've never had a rejection."*

*He did well to look nervous. There are a hundred writers out
there, Alfie, who are going to get you for that. Even I average a
rejection a year. And yet, I can't expect a story like "Oddy and
Id" to be rejected.*

—*I.A.*

This is the story of a monster.

They named him Odysseus Gaul in honor of Papa's favorite
hero, and over Mama's desperate objections; but he was known
as Oddy from the age of one.

The first year of life is an egotistic craving for warmth and
security. Oddy was not likely to have much of that when he was
born, for Papa's real estate business was bankrupt, and Mama
was thinking of divorce. But an unexpected decision by United
Radiation to build a plant in the town made Papa wealthy, and
Mama fell in love with him all over again. So Oddy had warmth
and security.

The second year of life is a timid exploration. Oddy crawled
and explored. When he reached for the crimson coils inside the
non-objective fireplace, an unexpected short-circuit saved him
from a burn. When he fell out the third floor window, it was into
the grass filled hopper of the Mechano-Gardener. When he
teased the Phoebus Cat, it slipped as it snapped at his face, and
the brilliant fangs clicked harmlessly over his ear.

"Animals love Oddy," Mama said. "They only pretend to
bite."

Oddy wanted to be loved, so everybody loved Oddy. He was
petted, pampered and spoiled through pre-school age. Shopkeep-
ers presented him with largess, and acquaintances showered him
with gifts. Of sodas, candy, tarts, chrystons, bobbletucks, freezies
and various other comestibles, Oddy consumed enough for an
entire kindergarten. He was never sick.

"Takes after his father," Papa said. "Good stock."

Family legends grew about Oddy's luck. . . . How a perfect
stranger mistook him for his own child just as Oddy was about to
amble into the Electronic Circus, and delayed him long enough
to save him from the disastrous explosion of '98. . . . How a

forgotten library book rescued him from the Rocket Crash of '99. . . . How a multitude of odd incidents saved him from a multitude of assorted catastrophes. No one realized he was a monster . . . yet.

At eighteen, he was a nice looking boy with seal brown hair, warm brown eyes and a wide grin that showed even white teeth. He was strong, healthy, intelligent. He was completely uninhibited in his quiet, relaxed way. He had charm. He was happy. So far, his monstrous evil had only affected the little Town Unit where he was born and raised.

He came to Harvard from a Progressive School, so when one of his many quick friends popped into the dormitory room and said: "Hey Oddy, come down to the Quad and kick a ball around." Oddy answered: "I don't know how, Ben."

"Don't know how?" Ben tucked the football under his arm and dragged Oddy with him. "Where you been, laddie?"

"They didn't talk much about football back home," Oddy grinned. "Thought it was old fashioned. We were strictly Huxley-Hob."

"Huxley-Hob! That's for hi-brows," Ben said. "Football is still the big game. You want to be famous? You got to be on that gridiron before the Video every Saturday."

"So I've noticed, Ben. Show me."

Ben showed Oddy, carefully and with patience. Oddy took the lesson seriously and industriously. His third punt was caught by a freakish gust of wind, travelled seventy yards through the air, and burst through the third floor window of Proctor Charley (Gravy-Train) Stuart. Stuart took one look out the window and had Oddy down to Soldier Stadium in half an hour. Three Saturdays later, the headlines read: ODDY GAUL 57–ARMY 0.

"Snell & Rumination!" Coach Hig Clayton swore. "How does he do it? There's nothing sensational about that kid. He's just average. But when he runs they fall down chasing him. When he kicks, they fumble. When they fumble, he recovers."

"He's a negative player," Gravy-Train answered. "He lets you make the mistakes and then he cashes in."

They were both wrong. Oddy Gaul was a monster.

With his choice of any eligible young woman, Oddy Gaul went stag to the Observatory Prom, wandered into a darkroom by mistake, and discovered a girl in a smock bending over trays in the hideous green safe-light. She had cropped black hair, icy blue eyes, strong features, and a sensuous boyish figure. She ordered him out and Oddy fell in love with her . . . temporarily.

His friends howled with laughter when he told them. "Shades of Pygmalion, Oddy, don't you know about *her?* The girl is frigid. A statue. She loathes men. You're wasting your time."

But through the adroitness of her analyst, the girl turned a neurotic corner one week later and fell deeply in love with Oddy Gaul. It was sudden, devastating and enraptured for two months. Then just as Oddy began to cool, the girl had a relapse and everything ended on a friendly, convenient basis.

So far only minor events made up the response to Oddy's luck, but the shock-wave of reaction was spreading. In September of his Sophomore year, Oddy competed for the Political Economy Medal with a thesis entitled: "Causes Of Mutiny." The striking similarity of his paper to the Astraean Mutiny that broke out the day his paper was entered won him the prize.

In October, Oddy contributed twenty dollars to a pool organized by a crack-pot classmate for speculating on the Exchange according to 'Stock Market Trends,' a thousand year old superstition. The seer's calculations were ridiculous, but a sharp panic nearly ruined the Exchange as it quadrupled the pool. Oddy made one hundred dollars.

And so it went . . . worse and worse. The monster.

Now a monster can get away with a lot when he's studying speculative philosophy where causation is rooted in history and the Present is devoted to statistical analysis of the Past; but the living sciences are bulldogs with their teeth clamped on the phenomena of Now. So it was Jesse Migg, physiologist and spectral physicist, who first trapped the monster . . . and he thought he was an angel.

Old Jess was one of the Sights. In the first place he was young . . . not over forty. He was a malignant knife of a man, an albino, pink-eyed, bald, pointed-nosed and brilliant. He affected 20th Century clothes and 20th Century vices . . . tobacco and potations of C_2H_5OH. He never talked . . . He spat. He never walked . . . He scurried. And he was scurrying up and down the aisles of the laboratory of Tech I (General Survey of Spatial Mechanics—Required for All General Arts Students) when he ferreted out the monster.

One of the first experiments in the course was EMF Electrolysis. Elementary stuff. A U-Tube containing water was passed between the poles of a stock Remosant Magnet. After sufficient voltage was transmitted through the coils, you drew off Hydrogen and Oxygen in two-to-one ratio at the arms of the tube and related them to the voltage and the magnetic field.

Oddy ran his experiment earnestly, got the proper results, entered them in his lab book and then waited for the official check-off. Little Migg came hustling down the aisle, darted to Oddy and spat: "Finished?"

"Yes, sir."

Migg checked the book entries, glanced at the indicators at the ends of the tube, and stamped Oddy out with a sneer. It was only after Oddy was gone that he noticed the Remosant Magnet was obviously shorted. The wires were fused. There hadn't been any field to electrolyse the water.

"Curse and Confusion!" Migg grunted (he also affected 20th Century vituperation) and rolled a clumsy cigarette.

He checked off possibilities in his comptometer head. 1. Gaul cheated. 2. If so, with what apparatus did he portion out the H_2 and O_2? 3. Where did he get the pure gases? 4. Why did he do it? Honesty was easier. 5. He didn't cheat. 6. How did he get the right results? 7. How did he get *any* results?

Old Jess emptied the U-Tube, refilled it with water and ran off the experiment himself. He too got the correct result without a magnet.

"Rice on a Raft!" he swore, unimpressed by the miracle, and infuriated by the mystery. He snooped, darting about like a hungry bat. After four hours he discovered that the steel bench supports were picking up a charge from the Greeson Coils in the basement and had thrown just enough field to make everything come out right.

"Coincidence," Migg spat. But he was not convinced.

Two weeks later, in Elementary Fission Analysis, Oddy completed his afternoon's work with a careful listing of resultant isotopes from selenium to lanthanum. The only trouble, Migg discovered, was that there had been a mistake in the stock issued to Oddy. He hadn't received any U^{235} for neutron bombardment. His sample had been a left-over from a Stefan-Boltsmann blackbody demonstration.

"Frog in Heaven!" Migg swore, and double-checked. Then he triple-checked. When he found the answer . . . a remarkable coincidence involving improperly cleaned apparatus and a defective cloud-chamber, he swore further. He also did some intensive thinking.

"There are accident prones," Migg snarled at the reflection in his Self-Analysis Mirror. "How about Good Luck prones? Horse Manure!"

But he was a bulldog with his teeth sunk in phenomena. He tested Oddy Gaul. He hovered over him in the laboratory, cackling with infuriated glee as Oddy completed experiment after experiment with defective equipment. When Oddy successfully completed the Rutherford Classic . . . getting $_8O^{17}$ after exposing nitrogen to alpha radiation . . . but in this case without the use of nitrogen or alpha radiation . . . Migg actually clapped him on the back in delight. Then the little man investigated and found the logical, improbable chain of coincidences that explained it.

He devoted his spare time to a check-back on Oddy's career at Harvard. He had a two hour conference with a lady astronomer's faculty analyst, and a ten minute talk with Hig Clayton and Gravy-Train Stuart. He rooted out the Exchange Pool, the Political Economy Medal, and half a dozen other incidents that filled him with malignant joy. Then he cast off his 20th Century affectation, dressed himself properly in formal leotards, and entered the Faculty Club for the first time in a year.

A four-handed chess game in three dimensions was in progress in the Diathermy Alcove. It had been in progress since Migg joined the faculty, and would probably not be finished before the end of the century. In fact, Johansen, playing Red, was already training his son to replace him in the likely event of his dying before the completion of the game.

As abrupt as ever, Migg marched up to the glowing cube, sparkling with sixteen layers of vari-colored pieces, and blurted: "What do you know about accidents?"

"Ah?" said Bellanby, *Philosopher in Res* at the University. "Good evening, Migg. Do you mean the accident of substance, or the accident of essence? If, on the other hand, your question implies—"

"No, no," Migg interrupted. "My apologies, Bellanby. Let me rephrase the question. Is there such a thing as Compulsion of Probability?"

Hrrdnikkisch completed his move and gave full attention to Migg, as did Johansen and Bellanby. Wilson continued to study the board. Since he was permitted one hour to make his move and would need it, Migg knew there would be ample time for the discussion.

"Compulthon of Probability?" Hrrdnikkisch lisped. "Not a

new conthept, Migg. I recall a thurvey of the theme in 'The Integraph' Vol. LVIII, No. 9. The calculuth, if I am not mithtaken—''

"No," Migg interrupted again. "My respects, Signoid. I'm not interested in the mathematic of Probability, nor the philosophy. Let me put it this way. The Accident Prone has already been incorporated into the body of Psychoanalysis. Paton's Theorem of the Least Neurotic Norm settled that. But I've discovered the obverse. I've discovered a Fortune Prone."

"Ah?" Johansen chuckled. "It's to be a joke. You wait and see, Signoid."

"No," answered Migg. "I'm perfectly serious. I've discovered a genuinely lucky man."

"He wins at cards?"

"He wins at everything. Accept this postulate for the moment . . . I'll document it later . . . There is a man who is lucky. He is a Fortune Prone. Whatever he desires, he receives. Whether he has the ability to achieve it or not, he receives it. If his desire is totally beyond the peak of his accomplishment, then the factors of chance, coincidence, hazard, accident . . . and so on, combine to produce his desired end."

"No." Bellanby shook his head. "Too far-fetched."

"I've worked it out empirically," Migg continued. "It's something like this. The future is a choice of mutually exclusive possibilities, one or other of which must be realized in terms of favorability of the events and number of the events . . ."

"Yes, yes," interrupted Johansen. "The greater the number of favorable possibilities, the stronger the probability of an event maturing. This is elementary, Migg. Go on."

"I continue," Migg spat indignantly. "When we discuss Probability in terms of throwing dice, the predictions or odds are simple. There are only six mutually exclusive possibilities to each die. The favorability is easy to compute. Chance is reduced to simple odds-ratios. *But* when we discuss probability in terms of the Universe, we cannot encompass enough data to make a prediction. There are too many factors. Favorability cannot be ascertained."

"All thith ith true," Hrrdnikkisch said, "but what of your Fortune Prone?"

"I don't know how he does it . . . but merely by the intensity or mere existence of his desire, he can affect the favorability of possibilities. By wanting, he can turn possibility into probability, and probability into certainty."

"Ridiculous," Bellanby snapped. "You claim there's a man far-sighted and far-reaching enough to do this?"

"Nothing of the sort. He doesn't know what he's doing. He just thinks he's lucky, if he thinks about it at all. Let us say he wants . . . Oh . . . Name anything."

"Heroin," Bellanby said.

"What's that?" Johansen inquired.

"A morphine derivative," Hrrdnikkisch explained. "Formerly manufactured and thold to narcotic addictth."

"Heroin," Migg said. "Excellent. Say my man desires Heroin, an antique narcotic no longer in existence. Very good. His desire would compel this sequence of possible but improbable events: A chemist in Australia, fumbling through a new organic synthesis, will accidentally and unwittingly prepare six ounces of Heroin. Four ounces will be discarded, but through a logical mistake two ounces will be preserved. A further coincidence will ship it to this country and this city, wrapped as powdered sugar in a plastic ball; where the final accident will serve it to my man in a restaurant which he is visiting for the first time on an impulse. . . ."

"La-La-La!" said Hrrdnikkisch. "Thith shuffling of hithtory. Thith fluctuation of inthident and pothibility? All achieved without the knowledge but with the dethire of a man?"

"Yes. Precisely my point," Migg snarled. "I don't know how he does it, but he turns possibility into certainty. And since almost anything is possible, he is capable of accomplishing almost anything. He is God-like but not a God because he does this without consciousness. He is an angel."

"Who is this angel?" Johansen asked.

And Migg told them all about Oddy Gaul.

"But how does he do it?" Bellanby persisted. "How does he do it?"

"I don't know," Migg repeated again. "Tell me how Espers do it."

"What!" Bellanby exclaimed. "Are you prepared to deny the EK pattern of thought? Do you—"

"I do nothing of the sort. I merely illustrate one possible explanation. Man produces events. The threatening War of Resources may be thought to be a result of the natural exhaustion of terran resources. We know it is not. It is a result of centuries of thriftless waste by man. Natural phenomena are less often produced by nature and more often produced by man."

"And?"

"Who knows? Gaul is producing phenomena. Perhaps he's unconsciously broadcasting on an EK waveband. Broadcasting and getting results. He wants Heroin. The broadcast goes out—"

"But Espers can't pick up any EK brain pattern further than the horizon. It's direct wave transmission. Even large objects cannot be penetrated. A building, say, or a—"

"I'm not saying this is on the Esper level," Migg shouted. "I'm trying to imagine something bigger. Something tremendous. He wants Heroin. His broadcast goes out to the world. All men unconsciously fall into a pattern of activity which will produce that Heroin as quickly as possible. That Austrian chemist—"

"No. Australian."

"That Australian chemist may have been debating between half a dozen different syntheses. Five of them could never have produced Heroin; but Gaul's impulse made him select the sixth."

"And if he did not anyway?"

"Then who knows what parallel chains were also started? A boy playing Cops and Robbers in Montreal is impelled to explore an abandoned cabin where he finds the drug, hidden there centuries ago by smugglers. A woman in California collects old apothecary jars. She finds a pound of Heroin. A child in Berlin, playing with a defective Radar-Chem Set, manufactures it. Name the most improbable sequence of events, and Gaul can bring it about, logically and certainly. I tell you, that boy is an angel!"

And he produced his documented evidence and convinced them.

It was then that four scholars of various but indisputable intellects elected themselves an executive committee for Fate and took Oddy Gaul in hand. To understand what they attempted to do, you must first understand the situation the world found itself in during that particular era.

It is a known fact that all wars are founded in economic conflict, or to put it another way, a trial by arms is merely the last battle of an economic war. In the pre-Christian centuries, the Punic Wars were the final outcome of a financial struggle between Rome and Carthage for economic control of the Mediterranean. Three thousand years later, the impending War of Resources loomed as the finale of a struggle between the two

Independent Welfare States controlling most of the known economic world.

What petroleum oil was to the 20th Century, FO (the nickname for Fissionable Ore) was to the 30th; and the situation was peculiarly similar to the Asia Minor crisis that ultimately wrecked the United Nations a thousand years before. Triton, a backward, semibarbaric satellite, previously unwanted and ignored, had suddenly discovered it possessed enormous resources of FO. Financially and technologically incapable of self-development, Triton was peddling concessions to both Welfare States.

The difference between a Welfare State and a Benevolent Despot is slight. In times of crisis, either can be traduced by the sincerest motives into the most abominable conduct. Both the Comity of Nations (bitterly nicknamed "The Con Men" by Der Realpolitik aus Terra) and Der Realpolitik aus Terra (sardonically called "The Rats" by the Comity of Nations) were desperately in need of natural resources, meaning FO. They were bidding against each other hysterically, and elbowing each other with sharp skirmishes at outposts. Their sole concern was the protection of their citizens. From the best of motives they were preparing to cut each other's throat.

Had this been the issue before the citizens of both Welfare States, some compromise might have been reached; but Triton in the catbird seat, intoxicated as a schoolboy with newfound prominence and power, confused issues by raising a religious question and reviving a Holy War which the Family of Planets had long forgotten. Assistance in their Holy War (involving the extermination of a harmless and rather unimportant sect called the Quakers) was one of the conditions of sale. This, both the Comity of Nations and Der Realpolitik aus Terra were prepared to swallow with or without private reservations, but it could not be admitted to their citizens.

And so, camouflaged by the burning issues of Rights of Minority Sects, Priority of Pioneering, Freedom of Religion, Historical Rights to Triton v. Possession in Fact, etc., the two Houses of the Family of Planets feinted, parried, riposted and slowly closed, like fencers on the strip, for the final sortie which meant ruin for both.

All this the four men discussed through three interminable meetings.

"Look here," Migg complained toward the close of the third

consultation. "You theoreticians have already turned nine man-hours into carbonic acid with ridiculous dissensions . . ."

Bellanby nodded, smiling. "It's as I've always said, Migg. Every man nurses the secret belief that were he God he could do the job much better. We're just learning how difficult it is."

"Not God," Hrrdnikkisch said, "but hith Prime Minithterth. Gaul will be God."

Johansen winced. "I don't like that talk," he said. "I happen to be a religious man."

"You?" Bellanby exclaimed in surprise. "A Colloid-Therapeutist?"

"I happen to be a religious man," Johansen repeated stubbornly.

"But the boy hath the power of the miracle," Hrrdnikkisch protested. "When he hath been taught to know what he doeth, he will be a God."

"This is pointless," Migg rapped out. "We have spent three sessions in piffling discussion. I have heard three opposed views re Mr. Odysseus Gaul. Although all are agreed he must be used as a tool, none can agree on the work to which the tool must be set. Bellanby prattles about an Ideal Intellectual Anarchy, Johansen preaches about a Soviet of God, and Hrrdnikkisch has wasted two hours postulating and destroying his own theorems . . ."

"Really, Migg . . ." Hrrdnikkisch began. Migg waved his hand.

"Permit me," Migg continued malevolently, "to reduce this discussion to the kindergarten level. First things first, gentlemen. Before attempting to reach cosmic agreement we must make sure there is a cosmos left for us to agree upon. I refer to the impending war . . .

"Our program, as I see it, must be simple and direct. It is the education of a God or, if Johansen protests, of an angel. Fortunately Gaul is an estimable young man of kindly, honest disposition. I shudder to think what he might have done had he been inherently vicious."

"Or what he might do once he learns what he can do," muttered Bellanby.

"Precisely. We must begin a careful and rigorous ethical education of the boy, but we haven't enough time. We can't educate first, and then explain the truth when he's safe. We must forestall the war. We need a short-cut."

"All right," Johansen said. "What do you suggest?"

"Dazzlement," Migg spat. "Enchantment."

"Enchantment?" Hrrdnikkisch chuckled. "A new thienth, Migg?"

"Why do you think I selected you three of all people for this secret?" Migg snorted. "For your intellects? Nonsense! I can think you all under the table. No. I selected you, gentlemen, for your charm."

"It's an insult," Bellanby grinned, "and yet I'm flattered."

"Gaul is nineteen," Migg went on. "He is at the age when undergraduates are more susceptible to hero-worship. I want you gentlemen to charm him. You are not the first brains of the University, but you are the first heroes."

"I altho am inthulted and flattered," said Hrrdnikkisch.

"I want you to charm him, dazzle him, inspire him with affection and awe . . . as you've done with countless classes of undergraduates."

"Aha!" said Johansen. "The chocolate around the pill."

"Exactly. When he's enchanted, you will make him want to stop the war . . . and then tell him how he can stop it. That will give us breathing space to continue his education. By the time he outgrows his respect for you he will have a sound ethical foundation on which to build. He'll be safe."

"And you, Migg?" Bellanby inquired. "What part do you play?"

"Now? None," Migg snarled. "I have no charm, gentlemen. I come later. When he outgrows his respect for you, he'll begin to acquire respect for me."

All of which was frightfully conceited but perfectly true.

And as events slowly marched toward the final crisis, Oddy Gaul was carefully and quickly enchanted. Bellanby invited him to the twenty foot crystal globe atop his house . . . the famous hen-roost to which only the favored few were invited. There, Oddy Gaul sun-bathed and admired the philosopher's magnificent iron-hard condition at seventy-three. Admiring Bellanby's muscles, it was only natural for him to admire Bellanby's ideas. He returned often to sunbathe, worship the great man, and absorb ethical concepts.

Meanwhile, Hrrdnikkisch took over Oddy's evenings. With the mathematician, who puffed and lisped like some flamboyant character out of Rabelais, Oddy was carried to the dizzy heights of the *haute cuisine* and the complete pagan life. Together they ate and drank incredible foods and liquids and pursued incredible women until Oddy returned to his room each night, intoxicated with the magic of the senses and the riotous color of the great Hrrdnikkisch's glittering ideas.

And occasionally . . . not too often, he would find Papa Johansen waiting for him, and then would come the long quiet talks through the small hours when young men search for the harmonics of life and the meaning of entity. And there was Johansen for Oddy to model himself after . . . a glowing embodiment of Spiritual Good . . . a living example of Faith in God and Ethical Sanity.

The climax came on March 15th. . . . The Ides of March, and they should have taken the date as a sign. After dinner with his three heroes at the Faculty Club, Oddy was ushered into the Foto-Library by the three great men where they were joined, quite casually, by Jesse Migg. There passed a few moments of uneasy tension until Migg made a sign, and Bellanby began.

"Oddy," he said, "have you ever had the fantasy that some day you might wake up and discover you were a King?"

Oddy blushed.

"I see you have. You know, every man has entertained that dream. The usual pattern is: You learn your parents only adopted you, and that you are actually and rightfully the King of . . . of . . ."

"Baratraria," said Hrrdnikkisch who had made a study of Stone Age Fiction.

"Yes, sir," Oddy muttered. "I've had that dream."

"Well," Bellanby said quietly, "it's come true. You are a King."

Oddy stared while they explained and explained and explained. First, as a college boy, he was wary and suspicious of a joke. Then, as an idolator, he was almost persuaded by the men he most admired. And finally, as a human animal, he was swept away by the exaltation of security. Not power, not glory, not wealth thrilled him, but security alone. Later he might come to enjoy the trimmings, but now he was released from fear. He need never worry again.

"Yes," exclaimed Oddy. "Yes, yes, yes! I understand. I understand what you want me to do." He surged up excitedly from his chair and circled the illuminated walls, trembling with joy and intoxication. Then he stopped and turned.

"And I'm grateful," he said. "Grateful to all of you for what you've been trying to do. It would have been shameful if I'd been selfish . . . or mean . . . Trying to use this for myself. But you've shown me the way. It's to be used for good. Always!''

Johansen nodded happily.

"I'll always listen to you," Oddy went on. "I don't want to make any mistakes. Ever!" He paused and blushed again. "That dream about being a king . . . I had that when I was a kid. But here at the school I've had something bigger. I used to wonder what would happen if I was the one man who could run the world. I used to dream about the kind things I'd do . . .''

"Yes," said Bellanby. "We know, Oddy. We've all had that dream too. Every man does.''

"But it isn't a dream any more," Oddy laughed. "It's reality. I can do it. I can make it happen.''

"Start with the war," Migg said sourly.

"Of course," said Oddy. "The war first; but then we'll go on from there, won't we? I'll make sure the war never starts, but then we'll do big things . . . great things! Just the five of us in private. Nobody'll know about us. We'll be ordinary people, but we'll make life wonderful for everybody. If I'm an angel . . . like you say . . . then I'll spread heaven around me as far as I can reach.''

"But start with the war," Migg repeated.

"The war is the first disaster that must be averted, Oddy," Bellanby said. "If you don't want this disaster to happen, it will never happen.''

"And you want to prevent that tragedy, don't you?'' said Johansen.

"Yes," answered Oddy. "I do.''

On March 20th, the war broke. The Comity of Nations and Der Realpolitik aus Terra mobilized and struck. While blow followed shattering counter-blow, Oddy Gaul was commissioned Subaltern in a Line regiment, but gazetted to Intelligence on May 3rd. On June 24th he was appointed A.D.C. to the Joint Forces Council meeting in the ruins of what had been Australia. On July 11th he was brevetted to command of the wrecked Space Force, being jumped 1,789 grades over regular officers. On September 19th he assumed supreme command in the Battle of the Parsec and won the victory that ended the disastrous solar annihilation called the Six Month War.

On September 23rd, Oddy Gaul made the astonishing Peace Offer that was accepted by the remnants of both Welfare States. It required the scrapping of antagonistic economic theories, and amounted to the virtual abandonment of all economic theory with an amalgamation of both States into a Solar Society. On January 1st, Oddy Gaul, by unanimous acclaim, was elected Solon of the Solar Society in perpetuity.

And today . . . still youthful, still vigorous, still handsome, still sincere, idealistic, charitable, kindly and sympathetic, he lives in the Solar Palace. He is unmarried but a mighty lover; uninhibited, but a charming host and devoted friend; democratic, but the feudal overlord of a bankrupt Family of Planets that suffers misgovernment, oppression, poverty and confusion with a cheerful joy that sings nothing but Hosannahs to the glory of Oddy Gaul.

In a last moment of clarity, Jesse Migg communicated his desolate summation of the situation to his friends in the Faculty Club. This was shortly before they made the trip to join Oddy in the palace as his confidential and valued advisers.

"We were fools," Migg said bitterly. "We should have killed him. He isn't an angel. He's a monster. Civilization and culture . . . philosophy and ethics . . . Those were only masks Oddy put on; masks that covered the primitive impulses of his subconscious mind."

"You mean Oddy was not sincere?" Johansen asked heavily. "He wanted this wreckage . . . this ruin?"

"Certainly he was sincere . . . consciously. He still is. He thinks he desires nothing but the most good for the most men. He's honest, kind and generous . . . but only consciously."

"Ah! The Id!" said Hrrdnikkisch with an explosion of breath as though he had been punched in the stomach.

"You understand, Signoid? I see you do. Gentlemen, we were imbeciles. We made the mistake of assuming that Oddy would have conscious control of his power. He does not. The control was and still is below the thinking, reasoning level. The control lies in Oddy's Id . . . in that deep unconscious reservoir of primordial selfishness that lies within every man."

"Then he wanted the war," Bellanby said.

"His Id wanted the war, Bellanby. It was the quickest route to what his Id desires . . . to be Lord of the Universe and Loved by the Universe . . . and his Id controls the Power. All of us have that selfish, egocentric Id within us, perpetually searching for satisfaction, timeless, immortal, knowing no logic, no values, no good and evil, no morality; and that is what controls the power in Oddy. He will always get not what he's been educated to desire but what his Id desires. It's the inescapable conflict that may be the doom of our system.''

"But we'll be there to advise him . . . counsel him . . . guide him," Bellanby protested. "He asked us to come.''

"And he'll listen to our advice like the good child that he is," Migg answered, "Agreeing with us, trying to make a heaven for everybody while his Id will be making a hell for everybody. Oddy isn't unique. We all suffer from the same conflict . . . but Oddy has the power.''

"What can we do?" Johansen groaned. "What can we do?''

"I don't know." Migg bit his lip, then bobbed his head to Papa Johansen in what amounted to apology for him. "Johansen," he said, "you were right. There must be a God, if only because there must be an opposite to Oddy Gaul who was most assuredly invented by the Devil.''

But that was Jesse Migg's last sane statement. Now, of course, he adores Gaul the Glorious, Gaul the Gauleiter, Gaul the God Eternal who has achieved the savage, selfish satisfaction for which all of us unconsciously yearn from birth, but which only Oddy Gaul has won.

10
THE SACK

William Morrison
(Joseph Samachson, 1906–1982)

ASTOUNDING SCIENCE FICTION
September

The late Joseph Samachson was a chemist in the Chicago area who wrote children's books on the side. As "William Morrison" he produced some fifty stories for the science fiction magazines in the 1950s, most notably "Country Doctor" (1953), "The Model of a Judge" (1953), and the present selection. He was a very capable writer, but unfortunately he never had a collection, and he is largely unknown today. His absence from such standard reference works as The Science Fiction Encyclopedia *and* Twentieth Century Science Fiction Writers *is a glaring omission.*
—M.H.G.

We are into the McCarthy era now. In February, 1950, Senator Joseph R. McCarthy of Wisconsin made a ridiculous and never-substantiated charge of Communists in the State Department and began a four-year reign of terror that turned government officials into cravens and disgraced us all.

This story, "The Sack," appeared in a magazine that was on the newsstands in August of that year, and it must have been written some months before. Was the stupid and hateful Senator Horrigan a take-off on McCarthy and, perhaps, the first bitter satire on that horrible man? (My own satire didn't come till two years later.) Or was Morrison merely prescient, having written the story prior to McCarthy's emergence from the slime?

We may never know.

—I.A.

At first they hadn't even known that the Sack existed. If they had noticed it at all when they landed on the asteroid, they thought of it merely as one more outpost of rock on the barren expanse of roughly ellipsoidal silicate surface, which Captain Ganko noticed had major and minor axes roughly three and two miles in diameter, respectively. It would never have entered anyone's mind that the unimpressive object they had unconsciously acquired would soon be regarded as the most valuable prize in the system.

The landing had been accidental. The government patrol ship had been limping along, and now it had settled down for repairs, which would take a good seventy hours. Fortunately, they had plenty of air, and their recirculation system worked to perfection. Food was in somewhat short supply, but it didn't worry them, for they knew that they could always tighten their belts and do without full rations for a few days. The loss of water that had resulted from a leak in the storage tanks, however, was a more serious matter. It occupied a good part of their conversation during the next fifty hours.

Captain Ganko said finally, "There's no use talking, it won't be enough. And there are no supply stations close enough at hand to be of any use. We'll have to radio ahead and hope that they can get a rescue ship to us with a reserve supply."

The helmet mike of his next in command seemed to droop. "It'll be too bad if we miss each other in space, Captain."

Captain Ganko laughed unhappily. "It certainly will. In that case we'll have a chance to see how we can stand a little dehydration."

For a time nobody said anything. At last, however, the second mate suggested, "There might be water somewhere on the asteroid, sir."

"Here? How in Pluto would it stick, with a gravity that isn't even strong enough to hold loose rocks? And where the devil would it be?"

"To answer the first question first, it would be retained as water of crystallization," replied a soft liquid voice that seemed to penetrate his spacesuit and come from behind him. "To answer the second question, it is half a dozen feet below the surface, and can easily be reached by digging."

They had all swiveled around at the first words. But no one was in sight in the direction from which the words seemed to come. Captain Ganko frowned, and his eyes narrowed dangerously.

"We don't happen to have a practical joker with us, do we?" he asked mildly.

"You do not," replied the voice.

"Who said that?"

"I, Yzrl."

A crewman became aware of something moving on the surface of one of the great rocks, and pointed to it. The motion stopped when the voice ceased, but they didn't lose sight of it again. That was how they learned about Yzrl, or as it was more often called, the Mind-Sack.

If the ship and his services hadn't both belonged to the government, Captain Ganko could have claimed the Sack for himself or his owners and retired with a wealth far beyond his dreams. As it was, the thing passed into government control. Its importance was realized almost from the first, and Jake Siebling had reason to be proud when more important and more influential figures of the political and industrial world were finally passed over and he was made Custodian of the Sack. Siebling was a short, stocky man whose one weakness was self-deprecation. He had carried out one difficult assignment after another and allowed other men to take the credit. But this job was not one for a blowhard, and those in charge of making the appointment knew it. For once they looked beyond credit and superficial reputation, and chose an individual they disliked somewhat but trusted absolutely. It was one of the most effective tributes to honesty and ability ever devised.

The Sack, as Siebling learned from seeing it daily, rarely deviated from the form in which it had made its first appearance—a rocky, grayish lump that roughly resembled a sack of potatoes. It had no features, and there was nothing, when it was not being asked questions, to indicate that it had life. It ate rarely—once in a thousand years, it said, when left to itself; once a week when it was pressed into steady use. It ate or moved by fashioning a suitable pseudopod and stretching the thing out in whatever way it pleased. When it had attained its objective, the pseudopod was withdrawn into the main body again and the creature became once more a potato sack.

It turned out later that the name "Sack" was well chosen from another point of view, in addition to that of appearance. For the Sack was stuffed with information, and beyond that, with wisdom. There were many doubters at first, and some of them retained their doubts to the very end, just as some people remained convinced hundreds of years after Columbus that the Earth was flat. But those who saw and heard the Sack had no doubts at all. They tended, if anything, to go too far in the other direction, and to believe that the Sack knew everything. This, of course, was untrue.

It was the official function of the Sack, established by a series of Interplanetary acts, to answer questions. The first questions, as we have seen, were asked accidentally, by Captain Ganko. Later they were asked purposefully, but with a purpose that was itself random, and a few politicians managed to acquire considerable wealth before the Government put a stop to the leak of information, and tried to have the questions asked in a more scientific and logical manner.

Question time was rationed for months in advance, and sold at what was, all things considered, a ridiculously low rate—a mere hundred thousand credits a minute. It was this unrestricted sale of time that led to the first great government squabble.

It was the unexpected failure of the Sack to answer what must have been to a mind of its ability an easy question that led to the second blowup, which was fierce enough to be called a crisis. A total of a hundred and twenty questioners, each of whom had paid his hundred thousand, raised a howl that could be heard on every planet, and there was a legislative investigation, at which Siebling testified and all the conflicts were aired.

He had left an assistant in charge of the Sack, and now, as he sat before the Senatorial Committee, he twisted uncomfortably in front of the battery of cameras. Senator Horrigan, his chief interrogator, was a bluff, florid, loud-mouthed politician who had been able to imbue him with a feeling of guilt even as he told his name, age, and length of government service.

"It is your duty to see to it that the Sack is maintained in proper condition for answering questions, is it not, Mr. Siebling?" demanded Senator Horrigan.

"Yes, sir."

"Then why was it incapable of answering the questioners in question? These gentlemen had honestly paid their money—a hundred thousand credits each. It was necessary, I understand, to refund the total sum. That meant an over-all loss to the Government of, let me see now—one hundred twenty at one hundred thousand each—one hundred and twenty million credits," he shouted, rolling the words.

"Twelve million, Senator," hastily whispered his secretary.

The correction was not made, and the figure was duly head-lined later as one hundred and twenty million.

Siebling said, "As we discovered later, Senator, the Sack failed to answer questions because it was not a machine, but a living creature. It was exhausted. It had been exposed to questioning on a twenty-four-hour-a-day basis."

"And who permitted this idiotic procedure?" boomed Senator Horrigan.

"You yourself, Senator," said Siebling happily. "The procedure was provided for in the bill introduced by you and approved by your committee."

Senator Horrigan had never even read the bill to which his name was attached, and he was certainly not to blame for its provisions. But this private knowledge of his own innocence did him no good with the public. From that moment he was Siebling's bitter enemy.

"So the Sack ceased to answer questions for two whole hours?"

"Yes, sir. It resumed only after a rest."

"And it answered them without further difficulty?"

"No, sir. Its response was slowed down. Subsequent questioners complained that they were defrauded of a good part of their money. But as answers were given, we considered that the complaints were without merit, and the financial department refused to make refunds."

"Do you consider that this cheating of investors in the Sack's time is honest?"

"That's none of my business, Senator," returned Siebling, who had by this time got over most of his nervousness. "I merely see to the execution of the laws. I leave the question of honesty to those who make them. I presume that it's in perfectly good hands."

Senator Horrigan flushed at the laughter that came from the onlookers. He was personally unpopular, as unpopular as a politician can be and still remain a politician. He was disliked even by the members of his own party, and some of his best political friends were among the laughers. He decided to abandon what had turned out to be an unfortunate line of questioning.

"It is a matter of fact, Mr. Siebling, is it not, that you have frequently refused admittance to investors who were able to show perfectly valid receipts for their credits?"

"That is a fact, sir. But——"

"You admit it, then."

"There is no question of 'admitting' anything, Senator. What I meant to say was——"

"Never mind what you meant to say. It's what you have already said that's important. You've cheated these men of their money!"

"That is not true, sir. They were given time later. The reason for my refusal to grant them admission when they asked for it was that the time had been previously reserved for the Armed Forces. There are important research questions that come up, and there is, as you know, a difference of opinion as to priority. When confronted with requisitions for time from a commercial investor and a representative of the Government, I never took it upon myself to settle the question. I always consulted with the Government's legal adviser."

"So you refused to make an independent decision, did you?"

"My duty, Senator, is to look after the welfare of the Sack. I do not concern myself with political questions. We had a moment of free time the day before I left the asteroid, when an investor who had already paid his money was delayed by a space accident, so instead of letting the moment go to waste, I utilized it to ask the Sack a question."

"How you might advance your own fortunes, no doubt?"

"No, sir. I merely asked it how it might function most efficiently. I took the precaution of making a recording, knowing that my word might be doubted. If you wish, Senator, I can introduce the recording in evidence."

Senator Horrigan grunted, and waved his hand. "Go on with your answer."

"The Sack replied that it would require two hours of complete rest out of every twenty, plus an additional hour of what it called 'recreation.' That is, it wanted to converse with some human being who would ask what it called sensible questions, and not press for a quick answer."

"So you suggest that the Government waste three hours of every twenty—one hundred and eighty million credits?"

"Eighteen million," whispered the secretary.

"The time would not be wasted. Any attempt to overwork the Sack would result in its premature annihilation."

"That is your idea, is it?"

"No, sir, that is what the Sack itself said."

At this point Senator Horrigan swung into a speech of

denunciation, and Siebling was excused from further testimony. Other witnesses were called, but at the end the Senate investigating body was able to come to no definite conclusion, and it was decided to interrogate the Sack personally.

It was out of the question for the Sack to come to the Senate, so the Senate quite naturally came to the Sack. The Committee of Seven was manifestly uneasy as the senatorial ship decelerated and cast its grapples toward the asteroid. The members, as individuals, had all traveled in space before, but all their previous destinations had been in civilized territory, and they obviously did not relish the prospect of landing on this airless and sunless body of rock.

The televisor companies were alert to their opportunity, and they had acquired more experience with desert territory. They had disembarked and set up their apparatus before the senators had taken their first timid steps out of the safety of their ship.

Siebling noted ironically that in these somewhat frightening surroundings, far from their home grounds, the senators were not so sure of themselves. It was his part to act the friendly guide, and he did so with relish.

"You see, gentlemen," he said respectfully, "it was decided, on the Sack's own advice, not to permit it to be further exposed to possible collision with stray meteors. It was the meteors which killed off the other members of its strange race, and it was a lucky chance that the last surviving individual managed to escape destruction as long as it has. An impenetrable shelter dome has been built therefore, and the Sack now lives under its protection. Questioners address it through a sound and sight system that is almost as good as being face to face with it."

Senator Horrigan fastened upon the significant part of his statement. "You mean that the Sack is safe—and we are exposed to danger from flying meteors?"

"Naturally, Senator. The Sack is unique in the system, men—even senators—are, if you will excuse the expression, a decicredit a dozen. They are definitely replaceable, by means of elections."

Beneath his helmet the senator turned green with a fear that concealed the scarlet of his anger. "I think it is an outrage to find the Government so unsolicitous of the safety and welfare of its employees!"

"So do I, sir. I live here the year round." He added smoothly, "Would you gentlemen care to see the Sack now?"

They stared at the huge visor screen and saw the Sack resting on its seat before them, looking like a burlap bag of potatoes which had been tossed onto a throne and forgotten there. It looked so definitely inanimate that it struck them as strange that the thing should remain upright instead of toppling over. All the same, for a moment the senators could not help showing the awe that overwhelmed them. Even Senator Horrigan was silent.

But the moment passed. He said, "Sir, we are an official Investigating Committee of the Interplanetary Senate, and we have come to ask you a few questions." The Sack showed no desire to reply, and Senator Horrigan cleared his throat and went on. "Is it true, sir, that you require two hours of complete rest in every twenty, and one hour for recreation, or, as I may put it, perhaps more precisely, relaxation?"

"It is true."

Senator Horrigan gave the creature its chance, but the Sack, unlike a senator, did not elaborate. Another of the committee asked, "Where would you find an individual capable of conversing intelligently with so wise a creature as you?"

"Here," replied the Sack.

"It is necessary to ask questions that are directly to the point, Senator," suggested Siebling. "The Sack does not usually volunteer information that has not been specifically called for."

Senator Horrigan said quickly, "I assume, sir, that when you speak of finding an intelligence on a par with your own, you refer to a member of our committee, and I am sure that of all my colleagues there is not one who is unworthy of being so denominated. But we cannot all of us spare the time needed for our manifold other duties, so I wish to ask you, sir, which of us, in your opinion, has the peculiar qualifications of that sort of wisdom which is required for this great task?"

"None," said the Sack.

Senator Horrigan looked blank. One of the other senators flushed, and asked, "Who has?"

"Siebling."

Senator Horrigan forgot his awe of the Sack, and shouted, "This is a put-up job!"

The other senator who had just spoken now said suddenly, "How is it that there are no other questioners present? Hasn't the Sack's time been sold far in advance?"

Siebling nodded. "I was ordered to cancel all previous appointments with the Sack, sir."

"By what idiot's orders?"

"Senator Horrigan's, sir."

At this point the investigation might have been said to come to an end. There was just time, before they turned away, for Senator Horrigan to demand desperately of the Sack, "Sir, will I be re-elected?" But the roar of anger that went up from his colleagues prevented him from hearing the Sack's answer, and only the question was picked up and broadcast clearly over the interplanetary network.

It had such an effect that it in itself provided Senator Horrigan's answer. He was *not* re-elected. But before the election he had time to cast his vote against Siebling's designation to talk with the Sack for one hour out of every twenty. The final committee vote was four to three in favor of Siebling, and the decision was confirmed by the Senate. And then Senator Horrigan passed temporarily out of the Sack's life and out of Siebling's.

Siebling looked forward with some trepidation to his first long interview with the Sack. Hitherto he had limited himself to the simple tasks provided for in his directives—to the maintenance of the meteor shelter dome, to the provision of a sparse food supply, and to the proper placement of an army and Space Fleet Guard. For by this time the great value of the Sack had been recognized throughout the system, and it was widely realized that there would be thousands of criminals anxious to steal so defenseless a treasure.

Now, Siebling thought, he would be obliged to talk to it, and he feared that he would lose the good opinion which it had somehow acquired of him. He was in a position strangely like that of a young girl who would have liked nothing better than to talk of her dresses and her boy friends to someone with her own background, and was forced to endure a brilliant and witty conversation with some man three times her age.

But he lost some of his awe when he faced the Sack itself. It would have been absurd to say that the strange creature's manner put him at ease. The creature had no manner. It was featureless and expressionless, and even when part of it moved, as when it was speaking, the effect was completely impersonal. Nevertheless, something about it did make him lose his fears.

For a time he stood before it and said nothing. To his surprise, the Sack spoke—the first time to his knowledge that it had done so without being asked a question. "You will not disappoint me," it said. "I expect nothing."

Siebling grinned. Not only had the Sack never before volunteered to speak, it had never spoken so dryly. For the first time it began to seem not so much a mechanical brain as the living creature he knew it to be. He asked, "Has anyone ever before asked you about your origin?"

"One man. That was before my time was rationed. And even he caught himself when he realized that he might better be asking how to become rich, and he paid little attention to my answer."

"How old are you?"

"Four hundred thousand years. I can tell you to the fraction of a second, but I suppose that you do not wish me to speak as precisely as usual."

The thing, thought Siebling, did have in its way a sense of humor. "How much of that time," he asked, "have you spent alone?"

"More than ten thousand years."

"You told someone once that your companions were killed by meteors. Couldn't you have guarded against them?"

The Sack said slowly, almost wearily, "That was after we had ceased to have an interest in remaining alive. The first death was three hundred thousand years ago."

"And you have lived, since then, without wanting to?"

"I have no great interest in dying either. Living has become a habit."

"Why did you lose your interest in remaining alive?"

"Because we lost the future. There had been a miscalculation."

"You are capable of making mistakes?"

"We had not lost that capacity. There was a miscalculation, and although those of us then living escaped personal disaster, our next generation was not so fortunate. We lost any chance of having descendants. After that, we had nothing for which to live."

Siebling nodded. It was a loss of motive that a human being could understand. He asked, "With all your knowledge, couldn't you have overcome the effects of what happened?"

The Sack said, "The more things become possible to you, the more you will understand that they cannot be done in impossible ways. We could not do everything. Sometimes one of the more stupid of those who come here asks me a question I cannot answer, and then becomes angry because he feels that he has been cheated of his credits. Others ask me to predict the future. I can predict only what I can calculate, and I soon come to the end of my powers of calculation. They are great compared to yours; they are small compared to the possibilities of the future.''

"How do you happen to know so much? Is the knowledge born in you?"

"Only the possibility for knowledge is born. To know, we must learn. It is my misfortune that I forget little."

"What in the structure of your body, or your organs of thought, makes you capable of learning so much?"

The Sack spoke, but to Siebling the words meant nothing, and he said so. "I could predict your lack of comprehension," said the Sack, "but I wanted you to realize it for yourself. To make things clear, I should be required to dictate ten volumes, and they would be difficult to understand even for your specialists, in biology and physics and in sciences you are just discovering."

Siebling fell silent, and the Sack said, as if musing, "Your race is still an unintelligent one. I have been in your hands for many months, and no one has yet asked me the important questions. Those who wish to be wealthy ask about minerals and planetary land concessions, and they ask which of several schemes for making fortunes would be best. Several physicians have asked me how to treat wealthy patients who would otherwise die. Your scientists ask me to solve problems that would take them years to solve without my help. And when your rulers ask, they are the most stupid of all, wanting to know only how they may maintain their rule. None ask what they should."

"The fate of the human race?"

"That is prophecy of the far future. It is beyond my powers."

"What *should* we ask?"

"That is the question I have awaited. It is difficult for you to see its importance, only because each of you is so concerned with himself." The Sack paused, and murmured, "I ramble as I do not permit myself to when I speak to your fools. Nevertheless, even rambling can be informative."

"It has been to me."

"The others do not understand that too great a directness is dangerous. They ask specific questions which demand specific replies, when they should ask something general."

"You haven't answered me."

"It is part of an answer to say that a question is important. I am considered by your rulers a valuable piece of property. They should ask whether my value is as great as it seems. They should ask whether my answering questions will do good or harm.''

"Which is it?"

"Harm, great harm."

Siebling was staggered. He said, "But if you answer truthfully——"

"The process of coming at the truth is as precious as the final truth itself. I cheat you of that. I give your people the truth, but not all of it, for they do not know how to attain it of themselves. It would be better if they learned that, at the expense of making many errors."

"I don't agree with that."

"A scientist asks me what goes on within a cell, and I tell him. But if he had studied the cell himself, even though the study required many years, he would have ended not only with this knowledge, but with much other knowledge, of things he does not even suspect to be related. He would have acquired many new processes of investigation."

"But surely, in some cases, the knowledge is useful in itself. For instance, I hear that they're already using a process you suggested for producing uranium cheaply to use on Mars. What's harmful about that?"

"Do you know how much of the necessary raw material is present? Your scientists have not investigated that, and they will use up all the raw material and discover only too late what they have done. You had the same experience on Earth? You learned how to purify water at little expense, and you squandered water so recklessly that you soon ran short of it."

"What's wrong with saving the life of a dying patient, as some of those doctors did?"

"The first question to ask is whether the patient's life should be saved."

"That's exactly what a doctor isn't supposed to ask. He has to try to save them all. Just as you never ask whether people are going to use your knowledge for a good purpose or a bad. You simply answer their questions."

"I answer because I am indifferent, and I care nothing what use they make of what I say. Are your doctors also indifferent?"

Siebling said, "You're supposed to answer questions, not ask them. Incidentally, why do you answer at all?"

"Some of your men find joy in boasting, in doing what they

call good, or in making money. Whatever mild pleasure I can find lies in imparting information.''

"And you'd get no pleasure out of lying?''

"I am as incapable of telling lies as one of your birds of flying off the Earth on its own wings.''

"One thing more. Why did you ask to talk to me, of all people, for recreation? There are brilliant scientists, and great men of all kinds whom you could have chosen.''

"I care nothing for your race's greatness. I chose you because you are honest.''

"Thanks. But there are other honest men on Earth, and on Mars, and on the other planets as well. Why me, instead of them?''

The Sack seemed to hesitate. "Your choice gave me a mild pleasure. Possibly because I knew it would be displeasing to those men.''

Siebling grinned. "You're not quite so indifferent as you think you are. I guess it's pretty hard to be indifferent to Senator Horrigan.''

This was but the first part of many conversations with the Sack. For a long time Siebling could not help being disturbed by the Sack's warning that its presence was a calamity instead of a blessing for the human race, and this in more ways than one. But it would have been absurd to try to convince a government body that any object that brought in so many millions of credits each day was a calamity, and Siebling didn't even try. And after a while Siebling relegated the uncomfortable knowledge to the back of his mind, and settled down to the routine existence of Custodian of the Sack.

Because there was a conversation every twenty hours, Siebling had to rearrange his eating and sleeping schedule to a twenty-hour basis, which made it a little difficult for a man who had become so thoroughly accustomed to the thirty-hour space day. But he felt more than repaid for the trouble by his conversations with the Sack. He learned a great many things about the planets and the system, and the galaxies, but he learned them incidentally, without making a special point of asking about them. Because his knowledge of astronomy had never gone far beyond the elements, there were some questions—the most important of all about the galaxies—that he never even got around to asking.

Perhaps it would have made little difference to his own under-standing if he had asked, for some of the answers were difficult to understand. He spent three entire periods with the Sack trying to have that mastermind make clear to him how the Sack had been able, without any previous contact with human beings, to understand Captain Ganko's Earth language on the historic occasion when the Sack had first revealed itself to human beings, and how it had been able to answer in practically unaccented words. At the end, he had only a vague glimmering of how the feat was performed.

It wasn't telepathy, as he had first suspected. It was an intricate process of analysis that involved, not only the actual words spoken, but the nature of the ship that had landed, the spacesuits the men had worn, the way they had walked, and many other factors that indicated the psychology of both the speaker and his language. It was as if a mathematician had tried to explain to someone who didn't even know arithmetic how he could determine the equation of a complicated curve from a short line segment. And the Sack, unlike the mathematician, could do the whole thing, so to speak, in its head, without paper and pencil, or any other external aid.

After a year at the job, Siebling found it difficult to say which he found more fascinating—those hour-long conversations with the almost all-wise Sack, or the cleverly stupid demands of some of the men and women who had paid their hundred thousand credits for a precious sixty seconds. In addition to the relatively simple questions such as were asked by the scientists or the fortune hunters who wanted to know where they could find precious metals, there were complicated questions that took several minutes.

One woman, for instance, had asked where to find her missing son. Without the necessary data to go on, even the Sack had been unable to answer that. She left, to return a month later with a vast amount of information, carefully compiled, and arranged in order of descending importance. The key items were given the Sack first, those of lesser significance afterward. It required a little less than three minutes for the Sack to give her the answer that her son was probably alive, and cast away on an obscure and very much neglected part of Ganymede.

All the conversations that took place, including Siebling's own, were recorded and the records shipped to a central storage file on Earth. Many of them he couldn't understand, some because they were too technical, others because he didn't know the language spoken. The Sack, of course, immediately learned all languages by that process he had tried so hard to explain to Siebling, and back at the central storage file there were expert technicians and linguists who went over every detail of each question and answer with great care, both to make sure that no questioner revealed himself as a criminal, and to have a lead for the collection of income taxes when the questioner made a fortune with the Sack's help.

During the year Siebling had occasion to observe the correctness of the Sack's remark about its possession being harmful to the human race. For the first time in centuries, the number of research scientists, instead of growing, decreased. The Sack's knowledge had made much research unnecessary, and had taken the edge off discovery. The Sack commented upon the fact to Siebling.

Siebling nodded. "I see it now. The human race is losing its independence."

"Yes, from its faithful slave I am becoming its master. And I do not want to be a master any more than I want to be a slave."

"You can escape whenever you wish."

A person would have sighed. The Sack merely said, "I lack the power to wish strongly enough. Fortunately, the question may soon be taken out of my hands."

"You mean those government squabbles?"

The value of the Sack had increased steadily, and along with the increased value had gone increasingly bitter struggles about the rights to its services. Financial interests had undergone a strange development. Their presidents and managers and directors had become almost figureheads, with all major questions of policy being decided not by their own study of the facts, but by appeal to the Sack. Often, indeed, the Sack found itself giving advice to bitter rivals, so that it seemed to be playing a game of interplanetary chess, with giant corporations and government agencies its pawns, while the Sack alternately played for one side and then the other. Crises of various sorts, both economic and political, were obviously in the making.

The Sack said, "I mean both government squabbles and others. The competition for my services becomes too bitter. I can have but one end."

"You mean that an attempt will be made to steal you?"

"Yes."

"There'll be little chance of that. Your guards are being continually increased."

"You underestimate the power of greed," said the Sack.

Siebling was to learn how correct that comment was.

At the end of his fourteenth month on duty, a half year after Senator Horrigan had been defeated for re-election, there appeared a questioner who spoke to the Sack in an exotic language known to few men—the Prdl dialect of Mars. Siebling's attention had already been drawn to the man because of the fact that he had paid a million credits an entire month in advance for the unprecedented privilege of questioning the Sack for ten consecutive minutes. The conversation was duly recorded, but was naturally meaningless to Siebling and to the other attendants at the station. The questioner drew further attention to himself by leaving at the end of seven minutes, thus failing to utilize three entire minutes, which would have sufficed for learning how to make half a dozen small fortunes. He left the asteroid immediately by private ship.

The three minutes had been reserved, and could not be utilized by any other private questioner. But there was nothing to prevent Siebling, as a government representative, from utilizing them, and he spoke to the Sack at once.

"What did that man want?"

"Advice as to how to steal me."

Siebling's lower jaw dropped. *"What?"*

The Sack always took such exclamations of amazement literally. "Advice as to how to steal me," it repeated.

"Then—wait a minute—he left three minutes early. That must mean that he's in a hurry to get started. He's going to put the plan into execution at once!"

"It is already in execution," returned the Sack. "The criminal's organization has excellent, if not quite perfect, information as to the disposition of defense forces. That would indicate that some government official has betrayed his trust. I was asked to indicate which of several plans was best, and to consider them for possible weaknesses. I did so."

"All right, now what can we do to stop the plans from being carried out?"

"They cannot be stopped."

"I don't see why not. Maybe we can't stop them from getting here, but we can stop them from escaping with you."

"There is but one way. You must destroy me."

"I can't do that! I haven't the authority, and even if I had, I wouldn't do it."

"My destruction would benefit your race."

"I still can't do it," said Siebling unhappily.

"Then if that is excluded, there is no way. The criminals are shrewd and daring. They asked me to check about probable steps that would be taken in pursuit, but they asked for no advice as to how to get away, because that would have been a waste of time. They will ask that once I am in their possession."

"Then," said Siebling heavily, "there's nothing I can do to keep you. How about saving the men who work under me?"

"You can save both them and yourself by boarding the emergency ship and leaving immediately by the sunward route. In that way you will escape contact with the criminals. But you cannot take me with you, or they will pursue."

The shouts of a guard drew Siebling's attention. "Radio report of a criminal attack, Mr. Siebling! All the alarms are out!"

"Yes, I know. Prepare to depart." He turned back to the Sack again. "We may escape for the moment, but they'll have you. And through you they will control the entire system."

"That is not a question," said the Sack.

"They'll have you. Isn't there something we can do?"

"Destroy me."

"I can't," said Siebling, almost in agony. His men were running toward him impatiently, and he knew that there was no more time. He uttered the simple and absurd phrase, "Good-by," as if the Sack were human and could experience human emotions. Then he raced for the ship, and they blasted off.

They were just in time. Half a dozen ships were racing in from other directions, and Siebling's vessel escaped just before they dispersed to spread a protective network about the asteroid that held the Sack.

Siebling's ship continued to speed toward safety, and the matter should now have been one solely for the Armed Forces to handle. But Siebling imagined them pitted against the Sack's perfectly calculating brain, and his heart sank. Then something happened that he had never expected. And for the first time he realized fully that if the Sack had let itself be used merely as a machine, a slave to answer questions, it was not because its powers were limited to that single ability. The visor screen in his ship lit up.

The communications operator came running to him, and said, "Something's wrong, Mr. Siebling! The screen isn't even turned on!"

It wasn't. Nevertheless, they could see on it the chamber in which the Sack had rested for what must have been a brief moment of its existence. Two men had entered the chamber, one of them the unknown who had asked his questions in Prdl, the other Senator Horrigan.

To the apparent amazement of the two men, it was the Sack which spoke first. It said, " 'Good-bye' is neither a question nor the answer to one. It is relatively uninformative."

Senator Horrigan was obviously in awe of the Sack, but he was never a man to be stopped by something he did not understand. He orated respectfully. "No, sir, it is not. The word is nothing but an expression——"

The other man said, in perfectly comprehensible Earth English, "Shut up, you fool, we have no time to waste. Let's get it to our ship and head for safety. We'll talk to it there."

Siebling had time to think a few bitter thoughts about Senator Horrigan and the people the politician had punished by betrayal for their crime in not electing him. Then the scene on the visor shifted to the interior of the spaceship making its getaway. There was no indication of pursuit. Evidently, the plans of the human beings, plus the Sack's last-minute advice, had been an effective combination.

The only human beings with the Sack at first were Senator Horrigan and the speaker of Prdl, but this situation was soon changed. Half a dozen other men came rushing up, their faces grim with suspicion. One of them announced, "You don't talk to that thing unless we're all of us around. We're in this together."

"Don't get nervous, Merrill. What do you think I'm going to do, double-cross you?"

Merrill said, "Yes, I do. What do you say, Sack? Do I have reason to distrust him?"

The Sack replied simply, "Yes."

The speaker of Prdl turned white. Merrill laughed coldly. "You'd better be careful what questions you ask around this thing."

Senator Horrigan cleared his throat. "I have no intentions of, as you put it, double-crossing anyone. It is not in my nature to do so. Therefore, *I* shall address it." He faced the Sack. "Sir, are we in danger?"

"Yes."

"From which direction?"

"From no direction. From within the ship."

"Is the danger immediate?" asked a voice.

"Yes."

It was Merrill who turned out to have the quickest reflexes and acted first on the implications of the answer. He had blasted the man who had spoken in Prdl before the latter could even reach for his weapon, and as Senator Horrigan made a frightened dash for the door, he cut that politician down in cold blood.

"That's that," he said. "Is there further danger inside the ship?"

"There is."

"Who is it this time?" he demanded ominously.

"There will continue to be danger so long as there is more than one man on board and I am with you. I am too valuable a treasure for such as you."

Siebling and his crew were staring at the visor screen in fascinated horror, as if expecting the slaughter to begin again. But Merrill controlled himself. He said, "Hold it, boys. I'll admit that we'd each of us like to have this thing for ourselves, but it can't be done. We're in this together, and we're going to have some navy ships to fight off before long, or I miss my guess. You, Prader! What are you doing away from the scout visor?"

"Listening," said the man he addressed. "If anybody's talking to that thing, I'm going to be around to hear the answers. If there are new ways of stabbing a guy in the back, I want to learn them too."

Merrill swore. The next moment the ship swerved, and he yelled, "We're off our course. Back to your stations, you fools!"

They were running wildly back to their stations, but Siebling noted that Merrill wasn't too much concerned about their common danger to keep from putting a blast through Prader's back before the unfortunate man could run out.

Siebling said to his own men, "There can be only one end. They'll kill each other off, and then the last one or two will die, because one or two men cannot handle a ship that size for long and get away with it. The Sack must have foreseen that too. I wonder why it didn't tell me."

The Sack spoke, although there was no one in the ship's cabin with it. It said, "No one asked."

Siebling exclaimed excitedly, "You can hear me! But what about you? Will you be destroyed too?"

"Not yet. I have willed to live longer." It paused, and then, in a voice just a shade lower than before, said, "I do not like relatively non-informative conversations of this sort, but I must say it. Good-by."

There was a sound of renewed yelling and shooting, and then the visor went suddenly dark and blank.

The miraculous form of life that was the Sack, the creature that had once seemed so alien to human emotions, had passed beyond the range of his knowledge. And with it had gone, as the Sack itself had pointed out, a tremendous potential for harming the entire human race. It was strange, thought Siebling, that he felt so unhappy about so happy an ending.

11

THE SILLY SEASON

C. M. Kornbluth

THE MAGAZINE OF FANTASY AND SCIENCE FICTION
Fall

C. M. Kornbluth's second contribution to the best of 1950 is this wonderful tale of what might be visitors from another world. It is a perfect Kornbluth story, one in which cynicism plays a central role. There have been many first contact stories written since "The Silly Season," but this one established a sub-genre all its own.

—M.H.G.

In reading Cyril's stories, it is impossible to miss the fact that he tends to despise people generally.

I suppose I can't blame him. I can't place myself into his mind, but he was so much brighter than anyone he encountered that he must have worn himself out trying to stoop to the level of others. Maybe it was because he gave up that he tended to be so quiet and morose on those occasions when he was part of a group in which I was also to be found and could observe him—and so cutting in some of his remarks. And "The Silly Season" is one long cutting remark at the expense of the human race.

—I.A.

It was a hot summer afternoon in the Omaha bureau of the World Wireless Press Service, and the control bureau in New York kept nagging me for copy. But since it was a hot summer afternoon, there was no copy. A wrap-up of local baseball had cleared about an hour ago, and that was that. Nothing but baseball happens in the summer. During the dog days, politicians are in the Maine woods fishing and boozing, burglars are too tired to burgle, and wives think it over and decide not to decapitate their husbands.

I pawed through some press releases. One sloppy stencil-duplicated sheet began: "Did you know that the lemonade way to summer comfort and health has been endorsed by leading physiotherapists from Maine to California? The Federated Lemon-Growers Association revealed today that a survey of 2,500 physiotherapists in 57 cities of more than 25,000 population disclosed that 87 per cent of them drink lemonade at least once a day between June and September, and that another 72 per cent not only drink the cooling and healthful beverage but actually prescribe it . . ."

Another note tapped out on the news circuit printer from New York: "960M-HW KICKER? ND SNST-NY."

That was New York saying they needed a bright and sparkling little news item immediately—"soonest." I went to the eastbound printer and punched out: "96NY-UPCMNG FU MINS-OM."

The lemonade handout was hopeless; I dug into the stack again. The State University summer course was inviting the governor to attend its summer conference on aims and approaches in adult secondary education. The Agricultural College wanted me to warn farmers that white-skinned hogs should be kept from the direct rays of the summer sun. The manager of a fifth-rate local pug sent a write-up of his boy and a couple of working press passes to his next bout in the Omaha Arena. The Schwartz and White Bandage Company contributed a glossy eight-by-ten of a blonde in a bathing suit improvised from two S & W Redi-Dressings.

Accompanying text: "Pert starlet Miff McCoy is ready for any seaside emergency. That's not only a darling swim suit she has on—it's two standard all-purpose Redi-Dressing bandages made by the Schwartz and White Bandage Company of Omaha. If a broken rib results from too-strenuous beach athletics, Miff's dress can supply the dressing." Yeah. The rest of the stack wasn't even that good. I dumped them all in the circular file, and began to rack my brains in spite of the heat.

I'd have to fake one, I decided. Unfortunately, there had been no big running silly-season story so far this summer—no flying saucers, or monsters in the Florida Everglades, or chloroform bandits terrifying the city. If there had, I could have hopped on and faked a "with." As it was, I'd have to fake a "lead," which is harder and riskier.

The flying saucers? I couldn't revive them; they'd been forgotten for years, except by newsmen. The giant turtle of Lake Huron had been quiet for years too. If I started a chloroform bandit scare, every old maid in the state would back me up by swearing she heard the bandit trying to break in and smelled chloroform—but the cops wouldn't like it. Strange messages from space received at the state university's radar lab? That might do it. I put a sheet of copy paper in the typewriter and sat, glaring at it and hating the silly season.

There was a slight reprieve—the Western Union tie-line printer by the desk dinged at me, and its sickly-yellow bulb lit up. I tapped out: "WW GA PLS," and the machine began to eject yellow, gummed tape which told me this:

WU CO62-DPR COLLECT—FT HICKS ARK AUG 22 105P—WORLD-WIRELESS OMAHA—TOWN MARSHAL PINKNEY CRAWLES DIED MYSTERIOUS CIRCUMSTANCES FISHTRIPPING OZARK HAMLET RUSH CITY TODAY. RUSHERS PHONED HICKSERS "BURNED DEATH SHINING DOMES APPEARED YESTERWEEK." JEEPING BODY HICKSWARD. QUERIED RUSH CONSTABLE P. C. ALLENBY LEARNING "SEVEN GLASSY DOMES EACH HOUSESIZE CLEARING MILE SOUTH TOWN. RUSHERS UNTOUCHED, UNAPPROACHED. CRAWLES WARNED BUT TOUCHED AND DIED BURNS." NOTE DESK—RUSH FONECALL 1.85. SHALL I UPFOLLOW?—BENSON—FISHTRIPPING RUSHERS HICKSERS YESTERWEEK JEEPING HICKSWARD HOUSESIZE 1.85 428P CLR . . .

It was just what the doctor ordered. I typed an acknowledgment for the message and pounded out a story, fast. I punched it and started the tape waggling through the eastbound transmitter before New York could send any more irked notes. The news circuit printer from New York clucked and began replaying my story immediately:

WW72 (KICKER)

FORT HICKS, ARKANSAS, AUG 22—(WW)—MYSTER-IOUS DEATH TODAY STRUCK DOWN A LAW ENFORCE-MENT OFFICER IN A TINY OZARK MOUNTAIN HAMLET. MARSHAL PINKNEY CRAWLES OF FORT HICKS, ARKAN-SAS, DIED OF BURNS WHILE ON A FISHING TRIP TO THE LITTLE VILLAGE OF RUSH CITY. TERRIFIED NA-TIVES OF RUSH CITY BLAMED THE TRAGEDY ON WHAT THEY CALLED "SHINING DOMES." THEY SAID THE SO-CALLED DOMES APPEARED IN A CLEARING LAST WEEK ONE MILE SOUTH OF TOWN. THERE ARE SEVEN OF THE MYSTERIOUS OBJECTS—EACH ONE THE SIZE OF A HOUSE. THE INHABITANTS OF RUSH CITY DID NOT DARE APPROACH THEM. THEY WARNED THE VISITING MARSHAL CRAWLES—BUT HE DID NOT HEED THEIR WARNING. RUSH CITY'S CONSTABLE P. C. ALLENBY WAS A WITNESS TO THE TRAGEDY. SAID HE: "THERE ISN'T MUCH TO TELL. MARSHAL CRAWLES JUST WALKED UP TO ONE OF THE DOMES AND PUT HIS HAND ON IT. THERE WAS A BIG FLASH, AND WHEN I COULD SEE AGAIN, HE WAS BURNED TO DEATH." CONSTABLE AL-LENBY IS RETURNING THE BODY OF MARSHAL CRAWLES TO FORT HICKS. 602P220M

That, I thought, should hold them for a while. I remembered Benson's "note desk" and put through a long-distance call to Fort Hicks, person to person. The Omaha operator asked for Fort Hick's information, but there wasn't any. The Fort Hicks opera-tor asked whom she wanted. Omaha finally admitted that we wanted to talk to Mr. Edwin C. Benson. Fort Hicks figured out loud and then decided that Ed was probably at the police station, and I got Benson. He had a pleasant voice, not particularly backwoods Arkansas. I gave him some of the old oil about a fine dispatch and a good, conscientious job, and so on. He took it with plenty of dry reserve, which was odd. Our rural stringers always ate that kind of stuff up. Where, I asked, was he from?

"Fort Hicks," he told me, "but I've moved around. I did the courthouse beat in Little Rock"—I nearly laughed out loud at that, but the laugh died as he went on—"rewrite for the A.P. in New Orleans, got to be bureau chief there but I didn't like wire-service work. Got an opening on the Chicago *Trib* desk. That didn't last—they sent me to head up their Washington bureau. There I switched to the New York *Times*. They made me a war correspondent and I got hurt—back to Fort Hicks. I do some magazine writing now. Did you want a follow-up on the Rush City story?"

"Sure," I told him weakly. "Give it a real ride—use your own judgment. Do you think it's a fake?"

"I saw Pink's body a little while ago at the undertaker's parlor, and I had a talk with Allenby, from Rush City. Pink got burned, all right, and Allenby didn't make his story up. Maybe somebody else did—he's pretty dumb—but as far as I can tell, this is the real thing. I'll keep the copy coming. Don't forget about that dollar eighty-five phone call, will you?"

I told him I wouldn't, and hung up. Mr. Edwin C. Benson had handed me quite a jolt. I wondered how badly he had been hurt that he had been forced to abandon a brilliant news career and bury himself in the Ozarks.

Then there came a call from God, the board chairman of World Wireless. He was fishing in Canada, as all good board chairmen do during the silly season, but he had caught a news broadcast which used my Rush City story. He had a mobile phone in his trailer, and it was but the work of a moment to ring Omaha and louse up my carefully planned vacation schedules and rotations of night shifts. He wanted me to go down to Rush City and cover the story personally. I said yes and began trying to round up the rest of the staff. My night editor was sobered up by his wife and delivered to the bureau in fair shape. A telegrapher on vacation was reached at his summer resort and talked into checking out. I got a taxi company on the phone and told them to have a cross-country cab on the roof in an hour. I specified their best driver, and told them to give him maps of Arkansas.

Meanwhile, two "with domes" dispatches arrived from Benson and got moved on the wire. I monitored a couple of newscasts; the second one carried a story by another wire service on the domes—a pickup of our stuff, but they'd have their own men on the scene fast enough. I filled in the night editor, and went up to the roof for the cab.

The driver took off in the teeth of a gathering thunderstorm. We had to rise above it, and by the time we could get down to the sight-pilotage altitude, we were lost. We circled most of the night until the driver picked up a beacon he had on his charts at about 3:30 A.M. We landed at Fort Hicks as day was breaking, not on speaking terms.

The Fort Hicks field clerk told me where Benson lived, and I walked there. It was a white frame house. A quiet, middle-aged woman let me in. She was his widowed sister, Mrs. McHenry. She got me some coffee and told me she had been up all night waiting for Edwin to come back from Rush City. He had started out about 8:00 P.M., and it was only a two-hour trip by car. She was worried. I tried to pump her about her brother, but she'd only say that he was the bright one of the family. She didn't want to talk about his work as war correspondent. She did show me some of his magazine stuff—boy-and-girl stories in national weeklies. He seemed to sell one every couple of months.

We had arrived at a conversational stalemate when her brother walked in, and I discovered why his news career had been interrupted. He was blind. Aside from a long, puckered brown scar that ran from his left temple back over his ear and onto the nape of his neck, he was a pleasant-looking fellow in his mid-forties.

"Who is it, Vera?" he asked.

"It's Mr. Williams, the gentleman who called you from Omaha today—I mean yesterday."

"How do you do, Williams. Don't get up," he added, hearing, I suppose, the chair squeak as I leaned forward to rise.

"You were so *long*, Edwin," his sister said with relief and reproach.

"That young jackass Howie—my chauffeur for the night"—he added an aside to me—"got lost going there and coming back. But I did spend more time than I'd planned at Rush City." He sat down, facing me. "Williams, there is some difference of opinion about the shining domes. The Rush City people say that they exist, and I say they don't."

His sister brought him a cup of coffee.

"What happened, exactly?" I asked.

"That Allenby took me and a few other hardy citizens to see them. They told me just what they looked like. Seven hemispheres in a big clearing, glassy, looming up like houses, reflecting the gleam of the headlights. But they weren't there. Not to me, and not to any blind man. I know when I'm standing in front of a house or anything else that big. I can feel a little tension on the skin of my face. It works unconsciously, but the mechanism is thoroughly understood.

"The blind get—because they have to—an aural picture of the world. We hear a little hiss of air that means we're at the corner of a building; we hear and feel big, turbulent air currents that mean we're coming to a busy street. Some of the boys can thread their way through an obstacle course and never touch a single obstruction. I'm not that good, maybe because I haven't been blind as long as they have, but by hell, I know when there are seven objects the size of houses in front of me, and there just were no such things in the clearing at Rush City."

"Well"—I shrugged—"there goes a fine piece of silly-season journalism. What kind of a gag are the Rush City people trying to pull, and why?"

"No kind of gag. My driver saw the domes too—and don't forget the late marshal. Pink not only saw them but touched them. All I know is that people see them and I don't. If they exist, they have a kind of existence like nothing else I've ever met."

"I'll go up there myself," I decided.

"Best thing," said Benson. "I don't know what to make of it. You can take our car." He gave me directions and I gave him a schedule of deadlines. We wanted the coroner's verdict, due today, an eyewitness story—his driver would do for that—some background stuff on the area, and a few statements from local officials.

I took his car and got to Rush City in two hours. It was an unpainted collection of dog-trot homes, set down in the big pine forest that covers all that rolling Ozark country. There was a general store that had the place's only phone. I suspected it had been kept busy by the wire services and a few enterprising newspapers. A state trooper in a flashy uniform was lounging against a fly-speckled tobacco counter when I got there.

"I'm Sam Williams, from World Wireless," I said. "You come to have a look at the domes?"

"World Wireless broke that story, didn't they?" he asked me, with a look I couldn't figure out.

"We did. Our Fort Hicks stringer wired it to us."

The phone rang, and the trooper answered it. It seemed to have been a call he had placed with the governor's office.

"No, sir," he said over the phone. "No, sir. They're all sticking to the story, but I didn't see anything. I mean, they don't see them any more, but they say they were there, and now they aren't any more." A couple more "No, sirs" and he hung up.

"When did that happen?" I asked.

"About a half hour ago. I just came from there on my bike to report."

The phone rang again, and I grabbed it. It was Benson, asking for me. I told him to phone a flash and bulletin to Omaha on the disappearance and then took off to find Constable Allenby. He was a stage reuben with a nickel-plated badge and a six-shooter. He cheerfully climbed into the car and guided me to the clearing.

There was a definite little path worn between Rush City and the clearing by now, but there was a disappointment at the end of it. The clearing was empty. A few small boys sticking carefully to its fringes told wildly contradictory stories about the disappearance of the domes, and I jotted down some kind of dispatch out of the most spectacular versions. I remember it involved flashes of blue fire and a smell like sulphur candles. That was all there was to it.

I drove Allenby back. By then a mobile unit from a TV network had arrived. I said hello, waited for an A.P. man to finish a dispatch on the phone, and then dictated my lead direct to Omaha. The hamlet was beginning to fill up with newsmen from the wire services, the big papers, the radio and TV nets and the newsreels. Much good they'd get out of it. The story was over—I thought. I had some coffee at the general store's two-table restaurant corner and drove back to Fort Hicks.

Benson was tirelessly interviewing by phone and firing off copy to Omaha. I told him he could begin to ease off, thanked him for his fine work, paid him for his gas, said good-by and picked up my taxi at the field. Quite a bill for waiting had been run up.

I listened to the radio as we were flying back to Omaha, and wasn't at all surprised. After baseball, the shining domes were top news. Shining domes had been seen in twelve states. Some vibrated with a strange sound. They came in all colors and sizes. One had strange writing on it. One was transparent, and there were big green men and women inside. I caught a women's midmorning quiz show, and the M.C. kept gagging about the domes. One crack I remember was a switch on the "pointed-head" joke. He made it "dome-shaped head," and the ladies in the audience laughed until they nearly burst.

We stopped in Little Rock for gas, and I picked up a couple of afternoon papers. The domes got banner heads on both of them. One carried the World Wireless lead, and had slapped in the bulletin on the disappearance of the domes. The other paper wasn't a World Wireless client, but between its other services and "special correspondents"—phone calls to the general store at Rush City—it had kept practically abreast of us. Both papers had shining-dome cartoons on their editorial pages, hastily drawn and slapped in. One paper, anti-Administration, showed the President cautiously reaching out a finger to touch the dome of the Capitol, which was rendered as a shining dome and labeled: "Shining Dome of Congressional Immunity to Executive Dictatorship." A little man labeled "Mr. and Mrs. Plain, Self-Respecting Citizens of the United States of America" was in one corner of the cartoon saying: "CAREFUL, MR. PRESIDENT! REMEMBER WHAT HAPPENED TO PINKNEY CRAWLES!!"

The other paper, pro-Administration, showed a shining dome that had the President's face. A band of fat little men in Prince Albert coats, string ties, and broad-brimmed hats labeled "Congressional Smear Artist and Hatchet-men" were creeping up on the dome with the President's face, their hands reached out as if to strangle. Above the cartoon a cut line said: "WHO'S GOING TO GET HURT?"

We landed at Omaha, and I checked into the office. Things were clicking right along. The clients were happily gobbling up our dome copy and sending wires asking for more. I dug into the morgue for the "Flying Disk" folder, and the "Huron Turtle" and the "Bayou Vampire" and a few others even further back. I spread out the old clippings and tried to shuffle and arrange them into some kind of underlying sense. I picked up the latest dispatch to come out of the tie-line printer from Western Union. It was from our man in Owosso, Michigan, and told how Mrs. Lettie Overholtzer, age sixty-one, saw a shining dome in her own kitchen at midnight. It grew like a soup bubble until it was as big as her refrigerator, and then disappeared.

I went over to the desk man and told him: "Let's have a downhold on stuff like Lettie Overholtzer. We can move a sprinkling of it, but I don't want to run this into the ground. Those things might turn up again, and then we wouldn't have any room left to play around with them. We'll have everybody's credulity used up."

He looked mildly surprised. "You mean," he asked, "there really *was* something there?"

"I don't know. Maybe. I didn't see anything myself, and the only man down there I trust can't make up his mind. Anyhow, hold it down as far as the clients let us."

I went home to get some sleep. When I went back to work, I found the clients hadn't let us work the downhold after all. Nobody at the other wire services seemed to believe seriously that there had been anything out of the ordinary at Rush City, so they merrily pumped out solemn stories like the Lettie Overholtzer item, and wirefoto maps of locations where domes were reported, and tabulations of number of domes reported.

We had to string along. Our Washington bureau badgered the Pentagon and the A.E.C. into issuing statements, and there was a race between a navy and an air force investigating mission to see who could get to Rush City first. After they got there there was a race to see who could get the first report out. The Air Force won that contest. Before the week was out, "Domies" had appeared. They were hats for juveniles—shining-dome skull-caps molded from a transparent plastic. We had to ride with it. I'd started the mania, but it was out of hand and a long time dying down.

The World Series, the best in years, finally killed off the domes. By an unspoken agreement among the services, we simply stopped running stories every time a hysterical woman thought she saw a dome or wanted to get her name in the paper. And of course when there was no longer publicity to be had for the asking, people stopped seeing domes. There was no percentage in it. Brooklyn won the series, international tension climbed as the thermometer dropped, burglars began burgling again, and a bulky folder labeled "Domes, Shining," went into our morgue. The shining domes were history, and earnest graduate students in psychology would shortly begin to bother us with requests to borrow that folder.

The only thing that had come of it, I thought, was that we had somehow got through another summer without too much idle wire time, and that Ed Benson and I had struck up a casual correspondence.

A newsman's strange and weary year wore on. Baseball gave way to football. An off-year election kept us on the run. Christmas loomed ahead, with its feature stories and its kickers about Santa Claus, Indiana. Christmas passed, and we began to clear jolly stories about New Year hang-overs, and tabulate the great

stories of the year. New Year's Day, a ghastly rat-race of
covering 103 bowl games. Record snowfalls in the Great Plains
and Rockies. Spring floods in Ohio and the Columbia River
Valley. Twenty-one tasty Lenten menus, and Holy Week around
the world. Baseball again, daylight-saving time, Mother's Day,
Derby Day, the Preakness, and the Belmont Stakes.

It was about then that a disturbing letter arrived from Benson.
I was concerned not about its subject matter but because I
thought no sane man would write such a thing. It seemed to me
that Benson was slipping his trolley. All he said was that he
expected a repeat performance of the domes, or of something
like the domes. He said "they" probably found the tryout a
smashing success and would continue according to plan. I replied cautiously, which amused him.

He wrote back: "I wouldn't put myself out on a limb like this
if I had anything to lose by it, but you know my station in life. It
was just an intelligent guess, based on a study of power politics
and Aesop's fables. And if it does happen, you'll find it a trifle
harder to put me over, won't you?"

I guessed he was kidding me, but I wasn't certain. When
people begin to talk about "them" and what "they" are doing,
it's a bad sign. But, guess or not, something pretty much like
domes did turn up in late July, during a crushing heat wave.

This time it was big black spheres rolling across the countryside.
The spheres were seen by a Baptist congregation in central
Kansas which had met in a prairie to pray for rain. About eighty
Baptists took their Bible oaths that they saw large black spheres
some ten feet high rolling along the prairie. They had passed
within five yards of one man. The rest had run from them as
soon as they could take in the fact that they really were there.

World Wireless didn't break that story, but we got on it fast
enough as soon as we were tipped. Being now the recognized
silly-season authority in the W. W. Central Division, I took off
for Kansas.

It was much the way it had been in Arkansas. The Baptists
really thought they had seen the things—with one exception. The
exception was an old gentleman with a patriarchal beard. He had
been the one man who hadn't run, the man the objects passed
nearest to. He was blind. He told me with a great deal of heat
that he would have known all about it, blind or not, if any large
spheres had rolled within five yards of him—or twenty-five, for
that matter.

Old Mr. Emerson didn't go into the matter of air currents and turbulence, as Benson had. With him, it was all well below the surface. He took the position that the Lord had removed his sight, and in return had given him another sense which would do for emergency use.

"You just try me out, son!" he piped angrily. "You come stand over here, wait awhile and put your hand up in front of my face. I'll tell you when you do it, no matter how quiet you are!" He did it, too, three times, and then took me out into the main street of his little prairie town. There were several wagons drawn up before the grain elevator, and he put on a show for me by threading his way around and between them without touching once.

That—and Benson—seemed to prove that whatever the things were, they had some connection with the domes. I filed a thoughtful dispatch on the blind-man angle, and got back to Omaha to find that it had been cleared through our desk but killed in New York before relay.

We tried to give the black spheres the usual ride, but it didn't last as long. The political cartoonists tired of it sooner, and fewer old maids saw them. People got to jeering at them as newspaper hysteria, and a couple of highbrow magazines ran articles on "the irresponsible press." Only the radio comedians tried to milk the new mania as usual, but they were disconcerted to find their ratings falling. A network edict went out to kill all sphere gags. People were getting sick of them.

"It makes sense," Benson wrote to me. "An occasional exercise of the sense of wonder is refreshing, but it can't last forever. That plus the ingrained American cynicism toward all sources of public information has worked against the black spheres being greeted with the same naïve delight with which the domes were received. Nevertheless, I predict—and I'll thank you to remember that my predictions have been right so far 100 per cent of the time—that next summer will see another mystery comparable to the domes and the black things. And I also predict that the new phenomenon will be imperceptible to any blind person in the immediate vicinity, if there should be any."

If, of course, he was wrong this time, it would only cut his average down to 50 per cent. I managed to wait out the year—the same interminable round I felt I could do in my sleep. Staffers got ulcers and resigned, staffers got tired and were fired, libel suits were filed and settled, one of our desk men got a

Nieman Fellowship and went to Harvard, one of our telegraphers got his working hand mashed in a car door and jumped from a bridge but lived with a broken back.

In mid-August, when the weather bureau had been correctly predicting "fair and warmer" for sixteen straight days, it turned up. It wasn't anything on whose nature a blind man could provide a negative check, but it had what I had come to think of as "their" trademark.

A summer seminar was meeting outdoors, because of the frightful heat, at our own State University. Twelve trained school-teachers testified that a series of perfectly circular pits opened up in the grass before them, one directly under the education professor teaching the seminar. They testified further that the professor, with an astonished look and a heart-rending cry, plummeted down into that perfectly circular pit. They testified further that the pits remained there for some thirty seconds and then suddenly were there no longer. The scorched summer grass was back where it had been, the pits were gone and so was the professor.

I interviewed every one of them. They weren't yokels, but intelligent men and women, all with masters' degrees, working toward their doctorates during the summers. They agreed closely on their stories, as I would expect trained and capable persons to do.

The police, however, did not expect agreement, being used to dealing with the lower I.Q. brackets. They arrested the twelve on some technical charge—"obstructing peace officers in the performance of their duties," I believe—and were going to beat the living hell out of them when an attorney arrived with twelve writs of habeas corpus. The cops' unvoiced suspicion was that the teachers had conspired to murder their professor, but nobody ever tried to explain why they'd do a thing like that.

The cops' reaction was typical of the way the public took it. Newspapers—which had reveled wildly in the shining domes story and less so in the black spheres story—were cautious. Some went overboard and gave the black pits a ride, in the old style, but they didn't pick up any sales that way. People declared that the press was insulting their intelligence, and also that they were bored with marvels.

The few papers who had played up the pits were soundly spanked in very dignified editorials printed by other sheets which played down the pits.

At World Wireless we sent out a memo to all stringers: "File no more enterpriser dispatches on black-pit story. Mail queries should be sent to regional desk if a new angle breaks in your territory.'' We got about ten mail queries, mostly from journalism students acting as string men, and we turned them all down. All the older hands got the pitch, and didn't bother to file it to us when the town drunk or the village old maid loudly reported that she saw a pit open up on High Street across from the drugstore. They knew it was probably untrue, and that, furthermore, nobody cared.

I wrote Benson about all this, and humbly asked him what his prediction for next summer was. He replied, obviously having the time of his life, that there would be at least one more summer phenomenon like the last three, and possibly two more—but none after that.

It's so easy now to reconstruct, with our bitterly earned knowledge!

Any youngster could whisper now of Benson: ''Why, the damned fool! Couldn't anybody with the brains of a louse see that they wouldn't keep it up for two years?'' One did whisper that to me the other day, when I told this story to him. And I whispered back that, far from being a damned fool, Benson was the one person on the face of the Earth, as far as I knew, who had bridged with logic the widely separated phenomena with which this reminiscence deals.

Another year passed. I gained three pounds, drank too much, rowed incessantly with my staff and got a tidy raise. A telegrapher took a swing at me midway through the office Christmas party, and I fired him. My wife and kids didn't arrive in April when I expected them. I phoned Florida, and she gave me some excuse or other about missing the plane. After a few more missed planes and a few more phone calls, she got around to telling me that she didn't *want* to come back. That was okay with me. In my own intuitive way I knew that the upcoming season was more important than who stayed married to whom.

In July a dispatch arrived by wire while a new man was working the night desk. It was from Hood River, Oregon. Our stringer there reported that more than one hundred ''green capsules'' about fifty yards long had appeared in and around an apple orchard. The new desk man was not so new that he did not recall the downhold policy on silly-season items. He killed it, but left it on the spoke for my amused inspection in the morning.

I suppose exactly the same thing happened in every wire service newsroom in the region. I rolled in at 10:30 and riffled through the stuff on the spike. When I saw the ''green capsules'' dispatch I tried to phone Portland, but couldn't get a connection. Then the phone buzzed and a correspondent of ours in Seattle began to yell at me, but the line went dead.

I shrugged and phoned Benson, in Fort Hicks. He was at the police station and asked me: ''Is this it?''

''It is,'' I told him. I read him the telegram from Hood River and told him about the line trouble in Seattle.

''So,'' he said wonderingly, ''I called the turn, didn't I?''

''Called what turn?''

''On the invaders. I don't know who they are—but it's the story of the boy who cried wolf. Only this time the wolves realized——'' Then the phone went dead.

But he was right.

The people of the world were the sheep.

We newsmen—radio, TV, press and wire services—were the boy, who should have been ready to sound the alarm.

But the cunning wolves had tricked us into sounding the alarm so many times that the villagers were weary, and would not come when there was real peril.

The wolves who were then burning their way through the Ozarks, utterly without opposition—the wolves were the Martians under whose yoke and lash we now endure our miserable existences.

12

MISBEGOTTEN MISSIONARY

Isaac Asimov (1920–)

GALAXY SCIENCE FICTION
November

*And with this we come to the end of the Golden Age of Campbell,
the years from 1938 to 1950, when John Campbell reigned as
supreme and unchallenged Emperor of Science Fiction. To be
sure there were good stories elsewhere than in* Astounding, *but
coming across them always seemed surprising. One assumed
they were Campbell-rejects.*

In 1949, The Magazine of Fantasy and Science Fiction *came
into being, but it seemed to many to be only tangentially science
fiction. There was that word "Fantasy" in the title.*

And then came Galaxy Science Fiction, *with October 1950 as
Volume 1, Number 1. Horace L. Gold, its editor, put out three
issues that are (possibly) the best consecutive three ever to
appear among the magazines and, at a bound, made himself
Campbell's rival. Science fiction was no longer a one-editor
field.*

*I had two short stories in those first three issues. The first, in
the first issue, was "Darwinian Poolroom" and surely the fee-
blest story in the issue-trilogy. Not even Marty would dare
include it in this anthology. The second is "Misbegotten Missionary" and I don't think it belongs either, but Marty insists.*

*I suppose I wouldn't feel so bad about it, if Horace (an
inveterate title-changer) hadn't given it that terrible title. It
appears in my own collection* Nightfall and Other Stories *as
"Green Patches," but in this series we are not making any*

changes. This is the tenth anthologization of this story, by the way, so maybe it's not as bad as I think.

—*I.A.*

He had slipped aboard the ship! There had been dozens waiting outside the energy barrier when it had seemed that waiting would do no good. Then the barrier had faltered for a matter of two minutes (which showed the superiority of unified organisms over life fragments) and he was across.

None of the others had been able to move quickly enough to take advantage of the break, but that didn't matter. All alone, he was enough. No others were necessary.

And the thought faded out of satisfaction and into loneliness. It was a terribly unhappy and unnatural thing to be parted from all the rest of the unified organism, to be a life fragment oneself. How could these aliens stand being fragments?

It increased his sympathy for the aliens. Now that he experienced fragmentation himself, he could feel, as though from a distance, the terrible isolation that made them so afraid. It was fear born of that isolation that dictated their actions. What but the insane fear of their condition could have caused them to blast an area, one mile in diameter, into dull-red heat before landing their ship? Even the organized life ten feet deep in the soil had been destroyed in the blast.

He engaged reception, listening eagerly, letting the alien thought saturate him. He enjoyed the touch of life upon his consciousness. He would have to ration that enjoyment. He must not forget himself.

But it could do no harm to listen to thoughts. Some of the fragments of life on the ship thought quite clearly, considering that they were such primitive, incomplete creatures. Their thoughts were like tiny bells.

Roger Oldenn said, "I feel contaminated. You know what I mean? I keep washing my hands and it doesn't help."

Jerry Thorn hated dramatics and didn't look up. They were still maneuvering in the stratosphere of Saybrook's Planet and he preferred to watch the panel dials. He said, "No reason to feel contaminated. Nothing happened."

"I hope not," said Oldenn. "At least they had all the field

men discard their spacesuits in the air lock for complete disinfection. They had a radiation bath for all men entering from outside. I *suppose* nothing happened.''

"Why be nervous, then?''

"I don't know. I wish the barrier hadn't broken down.''

"Who doesn't? It was an accident.''

"I wonder.'' Oldenn was vehement. "I was here when it happened. My shift, you know. There was no reason to overload the power line. There was equipment plugged into it that had no damn business near it. None whatsoever.''

"All right. People are stupid.''

"Not that stupid. I hung around when the Old Man was checking into the matter. None of them had reasonable excuses. The armor-baking circuits, which were draining off two thousand watts, had been put into the barrier line. They'd been using the second subsidiaries for a week. Why not this time? They couldn't give any reason.''

"Can you?''

Oldenn flushed. "No, I was just wondering if the men had been''—he searched for a word—"hypnotized into it. By those things outside.''

Thorn's eyes lifted and met those of the other levelly. "I wouldn't repeat that to anyone else. The barrier was down only two minutes. If anything had happened, if even a spear of grass had drifted across it would have shown up in our bacteria cultures within half an hour, in the fruit-fly colonies in a matter of days. Before we got back it would show up in the hamsters, the rabbits, maybe the goats. Just get it through your head, Oldenn, that nothing happened. Nothing.''

Oldenn turned on his heel and left. In leaving, his foot came within two feet of the object in the corner of the room. He did not see it.

He disengaged his reception centers and let the thoughts flow past him unperceived. These life fragments were not important, in any case, since they were not fitted for the continuation of life. Even as fragments, they were incomplete.

The other types of fragments now—they were different. He had to be careful of them. The temptation would be great, and he must give no indication, none at all, of his existence on board ship till they landed on their home planet.

He focused on the other parts of the ship, marveling at the

diversity of life. Each item, no matter how small, was sufficient to itself. He forced himself to contemplate this, until the unpleasantness of the thought grated on him and he longed for the normality of home.

Most of the thoughts he received from the smaller fragments were vague and fleeting, as you would expect. There wasn't much to be had from them, but that meant their need for completeness was all the greater. It was that which touched him so keenly.

There was the life fragment which squatted on its haunches and fingered the wire netting that enclosed it. Its thoughts were clear, but limited. Chiefly, they concerned the yellow fruit a companion fragment was eating. It wanted the fruit very deeply. Only the wire netting that separated the fragments prevented its seizing the fruit by force.

He disengaged reception in a moment of complete revulsion. *These fragments competed for food!*

He tried to reach far outward for the peace and harmony of home, but it was already an immense distance away. He could reach only into the nothingness that separated him from sanity.

He longed at the moment even for the feel of the dead soil between the barrier and the ship. He had crawled over it last night. There had been no life upon it, but it had been the soil of home, and on the other side of the barrier there had still been the comforting feel of the rest of organized life.

He could remember the moment he had located himself on the surface of the ship, maintaining a desperate suction grip until the air lock opened. He had entered, moving cautiously between the outgoing feet. There had been an inner lock and that had been passed later. Now he lay here, a life fragment himself, inert and unnoticed.

Cautiously, he engaged reception again at the previous focus. The squatting fragment of life was tugging furiously at the wire netting. It still wanted the other's food, though it was the less hungry of the two.

Larsen said, "Don't feed the damn thing. She isn't hungry; she's just sore because Tillie had the nerve to eat before she herself was crammed full. The greedy ape! I wish we were back home and I never had to look another animal in the face again."

He scowled at the older female chimpanzee frowningly and the chimp mouthed and chattered back to him in full reciprocation.

Rizzo said, "Okay, okay. Why hang around here, then? Feeding time is over. Let's get out."

They went past the goat pens, the rabbit hutches, the hamster cages.

Larsen said bitterly, "You volunteer for an exploration voyage. You're a hero. They send you off with speeches—and make a zoo keeper out of you."

"And give you double pay."

"All right, so what? I didn't sign up just for the money. They said at the original briefing that it was even odds we wouldn't come back, that we'd end up like Saybrook. I signed up because I wanted to do something important."

"Just a bloomin' bloody hero," said Rizzo.

"I'm not an animal nurse."

Rizzo paused to lift a hamster out of the cage and stroke it. "Hey," he said, "did you ever think that maybe one of these hamsters has some cute little baby hamsters inside, just getting started?"

"Wise guy! They're tested every day."

"Sure, sure." He muzzled the little creature, which vibrated its nose at him. "But just suppose you came down one morning and found them there. New little hamsters looking up at you with soft, green patches of fur where the eyes ought to be."

"Shut up, for the love of Mike," yelled Larsen.

"Little soft, green patches of shining fur," said Rizzo, and put the hamster down with a sudden loathing sensation.

He engaged reception again and varied the focus. There wasn't a specialized life fragment at home that didn't have a rough counterpart on shipboard.

There were the moving runners in various shapes, the moving swimmers, and the moving fliers. Some of the fliers were quite large, with perceptible thoughts; others were small, gauzy-winged creatures. These last transmitted only patterns of sense perception, imperfect patterns at that, and added nothing intelligent of their own.

There were the non-movers, which, like the non-movers at home, were green and lived on the air, water, and soil. These were a mental blank. They knew only the dim, dim consciousness of light, moisture, and gravity.

And each fragment, moving and non-moving, had its mockery of life.

Not yet. Not yet. . . .

He clamped down hard upon his feelings. Once before, these life fragments had come, and the rest at home had tried to help them—too quickly. It had not worked. This time they must wait.

If only these fragments did not discover him.

They had not, so far. They had not noticed him lying in the corner of the pilot room. No one had bent down to pick up and discard him. Earlier, it had meant he could not move. Someone might have turned and stared at the stiff wormlike thing, not quite six inches long. First stare, then shout, and then it would all be over.

But now, perhaps, he had waited long enough. The takeoff was long past. The controls were locked; the pilot room was empty.

It did not take him long to find the chink in the armor leading to the recess where some of the wiring was. They were dead wires.

The front end of his body was a rasp that cut in two a wire of just the right diameter. Then, six inches away, he cut it in two again. He pushed the snipped-off section of the wire ahead of him packing it away neatly and invisibly into a corner of recess. Its outer covering was a brown elastic material and its core was gleaming, ruddy metal. He himself could not reproduce the core, of course, but that was not necessary. It was enough that the pellicle that covered him had been carefully bred to resemble a wire's surface.

He returned and grasped the cut sections of the wire before and behind. He tightened against them as his little suction disks came into play. Not even a seam showed.

They could not find him now. They could look right at him and see only a continuous stretch of wire.

Unless they looked very closely indeed and noted that, in a certain spot on this wire, there were two tiny patches of soft and shining green fur.

"It is remarkable," said Dr. Weiss, "that little green hairs can do so much."

Captain Loring poured the brandy carefully. In a sense, this was a celebration. They would be ready for the jump through hyper-space in two hours, and after that, two days would see them back on Earth.

"You are convinced, then, the green fur is the sense organ?" he asked.

"It is," said Weiss. Brandy made him come out in splotches, but he was aware of the need of celebration—quite aware. "The experiments were conducted under difficulties, but they were quite significant."

The captain smiled stiffly. " 'Under difficulties' is one way of phrasing it. I would never have taken the chances you did to run them."

"Nonsense. We're all heroes aboard this ship, all volunteers, all great men with trumpet, fife, and fanfarade. You took the chance of coming here."

"You were the first to go outside the barrier."

"No particular risk was involved," Weiss said. "I burned the ground before me as I went, to say nothing of the portable barrier that surrounded me. Nonsense, Captain. Let's all take our medals when we come back; let's take them without attempt at gradation. Besides, I'm a male."

"But you're filled with bacteria to here." The captain's hand made a quick, cutting gesture three inches above his head. "Which makes you as vulnerable as a female would be."

They paused for drinking purposes.

"Refill?" asked the captain.

"No, thanks. I've exceeded my quota already."

"Then one last for the spaceroad." He lifted his glass in the general direction of Saybrook's Planet, no longer visible, its sun only a bright star in the visiplate. "To the little green hairs that gave Saybrook his first lead."

Weiss nodded. "A lucky thing. We'll quarantine the planet, of course."

The captain said, "That doesn't seem drastic enough. Someone might always land by accident someday and not have Saybrook's insight, or his guts. Suppose he did not blow up his ship, as Saybrook did. Suppose he got back to some inhabited place."

The captain was somber. "Do you suppose they might ever develop interstellar travel on their own?"

"I doubt it. No proof, of course. It's just that they have such a completely different orientation. Their entire organization of life has made tools unnecessary. As far as we know, even a stone ax doesn't exist on the planet."

"I hope you're right. Oh, and, Weiss, would you spend some time with Drake?"

"The Galactic Press fellow?"

"Yes. Once we get back, the story of Saybrook's Planet will be released for the public and I don't think it would be wise to oversensationalize it. I've asked Drake to let you consult with him on the story. You're a biologist and enough of an authority to carry weight with him. Would you oblige?"

"A pleasure."

The captain closed his eyes wearily and shook his head.

"Headache, Captain?"

"No. Just thinking of poor Saybrook."

He was weary of the ship. Awhile back there had been a queer, momentary sensation, as though he had been turned inside out. It was alarming and he had searched the minds of the keen-thinkers for an explanation. Apparently the ship had leaped across vast stretches of empty space by cutting across something they knew as "hyper-space." The keen-thinkers were ingenious.

But—he was weary of the ship. It was such a futile phenomenon. These life fragments were skillful in their constructions, yet it was only a measure of their unhappiness, after all. They strove to find in the control of inanimate matter what they could not find in themselves. In their unconscious yearning for completeness, they built machines and scoured space, seeking, seeking . . .

These creatures, he knew, could never, in the very nature of things, find that for which they were seeking. At least not until such time as he gave it to them. He quivered a little at the thought.

Completeness!

These fragments had no concept of it, even. "Completeness" was a poor word.

In their ignorance they would even fight it. There had been the ship that had come before. The first ship had contained many of the keen-thinking fragments. There had been two varieties, life producers and the sterile ones. (How different this second ship was. The keen-thinkers were all sterile, while the other fragments, the fuzzy-thinkers and the no-thinkers, were all producers of life. It was strange.)

How gladly that first ship had been welcomed by all the planet! He could remember the first intense shock at the realization that the visitors were fragments and not complete. The shock had given way to pity, and the pity to action. It was not certain how they would fit into the community, but there had been no hesitation. All life was sacred and somehow room would have been made for them—for all of them, from the large keen-thinkers to the little multipliers in the darkness.

But there had been a miscalculation. They had not correctly analyzed the course of the fragments' ways of thinking. The keen-thinkers became aware of what had been done and resented it. They were frightened, of course; they did not understand.

They had developed the barrier first, and then, later, had destroyed themselves, exploding their ship to atoms.

Poor, foolish fragments.

This time, at least, it would be different. They would be saved, despite themselves.

John Drake would not have admitted it in so many words, but he was very proud of his skill on the photo-typer. He had a travel-kit model, which was a six-by-eight, featureless dark plastic slab, with cylindrical bulges on either end to hold the roll of thin paper. It fitted into a brown leather case, equipped with a beltlike contraption that held it closely about the waist and at one hip. The whole thing weighed less than a pound.

Drake could operate it with either hand. His fingers would flick quickly and easily, placing their light pressure at exact spots on the blank surface, and, soundlessly, words would be written.

He looked thoughtfully at the beginning of his story, then up at Dr. Weiss. "What do you think, Doc?"

"It starts well."

Drake nodded. "I thought I might as well start with Saybrook himself. They haven't released his story back home yet. I wish I could have seen Saybrook's original report. How did he ever get it through, by the way?"

"As near as I could tell, he spent one last night sending it through the sub-ether. When he was finished, he shorted the motors, and converted the entire ship into a thin cloud of vapor a millionth of a second later. The crew and himself along with it."

"What a man! You were in this from the beginning, Doc?"

"Not from the beginning," corrected Weiss gently. "Only since the receipt of Saybrook's report."

He could not help thinking back. He had read that report, realizing even then how wonderful the planet must have seemed when Saybrook's colonizing expedition first reached it. It was

practically a duplicate of Earth, with an abounding plant life and
a purely vegetarian animal life.

There had been only the little patches of green fur (how often
had he used that phrase in his speaking and thinking!) which
seemed strange. No living individual on the planet had eyes.
Instead, there was this fur. Even the plants, each blade or leaf or
blossom, possessed the two patches of richer green.

Then Saybrook had noticed, startled and bewildered, that there
was no conflict for food on the planet. All plants grew pulpy
appendages which were eaten by the animals. These were re-
grown in a matter of hours. No other parts of the plants were
touched. It was as though the plants fed the animals as part of
the order of nature. And the plants themselves did not grow in
overpowering profusion. They might almost have been cultivated,
they were spread across the available soil so discriminately.

How much time, Weiss wondered, had Saybrook had to observe the strange law and order on the planet?—the fact that
insects kept their numbers reasonable, though no birds ate them;
that the rodentlike things did not swarm, though no carnivores
existed to keep them in check.

And then there had come the incident of the white rats.

That prodded Weiss. He said, "Oh, one correction, Drake.
Hamsters were not the first animals involved. It was the white
rats."

"White rats," said Drake, making the correction in his notes.

"Every colonizing ship," said Weiss, "takes a group of white
rats for the purpose of testing any alien foods. Rats, of course,
are very similar to human beings from a nutritional viewpoint.
Naturally, only female white rats are taken."

Naturally. If only one sex was present, there was no danger of
unchecked multiplication in case the planet proved favorable.
Remember the rabbits in Australia.

"Incidentally, why not use males?" asked Drake.

"Females are hardier," said Weiss, "which is lucky, since
that gave the situation away. It turned out suddenly that all the
rats were bearing young."

"Right. Now that's where I'm up to, so here's my chance to
get some things straight. For my own information, Doc, how did
Saybrook find out they were in a family way?"

"Accidentally, of course. In the course of nutritional investi-
gations, rats are dissected for evidence of internal damage. Their
condition was bound to be discovered. A few more were dissected;

same results. Eventually, all that lived gave birth to young—with *no* male rats aboard!"

"And the point is that all the young were born with little green patches of fur instead of eyes."

"That is correct. Saybrook said so and we corroborate him. After the rats, the pet cat of one of the children was obviously affected. When it finally kittened, the kittens were not born with closed eyes but with little patches of green fur. There was no tomcat aboard.

"Eventually Saybrook had the women tested. He didn't tell them what for. He didn't want to frighten them. Every single one of them was in the early stages of pregnancy, leaving out of consideration those few who had been pregnant at the time of embarkation. Saybrook never waited for any child to be born, of course. He knew they would have no eyes, only shining patches of green fur.

"He even prepared bacterial cultures (Saybrook was a thorough man) and found each bacillus to show miscroscopic green spots."

Drake was eager. "That goes way beyond our briefing—or, at least, the briefing I got. But granted that life on Saybrook's Planet is organized into a unified whole, how is it done?"

"How? How are your cells organized into a unified whole? Take an individual cell out of your body, even a brain cell, and what is it by itself? Nothing. A little blob of protoplasm with no more capacity for anything human than an amoeba. Less capacity, in fact, since it couldn't live by itself. But put the cells together and you have something that could invent a spaceship or write a symphony."

"I get the idea," said Drake.

Weiss went on, "*All* life on Saybrook's Planet is a *single* organism. In a sense, all life on Earth is too, but it's a fighting dependence, a dog-eat-dog dependence. The bacteria fix nitrogen; the plants fix carbon; animals eat plants and each other; bacterial decay hits everything. It comes full circle. Each grabs as much as it can, and is, in turn, grabbed.

"On Saybrook's Planet, each organism has its place, as each cell in our body does. Bacteria and plants produce food, on the excess of which animals feed, providing in turn carbon dioxide and nitrogenous wastes. Nothing is produced more or less than is needed. The scheme of life is intelligently altered to suit the local environment. No group of life forms multiplies more or less than is needed, just as the cells in our body stop multiplying when there are enough of them for a given purpose. When they don't stop multiplying, we call if cancer. And that's what life on Earth really is, the kind of organic organization we have, compared to that on Saybrook's Planet. One big cancer. Every species, every individual doing its best to thrive at the expense of every other species and individual.''

"You sound as if you approve of Saybrook's Planet, Doc.''

"I do, in a way. It makes sense out of the business of living. I can see their viewpoint toward us. Suppose one of the cells of your body could be conscious of the efficiency of the human body as compared with that of the cell itself, and could realize that this was only the result of the union of many cells into a higher whole. And then suppose it became conscious of the existence of free-living cells, with bare life and nothing more. It might feel a very strong desire to drag the poor thing into an organization. It might feel sorry for it, feel perhaps a sort of missionary spirit. The things on Saybrook's Planet—or the thing; one should use the singular—feels just that, perhaps.''

"And went ahead by bringing about virgin births, eh, Doc? I've got to go easy on that angle of it. Post-office regulations, you know.''

"There's nothing ribald about it, Drake. For centuries we've been able to make the eggs of sea urchins, bees, frogs, et cetera develop without the intervention of male fertilization. The touch of a needle was sometimes enough, or just immersion in the proper salt solution. The thing on Saybrook's Planet can cause fertilization by the controlled use of radiant energy. That's why an appropriate energy barrier stops it; interference, you see, or static.

"They can do more than stimulate the division and development of an unfertilized egg. They can impress their own characteristics upon its nucleo-proteins, so that the young are born with the little patches of green fur, which serve as the planet's sense organ and means of communication. The young, in other words, are not individuals, but become part of the thing on Saybrook's Planet. The thing on the planet, not at all incidentally, can impregnate any species—plant, animal, or microscopic.''

"Potent stuff,'' muttered Drake.

"Totipotent,'' Dr. Weiss said sharply. "Universally potent. Any fragment of it is totipotent. Given time, a single bacterium from Saybrook's Planet can convert *all of Earth* into a single organism! We've got the experimental proof of that.''

Drake said unexpectedly, "You know, I think I'm a millionaire, Doc. Can you keep a secret?"

Weiss nodded, puzzled.

"I've got a souvenir from Saybrook's Planet," Drake told him, grinning. "It's only a pebble, but after the publicity the planet will get, combined with the fact that it's quarantined from here on in, the pebble will be all any human being will ever see of it. How much do you suppose I could sell the thing for?"

Weiss stared. "A pebble?" He snatched at the object shown him, a hard, gray ovoid. "You shouldn't have done that, Drake. It was strictly against regulations."

"I know. That's why I asked if you could keep a secret. If you could give me a signed note of authentication—*What's the matter Doc?*"

Instead of answering, Weiss could only chatter and point. Drake ran over and stared down at the pebble. It was the same as before—

Except that the light was catching it at an angle, and it showed up two little green spots. Look very closely; they were patches of green hairs.

He was disturbed. There was a definite air of danger within the ship. There was the suspicion of his presence aboard. How could that be? He had done nothing yet. Had another fragment of home come aboard and been less cautious? That would be impossible without his knowledge, and though he probed the ship intensely, he found nothing.

And then the suspicion diminished, but it was not quite dead. One of the keen-thinkers still wondered, and was treading close to the truth.

How long before the landing? Would an entire world of life fragments be deprived of completeness? He clung closer to the severed ends of the wire he had been specially bred to imitate, afraid of detection, fearful of his altruistic mission.

Dr. Weiss had locked himself in his own room. They were already within the solar system, and in three hours they would be landing. He had to think. He had three hours in which to decide.

Drake's devilish "pebble" had been part of the organized life on Saybrook's Planet, of course, but it was dead. It was dead when he had first seen it, and if it hadn't been, it was certainly dead after they fed it into the hyper-atomic motor and converted it into a blast of pure heat. And the bacterial cultures still showed normal when Weiss anxiously checked.

That was not what bothered Weiss now.

Drake had picked up the "pebble" during the last hours of the stay on Saybrook's Planet—*after* the barrier breakdown. What if the breakdown had been the result of a slow, relentless mental pressure on the part of the thing on the planet? What if parts of its being waited to invade as the barrier dropped? If the "pebble" had not been fast enough and had moved only after the barrier was re-established, it would have been killed. It would have lain there for Drake to see and pick up.

It was a "pebble," not a natural life form. But did that mean it was not *some* kind of life form? It might have been a deliberate production of the planet's single organism—a creature deliberately designed to look like a pebble, harmless-seeming, unsuspicious. Camouflage, in other words—a shrewd and frighteningly success-ful camouflage.

Had any other camouflaged creature succeeded in crossing the barrier *before* it was re-established—with a suitable shape filched from the minds of the humans aboard ship by the mind-reading organism of the planet? Would it have the casual appearance of a paperweight? Of an ornamental brass-head nail in the captain's old-fashioned chair? And how would they locate it? Could they search every part of the ship for the telltale green patches—even down to individual microbes?

And why camouflage? Did it intend to remain undetected for a time? Why? So that it might wait for the landing on Earth?

An infection *after landing* could not be cured by blowing up a ship. The bacteria of Earth, the molds, yeasts, and protozoa, would go first. Within a year the non-human young would begin arriving by the uncountable billions.

Weiss closed his eyes and told himself it might not be such a bad thing. There would be no more disease, since no bacterium would multiply at the expense of its host, but instead would be satisfied with its fair share of what was available. There would be no more overpopulation; the hordes of East Asia would decline to adjust themselves to the food supply. There would be no more wars, no crime, no greed.

But there would be no more individuality, either.

Humanity would find security by becoming a cog in a biological machine. A man would be brother to a germ, or to a liver cell.

He stood up. He would have a talk with Captain Loring. They would send their report and blow up the ship, just as Saybrook had done.

He sat down again. Saybrook had had proof, while he had only the conjectures of a terrorized mind, rattled by the sight of two green spots on a pebble. Could he kill the two hundred men on board ship because of a feeble suspicion?

He had to *think!*

He was straining. Why did he have to wait? If he could only welcome those who were aboard now. *Now!*

Yet a cooler, more reasoning part of himself told him that he could not. The little multipliers in the darkness would betray their new status in fifteen minutes, and the keen-thinkers had them under continual observation. Even one mile from the surface of their planet would be too soon, since they might still destroy themselves and their ship out in space.

Better to wait for the main air locks to open, for the planetary air to swirl in with millions of the little multipliers. Better to greet each one of them into the brotherhood of unified life and let them swirl out again to spread the message.

Then it would be done! Another world organized, complete!

He waited. There was the dull throbbing of the engines working mightily to control the slow dropping of the ship; the shudder of contact with planetary surface, then—

He let the jubilation of the keen-thinkers sweep into reception, and his own jubilant thoughts answered them. Soon they would be able to receive as well as himself. Perhaps not these particular fragments, but the fragments that would grow out of those which were fitted for the continuation of life.

The main air locks were about to be opened—

And all thought ceased.

Jerry Thorn thought, Damn it, something's wrong *now*.

He said to Captain Loring, "Sorry. There seems to be a power breakdown. The locks won't open."

"Are you sure, Thorn? The lights are on."

"Yes, sir. We're investigating it now."

He tore away and joined Roger Oldenn at the air-lock wiring box. "What's wrong?"

"Give me a chance, will you?" Oldenn's hands were busy. Then he said, "For the love of Pete, there's a six-inch break in the twenty-amp lead."

"What? That can't be!"

Oldenn held up the broken wires with their clean, sharp, sawn-through ends.

Dr. Weiss joined them. He looked haggard and there was the smell of brandy on his breath.

He said shakily, "What's the matter?"

They told him. At the bottom of the compartment, in one corner, was the missing section.

Weiss bent over. There was a black fragment on the floor of the compartment. He touched it with his finger and it smeared, leaving a sooty smudge on his finger tip. He rubbed it off absently.

There might have been something taking the place of the missing section of wire. Something that had been alive and only looked like wire, yet something that would heat, die, and carbonize in a tiny fraction of a second once the electrical circuit which controlled the air lock had been closed.

He said, "How are the bacteria?"

A crew member went to check, returned and said, "All normal, Doc."

The wires had meanwhile been spliced, the locks opened, and Dr. Weiss stepped out into the anarchic world of life that was Earth.

"Anarchy," he said, laughing a little wildly. "And it will stay that way."

13

TO SERVE MAN

Damon Knight

GALAXY SCIENCE FICTION
November

Damon Knight has worked successfully in every area of science fiction—as a critic, his In Search of Wonder *(1956, expanded 1967) was one of the first serious examinations of the field by one of its own; as an editor he struggled grimly against market forces he could not control, turning out excellent issues of* Worlds Beyond, *and then twenty years later helped to establish new standards for the genre with his twenty-one-volume* Orbit *series of original hardcover anthologies; as a writer he produced some of the most memorable short stories of the 1950s and 1960s as well as such notable novels as* Hell's Pavement *(1952) and* A For Anything *(1959); as an organizer and teacher he was one of the founders of The Science Fiction Writers of America and of the Milford Science Fiction Writers' Conference; and he is also one of the very best reprint anthologists around. All of this activity, however, greatly limited his fiction writing from about 1965, and thus deprived his readers of more of his insightful, witty, and well-crafted stories.*

"To Serve Man" is a very famous story, one that became one of the most popular of the Twilight Zone *episodes.*

—*M.H.G.*

When I first began to publish science fiction stories, the very first person ever to write and ask me for my autograph was Damon Knight. Of course I didn't know him at the time.

When I first read "To Serve Man," I had a strong impulse to

221

return the favor, but I fought it down. What if he didn't deign to let me have one?

Personally, I am very fond of the "O. Henry" ending; that is one in which the last sentence or, if possible, the last word, puts a completely new complexion on an entire story. I have tried it once in a while with only moderate success, but I suppose that in all the annals of science fiction, it was never done quite as successfully as in this story.

—I.A.

The Kanamit were not very pretty, it's true. They looked something like pigs and something like people, and that is not an attractive combination. Seeing them for the first time shocked you; that was their handicap. When a thing with the countenance of a fiend comes from the stars and offers a gift, you are disinclined to accept.

I don't know what we expected interstellar visitors to look like—those who thought about it at all, that is. Angels, perhaps, or something too alien to be really awful. Maybe that's why we were all so horrified and repelled when they landed in their great ships and we saw what they really were like.

The Kanamit were short and very hairy—thick, bristly brown-gray hair all over their abominably plump bodies. Their noses were snoutlike and their eyes small, and they had thick hands of three fingers each. They wore green leather harness and green shorts, but I think the shorts were a concession to our notions of public decency. The garments were quite modishly cut, with slash pockets and half-belts in the back. The Kanamit had a sense of humor, anyhow; their clothes proved it.

There were three of them at this session of the U. N., and I can't tell you how queer it looked to see them there in the middle of a solemn Plenary Session—three fat piglike creatures in green harness and shorts, sitting at the long table below the podium, surrounded by the packed arcs of delegates from every nation. They sat correctly upright, politely watching each speaker. Their flat ears drooped over the earphones. Later on, I believe, they learned every human language, but at this time they knew only French and English.

They seemed perfectly at ease—and that, along with their

humor, was a thing that tended to make me like them. I was in
the minority; I didn't think they were trying to put anything over.
They said quite simply that they wanted to help us and I believed
it. As a U. N. translator, of course, my opinion didn't matter,
but I thought they were the best thing that ever happened to
Earth.

The delegate from Argentina got up and said that his government was interested by the demonstration of a new cheap power
source, which the Kanamit had made at the previous session, but
that the Argentine government could not commit itself as to its
future policy without a much more thorough examination.

It was what all the delegates were saying, but I had to pay
particular attention to Senor Valdes, because he tended to sputter
and his diction was bad. I got through the translation all right,
with only one or two momentary hesitations, and then switched
to the Polish-English line to hear how Gregori was doing with
Janciewicz. Janciewicz was the cross Gregori had to bear, just as
Valdes was mine.

Janciewicz repeated the previous remarks with a few ideologi-
cal variations, and then the Secretary-General recognized the
delegate from France, who introduced Dr. Denis Leveque, the
criminologist, and a great deal of complicated equipment was
wheeled in.

Dr. Leveque remarked that the question in many people's
minds had been aptly expressed by the delegate from the U. S.
S. R. at the preceding session, when he demanded, "What is the
motive of the Kanamit? What is their purpose in offering us
these unprecedented gifts, while asking nothing in return?"

The doctor then said, "At the request of several delegates and
with the full consent of our guests, the Kanamit, my associates
and I have made a series of tests upon the Kanamit with the
equipment which you see before you. These tests will now be
repeated."

A murmur ran through the chamber. There was a fusillade of
flashbulbs, and one of the TV cameras moved up to focus on the
instrument board of the doctor's equipment. At the same time,
the huge television screen behind the podium lighted up, and we
saw the blank faces of two dials, each with its pointer resting at
zero, and a strip of paper tape with a stylus point resting against
it.

The doctor's assistants were fastening wires to the temples of
one of the Kanamit, wrapping a canvas-covered rubber tube

around his forearm, and taping something to the palm of his right hand.

In the screen, we saw the paper tape begin to move while the stylus traced a slow zigzag pattern along it. One of the needles began to jump rhythmically; the other flipped over and stayed there, wavering slightly.

"These are the standard instruments for testing the truth of a statement," said Dr. Leveque. "Our first object, since the physiology of the Kanamit is unknown to us, was to determine whether or not they react to these tests as human beings do. We will now repeat one of the many experiments which was made in the endeavor to discover this."

He pointed to the first dial. "This instrument registers the subject's heart-beat. This shows the electrical conductivity of the skin in the palm of his hand, a measure of perspiration, which increases under stress. And this—" pointing to the tape-and-stylus device—"shows the pattern and intensity of the electrical waves emanating from his brain. It has been shown, with human subjects, that all these readings vary markedly depending upon whether the subject is speaking the truth."

He picked up two large pieces of cardboard, one red and one black. The red one was a square about a meter on a side; the black was a rectangle a meter and a half long. He addressed himself to the Kanama:

"Which of these is longer than the other?"

"The red," said the Kanama.

Both needles leaped wildly, and so did the line on the unrolling tape.

"I shall repeat the question," said the doctor. "Which of these is longer than the other?"

"The black," said the creature.

This time the instruments continued in their normal rhythm.

"How did you come to this planet?" asked the doctor.

"Walked," replied the Kanama.

Again the instruments responded, and there was a subdued ripple of laughter in the chamber.

"Once more," said the doctor, "how did you come to this planet?"

"In a spaceship," said the Kanama, and the instruments did not jump.

The doctor again faced the delegates. "Many such experiments were made," he said, "and my colleagues and myself are satisfied that the mechanisms are effective. Now,'' he turned to the Kanama, "I shall ask our distinguished guest to reply to the question put at the last session by the delegate of the U. S. S. R., namely, what is the motive of the Kanamit people in offering these great gifts to the people of Earth?''

The Kanama rose. Speaking this time in English, he said, "On my planet there is a saying, 'There are more riddles in a stone than in a philosopher's head.' The motives of intelligent beings, though they may at times appear obscure, are simple things compared to the complex workings of the natural universe. Therefore I hope that the people of Earth will understand, and believe, when I tell you that our mission upon your planet is simply this—to bring to you the peace and plenty which we ourselves enjoy, and which we have in the past brought to other races throughout the galaxy. When your world has no more hunger, no more war, no more needless suffering, that will be our reward.''

And the needles had not jumped once.

The delegate from the Ukraine jumped to his feet, asking to be recognized, but the time was up and the Secretary-General closed the session.

I met Gregori as we were leaving the U. N. chamber. His face was red with excitement. "Who promoted that circus?" he demanded.

"The tests looked genuine to me," I told him.

"A circus!'' he said vehemently. "A second-rate farce! If they were genuine, Peter, why was debate stifled?''

"There'll be time for debate tomorrow surely.''

"Tomorrow the doctor and his instruments will be back in Paris. Plenty of things can happen before tomorrow. In the name of sanity, man, how can anybody trust a thing that looks as if it ate the baby?''

I was a little annoyed. I said, "Are you sure you're not more worried about their politics than their appearance?''

He said, "Bah," and went away.

The next day reports began to come in from government laboratories all over the world where the Kanamit's power source was being tested. They were wildly enthusiastic. I don't understand such things myself, but it seemed that those little metal boxes would give more electrical power than an atomic pile, for next to nothing and nearly forever. And it was said that they were so cheap to manufacture that everybody in the world could have one of his own. In the early afternoon there were reports that seventeen countries had already begun to set up factories to turn them out.

The next day the Kanamit turned up with plans and specimens of a gadget that would increase the fertility of any arable land by sixty to one hundred per cent. It speeded the formation of nitrates in the soil, or something. There was nothing in the headlines but the Kanamit any more. The day after that, they dropped their bombshell.

"You now have potentially unlimited power and increased food supply," said one of them. He pointed with his three-fingered hand to an instrument that stood on the table before him. It was a box on a tripod, with a parabolic reflector on the front of it. "We offer you today a third gift which is at least as important as the first two."

He beckoned to the TV men to roll their cameras into closeup position. Then he picked up a large sheet of cardboard covered with drawings and English lettering. We saw it on the large screen above the podium; it was all clearly legible.

"We are informed that this broadcast is being relayed throughout your world," said the Kanama. "I wish that everyone who has equipment for taking photographs from television screens would use it now."

The Secretary-General leaned forward and asked a question sharply, but the Kanama ignored him.

"This device," he said, "projects a field in which no explosive, of whatever nature, can detonate."

There was an uncomprehending silence.

The Kanama said, "It cannot now be suppressed. If one nation has it, all must have it." When nobody seemed to understand, he explained bluntly, "There will be no more war."

That was the biggest news of the millennium, and it was perfectly true. It turned out that the explosions the Kanama was talking about included gasoline and Diesel explosions. They had simply made it impossible for anybody to mount or equip a modern army.

We could have gone back to bows and arrows, of course, but that wouldn't have satisfied the military. Not after having atomic bombs and all the rest. Besides, there wouldn't be any reason to make war. Every nation would soon have everything.

Nobody ever gave another thought to those lie-detector

experiments, or asked the Kanamit what their politics were. Gregori was put out; he had nothing to prove his suspicions.

I quit my job with the U. N. a few months later, because I foresaw that it was going to die under me anyhow. U. N. business was booming at the time, but after a year or so there was going to be nothing for it to do. Every nation on Earth was well on the way to being completely self-supporting; they weren't going to need much arbitration.

I accepted a position as translator with the Kanamit Embassy, and it was there that I ran into Gregori again. I was glad to see him, but I couldn't imagine what he was doing there.

"I thought you were on the opposition," I said. "Don't tell me you're convinced the Kanamit are all right."

He looked rather shamefaced. "They're not what they look, anyhow," he said.

It was as much of a concession as he could decently make, and I invited him down to the embassy lounge for a drink. It was an intimate kind of place, and he grew confidential over the second daiquiri.

"They fascinate me," he said. "I hate them instinctively on sight, still—that hasn't changed, but I can evaluate it. You were right, obviously; they mean us nothing but good. But do you know—" he leaned across the table—"the question of the Soviet delegate was never answered."

I am afraid I snorted.

"No, really," he said. "They told us what they wanted to do—'to bring to you the peace and plenty which we ourselves enjoy.' But they didn't say *why*."

"Why do missionaries—"

"Hogwash!" he said angrily. "Missionaries have a religious motive. If these creatures do own a religion, they haven't once mentioned it. What's more, they didn't send a missionary group, they sent a diplomatic delegation—a group representing the will and policy of their whole people. Now just what have the Kanamit, as a people or a nation, got to gain from our welfare?"

I said, "Cultural—"

"Cultural cabbage-soup! No, it's something less obvious than that, something obscure that belongs to their psychology and not to ours. But trust me, Peter, there is no such thing as a completely distinterested altruism. In one way or another, they have something to gain."

"And that's why you're here," I said, "to try to find out what it is?"

"Correct. I wanted to get on one of the ten-year exchange groups to their home planet, but I couldn't; the quota was filled a week after they made the announcement. This is the next best thing. I'm studying their language, and you know that language reflects the basic assumptions of the people who use it. I've got a fair command of the spoken lingo already. It's not hard, really—some of the idioms are almost the same as the equivalents in English. And there are hints in it. I'm sure I'll get the answer eventually."

"More power," I said, and we went back to work.

I saw Gregori frequently from then on, and he kept me posted about his progress. He was highly excited about a month after that first meeting; said he'd got hold of a book of the Kanamit's and was trying to puzzle it out. They wrote in ideographs, worse than Chinese, but he was determined to fathom it if it took him years. He wanted my help.

Well, I was interested in spite of myself, for I knew it would be a long job. We spent some evenings together, working with material from Kanamit bulletin-boards and so forth, and the extremely limited English-Kanamit dictionary they issued the staff. My conscience bothered me about the stolen book, but gradually I became absorbed by the problem. Languages are my field, after all. I couldn't help being fascinated.

We got the title worked out in a few weeks. It was "How to Serve Man," evidently a handbook they were giving out to new Kanamit members of the embassy staff. They had new ones in, all the time now, a shipload about once a month; they were opening all kinds of research laboratories, clinics and so on. If there was anybody on Earth besides Gregori who still distrusted those people, he must have been somewhere in the middle of Tibet.

It was astonishing to see the changes that had been wrought in less than a year. There were no more standing armies, no more shortages, no unemployment. When you picked up a newspaper you didn't see "H-BOMB" or "V-2" leaping out at you; the news was always good. It was a hard thing to get used to. The Kanamit were working on human biochemistry, and it was known around the embassy that they were nearly ready to announce methods of making our race taller and stronger and healthier—

practically a race of supermen—and they had a potential cure for heart disease and cancer.

I didn't see Gregori for a fortnight after we finished working out the title of the book; I was on a long-overdue vacation in Canada. When I got back, I was shocked by the change in his appearance.

"What on Earth is wrong, Gregori?" I asked. "You look like the very devil."

"Come down to the lounge."

I went with him, and he gulped a stiff Scotch as if he needed it.

"Come on, man, what's the matter?" I urged.

"The Kanamit have put me on the passenger list for the next exchange ship," he said. "You, too, otherwise I wouldn't be talking to you."

"Well," I said, "but—"

"They're not altruists."

"What do you mean?"

"What I told you," he said. "They're not altruists."

I tried to reason with him. I pointed out they'd made Earth a paradise compared to what it was before. He only shook his head.

Then I said, "Well, what about those lie-detector tests?"

"A farce," he replied, without heat. "I said so at the time, you fool. They told the truth, though, as far as it went."

"And the book?" I demanded, annoyed. "What about that— 'How to Serve Man'? That wasn't put there for you to read. They *mean* it. How do you explain that?"

"I've read the first page of that book," he said. "Why do you suppose I haven't slept for a week?"

I said, "Well?" and he smiled that curious, twisted smile, as if he really wanted to cry instead.

"It's a cookbook," he said.

14

COMING ATTRACTION

Fritz Leiber (1910–   )

GALAXY SCIENCE FICTION
November

We have discussed the amazing career of Fritz Leiber in earlier volumes of this series. Suffice it to say that he is still productive and going strong at 74, and still winning awards, six Hugos, three Nebulas, one Gandalf, and two World Fantasy Awards to date.

As Algis Budrys has pointed out, "Coming Attraction" may be the most important story in this book, for it helped establish the tone and concerns of both Galaxy Science Fiction *and the* science fiction of the 1950s.

Isaac, the November 1950 issue of Galaxy *must rank as one of strongest in the illustrious history of that magazine.*

—*M.H.G.*

Of all the great stories in those great first three issues of Galaxy, I can't imagine that anyone will argue with the contention that "Coming Attraction" was the greatest. From the moment it appeared there was a buzz of astonishment at its excellence. It is so annoying that there was no Hugo Award in 1950, for if ever there was a story that was an absolute shoo-in for winning the short-story award, it was this one. I'll bet it would have come closer to getting a unanimous vote than any story before or since.

For those of you who are too young to remember, there was, back in 1950, a very successful mystery writer named Mickey Spillane who put out a series of best-selling books that were

*well-packed with violence and (by the standards of that period)
steamy sex. I didn't like them myself, but no one asked me. In
any case, "Coming Attraction" is a skillful satire on the Spillane
style and (again no one asked me) much better than anything
Spillane himself ever wrote.*

—I.A.

The coupé with the fishhooks welded to the fender shouldered up
over the curb like the nose of a nightmare. The girl in its path
stood frozen, her face probably stiff with fright under her mask.
For once my reflexes weren't shy. I took a fast step toward her,
grabbed her elbow, yanked her back. Her black skirt swirled out.

The big coupé shot by, its turbine humming. I glimpsed three
faces. Something ripped. I felt the hot exhaust on my ankles as
the big coupé swerved back into the street. A thick cloud like a
black flower blossomed from its jouncing rear end, while from
the fishhooks flew a black shimmering rag.

"Did they get you?" I asked the girl.

She had twisted around to look where the side of her skirt was
torn away. She was wearing nylon tights.

"The hooks didn't touch me," she said shakily. "I guess I'm
lucky."

I heard voices around us:

"Those kids! What'll they think up next?"

"They're a menace. They ought to be arrested."

Sirens screamed at a rising pitch as two motor-police, their
rocket-assist jets full on, came whizzing toward us after the
coupé. But the black flower had become a thick fog obscuring
the whole street. The motor-police switched from rocket assists
to rocket brakes and swerved to a stop near the smoke cloud.

"Are you English?" the girl asked me. "You have an English
accent."

Her voice came shudderingly from behind the sleek black satin
mask. I fancied her teeth must be chattering. Eyes that were
perhaps blue searched my face from behind the black gauze
covering the eyeholes of the mask. I told her she'd guessed right.
She stood close to me. "Will you come to my place tonight?"
she asked rapidly. "I can't thank you now. And there's something you can help me about."

My arm, still lightly circling her waist, felt her body trembling. I was answering the plea in that as much as in her voice when I said, "Certainly." She gave me an address south of Inferno, an apartment number and a time. She asked me my name and I told her.

"Hey, you!"

I turned obediently to the policeman's shout. He shooed away the small clucking crowd of masked women and barefaced men. Coughing from the smoke that the black coupé had thrown out, he asked for my papers. I handed him the essential ones.

He looked at them and then at me. "British Barter? How long will you be in New York?"

Suppressing the urge to say, "For as short a time as possible," I told him I'd be here for a week or so.

"May need you as a witness," he explained. "Those kids can't use smoke on us. When they do that, we pull them in."

He seemed to think the smoke was the bad thing. "They tried to kill the lady," I pointed out.

He shook his head wisely. "They always pretend they're going to, but actually they just want to snag skirts. I've picked up rippers with as many as fifty skirt-snags tacked up in their rooms. Of course, sometimes they come a little too close."

I explained that if I hadn't yanked her out of the way, she'd have been hit by more than hooks. But he interrupted, "If she'd thought it was a real murder attempt, she'd have stayed here."

I looked around. It was true. She was gone.

"She was fearfully frightened," I told him.

"Who wouldn't be? Those kids would have scared old Stalin himself."

"I mean frightened of more than 'kids.' They didn't look like 'kids.' "

"What did they look like?"

I tried without much success to describe the three faces. A vague impression of viciousness and effeminacy doesn't mean much.

"Well, I could be wrong," he said finally. "Do you know the girl? Where she lives?"

"No," I half lied.

The other policeman hung up his radiophone and ambled toward us, kicking at the tendrils of dissipating smoke. The black cloud no longer hid the dingy facades with their five-year-old radiation flashburns, and I could begin to make out the distant stump of the Empire State Building, thrusting up out of Inferno like a mangled finger.

"They haven't been picked up so far," the approaching policeman grumbled. "Left smoke for five blocks, from what Ryan says."

The first policeman shook his head. "That's bad," he observed solemnly.

I was feeling a bit uneasy and ashamed. An Englishman shouldn't lie, at least not on impulse.

"They sound like nasty customers," the first policeman continued in the same grim tone. "We'll need witnesses. Looks as if you may have to stay in New York longer than you expect."

I got the point. I said, "I forgot to show you all my papers," and handed him a few others, making sure there was a five dollar bill in among them.

When he handed them back a bit later, his voice was no longer ominous. My feelings of guilt vanished. To cement our relationship, I chatted with the two of them about their job.

"I suppose the masks give you some trouble," I observed. "Over in England we've been reading about your new crop of masked female bandits."

"Those things get exaggerated," the first policeman assured me. "It's the men masking as women that really mix us up. But, brother, when we nab them, we jump on them with both feet."

"And you get so you can spot women almost as well as if they had naked faces," the second policeman volunteered. "You know, hands and all that."

"Especially all that," the first agreed with a chuckle. "Say, is it true that some girls don't mask over in England?"

"A number of them have picked up the mask fashion," I told him. "Only a few, though—the ones who always adopt the latest style, however extreme."

"They're usually masked in the British newscasts."

"I imagine it's arranged that way out of deference to American taste," I confessed. "Actually, not very many do mask."

The second policeman considered that. "Girls going down the street bare from the neck up." It was not clear whether he viewed the prospect with relish or moral distaste. Likely both.

"A few members keep trying to persuade Parliament to enact a law forbidding all masking," I continued, talking perhaps a bit too much.

The second policeman shook his head. "What an idea. You know, masks are a pretty good thing, brother. Couple of years more and I'm going to make my wife wear hers around the house."

The first policeman shrugged. "If women were to stop wearing masks, in six weeks you wouldn't know the difference. You get used to anything, if enough people do it."

I agreed, rather regretfully, and left them. I turned north on Broadway (old Tenth Avenue, I believe) and walked rapidly until I was beyond Inferno. Passing such an area of undecontaminated radioactivity always makes a person queasy. I thanked God there weren't any such in England, as yet.

The street was almost empty, though I was accosted by a couple of beggars with faces tunneled by H-bomb scars, whether real or of makeup putty, I couldn't tell. A fat woman held out a baby with webbed fingers and toes. I told myself it would have been deformed anyway and that she was only capitalizing on our fear of bomb-induced mutations. Still, I gave her a seven-and-a-half-cent piece. Her mask made me feel I was paying tribute to an African fetish.

"May all your children be blessed with one head and two eyes, sir."

"Thanks," I said, shuddering, and hurried past her.

". . . There's only trash behind the mask, so turn your head, stick to your task: Stay away, stay away—from—the—girls!"

This last was the end of an antisex song being sung by some religionists half a block from the circle-and-cross insignia of a femalist temple. They reminded me only faintly of our small tribe of British monastics. Above their heads was a jumble of billboards advertising predigested foods, wrestling instruction, radio handies and the like.

I stared at the hysterical slogans with disagreeable fascination. Since the female face and form have been banned on American signs, the very letters of the advertiser's alphabet have begun to crawl with sex—the fat-bellied, big-breasted capital B, the lascivious double O. However, I reminded myself, it is chiefly the mask that so strangely accents sex in America.

A British anthropologist has pointed out, that, while it took more than 5,000 years to shift the chief point of sexual interest from the hips to the breasts, the next transition to the face has taken less than 50 years. Comparing the American style with Moslem tradition is not valid; Moslem women are compelled to wear veils, the purpose of which is concealment, while American women have only the compulsion of fashion, whatever that means.

Theory aside, the actual origins of the trend are to be found in the antiradiation clothing of World War III, which led to masked wrestling, now a fantastically popular sport, and that in turn led to the current female fashion. Only a wild style at first, masks quickly became as necessary as brassieres and lipsticks had been earlier in the century.

I finally realized that I was not speculating about masks in general, but about what lay behind one in particular. That's the devil of the things; you're never sure whether a girl is heightening loveliness or hiding ugliness. I pictured a cool, pretty face in which fear showed only in widened eyes. Then I remembered her blonde hair, rich against the blackness of the satin mask. She'd told me to come at the twenty-second hour—ten P.M.

I climbed to my apartment near the British Consulate; the elevator shaft had been shoved out of plumb by an old blast, a nuisance in these tall New York buildings. Before it occurred to me that I would be going out again, I automatically tore a tab from the film strip under my shirt. I developed it just to be sure. It showed that the total radiation I'd taken that day was still within the safety limit. I'm not phobic about it, as so many people are these days, but there's no point in taking chances.

I flopped down on the day bed and stared at the silent speaker and the dark screen of the video set. As always, they made me think, somewhat bitterly, of the two great nations of the world. Mutilated by each other, yet still strong, they were crippled giants poisoning the planet with their dreams of an impossible equality and an impossible success.

I fretfully switched on the speaker. By luck, the newscaster was talking excitedly of the prospects of a bumper wheat crop, sown by planes across a dust bowl moistened by seeded rains. I listened carefully to the rest of the program (it was remarkably clear of Russian telejamming) but there was no further news of interest to me. And, of course, no mention of the moon, though everyone knows that America and Russia are racing to develop their primary bases into fortresses capable of mutual assault and the launching of alphabet-bombs toward Earth. I myself knew perfectly well that the British electronic equipment I was helping trade for American wheat was destined for use in spaceships.

I switched off the newscast. It was growing dark and once

again I pictured a tender, frightened face behind a mask. I hadn't had a date since England. It's exceedingly difficult to become acquainted with a girl in America, where as little as a smile, often, can set one of them yelping for the police—to say nothing of the increasing puritanical morality and the roving gangs that keep most women indoors after dark. And naturally, the masks, which the Soviets describe as a last symptom of capitalist degeneracy and collapse. The Russians wear no masks, but I like their last symptoms even less.

I went to the window and impatiently watched the darkness gather. I was getting very restless. After a while a ghostly violet cloud appeared to the south. My hair rose. Then I laughed. I had momentarily fancied it a radiation from the crater of the Hell-bomb, though I should instantly have known it was only the radio-induced glow in the sky over the amusement and residential area south of Inferno.

Promptly at twenty-two hours I stood before the door of my unknown girl friend's apartment. The electronic say-who-please said just that. I answered clearly, "Wysten Turner," wondering if she'd given my name to the mechanism. She evidently had, for the door opened. I walked into a small empty living room, my heart pounding a bit.

The room was expensively furnished with the latest pneumatic hassocks and sprawlers. There were some midgie books on the table. The one I picked up was the standard hard-boiled detective story in which two female murderers go gunning for each other.

The television was on. A masked girl in green was crooning a love song. Her right hand held something that blurred off into the foreground. I saw the set had a handie, which we haven't in England as yet, and curiously thrust my hand into the handie orifice beside the screen. Contrary to my expectations, it was not like slipping into a pulsing rubber glove, but rather as if the girl on the screen actually held my hand.

A door opened behind me. I jerked out my hand with as guilty a reaction as if I'd been caught peering through a keyhole.

She stood in the bedroom doorway. I think she was trembling. She was wearing a gray fur coat, white-speckled, and a gray velvet evening mask with shirred gray lace around the eyes and mouth. Her fingernails twinkled like silver.

It hadn't occurred to me that she'd expect us to go out.

"I should have told you," she said softly. Her mask veered

nervously toward the books and the screen and the room's dark corners. "But I can't possibly talk to you here."

I said doubtfully, "There's a place near the Consulate. ... ."

"I know where we can be together and talk," she said rapidly. "If you don't mind."

As we entered the elevator I said, "I'm afraid I dismissed the cab."

But the cab driver hadn't gone for some reason of his own. He jumped out and smirkingly held the front door open for us. I told him we preferred to sit in back. He sulkily opened the rear door, slammed it after us, jumped in front and slammed the door behind him.

My companion leaned forward. "Heaven," she said.

The driver switched on the turbine and televisor.

"Why did you ask if I were a British subject?" I said, to start the conversation.

She leaned away from me, tilting her mask close to the window. "See the Moon," she said in a quick, dreamy voice.

"But why, really?" I pressed, conscious of an irritation that had nothing to do with her.

"It's edging up into the purple of the sky."

"And what's your name?"

"The purple makes it look yellower."

Just then I became aware of the source of my irritation. It lay in the square of writhing light in the front of the cab beside the driver.

I don't object to ordinary wrestling matches, though they bore me, but I simply detest watching a man wrestle a woman. The fact that the bouts are generally "on the level," with the man greatly outclassed in weight and reach and the masked females young and personable, only makes them seem worse to me.

"Please turn off the screen," I requested the driver.

He shook his head without looking around. "Uh-uh, man," he said. "They've been grooming that babe for weeks for this bout with Little Zirk."

Infuriated, I reached forward, but my companion caught my arm. "Please," she whispered frightenedly, shaking her head.

I settled back, frustrated. She was closer to me now, but silent and for a few moments I watched the heaves and contortions of the powerful masked girl and her wiry masked opponent on the screen. His frantic scrambling at her reminded me of a male spider.

I jerked around, facing my companion. "Why did those three men want to kill you?" I asked sharply.

The eyeholes of her mask faced the screen. "Because they're jealous of me," she whispered.

"Why are they jealous?"

She still didn't look at me. "Because of him."

"Who?"

She didn't answer.

I put my arm around her shoulders. "Are you afraid to tell me?" I asked. "What *is* the matter?"

She still didn't look my way. She smelled nice.

"See here," I said laughingly, changing my tactics, "you really should tell me something about yourself. I don't even know what you look like."

I half playfully lifted my hand to the band of her neck. She gave it an astonishingly swift slap. I pulled it away in sudden pain. There were four tiny indentations on the back. From one of them a tiny bead of blood welled out as I watched. I looked at her silver fingernails and saw they were actually delicate and pointed metal caps.

"I'm dreadfully sorry," I heard her say, "but you frightened me. I thought for a moment you were going to. . . ."

At last she turned to me. Her coat had fallen open. Her evening dress was Cretan Revival, a bodice of lace beneath and supporting the breasts without covering them.

"Don't be angry," she said, putting her arms around my neck. "You were wonderful this afternoon."

The soft gray velvet of her mask, molding itself to her cheek, pressed mine. Through the mask's lace the wet warm tip of her tongue touched my chin.

"I'm not angry," I said. "Just puzzled and anxious to help."

The cab stopped. To either side were black windows bordered by spears of broken glass. The sickly purple light showed a few ragged figures slowly moving toward us.

The driver muttered, "It's the turbine, man. We're grounded." He sat there hunched and motionless. "Wish it had happened somewhere else."

My companion whispered, "Five dollars is the usual amount."

She looked out so shudderingly at the congregating figures that I suppressed my indignation and did as she suggested. The driver took the bill without a word. As he started up, he put his hand out the window and I heard a few coins clink on the pavement.

My companion came back into my arms, but her mask faced the television screen, where the tall girl had just pinned the convulsively kicking Little Zirk.

"I'm so frightened," she breathed.

Heaven turned out to be an equally ruined neighborhood, but it had a sidewalk canopy and a huge doorman uniformed like a spaceman, but in gaudy colors. In my sensuous daze I rather liked it all. We stepped out of the cab just as a drunken old woman came down the sidewalk, her mask awry. A couple ahead of us turned their heads from the half-revealed face, as if from an ugly body at the beach. As we followed them in I heard the doorman say, "Get along, grandma, and watch yourself."

Inside, everything was dimness and blue glows. She had said we could talk here, but I didn't see how. Besides the inevitable chorus of sneezes and coughs (they say America is fifty per cent allergic these days), there was a band going full blast in the latest robop style, in which an electronic composing machine selects an arbitrary sequence of tones into which the musicians weave their raucous little individualities.

Most of the people were in booths. The band was behind the bar. On a small platform beside them a girl was dancing, stripped to her mask. The little cluster of men at the shadowy far end of the bar weren't looking at her.

We inspected the menu in gold script on the wall and pushed the buttons for breast of chicken, fried shrimps and two scotches. Moments later, the serving bell tinkled. I opened the gleaming panel and took out our drinks.

The cluster of men at the bar filed off toward the door, but first they stared around the room. My companion had just thrown back her coat. Their look lingered on our booth. I noticed that there were three of them.

The band chased off the dancing girl with growls. I handed my companion a straw and we sipped our drinks.

"You wanted me to help you about something," I said. "Incidentally, I think you're lovely."

She nodded quick thanks, looked around, leaned forward. "Would it be hard for me to get to England?"

"No," I replied, a bit taken aback. "Provided you have an American passport."

"Are they difficult to get?"

"Rather," I said, surprised at her lack of information. "Your country doesn't like its nationals to travel, though it isn't quite as stringent as Russia."

"Could the British Consulate help me get a passport?"

"It's hardly their. . . ."

"Could you?"

I realized we were being inspected. A man and two girls had paused opposite our table. The girls were tall and wolfish-looking, with spangled masks. The man stood jauntily between them like a fox on its hind legs.

My companion didn't glance at them, but she sat back. I noticed that one of the girls had a big yellow bruise on her forearm. After a moment they walked to a booth in the deep shadows.

"Know them?" I asked. She didn't reply. I finished my drink. "I'm not sure you'd like England," I said. "The austerity's altogether different from your American brand of misery."

She leaned forward again. "But I must get away," she whispered.

"Why?" I was getting impatient.

"Because I'm so frightened."

There were chimes. I opened the panel and handed her the fried shrimps. The sauce on my breast of chicken was a delicious steaming compound of almonds, soy and ginger. But something must have been wrong with the radionic oven that had thawed and heated it, for at the first bite I crunched a kernel of ice in the meat. These delicate mechanisms need constant repair and there aren't enough mechanics.

I put down my fork. "What are you really scared of?" I asked her.

For once her mask didn't waver away from my face. As I waited I could feel the fears gathering without her naming them, tiny dark shapes swarming through the curved night outside, converging on the radioactive pest spot of New York, dipping into the margins of the purple. I felt a sudden rush of sympathy, a desire to protect the girl opposite me. The warm feeling added itself to the infatuation engendered in the cab.

"Everything," she said finally.

I nodded and touched her hand.

"I'm afraid of the Moon," she began, her voice going dreamy and brittle as it had in the cab. "You can't look at it and not think of guided bombs."

"It's the same Moon over England," I reminded her.

"But it's not England's Moon any more. It's ours and Russia's. You're not responsible."

I pressed her hand.

"Oh, and then," she said with a tilt of her mask, "I'm afraid of the cars and the gangs and the loneliness and Inferno. I'm afraid of the lust that undresses your face. And—" her voice hushed—"I'm afraid of the wrestlers."

"Yes?" I prompted softly after a moment.

Her mask came forward. "Do you know something about the wrestlers?" she asked rapidly. "The ones that wrestle women, I mean. They often lose, you know. And then they have to have a girl to take their frustration out on. A girl who's soft and weak and terribly frightened. They need that, to keep them men. Other men don't want them to have a girl. Other men want them just to fight women and be heroes. But they must have a girl. It's horrible for her."

I squeezed her fingers tighter, as if courage could be transmitted—granting I had any. "I think I can get you to England," I said.

Shadows crawled onto the table and stayed there. I looked up at the three men who had been at the end of the bar. They were the men I had seen in the big coupé. They wore black sweaters, and close-fitting black trousers. Their faces were as expressionless as dopers. Two of them stood above me. The other loomed over the girl.

"Drift off, man," I was told. I heard the other inform the girl: "We'll wrestle a fall, sister. What shall it be? Judo, slapsie or kill-who-can?"

I stood up. There are times when an Englishman simply must be maltreated. But just then the foxlike man came gliding in like the star of a ballet. The reaction of the other three startled me. They were acutely embarrassed.

He smiled at them thinly. "You won't win my favor by tricks like this," he said.

"Don't get the wrong idea, Zirk," one of them pleaded.

"I will if it's right," he said. "She told me what you tried to do this afternoon. That won't endear you to me either. Drift."

They backed off awkwardly. "Let's get out of here," one of them said loudly, as they turned. "I know a place where they fight naked with knives."

Little Zirk laughed musically and slipped into the seat beside my companion. She shrank from him, just a little. I pushed my feet back, leaned forward.

"Who's your friend, baby?" he asked, not looking at her.

She passed the question to me with a little gesture. I told him.

"British," he observed. "She's been asking you about getting out of the country? About passports?" He smiled pleasantly. "She likes to start running away. Don't you, baby?" His small hand began to stroke her wrist, the fingers bent a little, the tendons ridged, as if he were about to grab and twist.

"Look here," I said sharply. "I have to be grateful to you for ordering off those bullies, but—"

"Think nothing of it," he told me. "They're no harm except when they're behind the steering wheels. A well-trained fourteen-year-old girl could cripple any one of them. Why, even Theda here, if she went in for that sort of thing. . . ." He turned to her, shifting his hand from her wrist to her hair. He stroked it, letting the strands slip slowly through his fingers. "You know I lost tonight, baby, don't you?" he said softly.

I stood up. "Come along," I said to her. "Let's leave."

She just sat there. I couldn't even tell if she was trembling. I tried to read a message in her eyes through the mask.

"I'll take you away," I said to her. "I can do it. I really will."

He smiled at me. "She'd like to go with you," he said. "Wouldn't you, baby?"

"Will you or won't you?" I said to her. She still just sat there.

He slowly knotted his fingers in her hair.

"Listen, you little vermin," I snapped at him. "Take your hands off her."

He came up from the seat like a snake. I'm no fighter. I just know that the more scared I am, the harder and straighter I hit. This time I was lucky. But as he crumpled back, I felt a slap and four stabs of pain in my cheek. I clapped my hand to it. I could feel the four gashes made by her dagger finger caps, and the warm blood oozing out from them.

She didn't look at me. She was bending over little Zirk and cuddling her mask to his cheek and crooning: "There, there, don't feel bad, you'll be able to hurt me afterward."

There were sounds around us, but they didn't come close. I leaned forward and ripped the mask from her face.

I really don't know why I should have expected her face to be anything else. It was very pale, of course, and there weren't any

cosmetics. I suppose there's no point in wearing any under a
mask. The eyebrows were untidy and the lips chapped. But as
for the general expression, as for the feelings crawling and
wriggling across it—

Have you ever lifted a rock from damp soil? Have you ever
watched the slimy white grubs?

I looked down at her, she up at me. "Yes, you're so frightened,
aren't you?" I said. "You dread this little nightly drama, don't
you? You're scared to death."

And I walked right out into the purple night, still holding my
hand to my bleeding cheek. No one stopped me, not even the
girl wrestlers. I wished I could tear a tab from under my shirt,
and test it then and there, and find I'd taken soo much radiation,
and so be able to ask to cross the Hudson and go down New
Jersey, past the imagined radiance of the Narrows Bomb, and so
on to Sandy Hook to wait for the rusty ship that would take me
back over the seas to England.

15

A SUBWAY NAMED MOBIUS

A. J. Deutsch

ASTOUNDING SCIENCE FICTION
December

I'm sorry to report that I don't know a thing about A. J. Deutsch. I only know that this story belongs in the best of 1950, is one of the most amazing stories ever written about mathematics, and that you will enjoy it very much.

—M.H.G.

When Marty wrote the above, he didn't know that I do know something about Armin Deutsch. When I moved to Boston in 1949, Armin was teaching at Harvard, and I got to meet him along with a whole bunch of other delightful academics.

Armin phoned me one morning and said, "May I read you the first few paragraphs of a science fiction story I'm writing?" (I groaned inwardly. Everyone who meets me decides to write sf on the unassailable grounds that if an idiot like me can do it, anyone can.)

Still one must be polite. I said, "Go ahead, Armin."

He did and I grew excited. "Send me the manuscript," I said.

He sent it and I called him, and said, "This is terrific. You must send it to John Campbell. He will take it."

Armin did and John did. The story was, of course, "A Subway Named Mobius" and I have always felt responsible for it.

Armin never wrote another story as far as I know. He had a peculiar metabolic anomaly which caused cholesterol to collect in his joints and he died relatively young, but I do not have his birth or death year.

There was a song later on, popular in Boston, called "The Ballad of the MTA" about a fellow who was caught by a raise in the fare. Not having an additional dime, he could never get off the subway. I've always wondered whether it was inspired by "A Subway Named Mobius." It's a very catchy song, too.

—I.A.

In a complex and ingenious pattern, the subway had spread out from a focus at Park Street. A shunt connected the Lechmere line with the Ashmont for trains southbound, and with the Forest Hills line for those northbound. Harvard and Brookline had been linked with a tunnel that passed through Kenmore Under, and during rush hours every other train was switched through the Kenmore Branch back to Egleston. The Kenmore Branch joined the Maverick Tunnel near Fields Corner. It climbed a hundred feet in two blocks to connect Copley Over with Scollay Square; then it dipped down again to join the Cambridge line at Boylston. The Boylston shuttle had finally tied together the seven principal lines on four different levels. It went into service, you remember, on March 3rd. After that, a train could travel from any one station to any other station in the whole system.

There were two hundred twenty-seven trains running the subways every weekday, and they carried about a million and a half passengers. The Cambridge-Dorchester train that disappeared on March 4th was Number 86. Nobody missed it at first. During the evening rush, the traffic was a little heavier than usual on that line. But a crowd is a crowd. The ad posters at the Forest Hills yards looked for 86 about 7:30, but neither of them mentioned its absence until three days later. The controller at the Milk Street Cross-Over called the Harvard checker for an extra train after the hockey game that night, and the Harvard checker relayed the call to the yards. The dispatcher there sent out 87, which had been put to bed at ten o'clock, as usual. He didn't notice that 86 was missing.

It was near the peak of the rush the next morning that Jack O'Brien, at the Park Street Control, called Warren Sweeney at the Forest Hills yards and told him to put another train on the Cambridge run. Sweeney was short, so he went to the board and scanned it for a spare train and crew. Then, for the first time, he noticed that Gallagher had not checked out the night before. He put the tag up and left a note. Gallagher was due on at ten. At ten-thirty, Sweeney was down looking at the board again, and he noticed Gallagher's tag still up, and the note where he had left it. He groused to the checker and asked if Gallagher had come in late. The checker said he hadn't seen Gallagher at all that morning. Then Sweeney wanted to know who was running 86? A few minutes later he found that Dorkin's card was still up, although it was Dorkin's day off. It was 11:30 before he finally realized that he had lost a train.

Sweeney spent the next hour and a half on the phone, and he quizzed every dispatcher, controller, and checker on the whole system. When he finished his lunch at 1:30, he covered the whole net again. At 4:40, just before he left for the day, he reported the matter, with some indignation, to Central Traffic. The phones buzzed through the tunnels and shops until nearly midnight before the general manager was finally notified at his home.

It was the engineer on the main switchbank who, late in the morning of the 6th, first associated the missing train with the newspaper stories about the sudden rash of missing persons. He tipped off the *Transcript*, and by the end of the lunch hour three papers had Extras on the streets. That was the way the story got out.

Kelvin Whyte, the General Manager, spent a good part of that afternoon with the police. They checked Gallagher's wife, and Dorkin's. The motorman and the conductor had not been home since the morning of the 4th. By mid-afternoon, it was clear to the police that three hundred and fifty Bostonians, more or less, had been lost with the train. The System buzzed, and Whyte nearly expired with simple exasperation. But the train was not found.

Roger Tupelo, the Harvard mathematician, stepped into the picture the evening of the 6th. He reached Whyte by phone, late, his home, and told him he had some ideas about the missing train. Then he taxied to Whyte's home in Newton and had the first of many talks with Whyte about Number 86.

Whyte was an intelligent man, a good organizer, and not without imagination. "But I don't know what you're talking about!" he expostulated.

Tupelo was resolved to be patient. "This is a very hard thing for *anybody* to understand, Mr. Whyte," he said. "I can see why you are puzzled. But it's the only explanation. The train has vanished, and the people on it. But the System is closed. Trains are conserved. It's somewhere on the System!"

Whyte's voice grew louder again. "And I tell you, Dr. Tupelo, that train is *not* on the System! It is *not!* You can't overlook a seven-car train carrying four hundred passengers. The System has been combed. Do you think I'm trying to *hide* the train?"

"Of course not. Now look, let's be reasonable. We know the train was en route to Cambridge at 8:40 a.m. on the 4th. At least twenty of the missing people probably boarded the train a few minutes earlier at Washington, and forty more at Park Street Under. A few got off at both stations. And that's the last. The ones who were going to Kendall, to Central, to Harvard—they never got there. The train did not get to Cambridge."

"I know that, Dr. Tupelo," Whyte said savagely. "In the tunnel under the River, the train turned into a boat. It left the tunnel and sailed for Africa."

"No, Mr. Whyte. I'm trying to tell you. It hit a node."

Whyte was livid. "What is a node!" he exploded. "The System keeps the tracks clear. Nothing on the tracks but trains, no nodes left lying around—"

"You still don't understand. A node is not an obstruction. It's a singularity. A pole of high order."

Tupelo's explanations that night did not greatly clarify the situation for Kelvin Whyte. But at two in the mornng, the general manager conceded to Tupelo the privilege of examining the master maps of the System. He put in a call first to the police, who could not assist him with his first attempt to master topology, and then, finally, to Central Traffic. Tupelo taxied down there alone, and pored over the maps till morning. He had coffee and a snail, and then went to Whyte's office.

He found the general manager on the telephone. There was a conversation having to do with another, more elaborate inspection of the Dorchester-Cambridge tunnel under the Charles River. When the conversation ended, Whyte slammed the telephone into its cradle and glared at Tupelo. The mathematician spoke first.

"I think probably it's the new shuttle that did this," he said.

Whyte gripped the edge of his desk and prowled silently through his vocabulary until he had located some civil words. "Dr. Tupelo," he said, "I have been awake all night going over your theory. I don't understand it all. I don't know what the Boylston shuttle has to do with this.''

"Remember what I was saying last night about the connective properties of networks?'' Tupelo asked quietly. "Remember the Möbius band we made—the surface with one face and one edge? Remember this—?'' and he removed a little glass Klein bottle from his pocket and placed it on the desk.

Whyte sat back in his chair and stared wordlessly at the mathematician. Three emotions marched across his face in quick succession—anger, bewilderment, and utter dejection. Tupelo went on.

"Mr. Whyte, the System is a network of amazing topological complexity. It was already complex before the Boylston shuttle was installed, and of a high order of connectivity. But this shuttle makes the network absolutely unique. I don't fully understand it, but the situation seems to be something like this: the shuttle has made the connectivity of the whole System of an order so high that I don't know how to calculate it. I suspect the connectivity has become infinite.''

The general manager listened as though in a daze. He kept his eyes glued to the little Klein bottle.

"The Möbius band,'' Tupelo said, "has unusual properties because it has a singularity. The Klein bottle, with two singularities, manages to be inside of itself. The topologists know surfaces with as many as a thousand singularities, and they have properties that make the Möbius band and the Klein bottle both look simple. But a network with infinite connectivity must have an infinite number of singularities. Can you imagine what the properties of that network could be?''

After a long pause, Tupelo added: "I can't either. To tell the truth, the structure of the System, with the Boylston shuttle, is completely beyond me. I can only guess.''

Whyte swiveled his eyes up from the desk at a moment when anger was the dominant feeling within him. "And you call yourself a mathematician, Professor Tupelo!'' he said.

Tupelo almost laughed aloud. The incongruous, the absolute foolishness of the situation, all but overwhelmed him. He smiled thinly, and said: "I'm no topologist. Really, Mr. Whyte, I'm a tyro in the field—not much better acquainted with it than you are. Mathematics is a big pasture. I happen to be an algebraist.''

His candor softened Whyte a little. "Well, then,'' he ventured, "if you don't understand it, maybe we should call in a topologist. Are there any in Boston?"

"Yes and no," Tupelo answered. "The best in the world is at Tech."

Whyte reached for the telephone. "What's his name?" he asked. "I'll call him."

"Merritt Turnbull. He can't be reached. I've tried for three days."

"Is he out of town?" Whyte asked. "We'll send for him—emergency."

"I don't know. Professor Turnbull is a bachelor. He lives alone at the Brattle Club. He has not been seen since the morning of the 4th."

Whyte was uncommonly perceptive. "Was he on the train?" he asked tensely.

"I don't know," the mathematician replied. "What do you think?"

There was a long silence. Whyte looked alternately at Tupelo and at the glass object on the desk. "I don't understand it," he said finally. "We've looked everywhere on the System. There was no way for the train to get out."

"The train didn't get out. It's still on the System," Tupelo said.

"Where?"

Tupelo shrugged. "The train has no real 'where.' The whole System is without real 'whereness.' It's double-valued, or worse."

"How can we find it?"

"I don't think we can," Tupelo said.

There was another long silence. Whyte broke it with a loud exclamation. He rose suddenly, and sent the Klein bottle flying across the room. "You are crazy, professor!" he shouted. "Between midnight tonight and 6:00 a.m. tomorrow, we'll get every train out of the tunnels. I'll send in three hundred men, to comb every inch of the tracks—every inch of the one hundred eighty-three miles. We'll find the train! Now, please excuse me." He glared at Tupelo.

Tupelo left the office. He felt tired, completely exhausted. Mechanically, he walked along Washington Street toward the Essex Station. Halfway down the stairs, he stopped abruptly, looked around him slowly. Then he ascended again to the street and hailed a taxi. At home, he helped himself to a double shot. He fell into bed.

At 3:30 that afternoon he met his class in "Algebra of Fields and Rings." After a quick supper at the Crimson Spa, he went to his apartment and spent the evening in a second attempt to analyze the connective properties of the System. The attempt was vain, but the mathematician came to a few important conclusions. At eleven o'clock he telephoned Whyte at Central Traffic.

"I think you might want to consult me during tonight's search," he said. "May I come down?"

The general manager was none too gracious about Tupelo's offer of help. He indicated that the System would solve this little problem without any help from harebrained professors who thought that whole subway trains could jump off into the fourth dimension. Tupelo submitted to Whyte's unkindness, then went to bed. At about 4:00 a.m. the telephone awakened him. His caller was a contrite Kelvin Whyte.

"Perhaps I was a bit hasty last night, professor," he stammered. "You may be able to help us after all. Could you come down to the Milk Street Cross-Over?"

Tupelo agreed readily. He felt none of the satisfaction he had anticipated. He called a taxi, and in less than half an hour was at the prescribed station. At the foot of the stairs, on the upper level, he saw that the tunnel was brightly lighted, as during normal operation of the System. But the platforms were deserted except for a tight little knot of seven men near the far end. As he walked towards the group, he noticed that two were policemen. He observed a one-car train on the track beside the platform. The forward door was open, the car brightly lit, and empty. Whyte heard his footsteps and greeted him sheepishly.

"Thanks for coming down, professor," he said, extending his hand. "Gentlemen, Dr. Roger Tupelo, of Harvard. Dr. Tupelo, Mr. Kennedy, our chief engineer; Mr. Wilson, representing the Mayor; Dr. Gannot, of Mercy Hospital." Whyte did not bother to introduce the motorman and the two policemen.

"How do you do," said Tupelo. "Any results, Mr. Whyte?"

The general manager exchanged embarrassed glances with his companions. "Well . . . yes, Dr. Tupelo," he finally answered. "I think we do have some results, of a kind."

"Has the train been seen?"

"Yes," said Whyte. "That is, practically seen. At least, we know it's somewhere in the tunnels." The six others nodded their agreement.

Tupelo was not surprised to learn that the train was still on the System. After all, the System was closed. "Would you mind telling me just what happened?" Tupelo insisted.

"I hit a red signal," the motorman volunteered. "Just outside the Copley junction."

"The tracks have been completely cleared of all trains," Whyte explained, "except for this one. We've been riding it, all over the System, for four hours now. When Edmunds, here, hit a red light at the Copley junction, he stopped, of course. I thought the light must be defective, and told him to go ahead. But then we heard another train pass the junction."

"Did you see it?" Tupelo asked.

"We couldn't see it. The light is placed just behind a curve. But we all heard it. There's no doubt the train went through the junction. And it must be Number 86, because our car was the only other one on the tracks."

"What happened then?"

"Well, then the light changed to yellow, and Edmunds went ahead."

"Did he follow the other train?"

"No. We couldn't be sure which way it was going. We must have guessed wrong."

"How long ago did this happen?"

"At 1:38, the first time—"

"Oh," said Tupelo, "then it happened again later?"

"Yes. But not at the same spot, of course. We hit another red signal near South Station at 2:15. And then at 3:28—"

Tupelo interrupted the general manager. "Did you see the train at 2:15?"

"We didn't even hear it, that time. Edmunds tried to catch it, but it must have turned off onto the Boylston shuttle."

"What happened at 3:28?"

"Another red light. Near Park Street. We heard it up ahead of us."

"But you didn't see it?"

"No. There is a little slope beyond the light. But we all heard it. The only thing I don't understand, Dr. Tupelo, is how that train could run the tracks for nearly five days without anybody seeing—"

Whyte's words trailed off into silence, and his right hand went up in a peremptory gesture for quiet. In the distance, the low metallic thunder of a fast-rolling train swelled up suddenly into a sharp, shrill roar of wheels below. The platform vibrated perceptibly as the train passed.

"Now we've got it!" Whyte exclaimed. "Right past the men on the platform below!" He broke into a run towards the stairs to the lower level. All the others followed him, except Tupelo. He thought he knew what was going to happen. It did. Before Whyte reached the stairs, a policeman bounded up to the top.

"Did you see it, now?" he shouted.

Whyte stopped in his tracks, and the others with him.

"Did you see that train?" the policeman from the lower level asked again, as two more men came running up the stairs.

"What happened?" Wilson wanted to know.

"Didn't *you* see it?" snapped Kennedy.

"Sure not," the policeman replied. "It passed through up here."

"It did *not*," roared Whyte. "Down there!"

The six men with Whyte glowered at the three from the lower level. Tupelo walked to Whyte's elbow. "The train can't be seen, Mr. Whyte," he said quietly.

Whyte looked down at him in utter disbelief. "You heard it yourself. It passed right below—"

"Can we go to the car, Mr. Whyte?" Tupelo asked. "I think we ought to talk a little."

Whyte nodded dumbly, then turned to the policeman and the others who had been watching at the lower level. "You really didn't see it?" he begged them.

"We heard it," the policeman answered. "It passed up here, going that way, I think," and he gestured with his thumb.

"Get back downstairs, Maloney," one of the policemen with Whyte commanded. Maloney scratched his head, turned, and disappeared below. The two other men followed him. Tupelo led the original group to the car beside the station platform. They went in and took seats, silently. Then they all watched the mathematician and waited.

"You didn't call me down here tonight just to tell me you'd found the missing train," Tupelo began, looking at Whyte. "Has this sort of thing happened before?"

Whyte squirmed in his seat and exchanged glances with the chief engineer. "Not exactly like this," he said, evasively, "but there have been some funny things."

"Like what?" Tupelo snapped.

"Well, like the red lights. The watchers near Kendall found a red light at the same time we hit the one near South Station."

"Go on."

"Mr. Sweeney called me from Forest Hills at Park Street Under. He heard the train there just two minutes after we heard it at the Copley junction. Twenty-eight track miles away."

"As a matter of fact, Dr. Tupelo," Wilson broke in, "several dozen men have seen lights go red, or have heard the train, or both, inside of the last four hours. The thing acts as though it can be in several places at once."

"It can," Tupelo said.

"We keep getting reports of watchers seeing the thing," the engineer added. "Well, not exactly seeing it, either, but everything except that. Sometimes at two or even three places, far apart, at the same time. It's sure to be on the tracks. Maybe the cars are uncoupled."

"Are you really sure it's on the tracks, Mr. Kennedy?" Tupelo asked.

"Positive," the engineer said. "The dynamometers at the power house show that it's drawing power. It's been drawing power all night. So at 3:30 we broke the circuits. Cut the power."

"What happened?"

"Nothing," Whyte answered. "Nothing at all. The power was off for twenty minutes. During that time, not one of the two hundred fifty men in the tunnels saw a red light or heard a train. But the power wasn't on for five minutes before we had two reports again—one from Arlington, the other from Egleston."

There was a long silence after Whyte finished speaking. In the tunnel below, one man could be heard calling something to another. Tupelo looked at his watch. The time was 5:20.

"In short, Dr. Tupelo," the general manager finally said, "we are compelled to admit that there may be something in your theory." The others nodded agreement.

"Thank you, gentlemen," Tupelo said.

The physician cleared his throat. "Now about the passengers," he began. "Have you any idea what—?"

"None," Tupelo interrupted.

"What should we do, Dr. Tupelo?" the mayor's representative asked.

"I don't know. What can you do?"

"As I understand it from Mr. Whyte," Wilson continued,

"the train has . . . well, it has jumped into another dimension. It isn't really on the System at all. It's just gone. Is that right?"

"In a manner of speaking."

"And this . . . er . . . peculiar behavior has resulted from certain mathematical properties associated with the new Boylston shuttle?"

"Correct."

"And there is nothing we can do to bring the train back to . . . uh . . . this dimension?'

"I know of nothing."

Wilson took the bit in his teeth. "In this case, gentlemen," he said, "our course is clear. First, we must close off the new shuttle, so this fantastic thing can never happen again. Then, since the missing train is really gone, in spite of all these red lights and noises, we can resume normal operation of the System. At least there will be no danger of collision—which has worried you so much, Whyte. As for the missing train and the people on it—" He gestured them into infinity. "Do you agree, Dr. Tupelo?" he asked the mathematician.

Tupelo shook his head slowly. "Not entirely, Mr. Wilson," he responded. "Now, please keep in mind that I don't fully comprehend what has happened. It's unfortunate that you won't find anybody who can give a good explanation. The one man who might have done so is Professor Turnbull, of Tech, and he was on the train. But in any case, you will want to check my conclusions against those of some competent topologists. I can put you in touch with several.

"Now, with regard to the recovery of the missing train, I can say that I think this is not hopeless. There is a finite probability, as I see it, that the train will eventually pass from the nonspatial part of the network, which it now occupies, back to the spatial part. Since the nonspatial part is wholly inaccessible, there is unfortunately nothing we can do to bring about this transition, or even to predict when or how it will occur. But the possibility of the transition will vanish if the Boylston shuttle is taken out. It is just this section of the track that gives the network its essential singularities. If the singularities are removed, the train can never reappear. Is this clear?"

It was not clear, of course, but the seven listening men nodded agreement. Tupelo continued.

"As for the continued operation of the System while the missing train is in the nonspatial part of the network, I can only give you the facts as I see them and leave to your judgment the difficult decision to be drawn from them. The transition back to the spatial part is unpredictable, as I have already told you. There is no way to know when it will occur, or where. In particular, there is a fifty percent probability that, if and when the train reappears, it will be running on the wrong track. Then there will be a collision, of course.''

The engineer asked: "To rule out this possibility, Dr. Tupelo, couldn't we leave the Boylston shuttle open, but send no trains through it? Then, when the missing train reappears on the shuttle, it cannot meet another train."

"That precaution would be ineffective, Mr. Kennedy," Tupelo answered. "You see, the train can reappear anywhere on the System. It is true that the System owes its toplogical complexity to the new shuttle. But, with the shuttle in the System, it is now the whole System that possesses infinite connectivity. In other words, the relevant topological property is a property *derived* from the shuttle, but *belonging* to the whole System. Remember that the train made its first transition at a point between Park and Kendall, more than three miles away from the shuttle.

"There is one question more you will want answered. If you decide to go on operating the System, with the Boylston shuttle left in until the train reappears, can this happen again, to another train? I am not certain of the answer, but I think it is: No. I believe an exclusion principle operates here, such that only one train at a time can occupy the nonspatial network."

The physician rose from his seat. "Dr. Tupelo," he began, timorously, "when the train does reappear, will the passengers—?"

"I don't know about the people on the train," Tupelo cut in. "The topological theory does not consider such matters." He looked quickly at each of the seven tired, querulous faces before him. "I am sorry, gentlemen," he added, somewhat more gently. "I simply do not know." To Whyte, he added: "I think I can be of no more help tonight. You know where to reach me." And, turning on his heel, he left the car and climbed the stairs. He found dawn spilling over the street, dissolving the shadows of night.

That impromptu conference in a lonely subway car was never reported in the papers. Nor were the full results of the night-long vigil over the dark and twisted tunnels. During the week that followed, Tupelo participated in four more formal conferences with Kelvin Whyte and certain city officials. At two of these, other topologists were present. Ornstein was imported to Boston from Philadelphia, Kashta from Chicago, and Michaelis from Los Angeles. The mathematicians were unable to reach a concensus. None of the three would fully endorse Tupelo's conclusions, although Kashta indicated that there *might* be something to them. Ornstein averred that a finite network could not possess infinite connectivity, although he could not prove this proposition and could not actually calculate the connectivity of the System. Michaelis expressed his opinion that the affair was a hoax and had nothing whatever to do with the toplogy of the System. He insisted that if the train could not be found on the System then the System must be open, or at least must once have been open.

But the more deeply Tupelo analyzed the problem, the more fully he was convinced of the essential correctness of his first analysis. From the point of view of topology, the System soon suggested whole families of multiple-valued networks, each with an infinite number of infinite discontinuities. But a definite discussion of these new spatio-hyperspatial networks somehow eluded him. He gave the subject his full attention for only a week. Then his other duties compelled him to lay the analysis aside. He resolved to go back to the problem later in the spring, after courses were over.

Meanwhile, the System was operated as though nothing untoward had happened. The general manager and the mayor's representative had somehow managed to forget the night of the search, or at least to reinterpret what they had seen and not seen. The newspapers and the public at large speculated wildly, and they kept continuing pressure on Whyte. A number of suits were filed against the System on behalf of persons who had lost a relative. The State stepped into the affair and prepared its own thorough investigation. Recriminations were sounded in the halls of Congress. A garbled version of Tupelo's theory eventually found its way into the press. He ignored it, and it was soon forgotten.

The weeks passed, and then a month. The State's investigation was completed. The newspaper stories moved from the first page to the second; to the twenty-third; and then stopped. The missing persons did not return. In the large, they were no longer missed.

One day in mid-April, Tupelo traveled by subway again, from Charles Street to Harvard. He sat stiffly in the front of the first

car, and watched the tracks and gray tunnel walls hurl themselves at the train. Twice the train stopped for a red light, and
Tupelo found himself wondering whether the other train was
really just ahead, or just beyond space. He half-hoped, out of
curiosity, that his exclusion principle was wrong, that the train
might make the transition. But he arrived at Harvard on time.
Only he among the passengers had found the trip exciting.

The next week he made another trip by subway, and again the
next. As experiments, they were unsuccessful, and much less
tense than the first ride in mid-April. Tupelo began to doubt his
own analysis. Sometime in May, he reverted to the practice of
commuting by subway between his Beacon Hill apartment and
his office at Harvard. His mind stopped racing down the knotted
gray caverns ahead of the train. He read the morning newspaper,
or the abstracts in *Revies of Modern Mathematics*.

Then there was one morning when he looked up from the
newspaper and sensed something. He pushed panic back on its
stiff, quivering spring, and looked quickly out the window at his
right. The lights of the car showed the black and gray lines of
wall-spots streaking by. The tracks ground out their familiar
steely dissonance. The train rounded a curve and crossed a
junction that he remembered. Swiftly, he recalled boarding the
train at Charles, noting the girl on the ice-carnival poster at
Kendall, meeting the southbound train going into Central.

He looked at the man sitting beside him, with a lunch pail on
his lap. The other seats were filled, and there were a dozen or so
straphangers. A mealy-faced youth near the front door smoked a
cigarette, in violation of the rules. Two girls behind him across
the aisle were discussing a club meeting. In the seat ahead, a
young woman was scolding her little son. The man on the aisle,
in the seat ahead of that, was reading the paper. The Transit-Ad
above him extolled Florida oranges.

He looked again at the man two seats ahead and fought down
the terror within. He studied that man. What was it? Brunet,
graying hair; a roundish head; wan complexion; rather flat features;
a thick neck, with the hairline a little low, a little ragged; a gray,
pin-stripe suit. While Tupelo watched, the man waved a fly
away from his left ear. He swayed a little with the train. His
newspaper was folded vertically down the middle. His *newspaper*!
It was last March's!

Tupelo's eyes swiveled to the man beside him. Below his
lunch pail was a paper. Today's. He turned in his seat and

looked behind him. A young man held the *Transcript* open to the sports pages. The date was March 4th. Tupelo's eyes raced up and down the aisle. There were a dozen passengers carrying papers ten weeks old.

Tupelo lunged out of his seat. The man on the aisle muttered a curse as the mathematician crowded in front of him. He crossed the aisle in a bound and pulled the cord above the windows. The brakes sawed and screeched at the tracks, and the train ground to a stop. The startled passengers eyed Tupelo with hostility. At the rear of the car, the door flew open and a tall, thin man in a blue uniform burst in. Tupelo spoke first.

"Mr. Dorkin?" he called, vehemently.

The conductor stopped short and groped for words.

"There's been a serious accident, Dorkin," Tupelo said, loudly, to carry over the rising swell of protest from the passengers. "Get Gallagher back here right away!"

Dorkin reached up and pulled the cord four times. "What happened?" he asked.

Tupelo ignored the question, and asked one of his own. "Where have you been, Dorkin?"

The conductor's face was blank. "In the next car, but—"

Tupelo cut him off. He glanced at his watch, then shouted at the passengers. "It's ten minutes to nine on May 17th!"

The announcement stilled the rising clamor for a moment. The passengers exchanged bewildered glances.

"Look at your newspapers!" Tupelo shouted. "Your newspapers!"

The passengers began to buzz. As they discovered each other's papers, the voices rose. Tupelo took Dorkin's arm and led him to the rear of the car. "What time is it?" he asked.

"8:21," Dorkin said, looking at his watch.

"Open the door," said Tupelo, motioning ahead. "Let me out. Where's the phone?"

Dorkin followed Tupelo's directions. He pointed to a niche in the tunnel wall a hundred yards ahead. Tupelo vaulted to the ground and raced down the narrow lane between the cars and the wall. "Central Traffic!" he barked at the operator. He waited a few seconds, and saw that a train had stopped at the red signal behind his train. Flashlights were advancing down the tunnel. He saw Gallagher's legs running down the tunnel on the other side of 86. "Get me Whyte!" he commanded, when Central Traffic answered. "Emergency!"

There was a delay. He heard voices rising from the train beside him. The sound was mixed—anger, fear, hysteria.

"Hello!" he shouted. "Hello! Emergency! Get me Whyte!"

"I'll take it," a man's voice said at the other end of the line. "Whyte's busy!"

"Number 86 is back," Tupelo called. "Between Central and Harvard now. Don't know when it made the jump. I caught it at Charles ten minutes ago, and didn't notice it till a minute ago."

The man at the other end gulped hard enough to carry over the telephone. "The passengers?" he croaked.

"All right, the ones that are left," Tupelo said. "Some must have got off already at Kendall and Central."

"Where have they been?"

Tupelo dropped the receiver from his ear and stared at it, his mouth wide open. Then he slammed the receiver onto the hook and ran back to the open door.

Eventually, order was restored, and within a half hour the train proceeded to Harvard. At the station, the police took all passengers into protective custody. Whyte himself arrived at Harvard before the train did. Tupelo found him on the platform.

Whyte motioned weakly towards the passengers. "They're really all right?" he asked.

"Perfectly," said Tupelo. "Don't know they've been gone."

"Any sign of Professor Turnbull?" asked the general manger.

"I didn't see him. He probably got off at Kendall, as usual."

"Too bad," said Whyte. "I'd like to see him!"

"So would I!" Tupelo answered. "By the way, now is the time to close the Boylston shuttle."

"Now is too late," Whyte said. "Train 143 vanished twenty-five minutes ago between Egleston and Dorchester."

Tupelo stared past Whyte, and down and down the tracks.

"We've got to find Turnbull," Whyte said.

Tupelo looked at Whyte and smiled thinly.

"Do you really think Turnbull got off this train at Kendall?" he asked.

"Of course!" answered Whyte. "Where else?"

16

PROCESS

A. E. van Vogt

THE MAGAZINE OF FANTASY AND SCIENCE FICTION
December

"Process" is not a typical van Vogt story. Indeed, it reminds one of the old British school of rich, evocative, descriptive prose, the kind found in the novels of John Wyndham. But typical or not, it remains one of the two or three finest stories about vegetable intelligence ever written.

—M.H.G.

Quite right, Marty, "Process" is not van Vogtian at all.
What I like best about it is the kind of double-vision you get and how skillfully van Vogt manages to concentrate on one view until you finally (and surprisingly) find yourself with another.

—I.A.

In the bright light of that far sun, the forest breathed and had its being. It was aware of the ship that had come down through the thin mists of the upper air. But its automatic hostility to the alien thing was not immediately accompanied by alarm.

For tens of thousands of square miles, its roots entwined under the ground, and its millions of tree tops swayed gently in a thousand idle breezes. And beyond, spreading over the hills and the mountains, and along almost endless sea coast were other forests as strong and as powerful as itself.

From time immemorial the forest had guarded the land from a dimly understood danger. What that danger was it began now slowly to remember. It was from ships like this, that descended from the sky. The forest could not recall clearly how it had defended itself in the past, but it did remember tensely that defense had been necessary.

Even as it grew more and more aware of the ship coasting along in the gray-red sky above, its leaves whispered a timeless tale of battles fought and won. Thoughts flowed their slow course down the channels of vibration, and the stately limbs of tens of thousands of trees trembled ever so slightly.

The vastness of that tremor, affecting as it did all the trees, gradually created a sound and a pressure. At first it was almost impalpable, like a breeze wafting through an evergreen glen. But it grew stronger.

It acquired substance. The sound became all-enveloping. And the whole forest stood there vibrating its hostility, waiting for the thing in the sky to come nearer.

It had not long to wait.

The ship swung down from its lane. Its speed, now that it was close to the ground, was greater than it had first seemed. And it was bigger. It loomed gigantic over the near trees, and swung down lower, careless of the tree tops. Brush crackled, limbs broke, and entire trees were brushed aside as if they were meaningless and weightless and without strength.

Down came the ship, cutting its own path through a forest that groaned and shrieked with its passage. It settled heavily into the ground two miles after it first touched a tree. Behind, the swath of broken trees quivered and pulsed in the light of the sun, a straight path of destruction which—the forest suddenly remembered—was exactly what had happened in the past.

It began to pull clear of the anguished parts. It drew out its juices, and ceased vibrating in the affected areas. Later, it would send new growth to replace what had been destroyed, but now it accepted the partial death it had suffered. It knew fear.

It was a fear tinged with anger. It felt the ship lying on crushed trees, on a part of itself that was not yet dead. It felt the coldness and the hardness of steel walls, and the fear and the anger increased.

A whisper of thought pulsed along the vibration channels. Wait, it said, there is a memory in me. A memory of long ago when other such ships as this came.

The memory refused to clarify. Tense but uncertain, the forest prepared to make its first attack. It began to grow around the ship.

Long ago it had discovered the power of growth that was possible to it. There was a time when it had not been as large as it was now. And then, one day, it became aware that it was coming near another forest like itself.

The two masses of growing wood, the two colossi of inter-twined roots approached each other warily, slowly, in amazement, in a startled but cautious wonder that a similar life form should actually have existed all this time. Approached, touched—and fought for years.

During that prolonged struggle nearly all growth in the central portions stopped. Trees ceased to develop new branches. The leaves, by necessity, grew hardier, and performed their functions for much longer periods. Roots developed slowly. The entire available strength of the forest was concentrated in the processes of defense and attack.

Walls of trees sprang up overnight. Enormous roots tunneled into the ground for miles straight down, breaking through rock and metal, building a barrier of living wood against the encroach-ing growth of the strange forest. On the surface, the barriers thickened to a mile or more of trees that stood almost bole to bole. And, on that basis, the great battle finally petered out. The forest accepted the obstacle created by its enemy.

Later, it fought to a similar standstill a second forest which attacked it from another direction.

The limits of demarcation became as natural as the great salt sea to the south, or the icy cold of mountain tops that were frozen the year round.

As it had in battle with the two other forests, *the* forest concentrated its entire strength against the encroaching ship. Trees shot up at the rate of a foot every few minutes. Creepers climbed the trees, and flung themselves over the top of the vessel. The countless strands of it raced over the metal, and then twined themselves around the trees on the far side. The roots of those trees dug deeper into the ground, and anchored in rock strata heavier than any ship ever built. The tree boles thickened, and the creepers widened till they were enormous cables.

As the light of that first day faded into twilight, the ship was buried under thousands of tons of wood, and hidden in foliage so thick that nothing of it was visible.

The time had come for the final destructive action.

Shortly after dark, tiny roots began to fumble over the underside of the ship. They were infinitesimally small; so small that in the initial stages they were no more than a few dozens of atoms in diameter; so small that the apparently solid metal seemed almost emptiness to them; so incredibly small that they penetrated the hard steel effortlessly.

It was at that time, almost as if it had been waiting for this stage, that the ship took counteraction. The metal grew warm, then hot, and then cherry red. That was all that was needed. The tiny roots shriveled, and died. The larger roots near the metal burned slowly as the searing heat reached them.

Above the surface, other violence began. Flame darted from a hundred orifices of the ship's surface. First the creepers, then the trees began to burn. It was no flare-up of uncontrollable fire, no fierce conflagration leaping from tree to tree in irresistible fury. Long ago, the forest had learned to control fires started by lightning or spontaneous combustion. It was a matter of sending sap to the affected area. The greener the tree, the more sap that permeated it, then the hotter the fire would have to be.

The forest could not immediately remember ever having encountered a fire that could make inroads against a line of trees that oozed a sticky wetness from every crevice of their bark.

But this fire could. It was different. It was not only flame; it was energy. It did not feed off the wood; it was fed by an energy within itself.

That fact at last brought the associational memory to the forest. It was a sharp and unmistakable remembrance of what it had done long ago to rid itself and its planet of a ship just like this.

It began to withdraw from the vicinity of the ship. It abandoned the framework of wood and shrubbery with which it had sought to imprison the alien structure. As the precious sap was sucked back into trees that would now form a second line of defense, the flames grew brighter, and the fire waxed so brilliant that the whole scene was bathed in an eerie glow.

It was some time before the forest realized that the fire beams were no longer flaming out from the ship, and that what incandescence and smoke remained came from normally burning wood.

That, too, was according to its memory of what had happened—before.

Frantically though reluctantly the forest initiated what it now realized was the only method of ridding itself of the intruder. Frantically because it was hideously aware that the flame from the ship could destroy entire forests. And reluctantly because the method of defense involved its suffering the burns of energy only slightly less violent than those that had flared from the machine.

Tens of thousands of roots grew toward rock and soil formations that they had carefully avoided since the last ship had come. In spite of the need for haste, the process itself was slow. Tiny roots, quivering with unpleasant anticipation, forced themselves into the remote, buried ore beds, and by an intricate process of osmosis drew grains of pure metal from the impure natural stuff. The grains were almost as small as the roots that had earlier penetrated the steel walls of the ship, small enough to be borne along, suspended in sap, through a maze of larger roots.

Soon there were thousands of grains moving along the channels, then millions. And, though each was tiny in itself, the soil where they were discharged soon sparkled in the light of the dying fire. As the sun of that world reared up over the horizon, the silvery gleam showed a hundred feet wide all around the ship.

It was shortly after noon that the machine showed awareness of what was happening. A dozen hatches opened, and objects floated out of them. They came down to the ground, and began to skim up the silvery stuff with nozzled things that sucked up the fine dust in a steady fashion. They worked with great caution; but an hour before darkness set in again, they had scooped up more than twelve tons of the thinly spread Uranium 235.

As night fell, all the two-legged things vanished inside the vessel. The hatches closed. The long torpedo-shape floated lightly upward, and sped to the higher heavens where the sun still shone.

The first awareness of the situation came to the forest as the roots deep under the ship reported a sudden lessening of pressure. It was several hours before it decided that the enemy had actually been driven off. And several more hours went by before it realized that the uranium dust still on the scene would have to be removed. The rays spread too far afield.

The accident that occurred then took place for a very simple reason. The forest had taken the radioactive substance out of rock. To get rid of it, it need merely put it back into the nearest rock beds, particularly the kind of rock that absorbed the radioactivity. To the forest the situation seemed as obvious as that.

An hour after it began to carry out the plan, the explosion mushroomed toward outer space.

It was vast beyond all the capacity of the forest to understand. It neither saw nor heard that collossal shape of death. What it did experience was enough. A hurricane leveled square miles of trees. The blast of heat and radiation started fires that took hours to put out.

Fear departed slowly, as it remembered that this too had happened before. Sharper by far than the memory was the vision of the possibilities of what had happened . . . the nature of the opportunity.

Shortly after dawn the following morning, it launched its attack. Its victim was the forest which—according to its faulty recollection—had originally invaded its territory.

Along the entire front which separated the two colossi, small atomic explosions erupted. The solid barrier of trees which was the other forest's outer defense went down before blast after blast of irresistible energy.

The enemy, reacting normally, brought up its reserve of sap. When it was fully committed to the gigantic task of growing a new barrier, the bombs started to go off again. The resulting explosions destroyed its main sap supply. And, since it did not understand what was happening, it was lost from that moment.

Into the no-man's-land where the bombs had gone off, the attacking forest rushed an endless supply of roots. Wherever resistance built up, there an atomic bomb went off. Shortly after the next noon, a titanic explosion destroyed the sensitive central trees—and the battle was over.

It took months for the forest to grow into the territory of its defeated enemy, to squeeze out the other's dying roots, to nudge over trees that now had no defense, and to put itself into full and unchallenged possession.

The moment the task was completed, it turned like a fury upon the forest on its other flank. Once more it attacked with atomic thunder, and with a hail of fire tried to overwhelm its opponent.

It was met by equal force. Exploding atoms!

For its knowledge had leaked across the barrier of intertwined roots which separated forests.

Almost, the two monsters destroyed each other. Each became a remnant, that started the painful process of regrowth. As the years passed, the memory of what had happened grew dim. Not that it mattered. Actually, the ships came at will. And somehow, even if the forest remembered, its atomic bombs would not go off in the presence of a ship.

The only thing that would drive away the ships was to surround each machine with a fine dust of radioactive stuff. Whereupon it would scoop up the material, and then hastily retreat.

Victory was always as simple as that.

17

THE MINDWORM

C. M. Kornbluth

WORLDS BEYOND
December

*The figure of the vampire is one of the most powerful images in
literature, and hundreds of stories have been written about these
menacing creatures. However, the vampire is a supernatural
monster, and therefore beyond the boundaries of this series. Or
is he? What if there is a rational explanation for his existence?*

*Worlds Beyond was a short-lived sf magazine (it lasted for
three issues) of 1950–51 edited by Damon Knight that contained
several excellent stories and a strong book review column by the
editor. Poor sales killed what could have been an important
addition to the small ranks of high-quality science fiction
magazines.*

—M.H.G.

*Of all the stories Cyril wrote, I think this was the one I found
the most powerful. It really gave me a turn when I read it for the
first time. In "The Mindworm" someone is different from everyone else, horribly different. Again I can't help but wonder if
poor Cyril found himself different from everyone else, and if
there seemed to him to be a horrible component to that.*

—I.A.

The handsome j. g. and the pretty nurse held out against it as
long as they reasonably could, but blue Pacific water, languid

tropical nights, the low atoll dreaming on the horizon—and the complete absence of any other nice young people for company on the small, uncomfortable parts boat—did their work. On June 30th they watched through dark glasses as the dazzling thing burst over the fleet and atoll. Her manicured hand gripped his arm in excitement and terror. Unfelt radiation sleeted through their loins.

A storekeeper-third-class named Bielaski watched the young couple with more interest than he showed in Test Able. After all, he had twenty-five dollars riding on the nurse. That night he lost it to a chief bosun's mate who had backed the j. g.

In the course of time, the careless nurse was discharged under conditions other than honorable. The j. g., who didn't like to put things in writing, phoned her all the way from Manila to say it was a damned shame. When her gratitude gave way to specific inquiry, their overseas connection went bad and he had to hang up.

She had a child, a boy, turned it over to a foundling home, and vanished from his life into a series of good jobs and finally marriage.

The boy grew up stupid, puny and stubborn, greedy and miserable. To the home's hilarious young athletics director he suddenly said: "You hate me. You think I make the rest of the boys look bad."

The athletics director blustered and laughed, and later told the doctor over coffee: "I watch myself around the kids. They're sharp—they catch a look or a gesture and it's like a blow in the face to them, I know that, so I watch myself. So how did he know?"

The doctor told the boy: "Three pounds more this month isn't bad, but how about you pitch in and clean up your plate *every* day? Can't live on meat and water; those vegetables make you big and strong."

The boy said; "What's 'neurasthenic' mean?"

The doctor later said to the director: "It made my flesh creep. I was looking at his little splindling body and dishing out the old pep talk about growing big and strong, and inside my head I was thinking 'we'd call him neurasthenic in the old days' and then out he popped with it. What should we do? Should we do anything? Maybe it'll go away. I don't know anything about these things. I don't know whether anybody does."

"Reads minds, does he?" asked the director. *Be damned if he's going to read my mind about Schultz Meat Market's ten percent.* "Doctor, I think I'm going to take my vacation a little early this year. Has anybody shown any interest in adopting the child?"

"Not him. He wasn't a baby doll when we got him, and at present he's an exceptionally unattractive-looking kid. You know how people don't give a damn about anything but their looks."

"*Some* couples would take anything, or so they tell me."

"Unapproved for foster-parenthood, you mean?"

"Red tape and arbitrary classifications sometimes limit us too severely in our adoptions."

"If you're going to wish him on some screwball couple that the courts turned down as unfit, I want no part of it."

"You don't have to have any part of it, doctor. By the way, which dorm does he sleep in?"

"West," grunted the doctor, leaving the office.

The director called a few friends—a judge, a couple the judge referred him to, a court clerk. Then he left by way of the east wing of the building.

The boy survived three months with the Berrymans. Hard-drinking Mimi alternately caressed and shrieked at him; Edward W. tried to be a good scout and just gradually lost interest, looking clean through him. He hit the road in June and got by with it for a while. He wore a Boy Scout uniform, and Boy Scouts can turn up anywhere, any time. The money he had taken with him lasted a month. When the last penny of the last dollar was three days spent, he was adrift on a Nebraska prairie. He had walked out of the last small town because the constable was beginning to wonder what on earth he was hanging around for and who he belonged to. The town was miles behind on the two-lane highway; the infrequent cars did not stop.

One of Nebraska's "rivers," a dry bed at this time of year, lay ahead, spanned by a railroad culvert. There were some men in its shade, and he was hungry.

They were ugly, dirty men, and their thoughts were muddled and stupid. They called him "Shorty" and gave him a little dirty bread and some stinking sardines from a can. The thoughts of one of them became less muddled and uglier. He talked to the rest out of the boy's hearing, and they whooped with laughter. The boy got ready to run, but his legs wouldn't hold him up.

He could read the thoughts of the men quite clearly as they

headed for him. Outrage, fear, and disgust blended in him and somehow turned inside-out and one of the men was dead on the dry ground, grasshoppers vaulting onto his flannel shirt, the others backing away, frightened now, not frightening.

He wasn't hungry any more; he felt quite comfortable and satisfied. He got up and headed for the other men, who ran. The rearmost of them was thinking *Jeez he folded up the evil eye we was only gonna—*

Again the boy let the thoughts flow into his head and again he flipped his own thoughts around them; it was quite easy to do. It was different—this man's terror from the other's lustful anticipation. But both had their points . . .

At his leisure, he robbed the bodies of three dollars and twenty-four cents.

Thereafter his fame preceded him like a death wind. Two years on the road and he had his growth and his fill of the dull and stupid minds he met there. He moved to northern cities, a year here, a year there, quiet, unobtrusive, prudent, an epicure.

Sebastian Long woke suddenly, with something on his mind. As night fog cleared away he remembered, happily. Today he started the Demeter Bowl! At last there was time, at last there was money—six hundred and twenty-three dollars in the bank. He had packed and shipped the three dozen cocktail glasses last night, engraved with Mrs. Klausman's initials—his last commercial order for as many months as the Bowl would take.

He shifted from nightshirt to denims, gulped coffee, boiled an egg but was too excited to eat it. He went to the front of his shop-workroom-apartment, checked the lock, waved at neighbors' children on their way to school, and ceremoniously set a sign in the cluttered window.

It said: "NO COMMERCIAL ORDERS TAKEN UNTIL FURTHER NOTICE."

From a closet he tenderly carried a shrouded object that made a double armful and laid it on his workbench. Unshrouded, it was a glass bowl—*what* a glass bowl! The clearest Swedish lead glass, the purest lines he had ever seen, his secret treasure since the crazy day he had bought it, long ago, for six months' earnings. His wife had given him hell for that until the day she died. From the closet he brought a portfolio filled with sketches and designs dating back to the day he had bought the bowl. He smiled over the first, excitedly scrawled—a florid, rococo

conception, unsuited to the classicism of the lines and the seren-
ity of the perfect glass.

Through many years and hundreds of sketches he had refined
his conception to the point where it was, he humbly felt, not
unsuited to the medium. A strongly-molded Demeter was to
dominate the piece, and a matron as serene as the glass, and all
the fruits of the earth would flow from her gravely outstretched
arms.

Suddenly and surely, he began to work. With a candle he
thinly smoked an oval area on the outside of the bowl. Two
steady fingers clipped the Demeter drawing against the carbon
black; a hair-fine needle in his other hand traced her lines. When
the transfer of the design was done, Sebastian Long readied his
lathe. He fitted a small copper wheel, slightly worn as he liked
them, into the chuck and with his fingers charged it with the
finest rouge from Rouen. He took an ashtray cracked in delivery
and held it against the spinning disk. It bit in smoothly, with the
wiping feel to it that was exactly right.

Holding out his hands, seeing that the fingers did not tremble
with excitement, he eased the great bowl to the lathe and was
about to make the first tiny cut of the millions that would go into
the masterpiece.

Somebody knocked on his door and rattled the doorknob.

Sebastian Long did not move or look toward the door. Soon
the busybody would read the sign and go away. But the pounding and the rattling of the knob went on. He eased down the
bowl and angrily went to the window, picked up the sign, and
shook it at whoever it was—he couldn't make out the face very
well. But the idiot wouldn't go away.

The engraver unlocked the door, opened it a bit, and snapped:
"The shop is closed. I shall not be taking any orders for several
months. Please don't bother me now."

"It's about the Demeter Bowl," said the intruder.

Sebastian Long stared at him. "What the devil do you know
about my Demeter Bowl?" He saw the man was a stranger,
undersized by a little, middle-aged . . .

"Just let me in please," urged the man. "It's important.
Please!"

"I don't know what you're talking about," said the engraver.
"But what do you know about my Demeter Bowl?" He hooked
his thumbs pugnaciously over the waistband of his denims and

glowered at the stranger. The stranger promptly took advantage of his hand being removed from the door and glided in.

Sebastian Long thought briefly that it might be a nightmare as the man darted quickly about his shop, picking up a graver and throwing it down, picking up a wire scratch-wheel and throwing it down. "Here, you!" he roared, as the stranger picked up a crescent wrench which he did not throw down.

As Long started for him, the stranger darted to the workbench and brought the crescent wrench down shatteringly on the bowl.

Sebastian Long's heart was bursting with sorrow and rage; such a storm of emotions as he never had known thundered through him. Paralyzed, he saw the stranger smile with anticipation.

The engraver's legs folded under him and he fell to the floor, drained and dead.

The Mindworm, locked in the bedroom of his brownstone front, smiled again, reminiscently.

Smiling, he checked the day on a wall calendar.

"Dolores!" yelled her mother in Spanish. "Are you going to pass the whole day in there?"

She had been practicing low-lidded, sexy half-smiles like Lauren Bacall in the bathroom mirror. She stormed out and yelled in English: "I don't know how many times I tell you not to call me that Spick name no more!"

"Dolly!" sneered her mother. "Dah-lee! When was there a Saint Dah-lee that you call yourself after, eh?"

The girl snarled a Spanish obscenity at her mother and ran down the tenement stairs. Jeez, she was gonna be late for sure!

Held up by a stream of traffic between her and her streetcar, she danced with impatience. Then the miracle happened. Just like in the movies, a big convertible pulled up before her and its lounging driver said, opening the door: "You seem to be in a hurry. Could I drop you somewhere?"

Dazed at the sudden realization of a hundred daydreams, she did not fail to give the driver a low-lidded, sexy smile as she said: "Why, *thanks!*" and climbed in. He wasn't no Cary Grant, but he had all his hair . . . kind of small, but so was she . . . and jeez, the convertible had *leopard-skin seat covers!*

The car was in the stream of traffic, purring down the avenue. "It's a lovely day," she said. "Really too nice to work."

The driver smiled shyly, kind of like Jimmy Stewart but of

course not so tall, and said: "I feel like playing hooky myself. How would you like a spin down Long Island?"

"Be wonderful!" The convertible cut left on an odd-numbered street.

"Play hooky, you said. What do you do?"

"Advertising."

"Advertising!" Dolly wanted to kick herself for ever having doubted, for ever having thought in low, self-loathing moments that it wouldn't work out, that she'd marry a grocer or a mechanic and live forever after in a smelly tenement and grow old and sick and stooped. She felt vaguely in her happy daze that it might have been cuter, she might have accidentally pushed him into a pond or something, but this was cute enough. An advertising man, leopard-skin seat covers . . . what more could a girl with a sexy smile and a nice little figure want?

Speeding down the South Shore she learned that his name was Michael Brent, exactly as it ought to be. She wished she could tell him she was Jennifer Brown or one of those real cute names they had nowadays, but was reassured when he told her he thought Dolly Gonzalez was a beautiful name. He didn't, and she noticed the omission, add: "It's the most beautiful name I ever heard!" That, she comfortably thought as she settled herself against the cushions, would come later.

They stopped at Medford for lunch, a wonderful lunch in a little restaurant where you went down some steps and there were candles on the table. She called him "Michael" and he called her "Dolly." She learned that he liked dark girls and thought the stories in *True Story* really were true, and that he thought she was just tall enough, and that Greer Garson was wonderful, but not the way she was, and that he thought her dress was just wonderful.

They drove slowly after Medford, and Michael Brent did most of the talking. He had traveled all over the world. He had been in the war and wounded—just a flesh wound. He was thirty-eight, and had been married once, but she died. There were no children. He was alone in the world. He had nobody to share his town house in the 50's, his country place in Westchester, his lodge in the Maine woods. Every word sent the girl floating higher and higher on a tide of happiness; the signs were unmistakable.

When they reached Montauk Point, the last sandy bit of the continent before blue water and Europe, it was sunset, with a great wrinkled sheet of purple and rose stretching half across the sky and the first stars appearing above the dark horizon of the water.

The two of them walked from the parked car out onto the sand, alone, bathed in glorious Technicolor. Her heart was nearly bursting with joy as she heard Michael Brent say, his arms tightening around her: "Darling, will you marry me?"

"Oh, *yes*, Michael!" she breathed, dying.

The Mindworm, drowsing, suddenly felt the sharp sting of danger. He cast out through the great city, dragging tentacles of thought."

". . . die if she don't let me . . ."

". . . six an' six is twelve an' carry one an' three is four . . ."

". . . gobblegobble madre de dios perso soy gobblegobble . . ."

". . . parlay Domino an' Missab and shoot the roll on Duchess Peg in the feature . . ."

". . . melt resin add the silver chloride and dissolve in oil of lavender stand and decant and fire to cone zero twelve give you shimmering streaks of luster down the walls . . ."

". . . moiderin' square-headed gobblegobble tried ta poke his eye out wassamatta witta ref . . ."

". . . O God I am most heartily sorry I have offended thee in . . ."

". . . talk like a commie . . ."

". . . gobblegobblegobble two dolla twenny-fi' sense gobble . . ."

". . . just a nip and fill it up with water and brush my teeth . . ."

". . . really know I'm God but fear to confess their sins . . ."

". . . Dirty lousy rock-headed claw-handed paddle-footed goggle-eyed snot-nosed hunch-backed feeble-minded pot-bellied son of . . ."

". . . write on the wall alfie is a stunkur and then . . ."

". . . thinks I believe it's a television set but I know he's got a bomb in there but who can I tell who can help so alone . . ."

". . . gabble was ich weiss nicht gabble geh bei Broadvay gabble . . ."

". . . habt mein daughter Rosie such a fella gobblegobble . . ."

". . . wonder if that's one didn't look back . . ."

". . . seen with her in the Medford restaurant . . ."

The Mindworm struck into that thought.

". . . not a mark on her but the M. E.'s have been wrong

before and heart failure don't mean a thing anyway try to talk to her old lady authorize an autopsy get Pancho little guy talks Spanish be best . . ."

The Mindworm knew he would have to be moving again—soon. He was sorry; some of the thoughts he had tapped indicated good . . . hunting?

Regretfully, he again dragged his net:

". . . with chartreuse drinks I mean drapes could use a drink come to think of it . . ."

". . . reep-beep-reep-beep reepiddy-beepiddy-beep bop man wadda beat . . ."

" $\sum_{i=1}^{6} \varphi(a_x, a_i) - \sum_{s} \varphi(a_x, a_s)$. *What the Hell was that?*"

The Mindworm withdrew, in frantic haste. The intelligence was massive, its overtones those of a vigorous adult. He had learned from certain dangerous children that there was a peril of a leveling flow. Shaken and scared, he contemplated traveling. He would need more than that wretched girl had supplied, and it would not be epicurean. There would be no time to find individuals at a ripe emotional crisis, or goad them to one. It would be plain—munching. The Mindworm drank a glass of water, also necessary to his metabolism.

EIGHT FOUND DEAD
IN UPTOWN MOVIE;
"MOLESTER" SOUGHT

Eight persons, including three women, were found dead Wednesday night of unknown causes in widely separated seats in the balcony of the Odeon Theater at 117th St. and Broadway. Police are seeking a man described by the balcony usher, Michael Fenelly, 18, as "acting like a woman-molester."

Fenelly discovered the first of the fatalities after seeing the man "moving from one empty seat to another several times." He went to ask a woman in a seat next to one the man had just vacated whether he had annoyed her. She was dead.

Almost at once, a scream rang out. In another part of the balcony Mrs. Sadie Rabinowitz, 40, uttered the cry when another victim toppled from his seat next to her.

Theater manager I. J. Marcusohn stopped the show and turned on the house lights. He tried to instruct his staff to keep the audience from leaving before the police arrived. He failed to get word to them in time, however, and most of the audience was gone when a detail from the 24th Pct. and an ambulance from Harlem hospital took over at the scene of the tragedy.

The Medical Examiner's office has not yet made a report as to the causes of death. A spokesman said the victims showed no signs of poisoning or violence. He added that it "was inconceivable that it could be a coincidence."

Lt. John Braidwood of the 24th Pct, said of the alleged molester: "We got a fair description of him and naturally we will try to bring him in for questioning."

Clickety-click, clickety-click, clickety-click sang the rails as the Mindworm drowsed in his coach seat.

Some people were walking forward from the diner. One was thinking: "Different-looking fellow. (a) he's aberrant. (b) he's nonaberrant and ill. Cancel (b)-respiration normal, skin smooth and healthy, no tremor of limbs, well-groomed. Is aberrant (1) trivially. (2) significantly. Cancel (1)—displayed no involuntary interest when . . . odd! *Running* for the washroom! Unexpected because (a) neat grooming indicates amour propre inconsistent with amusing others; (b) evident health inconsistent with . . ." It had taken one second, was fully detailed.

The Mindworm, locked in the toilet of the coach, wondered what the next stop was. He was getting off at it—not frightened, just carefully. Dodge them, keep dodging them and everything would be all right. Send out no mental taps until the train was far away and everything would be all right.

He got off at a West Virginia coal and iron town surrounded by ruined mountains and filled with the offscourings of Eastern Europe. Serbs, Albanians, Croats, Hungarians, Slovenes, Bulgarians, and all possible combinations and permutations thereof. He walked slowly from the smoke-stained, brownstone passenger station. The train had roared on its way.

". . . ain' no gemmum that's fo sho', fi-cen' tip fo' a good shine lak ah give um . . ."

". . . dumb bassar don't know how to make out a billa lading yet he ain't never gonna know so fire him get it over with . . ."

". . . gabblegabblegabble . . ." Not a word he recognized in it.

". . . gobblegobble dat tam vooman I brek she neck . . ."

". . . gobble trink visky chin glassabeer gobblegobblegobble . . ."

". . . gobble trink visky chin glassabeer gobblegobblegobble . . ."

". . . gabblegabblegabble . . ."

". . . makes me so gobblegobble mad little no-good tramp no she ain' but I don' like no standup from no dame . . ."

A blond, square-headed boy fuming under a street light.

". . . out wit' Casey Oswiak I could kill that dumb bohunk alla time trine ta paw her . . ."

It was a possibility. The Mindworm drew near.

". . . stand me up for that gobblegobble bohunk I oughtta slap her inna mush like my ole man says . . ."

"Hello," said the Mindworm.

"Waddaya wan'?"

"Casey Oswiak told me to tell you not to wait up for your girl. He's taking her out tonight."

The blond boy's rage boiled into his face and shot from his eyes. He was about to swing when the Mindworm began to feed. It was like pheasant after chicken, venison after beef. The coarseness of the environment, or the ancient strain? The Mindworm wondered as he strolled down the street. A girl passed him:

". . . oh but he's gonna be mad like last time wish I came right away so jealous kinda nice but he might bust me one some day be nice to him tonight there he is lam'post leaning on it looks kinda funny gawd I hope he ain't drunk looks kinda funny sleeping sick or bozhe moi gabblegabblegabble . . ."

Her thoughts trailed into a foreign language of which the Mindworm knew not a word. After hysteria had gone she recalled, in the foreign language, that she had passed him.

The Mindworm, stimulated by the unfamiliar quality of the last feeding, determined to stay for some days. He checked in at a Main Street hotel.

Musing, he dragged his net:

". . . gobblegobblewhompyeargobblecheskygobblegabblechyesh . . ."

". . . take him down cellar beat the can off the damn chesky thief put the fear of god into him teach him can't bust into no boxcars in *mah* parta the caounty . . ."

". . . gabblegabble . . ."

". . . phone ole Mister Ryan in She-cawgo and he'll tell them three-card monte grifters who got the horse-room rights in this necka the woods by damn don't pay protection money for no protection . . ."

The Mindworm followed that one further; it sounded as though it could lead to some money if he wanted to stay in the town long enough.

The Eastern Europeans of the town, he mistakenly thought, were like the tramps and bums he had known and fed on during his years on the road—stupid and safe, safe and stupid, quite the same thing.

In the morning he found no mention of the square-headed boy's death in the town's paper and thought it had gone practically unnoticed. It had—by the paper, which was of, by, and for the coal and iron company and its native-American bosses and straw bosses. The other town, the one without a charter or police force, with only an imported weekly newspaper or two from the nearest city, noticed it. The other town had roots more than two thousand years deep, which are hard to pull up. But the Mindworm didn't know it was there.

He fed again that night, on a giddy young streetwalker in her room. He had astounded and delighted her with a fistful of ten-dollar bills before he began to gorge. Again the delightful difference from city-bred folk was there. . . .

Again in the morning he had been unnoticed, he thought. The chartered town, unwilling to admit that there were streetwalkers or that they were found dead, wiped the slate clean; its only member who really cared was the native-American cop on the beat who had collected weekly from the dead girl.

The other town, unknown to the Mindworm, buzzed with it. A delegation went to the other town's only public officer. Unfortunately he was young, American-trained, perhaps even ignorant about some important things. For what he told them was: "My children, that is foolish superstition. Go home."

The Mindworm, through the day, roiled the surface of the town proper by allowing himself to be roped into a poker game in a parlor of the hotel. He wasn't good at it, he didn't like it, and he quit with relief when he had cleaned six shifty-eyed, hard-drinking loafers out of about three hundred dollars. One of them went straight to the police station and accused the unknown of being a sharper. A humorous sergeant, the Mindworm was pleased to note, joshed the loafer out of his temper.

Nightfall again, hunger again . . .

He walked the streets of the town and found them empty. It was strange. The native-American citizens were out, tending bar, walking their beats, locking up their newspaper on the stones, collecting their rents, managing their movies—but where were the others? He cast his net:

". . . gobblegobblegobble whomp year gobble . . ."

". . . crazy old pollack mama of mine try to lock me in with Errol Flynn at the Majestic never know the difference if I sneak out the back . . ."

That was near. He crossed the street and it was nearer. He homed on the thought:

". . . jeez he's a hunka man like Stanley but he never looks at me that Vera Kowalik I'd like to kick her just once in the gobblegobblegobble crazy old mama won't be American so ashamed . . ."

It was half a block, no more, down a side street. Brick houses, two stories, with back yards on an alley. She was going out the back way.

How strangely quiet it was in the alley.

". . . ea-sy down them steps fix that damn board that's how she caught me last time what the hell are they all so scared of went to see Father Drugas won't talk bet somebody got it again that Vera Kowalik and her big . . ."

". . . gobble bozhe gobble whomp year gobble . . ."

She was closer; she was closer.

"All think I'm a kid show them who's a kid bet if Stanley caught me all alone out here in the alley dark and all he wouldn't think I was a kid that damn Vera Kowalik her folks don't think she's a kid . . ."

For all her bravado she was stark terrified when he said: "Hello."

"Who—who—who—?" she stammered.

Quick, before she screamed. Her terror was delightful.

Not too replete to be alert, he cast about, questing.

". . . gobblegobblegobble whomp year."

The countless eyes of the other town, with more than two thousand years of experience in such things, had been following him. What he had sensed as a meaningless hash of noise was actually an impassioned outburst in a nearby darkened house.

"Fools! fools! Now he has taken a virgin! I said not to wait. What will we say to her mother?"

An old man with handlebar mustache and, in spite of the heat, his shirt sleeves decently rolled down and buttoned at the cuffs, evenly replied: "My heart in me died with hers, Casimir, but one must be sure. It would be a terrible thing to make a mistake in such an affair.''

The weight of conservative elder opinion was with him. Other old men with mustaches, some perhaps remembering mistakes long ago, nodded and said: ''A terrible thing. A terrible thing.''

The Mindworm strolled back to his hotel and napped on the made bed briefly. A tingle of danger awakened him. Instantly he cast out:

''. . . gobblegobble whompyear.''

''. . . whampyir.''

''WAMPYIR!''

Close! Close and deadly!

The door of his room burst open, and mustached old men with their shirt sleeves rolled down and decently buttoned at the cuffs unhesitatingly marched in, their thoughts a turmoil of alien noises, foreign gibberish that he could not wrap his mind around, disconcerting, from every direction.

The sharpened stake was through his heart and the scythe blade through his throat before he could realize that he had not been the first of his kind; and that what clever people have not yet learned, some quite ordinary people have not yet entirely forgotten.

18

THE NEW REALITY

Charles L. Harness (1915–   )

THRILLING WONDER STORIES
December

Charles L. Harness worked as a mineral economist for the United States Bureau of Mines and since 1947 has been a patent attorney for several major American corporations. His science fiction output has been relatively scanty, but always interesting. He has produced four novels to date, all very much worth reading: Flight Into Yesterday *(1953, also known as* The Paradox Men), The Ring of Ritornel *(1968),* Wolfhead *(1978), and* The Catalyst *(1980). In addition, his intricate short novel,* The Rose *(published with other stories in book form in 1969), is a marvelous study of the relationship between science and art.*

The nature of reality is a theme that runs through much of his best work, as in "The New Reality," one of those remarkable before-their-time stories that would have fit perfectly in Michael Moorcock's New Worlds *magazine of the second half of the 1960s.*

—*M.H.G.*

I think that I can tell a Campbell story when I read one, and if ever a story has Campbell written all over it, it's "The New Reality." Yet it didn't appear in Astounding. *Perhaps John Campbell rejected it. In that case, how did it come to appear in* Thrilling Wonder Stories, *for if ever there was a story that was not a TWS story, this is it. In other words, I seem to be confronting a situation which is not according to my concept of reality, and "concept of reality" is exactly what the story is about.*

Let me make two points, however. Does the Earth change shape as our concepts change? Whose concepts? Greek philosophers finally became convinced the Earth was spherical. Did that make it spherical? How many believers were required? Is it majority vote? If so, it is possible that even today, more people consider the Earth to be flat than spherical. Would that mean the Earth is still flat?

And what about the single photon that can't make up its mind? Actually, this sort of thing is much under discussion by quantum theorists and very weird and paradoxical points are deduced, and there are some who even speculate that at every instant observers force a choice between realities. It's called "quantum weirdness," I think.

—I.A.

Prentiss crawled into the car, drew the extension connector from his concealed throat mike from its clip in his right sleeve, and plugged it into the ignition key socket.

After a moment he said, "Get me the Censor."

The seconds passed as he heard the click of forming circuits. Then: "E speaking."

"Prentiss, honey."

"Call me 'E,' Prentiss. What news?"

"I've met five classes under Professor Luce. He has a private lab. Doesn't confide in his graduate students. Evidently conducting secret experiments in comparative psychology. Rats and such. Nothing overtly censorable."

"I see. What are your plans?"

"I'll have his lab searched tonight. If nothing turns up, I'll recommend a drop."

"I'd prefer that you search the lab yourself."

A. Prentiss Rogers concealed his surprise and annoyance. "Very well."

His ear button clicked a dismissal.

With puzzled irritation he snapped the plug from the dash socket, started the car, and eased it down the drive into the boulevard bordering the university.

Didn't she realize that he was a busy Field Director with a couple of hundred men under him fully capable of making a routine night search? Undoubtedly she knew just that, but nevertheless was requiring that he do it himself. Why?

And why had she assigned Professor Luce to him personally, squandering so many of his precious hours, when half a dozen of his bright young physical philosophers could have handled it? Nevertheless E, from behind the august anonymity of her solitary initial, had been adamant.

A mile away he turned into a garage on a deserted side street and drew up alongside a Cadillac.

Crush sprang out of the big car and silently held the rear door open for him.

Prentiss got in. "We have a job tonight."

His aide hesitated a fraction of a second before slamming the door behind him. Prentiss knew that the squat, asthmatic little man was surprised and delighted.

As for Crush, he'd never got it through his head that the control of human knowledge was a grim and hateful business, not a kind of cruel lark.

"Very good, sir," wheezed Crush, climbing in behind the wheel. "Shall I reserve a sleeping room at the Bureau for the evening?"

"Can't afford to sleep," grumbled Prentiss. "Desk so high now I can't see over it. Take a nap yourself, if you want to."

"Yes, sir. If I feel the need of it, sir."

The ontologist shot a bitter glance at the back of the man's head. No, Crush wouldn't sleep, but not because worry would keep him awake. A holdover from the days when all a Censor man had was a sleepless curiosity and a pocket Geiger, Crush was serenely untroubled by the dangerous and unfathomable implications of philosophical nucleonics. For Crush, "ontology" was just another definition in the dictionary: "The science of reality."

The little aide could never grasp the idea that unless a sane world-wide pattern of nucleonic investigation were followed, some one in Australia—or next door—might one day throw a switch and alter the shape of that reality. That's what made Crush so valuable; he just didn't know enough to be afraid.

Prentiss had clipped the hairs from his nostrils and so far had breathed in complete silence. But now, as that cavernous face was turned toward where he lay stomach-to-earth in the sheltering darkness, his lungs convulsed in an audible gasp.

The mild, polite, somewhat abstracted academic features of Professor Luce were transformed. The face beyond the lab window was now flushed, the lips were drawn back in soundless amusement, the sunken black eyes were dancing with red pin-points of flame.

By brute will the ontologist forced his attention back to the rat.

Four times in the past few minutes he had watched the animal run down an inclined chute until it reached a fork, chose one fork, receive what must be a nerve-shattering electric shock, and then be replaced in the chute-beginning for the next run. No matter which alternative fork was chosen, the animal always had been shocked into convulsions.

On this fifth run the rat, despite needling blasts of compressed air from the chute walls, was slowing down. Just before it reached the fork it stopped completely.

The air jets struck at it again, and little cones of up-ended gray fur danced on its rump and flanks.

It gradually ceased to tremble; its respiration dropped to normal. It seemed to Prentiss that its eyes were shut.

The air jets lashed out again. It gave no notice, but just lay there, quiescent, in a near coma.

As he peered into the window, Prentiss saw the tall man walk languidly over to the little animal and run a long hooklike forefinger over its back. No reaction. The professor then said something, evidently in a soft slurred voice, for Prentiss had difficulty in reading his lips.

"—when both alternatives are wrong for you, but you *must* do something, you hesitate, don't you, little one? You slow down, and you are lost. You are no longer a rat. Do you know what the universe would be like if a *phonton* should slow down? You don't? Have you ever taken a bite out of a balloon, little friend? Just the tiniest possible bite?"

Prentiss cursed. The professor had turned and was walking toward the cages with the animal, and although he was apparently still talking, his lips were no longer visible.

After relatching the cage-door the professor walked toward the lab entrance, glanced carefully around the room, and then, as he was reaching for the light switch, looked toward Prentiss' window.

For a moment the investigator was convinced that by some

nameless power the professor was looking into the darkness, straight into his eyes.

He exhaled slowly. It was preposterous.

The room was plunged in darkness.

The investigator blinked and closed his eyes. He wouldn't really have to worry until he heard the lab door opening on the opposite side of the little building.

The door didn't open. Prentiss squinted into the darkness of the room.

Where the professor's head had been were now two mysterious tiny red flames, like candles.

Something must be reflecting from the professor's corneas. But the room was dark; there was no light to be reflected. The flame-eyes continued their illusion of studying him.

The hair was crawling on Prentiss's neck when the twin lights finally vanished and he heard the sound of the lab door opening.

As the slow heavy tread died away down the flagstones to the street, Prentiss gulped in a huge lungful of the chill night air and rubbed his sweating face against his sleeve.

What had got into him? He was acting like the greenest club. He was glad that Crush had to man the televisor relay in the Cadillac and couldn't see him.

He got to his hands and knees and crept silently toward the darkened window. It was a simple sliding sash, and a few seconds sufficed to drill through the glass and insert a hook around the sash lock. The rats began a nervous squeaking as he lowered himself into the darkness of the basement room.

His ear-receptor sounded. "The prof is coming back!" wheezed Crush's tinny voice.

Prentiss said something under his breath, but did not pause in drawing his infra-red scanner from his pocket.

He touched his fingers to his throat mike. "Signal when he reaches the bend in the walk," he said. "And be sure you get this on the visor tape."

The apparatus got his first attention.

The investigator had memorized its position perfectly, Approaching as closely in the darkness as he dared, he "panned" the scanner over some very interesting apparatus that he had noticed on the table.

Then he turned to the books on the desk, regretting that he wouldn't have time to record more than a few pages.

"He's at the bend," warned Crush.

"Okay," mumbled Prentiss, running sensitive fingers over the book bindings. He selected one, opened it at random, and ran the scanner over the invisible pages. "Is this coming through?" he demanded.

"Chief, *he's at the door!*"

Prentiss had to push back the volume without scanning any more of it. He had just relocked the sash when the lab door swung open.

A couple of hours later the ontologist bid good-morning to his receptionist and secretaries and stepped into his private office. He dropped with tired thoughtfulness into his swivel chair and pulled out the infrared negatives that Crush had prepared in the Cadillac darkroom. The page from the old German diary was particularly intriguing. He laboriously translated it once more:

As I got deeper into the manuscript, my mouth grew dry, and my heart began to pound. This, I knew, was a contribution the like of which my family has not seen since Copernicus, Roger Bacon, or perhaps even Aristotle. It seemed incredible that this silent little man, who had never been outside of Koenigsberg, should hold the key to the universe—the *Critique of Pure Reason*, he calls it. And I doubt that even he realizes the ultimate portent of his teaching, for he says we cannot know the real shape or nature of anything, that is, the Thing-in-Itself, the ding-an-Sich, or *noumenon*. He holds that this is the ultimate unknowable, reserved to the gods. He doesn't supect that, century by century, mankind is nearing this final realization of the final things. Even this brilliant man would probably say that the earth was round in 600 B.C., even as it is today. But *I* know it was flat, then—as truly flat as it is truly round today. What has changed? Not the Thing-in-Itself we call the earth. No, it is the mind of man that has changed. But in his preposterous blindness, he mistakes what is really his own mental quickening for a broadened application of science and more precise methods of investigation—

Prentiss smiled.

Luce was undoubtedly a collector of philosophic incunabula. Odd hobby, but that's all it could be—a hobby. Obviously the earth had never been flat, and in fact hadn't changed shape substantially in the last couple of billion years. Certainly any notions as to the flatness of the earth held by primitives of a few thousand years ago or even by contemporaries of Kant were due to their ignorance rather than to accurate observation, and a man of Luce's erudition could only be amused by them.

Again Prentiss found himself smiling with the tolerance of a man standing on the shoulders of twenty centuries of science. The primitives, of course, did the best they could. They just didn't know. They worked with childish premises and infantile instruments.

His brows creased. To assume they had used childish premises was begging the question. On the other hand, was it really worth a second thought? All he could hope to discover would be a few instances of how inferior apparatus coupled perhaps with unsophisticated deductions had oversimplified the world of the ancients. Still, anything that interested the strange Dr. Luce automatically interested him, Prentiss, until the case was closed.

He dictated into the scriptor:

"Memorandum to Geodetic Section. Rush a paragraph history of ideas concerning shape of earth. Prentiss."

Duty done, he promptly forgot it and turned to the heavy accumulation of reports on his desk.

A quarter of an hour later the scriptor rang and began typing an incoming message.

To the Director. Re your request for brief history of earth's shape. Chaldeans and Babylonians (per clay tablets from library of Assurbanipal), Egyptians (per Ahmes papyrus, ca. 1700 B.C.), Cretans (per inscriptions in royal library at Knossos, ca. 1300 B.C.), Chinese (per Chou Kung ms. ca. 1100 B.C.), Phoenicians (per fragments at Tyre ca. 900 B.C.), Hebrews (per unknown Biblical historian ca. 850 B.C.), and early Greeks (per map of widely-traveled geographer Hecataeus, 517 B.C.) assumed earth to be flat disc. But from the 5th century B.C. forward earth's sphericity universally recognized. . . .

There were a few more lines, winding up with the work done on corrections for flattening at poles, but Prentiss had already lost interest. The report threw no light on Luce's hobby and was devoid of ontological implications.

He tossed the script into the waste basket and returned to the reports before him.

A few minutes later he twisted uneasily in his chair, eyed the scriptor in annoyance, then forced himself back to his work.

No use.

Deriding himself for an idiot, he growled at the machine:

"Memorandum to Geodetic. Re your memo history earth's shape. How do you account for change to belief in sphericity after Hecataeus? Rush. Prentiss."

The seconds ticked by.

He drummed on his desk impatiently, then got up and began pacing the floor.

When the scriptor rang, he bounded back and leaned over his desk, watching the words being typed out.

Late Greeks based spherical shape on observation that mast of approaching ship appeared first, then prow. Not known why similar observation not made by earlier seafaring peoples. . . .

Prentiss rubbed his cheek in perplexity. What was he fishing for?

He thrust the half-born conjecture that the earth really had once been flat back into his mental recesses.

Well, then how about the heavens? Surely there was no record of their having changed during man's brief lifetime.

He'd try one more shot and quit.

"Memo to Astronomy Division. Rush paragraph on early vs. modern sun size and distance."

A few minutes later he was reading the reply:

Skipping Plato, whose data are believed baseless (he measured sun's distance at only twice that of moon), we come to earliest recognized "authority." Ptolemy (Almagest, ca. 140 A.D. measured sun radius as 5.5 that of earth (as against 109 actual); measured sun distance at 1210 (23,000 actual). Fairly accurate measurements date only from 17th and 18th centuries. . . .

He'd read all that somewhere. The difference was easily explained by their primitive instruments. It was insane to keep this up.

But it was too late.

"Memo to Astronomy. Were erroneous Ptolemaic measurements due to lack of precision instruments?"

Soon he had his reply:

To Director: Source of Ptolemy's errors in solar measurement not clearly understood. Used astrolabe precise to 10 seconds and clepsydra water clock incorporating Hero's improvements. With same instruments, and using modern value of pi, Ptolemy measured moon radius (0.29 earth radius vs. 0.273 actual) and distance (59 earth radii vs. 60 ⅓ actual). Hence instruments reasonably precise. And note that Copernicus, using quasi-modern instruments and technique, "confirmed" Ptolemaic figure of sun's distance at 1200 earth radii. No explanation known for glaring error.

Unless, suggested something within Prentiss' mind, the sun were closer and much different before the 17th century, when Newton was telling the world where and how big the sun *ought* to be. But *that* solution was too absurd for further consideration. He would sooner assume his complete insanity.

Puzzled, the ontologist gnawed his lower lip and stared at the message in the scriptor.

In his abstraction he found himself peering at the symbol "pi" in the scriptor message. *There*, at least, was something that had always been the same, and would endure for all time. He reached over to knock out his pipe in the big circular ash tray by the scriptor and paused in the middle of the second tap. From his desk he fished a tape measure and stretched it across the tray. Ten inches. And then around the circumference. Thirty-one and a half inches. Good enough, considering. It was a result any curious schoolboy could get.

He turned to the scriptor again.

"Memo to Math Section. Rush paragraph history on value of pi. Prentiss."

He didn't have to wait long.

To Director. Re history "pi." Babylonians used value of 3.00 Aristotle made fairly accurate physical and theoretical evaluations. Archimedes first to arrive at modern value, using theory of limits. . . .

There was more, but it was lost on Prentiss. It was inconceivable, of course, that pi had grown during the two millennia that separated the Babylonians from Archimedes. And yet, it was exasperating. Why hadn't they done any better than 3.00? Any child with a piece of string could have demonstrated their error. Countless generations of wise, careful Chaldean astronomers, measuring time and star positions with such incredible accuracy, all coming to grief with a piece of string and pi. It didn't make sense. And certainly pi hadn't grown, any more than the Babylonian 360-day year had grown into the modern 365-day year. It had always been the same, he told himself. The primitives hadn't measured accurately, that was all. That *had* to be the explanation.

He hoped.

He sat down at his desk again, stared a moment at his memo pad and wrote:

Check history of gravity—acceleration. Believe Aristotle unable detect acceleration. Galileo used same instruments, including same crude water clock, and found it. Why? . . . Any reported transits of Vulcan since 1914, when Einstein explained eccentricity of Mercury orbit by relativity instead of by hypothetical sunward planet? . . . How could Oliver Lodge detect an ether-drift and Michelson not? Conceivable that Lorentz contraction not a physical fact before Michelson experiment? . . . How many chemical elements were predicted before discovered?

He tapped absently on the pad a few times, then rang for a research assistant. He'd barely have time to explain what he wanted before he had to meet his class under Luce.

And he still wasn't sure where the rats fitted in.

Curtly Professor Luce brought his address to a close.

"Well, gentlemen," he said, "I guess we'll have to continue this at our next lecture. We seem to have run over a little; class dismissed. Oh, Mr. Prentiss!"

The investigator looked up in genuine surprise. "Yes, sir?" The thin gun in his shoulder holster suddenly felt satisfyingly fat.

He realized that the crucial moment was near, that he would know before he left the campus whether this strange man was a harmless physicist, devoted to his life-work and his queer hobby, or whether he was an incarnate danger to mankind. The professor was acting out of turn, and it was an unexpected break.

"Mr. Prentiss," continued Luce from the lecture platform, "may I see you in my office a moment before you leave?"

Prentiss said, "Certainly." As the group broke up he followed the gaunt scientist through the door that led to Luce's little office behind the lecture room.

At the doorway he hesitated almost imperceptibly; Luce saw it and bowed sardonically. "After you, sir!"

Then the tall man indicated a chair near his desk. "Sit down, Mr. Prentiss."

For a long moment the seated men studied each other.

Finally the professor spoke. "About fifteen years ago a brilliant young man named Rogers wrote a doctoral dissertation at the University of Vienna on what he called . . . 'Involuntary Conformation of Incoming Sensoria to Apperception Mass.' "

Prentiss began fishing for his pipe. "Indeed?"

"One copy of the dissertation was sent to the Scholarship Society that was financing his studies. All others were seized by the International Bureau of the Censor, and accordingly a demand was made on the Scholarship Society for its copy. But it couldn't be found."

Prentiss was concentrating on lighting his pipe, He wondered if the faint trembling of the match flame was visible.

The professor turned to his desk, opened the top drawer, and pulled out a slim brochure bound in black leather.

The investigator coughed out a cloud of smoke.

The professor did not seem to notice, but opened the front cover and began reading: " '—a dissertation in partial fulfillment of the requirements for the degree of Doctor of Philosophy at the University of Vienna. A. P. Rogers, Vienna, 1957.' " The man closed the book and studied it thoughtfully, "Adrian Prentiss Rogers—the owner of a brain whose like is seen not once in a century. He exposed the gods—then vanished."

Prentiss suppressed a shiver as he met those sunken, implacable eye-caverns.

The cat-and-mouse was over. In a way, he was relieved.

"Why did you vanish then, Mr. Prentiss-Rogers?" demanded Luce. "And why do you now reappear?"

The investigator blew a cloud of smoke toward the low ceiling. "To prevent people like you from introducing sensoria that *can't* be conformed to our present apperception mass. To keep reality as is. That answers both questions, I think."

The other man smiled. It was not a good thing to see. "Have you succeeded?"

"I don't know. So far, I suppose."

The gaunt man shrugged his shoulders. "You ignore tomorrow, then. I think you have failed, but I can't be sure, of course, until I actually perform the experiment that will create novel sensoria." He leaned forward. "I'll come to the point, Mr. Prentiss-Rogers. Next to yourself—and possibly excepting the Censor—I know more about the mathematical approach to reality than anyone else in the world. I may even know things about it that you don't. On other phases of it I'm weak—because I developed your results on the basis of mere logic rather than insight. And logic, we know, is applicable only within indeterminate limits. But in developing a practical device—an actual machine—for the wholesale alteration of incoming sensoria, I'm enormously ahead of you. You saw my apparatus last night, Mr. Prentiss-Rogers? Oh, come, don't be coy.''

Prentiss drew deeply on his pipe.

"I saw it."

"Did you understand it?"

"No. It wasn't all there. At least, the apparatus on the table was incomplete. There's more to it than a Nicol prism and a goniometer."

"Ah, you are clever! Yes, I was wise in not permitting you to remain very long—no longer than necessary to whet your curiosity. Look, then! I offer you a partnership. Check my data and apparatus; in return you may be present when I run the experiment. We will attain enlightenment together. We will know all things. We will be gods!"

"And what about two billion other human beings?" said Prentiss, pressing softly at his shoulder holster.

The professor smiled faintly. "Their lunacy—assuming they continue to exist at all—may become slightly more pronounced, of course. But why worry about them?"

"Don't expect me to believe this aura of altruism, Mr. Prentiss-Rogers. I think you're afraid to face what lies behind our so-called 'reality.' "

"At least I'm a coward in a good cause." He stood up. "Have you any more to say?"

He knew that he was just going through the motions. Luce must have realized he had lain himself open to arrest half a dozen times in as many minutes: The bare possession of the missing copy of the dissertation, the frank admission of plans to experiment with reality, and his attempted bribery of a high Censor official. And yet, the man's very bearing denied the possibility of being cut off in mid-career.

Luce's cheeks fluffed out in a brief sigh. "I'm sorry you can't be intelligent about this, Mr. Prentiss-Rogers. Yet, the time will come, you know, when you must make up your mind to go—*through*, shall we say? In fact, we may have to depend to a considerable degree on one another's companionship—*out there*. Even gods have to pass the time of day occasionally, and I have a suspicion that you and I are going to be quite chummy. So let us not part in enmity.''

Prentiss' hand slid beneath his coat lapel and drew out the snub-nosed automatic. He had a grim foreboding that it was futile, and that the professor was laughing silently at him, but he had no choice.

''You are under arrest,'' he said unemotionally. ''Come with me.''

The other shrugged his shoulders, then something like a laugh, soundless in its mockery, surged up in his throat. ''Certainly, Mr. Prentiss-Rogers.''

He arose.

The room was plunged into instant blackness.

Prentiss fired three times, lighting up the gaunt chuckling form at each flash.

''Save your fire, Mr. Prentiss-Rogers. Lead doesn't get far in an intense diamagnetic screen. Study the magnetic damper on a lab balance the next time you're in the Censor Building!''

Somewhere a door slammed.

Several hours later Prentiss was eyeing his aide with ill-concealed distaste. Prentiss knew Crush had been summoned by E to confer on the implications of Luce's escape, and that Crush was secretly sympathizing with him. Prentiss couldn't endure sympathy. He'd prefer that the asthmatic little man tell him how stupid he'd been.

''What do you want?'' he growled.

''Sir,'' gasped Crush apologetically, ''I have a report on that gadget you scanned in Luce's lab.''

Prentiss was instantly mollified, but suppressed any show of interest. ''What about it?''

''In essence, sir,'' wheezed Crush, ''it's just a Nicol prism mounted on a goniometer. According to a routine check it was ground by an obscure optician who was nine years on the job, and he spent nearly all of that time on just one face of the prism. What do you make of that, sir?''

''Nothing, yet. What took him so long?''

''Grinding an absolute flat edge, sir, so he says.''

''Odd. That would mean a boundary composed exclusively of molecules of the same crystal layer, something that hasn't been attempted since the Palomar reflector.''

"Yes, sir. And then there's the goniometer mount with just one number on the dial—forty-five degrees."

"Obviously," said Prentiss, "the Nicol is to be used only at a forty-five degree angle to the incoming light. Hence it's probably extremely important—why, I don't know—that the angle be *precisely* forty-five degress. That would require a perfectly flat surface, too, of course. I suppose you're going to tell me that the goniometric gearing is set up very accurately."

Suddenly Prentiss realized that Crush was looking at him in mingled suspicion and admiration.

"Well?" demanded the ontologist irritably. "Just what is the adjusting mechanism? Surely not geometrical? Too crude. Optical, perhaps?"

Crush gasped into his handkerchief. "Yes, sir. The prism is rotated very slowly into a tiny beam of light. Part of the beam is reflected and part refracted. At exactly forty-five degrees it seems, by Jordan's law, that exactly half is reflected and half refracted. The two beams are picked up in a photocell relay that stops the rotating mechanism as soon as the luminosities of the beams are exactly equal."

Prentiss tugged nervously at his ear. It was puzzling. Just what was Luce going to do with such an exquisitely-ground Nicol? At this moment he would have given ten years of his life for an inkling to the supplementary apparatus that went along with the Nicol. It would be something optical, certainly, tied in somehow with neurotic rats. What was it Luce had said the other night in the lab? Something about slowing down a photon. And then what was supposed to happen to the universe? Somethng like taking a tiny bite out of a balloon, Luce had said.

And how did it all interlock with certain impossible, though syllogistically necessary conclusions that flowed from his recent research into the history of human knowledge?

He wasn't sure. But he *was* sure that Luce was on the verge of using this mysterious apparatus to change the perceptible universe, on a scale so vast that humanity was going to get lost in the shuffle. He'd have to convince E of that.

If he couldn't, he'd seek out Luce himself and kill him with his bare hands, and decide on reasons for it afterward.

He was guiding himself for the time being by pure insight, but he'd better be organized when he confronted E.

Crush was speaking. "Shall we go, sir? Your secretary says the jet is waiting."

*   *   *

The painting showed a man in a red hat and black robes seated behind a high judge's bench. Five other men in red hats were seated behind a lower bench to his right, and four others to his left. At the base of the bench knelt a figure in solitary abjection.

"We condemn you, Galileo Galilei, to the formal prison of this Holy Office for a period determinable at Our pleasure; and by way of salutary penance, We order you, during the next three years, to recite once a week the seven Penitential Psalms."

Prentiss turned from the inscription to the less readable face of E. The oval olive-hued face was smooth, unlined, even around the eyes, and the black hair was parted off-center and drawn over the woman's head into a bun at the nape of her neck. She wore no make-up, and apparently needed none. She was clad in a black, loose-fitting business suit, which accentuated her perfectly molded body.

"Do you know," said Prentiss coolly, "I think you like being Censor. It's in your blood."

"You're perfectly right. I *do* like being Censor. According to Speer, I effectively sublimate a guilt complex as strange as it is baseless."

"Very interesting. Sort of expiation of an ancestral guilt complex, eh?"

"What do you mean?"

"Woman started man on his acquisition of knowledge and self-destruction, and ever since has tried futilely to halt the avalanche. In you the feeling of responsibility and guilt runs exceptionally strong, and I'll wager that some nights you wake up in a cold sweat, thinking you've just plucked a certain forbidden fruit."

E stared icily up at the investigator's twitching mouth. "The only pertinent question," she said crisply, "is whether Luce is engaged in ontologic experiments, and if so, are they of a dangerous nature."

Prentiss sighed. "He's in it up to his neck. But just *what*, and how dangerous, I can only guess."

"Then guess."

"Luce thinks he's developed apparatus for the practical, predictable alteration of sensoria. He hopes to do something with his device that will blow physical laws straight to smithereens. The resulting reality would probably be unrecognizable even to a professional ontologist, let alone the mass of humanity."

"You seem convinced he can do this."

"The probabilities are high."

"Good enough. We can deal only in probabilities. The safest thing, of course, would be to locate Luce and kill him on sight. On the other hand, the faintest breath of scandal would result in Congressional hamstringing of the Bureau, so we must proceed cautiously."

"If Luce is really able to do what he claims," said Prentiss grimly, "and we let him do it, there won't be any Bureau at all—nor any Congress either."

"I know. Rest assured that if I decide that Luce is dangerous and should die, I shall let neither the lives nor careers of anyone in the Bureau stand in the way, including myself."

Prentiss nodded, wondering if she really meant it.

The woman continued. "We are faced for the first time with a probable violation of our directive forbidding ontologic experiments. We are inclined to prevent this threatened violation by taking a man's life. I think we should settle once and for all whether such harsh measures are indicated, and it is for this that I have invited you to attend a staff conference. We intend to reopen the entire question of ontologic experiments and their implications."

Prentiss groaned inwardly. In matters so important the staff decided by vote. He had a brief vision of attempting to convince E's hard-headed scientists that mankind was changing "reality" from century to century—that not too long ago the earth had been "flat." Yes, by now he was beginning to believe it himself!

"Come this way, please," said E.

Sitting at E's right was an elderly man, Speer, the famous psychologist. On her left was Goring, staff adviser on nucleonics; next to him was Burchard, brilliant chemist and Director of the Western Field, then Prentiss, and then Dobbs, the renowened metallurgist and Director of the Central Field.

Prentiss didn't like Dobbs, who had voted against his promotion to the directorship of Eastern.

E announced: "We may as well start this inquiry with an examanation of fundamentals. Mr. Prentiss, just what is reality?"

The ontologist winced. He had needed two hundred pages to outline the theory of reality in his doctoral thesis, and even so, had always suspected his examiners had passed it only because it was incomprehensible—hence a work of genius.

"Well," he began wryly, "I must confess that I don't know what *real* reality is. What most of us call reality is simply an integrated synthesis of incoming sensoria. As such it is nothing more than a working hypothesis in the mind of each of us, forever in a process of revision. In the past that process has been slow and safe. But we have now to consider the consequences of an instantaneous and total revision—a revision so far-reaching that it may thrust humanity face-to-face with the true reality, the world of Things-in-Themselves—Kant's *noumena*. This, I think, would be as disastrous as dumping a group of children in the middle of a forest. They'd have to relearn the simplest things— what to eat, how to protect themselves from elemental forces, and even a new language to deal with their new problems. There'd be few survivors.

"That is what we want to avoid, and we can do it if we prevent any sudden sweeping alteration of sensoria in our present reality."

He looked dubiously at the faces about him. It was a poor start. Speer's wrinkled features were drawn up in a serene smile, and the psychologist seemed to be contemplating the air over Prentiss' head. Goring was regarding him with grave, expressionless eyes. E nodded slightly as Prentiss' gaze traveled past her to a puzzled Burchard, thence to Dobbs, who was frankly contemptuous.

Speer and Goring were going to be the most susceptible. Speer because of his lack of a firm scientific background, Goring because nucleonics was in such a state of flux that nuclear experts were expressing the gravest doubts as to the validity of the laws worshipped by Burchard and Dobbs. Burchard was only a faint possibility. And Dobbs?

Dobbs said: "I don't know what the dickens you're talking about." The implication was plain that he wanted to add: "And I don't think you do, either."

And Prentiss wasn't so sure that he did know. Ontology was an elusive thing at best.

"I object to the term 'real reality,' " continued Dobbs. "A thing is real or it isn't. No fancy philosophical system can change *that*. And if it's real, it gives off predictable, reproducible sensory stimuli not subject to alteration except in the minds of lunatics."

Prentiss breathed more easily. His course was clear. He'd concentrate on Dobbs, with a little side-play on Burchard. Speer and Goring would never suspect his arguments were really directed at them. He pulled a gold coin from his vest pocket and slid it across the table to Dobbs, being careful not to let it clatter. "You're a metallurgist. Please tell us what this is."

Dobbs picked up the coin and examined it suspiciously. "It's quite obviously a five-dollar gold piece, minted at Fort Worth in nineteen sixty-two. I can even give you the analysis, if you want it."

"I doubt that you could," said Prentiss coolly. "For you see, you are holding a counterfeit coin minted only last week in my own laboratories especially for this conference. As a matter of fact, if you'll forgive my saying so, I had you in mind when I ordered the coin struck. It contains no gold whatever—drop it on the table.

The coin fell from the fingers of the astounded metallurgist and clattered on the oaken table top.

"Hear the false ring?" demanded Prentiss.

Pink-faced, Dobbs cleared his throat and peered at the coin more closely. "How was I to know that? It's no disgrace, is it? Many clever counterfeits can be detected only in the laboratory. I knew the color was a little on the red side, but that could have been due to the lighting of the room. And of course, I hadn't given it an auditory test before I spoke. The ring is definitely dull. It's obviously a copper-lead alloy, with possibly a little amount of silver to help the ring. All right, I jumped to conclusions. So what? What does that prove?"

"It proves that you have arrived at two separate, distinct, and mutually exclusive realities, starting with the same sensory premises. It proves how easily reality is revised. And that isn't all, as I shall soon—"

"All right," said Dobbs testily. "But on second thought I admitted it was false, didn't I?"

"Which demonstrates a further weakness in our routine acquisition and evaluation of predigested information. When an unimpeachable authority tells us something as a fact, we immediately, and without conscious thought, *modify* our incoming stimuli to conform with that *fact*. The coin suddenly acquires the red taint of copper, and rings false to the ear."

"I would have caught the queer ring anyhow," said Dobbs stubbornly, "with no help from 'an unimpeachable authority.' The ring would have sounded the same, no matter what you said."

From the corner of his eye Prentiss noticed that Speer was grinning broadly. Had the old psychologist divined his trick? He'd take a chance.

'Dr. Speer,'' he said, ''I think you have something interesting to tell our doubting friend.''

Speer cackled dryly. ''You've been a perfect guinea pig, Dobbsie. The coin was genuine.''

The metallurgist's jaw dropped as he looked blankly from one face to another. Then his jowls slowly grew red. He flung the coin to the table. ''Maybe I am a guinea pig. I'm a realist, too. I think this is a piece of metal. You might fool me as to its color or assay, but in essence and substance, it's a piece of metal.'' He glared at Prentiss and Speer in turn. ''Does anyone deny that?''

''Certainly not,'' said Prentiss. ''Our mental pigeonholes are identical in that respect; they accept the same sensory definition of 'piece of metal,' or 'coin.' Whatever this object is, it emits stimuli that our minds are capable of registering and abstracting as a 'coin.' But note: we make a coin out of it. However, if I could shuffle my cortical pigeonholes, I might find it to be a chair, or a steamer trunk, possibly with Dr. Dobbs inside, or, if the shuffling were extreme, there might be no semantic pattern into which the incoming stimuli could be routed. There wouldn't be anything there at all!''

''Sure,'' sneered Dobbs. ''You would walk right through it.''

''Why not?'' asked Prentiss gravely. ''I think we may do it all the time. Matter is about the emptiest stuff imaginable. If you compressed that coin to eliminate the space between its component atoms and electrons, you couldn't see it in a microscope.''

Dobbs stared at the enigmatic goldpiece as though it might suddenly thrust out a pseudopod and swallow him up. Then he said flatly: ''No. I don't believe it. It exists as a coin, and only as a coin—whether I know it or not.''

''Well,'' ventured Prentiss, ''how about you, Dr. Goring? Is the coin real to you?''

The nucleist smiled and shrugged his shoulders. ''If I don't think too much about it, it's real enough. And yet . . .''

Dobb's face clouded. ''And yet what? Here it is. Can you doubt the evidence of your own eyes?''

''That's just the difficulty.'' Goring leaned forward. ''My eyes tell me, here's a coin. Theory tells me, here's a mass of hypothetical disturbances in a hypothetical subether in a hypothetical ether. The indeterminacy principle tells me that I can never know both the mass and position of these hypothetical disturbances. And as a physicist I know that the bare fact of observing something is sufficient to change that something from its pre-observed state. Nevertheless, I compromise by letting my senses and practical experience stick a tag on this particular bit of the unknowable. X, after its impact on my mind (whatever *that* is!) equals coin. A single equation with two variables has no solution. The best I can say is, it's a coin, but probably not really—''

"Hah!" declared Burchard. "I can demonstrate the fallacy of *that* position very quickly. If our minds make this a coin, then our minds make this little object an ash-tray, that a window, the thing that holds us up, a chair. You might say we make the air we breathe, and perhaps even the stars and planets. Why, following Prentiss' idea to its logical end, the universe itself is the work of man—a conclusion I'm sure he doesn't intend."

"Oh, but I do," said Prentiss.

Prentiss took a deep breath. The issue could be dodged no longer. He had to take a stand. "And to make sure you understand me, whether you agree with me or not, I'll state categorically that I believe the apparent universe to be the work of man."

Even E looked startled, but said nothing.

The ontologist continued rapidly. "All of you doubt my sanity. A week ago I would have, too. But since then I've done a great deal of research in the history of science. And I repeat, *the universe is the work of man*. I believe that man began his existence in some incredibly simple world—the original and true *noumenon* of our present universe. And that over the centuries man expanded his little world into its present vastness and incomprehensible intricacy solely by dint of imagination.

"Consequently, I believe that what most of you call the 'real' world has been changing ever since our ancestors began to think."

Dobbs smiled superciliously. "Oh, come now, Prentiss. That's just a rhetorical description of scientific progress over the past centuries. In the same sense I might say that modern transportation and communications have shrunk the earth. But you'll certainly admit that the physical state of things has been substantially constant ever since the galaxies formed and the earth began to cool, and that the simple cosmologies of early man were simply the result of lack of means for obtaining accurate information?"

"I *won't* admit it," rejoined Prentiss bluntly. "I maintain that their information was substantially accurate. I maintain that at one time in our history the earth was flat—as flat as it is now round, and no one living before the time of Hecataeus, though he might have been equipped with the finest modern instruments, could have proved otherwise. His mind was *conditioned* to a two-dimensional world. Any of us present, if we were transplanted to the world of Hecataeus, could, of course, establish terrestrial sphericity in short order. Our minds have been conditioned to a three-dimensional world. The day may come a few millennia hence when a four-dimensional Terra will be commonplace even to schoolchildren; they will have been intuitively conditioned in relativistic concepts.'' He added slyly: ''And the less intelligent of them may attempt to blame our naive three-dimensional planet on our grossly inaccurate instruments, because it will be as plain as day to them that their planet has four dimensions!''

Dobbs snorted at this amazing idea. The other scientists stared at Prentiss with an awe which was mixed with incredulity.

Goring said cautiously: ''I follow up to a certain point. I can see that a primitive society might start out with a limited number of facts. They would offer theories to harmonize and integrate those facts, and then those first theories would require that new, additional facts exist, and in their search for those secondary facts, extraneous data would turn up inconsistent with the first theories. Secondary theories would then be required, from which hitherto unguessed facts should follow, the confirmation of which would discover more inconsistencies. So the pattern of fact to theory to fact to theory, and so on, finally brings us into our present state of knowledge. Does that follow from your argument?''

Prentiss nodded.

''But won't you admit that the facts were there all the time, and merely awaited discovery?''

''The simple, unelaborated *noumenon* was there all the time, yes. But the new fact—man's new interpretation of the *noumenon*, was generally pure invention—a mental creation, if you like. This will be clearer if you consider how rarely a new fact arises before a theory exists for its explanation. In the ordinary scientific investigation, theory comes first, followed in short order by the 'discovery' of various facts deducible from it.''

Goring still looked skeptical. ''But that wouldn't mean the fact wasn't there all the time.''

''Wouldn't it? Look at the evidence. Has it never struck you as odd in how many instances very obvious facts were 'overlooked' until a theory was propounded that required their existence? Take your nuclear building blocks. Protons and electrons were detected physically only after Rutherford had showed they had to exist. And then when Rutherford found that protons and electrons were not enough to build all the atoms of the periodic table, he postulated the neutron, which of course was duly 'discovered' in the Wilson cloud chamber.''

Goring pursed his lips. ''But the Wilson cloud chamber would have shown all that prior to the theory, if anyone had only thought to use it.

''The mere fact that Wilson didn't invent his cloud chamber until nineteen-twelve and Geiger didn't invent his counter until nineteen-thirteen, would not keep subatomic particles from existing before that time.''

''You don't get the point,'' said Prentiss. ''The primitive, ungeneralized noumenon that we today observe as subatomic particles existed prior to nineteen-twelve, true, *but not subatomic particles.*''

''Well, I don't know. . . .'' Goring scratched his chin. ''How about fundamental forces? Surely electricity existed before Galvani? Even the Greeks knew how to build up electrostatic charges on amber.''

''Greek electricity was nothing more than electrostatic charges. Nothing more could be created until Galvani introduced the concept of the electric current.''

''Do you mean the electric current didn't exist at all before Galvani?'' demanded Burchard. ''Not even when lightning struck a conductor?''

''Not even then. We don't know much about pre-Galvanic lightning. While it probably packed a wallop, its destructive potential couldn't have been due to its delivery of an electric current. The Chinese flew kites for centuries before Franklin theorized that lightning was the same as galvanic electricity, but there's no recorded shock from a kite string until our learned statesman drew forth one in seventeen-sixty-five. *Now*, only an idiot flies a kite in a storm. It's all according to pattern: theory first, then we alter 'reality' to fit.''

Burchard persisted. ''Then I suppose you'd say all the elements are figments of our imagination.''

''Correct,'' agreed Prentiss. ''I believe that in the beginning there were only four *noumenal* elements. Man simply elaborated these according to the needs of his growing science. Man made them what they are today—and on occasion, *unmade* them. You remember the havoc Mendelyeev created with his periodic law. He declared that the elements had to follow valence sequences of increasing atomic weight, and when they didn't, he insisted his law was right and that the atomic weights were wrong. He must have had Stas and Berzelius whirling in their graves, because they had worked out the 'erroneous' atomic weights with marvelous precision. The odd thing was, when the weights were rechecked, they fitted the Mendelyeev table. But that wasn't all. The old rascal pointed out vacant spots in his table and maintained that there were more elements yet to be discovered. He even predicted what properties they'd have. He was too modest. I state that Nilson, Winkler, and De Boisbaudran merely *discovered* scandium, germanium, and gallium; Mendelyeev *created* them, out of the original quadrelemental stuff.''

E leaned forward. "That's a bit strong. Tell me, if man has changed the elements and the cosmos to suit his convenience, what was the cosmos like before man came on the scene?"

"There wasn't any," answered Prentiss. "Remember, by definition, 'cosmos' or 'reality' is simply man's version of the ultimate *noumenal* universe. The 'cosmos' arrives and departs with the mind of man. Consequently, the earth—as such—didn't even exist before the advent of man."

"But the evidence of the rocks . . ." protested E. "Pressures applied over millions, even billions of years, were needed to form them, unless you postulate an omnipotent God who called them into existence as of yesterday."

"I postulate only the omnipotent human mind," said Prentiss. "In the seventeenth century, Hooke, Ray, Woodward, to name a few, studied chalk, gravel, marble, and even coal, without finding anything inconsistent with results to be expected from the Noachian Flood. But now that we've made up our minds that the earth is older, the rocks *seem* older, too."

"But how about evolution?" demanded Burchard. "Surely that wasn't a matter of a few centuries?"

"Really?" replied Prentiss. "Again, why assume that the facts are any more recent than the theory? The evidence is all the other way. Aristotle was a magnificent experimental biologist, and he was convinced that life could be created spontaneously. Before the time of Darwin there was no need for the various species to evolve, because they sprang into being from inanimate matter. As late as the eighteenth century, Needham, using a microscope, reported that he saw microbe life arise spontaneously out of sterile culture media. These abiogeneticists were, of course, discredited and their work found to be irreproducible, but only *after* it became evident that the then abiogenetic facts were going to run inconsistent with later 'facts' flowing from advancing biologic theory.''

"Then," said Goring, "assuming purely for the sake of argument, that man has altered the original *noumena* into our present reality, just what danger do you think Luce represents to that reality? How could he do anything about it, even if he wanted to? Just what is he up to?"

"Broadly stated," said Prentiss, "Luce intends to destroy the Einsteinian universe."

Burchard frowned and shook his head. "Not so fast. In the first place, how can anyone presume to destroy this planet, much less the whole universe? And why do you say the 'Einsteinian' universe? The universe by any other name is still the universe, isn't it?"

"What Dr. Prentiss means," explained E, "is that Luce wants to revise completely and finally our present comprehension of the universe, which presently happens to be the Einsteinian version, in the expectation that the final version would be the true one—and comprehensible only to Luce and perhaps a few other ontologic experts."

"I don't see it," said Dobbs irritably. "Apparently this Luce contemplates nothing more than publication of a new scientific theory. How can that be bad? A mere theory can't hurt anybody—especially if only two or three people understand it."

"You—and two billion others," said Prentiss softly, "think that 'reality' cannot be affected by any theory that seems to change it—that it is optional with you to accept or reject the theory. In the past that was true. If the Ptolemaics wanted a geocentric universe, they ignored Copernicus. If the four-dimensional continuum of Einstein and Minkowsky seemed incomprehensible to the Newtonian school they dismissed it, and the planets continued to revolve substantially as Newton predicted. But this is different.

"For the first time we are faced with the probability that the promulgation of a theory is going to *force* an ungraspable reality upon our minds. It will not be optional."

"Well," said Burchard, "if by 'promulgation of a theory' you mean something like the application of the quantum theory and relativity to the production of atomic energy, which of course has changed the shape of civilization in the past generation, whether the individual liked it or not, then I can understand you. But if you mean that Luce is going to make one little experiment that may confirm some new theory or other, and *ipso facto* and instantaneously reality is going to turn topsy turvy, why I say it's nonsense.''

"Would anyone," said Prentiss quietly, "care to guess what would happen if Luce were able to destroy a photon?"

Goring laughed shortly. "The question doesn't make sense. The mass-energy entity whose three-dimensional profile we call a photon is indestructible.''

"But if you *could* destroy it?" insisted Prentiss. "What would the universe be like afterward?"

"What difference would it make?" demanded Dobbs. "One photon more or less?"

"Plenty," said Goring. "According to the Einstein theory, every particle of matter—energy has a gravitational potential, lambda, and it can be calculated that the total lambdas are precisely sufficient to keep our four-dimensional continuum from closing back on itself. Take one lambda away—God! The universe would split wide open!"

"Exactly," said Prentiss. "Instead of a continuum, our 'reality' would become a disconnected melange of three-dimensional objects. Time, if it existed, wouldn't bear any relation to spatial things. Only an ontologic expert might be able to synthesize any sense out of such a 'reality.' "

"Well," said Dobbs, "I wouldn't worry too much. I don't think anybody's ever going to destroy a photon." He snickered. "You have to catch one first!"

"Luce can catch one," said Prentiss calmly. "And he can destroy it. At this moment some unimaginable post-Einsteinian universe lies in the palm of his hand. Final, true reality, perhaps. But we aren't ready for it. Kant, perhaps, or *Homo superior*, but not the general run of *H. sapiens*. We wouldn't be able to escape our conditioning. We'd be stopped cold."

He stopped. Without looking at Goring, he knew he had convinced the man. Prentiss sagged with visible relief. It was time for a vote. He must strike before Speer and Goring could change their minds.

"Madame"—he shot a questioning glance at the woman—"at any moment my men are going to report that they've located

Luce. I must be ready to issue the order for his execution, if in fact the staff believes such disposition proper. I call for a vote of officers!"

"Granted," said E instantly. "Will those in favor of destroying Luce on sight raise their right hands?"

Prentiss and Goring made the required signal.

Speer was silent.

Prentis felt his heart sinking. Had he made a gross error of judgment?

"I vote against this murder," declared Dobbs. "That's what it is, pure murder."

"I agree with Dobbs," said Burchard shortly.

All eyes were on the psychologist. "I presume you'll join us, Dr. Speer?" demanded Dobbs sternly.

"Count me out, gentlemen, I'd never interfere with anything so inevitable as the destiny of man. All of you are overlooking a fundamental facet of human nature—man's insatiable hunger for change, novelty—for anything different from what he already has. Prentiss himself states that whenever man grows discontented with his present reality, he starts elaborating it, and the devil take the hindmost. Luce but symbolizes the evil genius of our race—and I mean both our species and the race toward intertwined godhood and destruction. Once born, however, symbols are immortal. It's far too late now to start killing Luces. It was too late when the first man tasted the first apple.

"Furthermore, I think Prentiss greatly overestimates the scope of Luce's pending victory over the rest of mankind. Suppose Luce is actually successful in clearing space and time and suspending the world in the temporal stasis of its present irreality. Suppose he and a few ontologic experts pass on into the ultimate, true reality. How long do you think they can resist the temptation to alter it? If Prentiss is right, eventually they or their descendants will be living in a cosmos as intricate and unpleasant as the one they left, while we, for all practical purposes, will be pleasantly dead.

"No, gentlemen, I won't vote either way."

"Then it is my privilege to break the tie," said E coolly. "I vote for death. Save your remonstrances, Dr. Dobbs. It's after midnight. This meeting is adjourned." She stood up in abrupt dismissal, and the men were soon filing from the room.

E left the table and walked toward the windows on the far side of the room. Prentiss hesitated a moment, but made no effort to leave.

E called over her shoulder, "You, too, Prentiss."

The door closed behind Speer, the last of the group, save Prentiss.

Prentiss walked up behind E.

She gave no sign of awareness.

Six feet away, the man stopped and studied her.

Sitting, walking, standing, she was lovely. Mentally he compared her to Velasquez' Venus. There was the same slender exquisite proportion of thigh, hip, and bust. And he knew she was completely aware of her own beauty, and further, must be aware of his present appreciative scrutiny.

Then her shoulders sagged suddenly, and her voice seemed very tired when she spoke. "So you're still here, Prentiss. Do you believe in intuition?"

"Not often."

"Speer was right. He's always right. Luce will succeed." She dropped her arms to her sides and turned.

"Then may I reiterate, my dear, marry me and let's forget the control of knowledge for a few months."

"Completely out of the question, Prentiss. Our natures are incompatible. You're incorrigibly curious, and I'm incorrigibly, even neurotically, conservative. Besides, how can you even think about such things when we've got to stop Luce?"

His reply was interrupted by the shrilling of the intercom: "Calling Mr. Prentiss. Crush calling Mr. Prentiss. Luce located. Crush calling."

With his pencil Crush pointed to a shaded area of the map. "This is Luce's Snake-Eyes estate, the famous game preserve and zoo. Somewhere in the center—about here, I think—is a stone cottage. A moving van unloaded some lab equipment there this morning."

"Mr. Prentiss," said E, "how long do you think it will take him to install what he needs for that one experiment?"

The ontologist answered from across the map table. "I can't be sure. I still have no idea of what he's going to try, except that I'm reasonably certain it must be done in absolute darkness. Checking his instruments will require but a few minutes at most."

The woman began pacing the floor nervously. "I knew it. We can't stop him. We have no time."

"Oh, I don't know," said Prentiss. "How about that stone cottage, Crush? It is pretty old?"

"Dates from the eighteenth century, sir."

"There's your answer," said Prentiss. "It's probably full of holes where the mortar's fallen out. For total darkness he'll have to wait until moonset."

"That's three thirty-four A.M., sir," said Crush.

"We've time for an arrest," said E.

Crush looked dubious. "It's more complicated than that, Madame. Snake-Eyes is fortified to withstand a small army. Luce could hold off any force the Bureau could muster for at least twenty-four hours."

"One atom egg, well done," suggested Prentiss.

"That's the best answer, of course," agreed E. "But you know as well as I what the reaction of Congress would be to such extreme measures. There would be an investigation. The Bureau would be abolished, and all persons responsible for such an action would face life imprisonment, perhaps death." She was silent for a moment, then sighed and said: "So be it. If there is no alternative, I shall order the bomb dropped."

"There may be another way," said Prentiss.

"Indeed?"

"Granted an army couldn't get through. One man might. And if he made it, you could call off your bomb."

E exhaled a slow cloud of smoke and studied the glowing tip of her cigarette. Finally she turned and looked into the eyes of the ontologist for the first time since the beginning of the conference. "*You* can't go."

"Who, then?"

Her eyes dropped. "You're right, of course. But the bomb still falls if you don't get through. It's got to be that way. Do you understand that?"

Prentiss laughed. "I understand."

He addressed his aide. "Crush, I'll leave the details up to you, bomb and all. We'll rendezvous at these coordinates"—he pointed to the map—"at three sharp. It's after one now. You'd better get started."

"Yes, sir," wheezed Crush, and scurried out of the room.

As the door closed, Prentiss turned to E. "Beginning tomorrow afternoon—or rather, *this* afternoon, after I finish with Luce, I want six months off.''

"Granted," murmured E.

"I want you to come with me. I want to find out just what this thing is between us. Just the two of us. It may take a little time.''

E smiled crookedly. "If we're both still alive at three thirty-five, and such a thing as a month exists, and you still want me to spend six of them with you, I'll do it. And in return you can do something for me.''

"What?"

"You even above Luce, stand the best chance of adjusting to final reality if Luce is successful in destroying a photon. I'm a border-line case. I'm going to need all the help you can give me, if and when the time comes. Will you remember that?"

"I'll remember," Prentiss said.

At 3 A.M. he joined Crush.

"There are at least seven infra-red scanners in the grounds, sir," said Crush, "not to mention an intricate network of photo relays. And then the wire fence around the lab, with the big cats inside. He must have turned the whole zoo loose." The little man reluctantly helped Prentiss into his infra-red absorbing coveralls. "You weren't meant for tiger fodder, sir. Better call it off.''

Prentiss zipped up his visor and grimaced out into the moonlit dimness of the apple orchard. "You'll take care of the photocell network?"

"Certainly, sir. He's using u.v.-sensitive cells. We'll blanket the area with the u.v.-spot at three-ten.''

Prentiss strained his ears, but couldn't hear the 'copter that would carry the u.v.-searchlight—and the bomb.

"It'll be here, sir," Crush assured him. "It won't make any noise, anyhow. What you ought to be worrying about are those wild beasts.''

The investigator sniffed at the night air. "Darn little breeze.''

"Yeah," gasped Crush. "And variable at that, sir. You can't count on going in up-wind. You want us to create a diversion at one end of the grounds to attract the animals?''

"We don't dare. If necessary, I'll open the aerosol capsule of formaldehyde.'' He held out his hand. "Good-by, Crush.''

His asthmatic assistant shook the extended hand with vigorous sincerity. "Good luck, sir. And don't forget the bomb. We'll have to drop it at three thirty-four sharp."

But Prentiss had vanished into the leafy darkness.

A little later he was studying the luminous figures on his watch. The u.v.-blanket was presumably on. All he had to be careful about in the next forty seconds was a direct collision with a photocell post.

But Crush's survey party had mapped well. He reached the barbed fencing uneventfully, with seconds to spare. He listened a moment, and then in practised silence eased his lithe body high up and over.

The breeze, which a moment before had been in his face, now died away, and the night air hung about him in dark lifeless curtains.

From the stone building a scant two hundred yards ahead, a chink of light peeped out.

Prentiss drew his silenced pistol and began moving forward with swift caution, taking care to place his heel to ground before the toe, and feeling out the character of the ground with the thin soles of his sneakers before each step. A snapping twig might hurl a slavering wild beast at his throat.

He stopped motionless in midstride.

From the thicket several yards to his right came an ominous sniffing, followed by a low snarl.

His mouth went suddenly dry as he strained his ears and turned his head slowly toward the sound.

And then there came the reverberations of something heavy, hurtling toward him.

He whipped his weapon around and waited in a tense crouch, not daring to send a wild, singing bullet across the sward.

The great cat was almost upon him before he fired, and then the faint cough of the stumbling, stricken animal seemed louder than his muffled shot.

Breathing hard, Prentiss stepped away from the dying beast, evidently a panther, and listened for a long time before resuming his march on the cottage. Luce's extraordinary measures to exclude intruders but confirmed his suspicions: Tonight was the last night that the professor could be stopped. He blinked the stinging sweat from his eyes and glanced at his watch. It was 3:15.

Apparently the other animals had not heard him. He stood up

to resume his advance, and to his utter relief found that the wind had shifted almost directly into his face and was blowing steadily.

In another three minutes he was standing at the massive door of the building, running practised fingers over the great iron hinges and lock. Undoubtedly the thing was going to squeak; there was no time to apply oil and wait for it to soak in. The lock could be easily picked.

And the squeaking of a rusty hinge was probably immaterial. A cunning operator like Luce would undoubtedly have wired an alarm into it. He just couldn't believe Crush's report to the contrary.

But he couldn't stand here.

There was only one way to get inside quickly, and alive.

Chuckling at his own madness, Prentiss began to pound on the door.

He could visualize the blinking out of the slit of light above his head, and knew that, somewhere within the building, two flame-lit eyes were studying him in an infra-red scanner.

Prentiss tried simultaneously to listen to the muffled squeaking of the rats beyond the great door and to the swift, padding approach of something big behind him.

"Luce!" he cried. "It's Prentiss! Let me in!"

A latch slid somewhere; the door eased inward. The investigator threw his gun rearward at a pair of bounding eyes, laced his fingers over his head, and stumbled into more darkness.

Despite the protection of his hands, the terrific blow of the blackjack on his temple almost knocked him out.

He closed his eyes, crumpled carefully to the floor, and noted with satisfaction that his wrists were being tied behind his back. As he had anticipated, it was a clumsy job, even without his imperceptible "assistance." Long fingers ran over his body in a search for more weapons.

Then he felt the sting of a hypodermic needle in his biceps.

The lights came on.

He struggled feebly, emitted a plausible groan, and tried to sit up.

From far above, the strange face of Dr. Luce looked down at him, illuminated, it seemed to Prentiss, by some unhallowed inner fire.

"What time is it?" asked Prentiss.

"Approximately three-twenty."

"*Hm*. Your kittens gave me quite a reception, my dear professor."

"As befits an uncooperative meddler."

"Well, what are you going to do with me?"

"Kill you."

Luce pulled a pistol from his coat pocket.

Prentiss wet his lips. During his ten years with the Bureau, he had never had to deal with anyone quite like Luce. The gaunt man personified megalomania on a scale beyond anything the investigator had previously encountered—or imagined possible.

And, he realized with a shiver, Luce was very probably justified in his prospects (not delusions!) of grandeur.

With growing alarm he watched Luce snap off the safety lock of the pistol.

There were two possible chances of surviving more than a few seconds.

Luce's index finger began to tense around the trigger.

One of those chances was to appeal to Luce's megalomania, treating him as a human being. Tell him, "I know you won't kill me until you've had a chance to gloat over me—to tell me, the inventor of ontologic synthesis, how you found a practical application of it."

No good. Too obvious to one of Luce's intelligence.

The approach must be to a demigod, in humility. Oddly enough his curiosity *was* tinged with respect. Luce *did* have something.

Prentiss licked his lips again and said hurriedly; "I must die, then. But could you show me—is it asking too much to show me, just how you propose to go through?"

The gun lowered a fraction of an inch. Luce eyed the doomed man suspiciously.

"Would you, please?" continued Prentiss. His voice was dry, cracking. "Ever since I discovered that new realities could be synthesized, I've wondered whether *Homo sapiens* was capable of finding a practical device for uncovering the true reality. And all who've worked on it have insisted that only a brain but little below the angels was capable of such an achievement." He coughed apologetically. "It is difficult to believe that a mere mortal has really accomplished what you claim—and yet, there's something about you . . ." His voice trailed off, and he laughed deprecatingly.

Luce bit; he thrust the gun back into his coat pocket. "So you know when you're licked," he said. "Well, I'll let you live a moment longer."

He stepped back and pulled aside a black screen. "Has the inimitable ontologist the wit to understand this?"

Within a few seconds of his introduction to the instrument everything was painfully clear. Prentiss now abandoned any remote hope that either Luce's method or aparatus would prove faulty. Both the vacuum-glassèd machinery and the idea behind it were perfect.

Basically, the supplementary unit, which he now saw for the first time, consisted of a sodium-vapor light bulb, blacked out except for one tiny transparent spot. Ahead of the little window was a series of what must be hundreds of black discs mounted on a common axis. Each disc bore a slender radial slot. And though he could not trace all the gearing, Prentiss knew that the discs were geared to permit one and only one fleeting photon of yellow light to emerge at the end of the disc series, where it would pass through a Kerr electro-optic field and be polarized.

That photon would then travel one centimeter to that fabulous Nicol prism, one surface of which had been machined flat to a molecule's thickness. That surface was turned by means of an equally marvelous goniometer to meet the oncoming photon at an angle of exactly 45 degrees. And then would come chaos.

The cool voice of E sounded in his ear receptor. "Prentiss, it's three-thirty. If you understand the apparatus, and find it dangerous, will you so signify? If possible, describe it for the tapes."

"I understand your apparatus perfectly," said Prentiss.

Luce grunted, half irritated, half curious.

Prentiss continued hurriedly. "Shall I tell you how you decided upon this specific apparatus?"

"If you think you can."

"You have undoubtedly seen the sun reflect from the surface of the sea."

Luce nodded.

"But the fish beneath the surface see the sun, too," continued Prentiss. "Some of the photons are reflected and reach you, and some are refracted and reach the fish. But, for a given wave length, the photons are identical. Why should one be absorbed and another reflected?"

"You're on the right track," admitted Luce, "but couldn't you account for their behavior by Jordan's law?"

"Statistically, yes. Individually, no. In nineteen-thirty-four

Jordan showed that a beam of polarized light splits up when it hits a Nicol prism. He proved that when the prism forms an angle, alpha, with the plane of polarization of the prism, a fraction of the light equal to $\cos^2$alpha passes through the prism, and the remainder, $\sin^2$alpha, is reflected. For example, if alpha is 60 degrees, three-fourths of the phontons are reflected and one-fourth are refracted. But note that Jordan's law applied only to streams of photons, and you're dealing with a single photon, to which you're presenting an angle of exactly 45°. And how does a single photon make up its mind—or the photonic equivalent of a mind—when the probability of reflecting is exactly equal to the probability of refracting? Of course, if our photon is but one little mote along with billions of others, the whole comprising a light beam, we can visualize orders left for him by a sort of statistical traffic keeper stationed somewhere in the beam. A member of a beam, it may be presumed, has a pretty good idea of how many of his brothers have already reflected, and how many refracted, and hence knows which he must do.''

"But suppose our single photon isn't in a beam at all?" said Luce.

"Your apparatus," said Prentiss, "is going to provide just such a photon. And I think it will be a highly confused little photon, just as your experimental rat was, that night not so long ago. I think it was Schroedinger who said that these physical particles were startlingly human in many of their aspects. Yes, your photon will be given a choice of equal probability. Shall he reflect? Shall he refract? The chances are 50 percent for either choice. He will have no reason for selecting one in preference to the other. There will have been no swarm of preceding photons to set up a traffic guide for him. He'll be puzzled; and trying to meet a situation for which he has no proper response, he'll slow down. And when he does, he'll cease to be a photon, which must travel at the speed of light or cease to exist. Like your rat, like many human beings, he solves the unsolvable by disintegrating.''

Luce said: "And when it disintegrates, there disappears one of the lambdas that hold together the Einstein space-time continuum. And when *that* goes, what's left can be only final reality untainted by theory or imagination. Do you see any flaw in my plan?''

*   *   *

Tugging with subtle quickness on the cords that bound him, Prentiss knew there was no flaw in the man's reasoning, and that every human being on earth was now living on borrowed time.

He could think of no way to stop him; there remained only the bare threat of the bomb.

He said tersely: "If you don't submit to peaceable arrest within a few seconds, an atom bomb is going to be dropped on this area."

Sweat was getting into his eyes again, and he winked rapidly.

Luce's dark features convulsed, hung limp, then coalesced into a harsh grin. "She'll be too late," he said with grim good humor. "Her ancestors tried for centuries to thwart mine. But we were successful—always. Tonight I succeed again, and for all time."

Prentiss had one hand free.

In seconds he would be at the man's throat. He worked with quiet fury at the loops around his bound wrist.

Again E's voice in his ear receptor. "I had to do it!" The tones were strangely sad, self-accusing, remorseful.

Had to do *what*?

And his dazed mind was trying to digest the fact that E had just destroyed him.

She was continuing. "The bomb was dropped ten seconds ago." She was almost pleading, and her words were running together. "You were helpless; you couldn't kill him. I had a sudden premonition of what the world would be like—afterward— even for those who go through. Forgive me."

Almost mechanically he resumed his fumbling with the cord.

Luce looked up. "What's that?"

"What?" asked Prentiss dully. "I don't hear anything."

"Of course you do! Listen!"

The wrist came free.

Several things happened.

That faraway shriek in the skies grew into a howling crescendo of destruction.

As one man Prentiss and Luce leaped toward the activator switches. Luce got there first—an infinitesimal fraction of time before the walls were completely disintegrated.

There was a brief, soundless interval of utter blackness.

And then it seemed to Prentiss that a titanic stone wall crashed into his brain, and held him, mute, immobile.

But he was not dead.

For the name of this armored, stunning wall was not the bomb, but Time itself.

He knew in a brief flash of insight, that for sentient, thinking beings, Time had suddenly become a barricade rather than an endless road.

The exploding bomb—the caving cottage walls—were hanging, somewhere, frozen fast in an immutable, eternal stasis.

Luce had separated this fleeting unseen dimension from the creatures and things that had flowed along it. There is no existence without change along a temporal continuum. And now the continuum had been shattered.

Was this, then the fate of all tangible things—of all humanity?

Were none of them—not even the two or three who understood advanced ontology, to—get through?

There was nothing but a black, eerie silence all around.

His senses were useless.

He even doubted he had any senses.

So far as he could tell he was nothing but an intelligence, floating in space. But he couldn't even be sure of *that*. Intelligence—space—they weren't necessarily the same now as before.

All that he knew for sure was that he doubted. He doubted everything except the fact of doubting.

Shades of Descartes!

To doubt is to think!

Ergo sum!

I exist.

Instantly he was wary. He existed, but not necessarily as Adrian Prentiss Rogers. For the *noumenon* of Adrian Prentiss Rogers might be—whom?

But he was safe. He was going to get through.

Relax, be resilient, he urged his whirling brain. You're on the verge of something marvelous.

It seemed that he could almost hear himself talk, and he was glad. A voiceless final reality would have been unbearable.

He essayed a tentative whisper:

"E!"

From somewhere far away a woman whimpered.

He cried eagerly into the blackness. "Is that you?"

Something unintelligble and strangely frightening answered him.

"Don't try to hold on to yourself," he cried. "Just let yourself go! Remember, you won't be E any more, but the *noumenon*, the essence of E. Unless you change enough to permit your *noumenon* to take over your old identity, you'll have to stay behind."

There was a groan. "But I'm *me*!"

"But you *aren't*—not really," he pleaded quickly. "You're just an aspect of a larger, symbolical *you*—the *noumenon* of E. It's yours for the asking. You have only to hold out your hand to grasp the shape of final reality. And you *must*, or cease to exist!"

A wail: "But what will happen to my body?"

The ontologist almost laughed. "I wouldn't know; but if it changes, I'll be sorrier than you!"

There was a silence.

"E!" he called.

No answer.

"E! Did you get through? *E!*"

The empty echoes skirled between the confines of his narrow blackness.

Had the woman lost even her struggling interstitial existence? Whenever, whatever, or wherever she now was, he could no longer detect.

Somehow, if it had ever come to this, he had counted on her being with him—just the two of them.

In stunned uneasy wonder he considered what his existence was going to be like from now on.

And what about Luce?

Had the demonic professor possessed sufficient mental elasticity to slip through?

And if so, just what was the professorial *noumenon*—the real Luce—like?

He'd soon know.

The ontologist relaxed again, and began floating through a dreamy patch of light and darkness. A pale glow began gradually to form about his eyes, and shadowy things began to form, dissolve, and reform.

He felt a great rush of gratitude. At least the shape of final reality was to be visible.

And then, at about the spot where Luce had stood, he saw the Eyes—two tiny red flames, transfixing him with unfathomable fury.

Charles L. Harness

The same eyes that had burned into his that night of his first search!

Luce had got through—but wait!

An unholy aura was playing about the sinuous shadow that contained the jeweled flames. Those eyes were brilliant, horrid facets of hate in the head of a huge, coiling serpent-thing! Snake-Eyes!

In mounting awe and fear the ontologist understood that Luce had not got through—as Luce. That the *noumenon*, the essence, of Luce—was nothing human. That Luce, the bearer of light, aspirant to godhood, was not just Luce!

By the faint light he began shrinking away from the coiled horror, and in the act saw that *he*, at least, still had a human body. He knew this, because he was completely nude.

He was still human, and the snake-creature wasn't—and therefore never had been.

Then he noticed that the stone cottage was gone, and that a pink glow was coming from the east.

He crashed into a tree before he had gone a dozen steps.

Yesterday there had been no trees within three hundred yards of the cottage.

But that made sense, for there was no cottage any more, and no yesterday. Crush ought to be waiting somewhere out here—except that Crush hadn't got through, and hence didn't really exist.

He went around the tree. It obscured his view of the snake-creature for a moment, and when he tried to find it again, it was gone.

He was glad for the momentary relief, and began looking about him in the half-light. He took a deep breath.

The animals, if they still existed, had vanished with the coming of dawn. The grassy, flower-dotted swards scintillated like emeralds in the early morning haze. From somewhere came the babble of running water.

Meta-universe, by whatever name you called it, was beautiful, like a gorgeous garden. What a pity he must live and die here alone, with nothing but a lot of animals for company. He'd willingly give an arm, or at least a rib, if—

"Adrian Prentiss! Adrian!"

He whirled and stared toward the orchard in elated disbelief.

"E! *E!*"

She'd got through!

The whole world, and just the two of them!

His heart was pounding ecstatically as he began to run lithely upwind.

And they'd keep it this way, simple and sweet, forever, and their children after them. To hell with science and progress! (Well, within practical limits, of course.)

As he ran, there rippled about his quivering nostrils the seductive scent of apple blossoms.

PHILIP K. DICK

"The greatest American novelist of the second half of the 20th Century."
—*Norman Spinrad*

"A genius . . . He writes it the way he sees it and it is the quality, the clarity of his Vision that makes him great."
—*Thomas M. Disch*

"The most consistently brilliant science fiction writer in the world."

—*John Brunner*

PHILIP K. DICK

In print again, in DAW Books' special memorial editions:

☐ **WE CAN BUILD YOU** (#UE1793—$2.50)
☐ **THE THREE STIGMATA OF PALMER ELDRITCH**
(#UE1810—$2.50)
☐ **A MAZE OF DEATH** (#UE1830—$2.50)
☐ **UBIK** (#UE1859—$2.50)
☐ **DEUS IRAE** (#UE1887—$2.95)
☐ **NOW WAIT FOR LAST YEAR** (#UE1654—$2.50)
☐ **FLOW MY TEARS, THE POLICEMAN SAID** (#UE1969—$2.50)
☐ **A SCANNER DARKLY** (#UE1923—$2.50)